Dead of Winter

Dead of Winter

A Lily Dale Mystery

Wendy Corsi Staub

CROOKED
LANE

NEW YORK

Published in the United States by Crooked Lane Books, an imprint of The Quick Brown Fox & Company LLC.

Crooked Lane Books and its logo are trademarks of The Quick Brown Fox & Company LLC.

Library of Congress Catalog-in-Publication data available upon request.

ISBN (hardcover): 978-1-68331-333-5
ISBN (ePub): 978-1-68331-334-2
ISBN (ePDF): 978-1-68331-336-6

Cover design by Melanie Sun
Book design by Jennifer Canzone

Printed in the United States.

www.crookedlanebooks.com

Crooked Lane Books
34 West 27th St., 10th Floor
New York, NY 10001

First Edition: November 2017

10 9 8 7 6 5 4 3 2 1

For Anita,
with wishes for a sunny, beachy,
margarita-splashed holiday;

for Elvis—I mean, Paul—
with a future dance floor date, '80s-style;

for Poppo-Claus,
with love and gratitude for a lifetime
of merry Christmases;

for the real Chance the Cat, Li'l Chap, and Sanchez;

and for my greatest gifts, my three wise men:
Mark, Morgan, and Brody.

Chapter One

Bella Jordan squints and takes aim. Just as she presses the trigger, a voice bellows, "Mom!"

Jolted, she misses the target.

A fat white blob lands in the middle of a newly installed tile instead of in the seam along the countertop. With a sigh, she sets aside the caulk gun and grabs a rag.

"Mom!"

"What is it, Max?"

Her six-year-old son offers an unintelligible response from the small TV room off the front parlor.

"Max! Come in here if you need something!"

Hastily wiping her gooey mistake from the gleaming white porcelain, she checks the stove clock, does a double take, and sighs.

It's challenging to keep track of time here in western New York in mid-December. Dusk was already falling when Max got off the school bus, and she'd lost an hour to a shopping excursion for social studies project supplies. Back home, they had painstakingly cut out shapes depicting the original thirteen colonies and pasted them to a piece of poster board—another hour gone.

Now two more have disappeared, and suppertime has all but given way to bedtime.

Footsteps pad into the room. Max looks just like his dad, with the same brown eyes, same glasses, same sandy brown hair, and even the same cowlick.

1

"I just saw a commercial, and it made me hungry for spaghetti and meatballs," he tells her. "Can we have some?"

"You were supposed to be watching PBS, kiddo."

"I was."

"Not if there are spaghetti and meatball commercials."

"How do you know that?"

"I know everything."

He doesn't dispute that, though Bella is one of the few locals whose livelihood doesn't involve omniscience.

Like many vintage summer cottage colonies in this rural corner of New York, Lily Dale's entrance is marked by a small gatehouse. Like the other communities, it's perched on a small, picturesque lake, with a network of ancient, rutted lanes more suited to foot traffic than automobiles and lined with weather-beaten ginger-bread cottages and stands of towering trees. It, too, lies dormant between Labor Day and Columbus Day, nearly deserted for six months as brutal midwestern blizzards barrel across the Great Lakes. And it, too, stirs to life between Mother's Day and Memorial Day.

But here, the "season" isn't dictated by calendar or weather. The Lily Dale season is an official Season—a ten-week schedule of daily events that draw people from around the globe. Visitors aren't vacationing as much as they're making a pilgrimage, like gamblers to Vegas or aspiring starlets to Hollywood.

Lily Dale is an industry town, and its industry is communicating with the dead. Founded in the dawn of the nineteenth-century spiritualist movement, the Dale remains populated by psychic mediums.

Six months ago, Bella had never even heard of this place. She'd just lost her teaching job, and her landlord had sold the house back in Bedford where she'd lived all her married life. On their last day, as she and Max were packing their belongings, a very pregnant stray tabby had parked herself on their doorstep.

Max had wanted to keep her, but that was out of the question. They were headed to Chicago to stay with Sam's mother, Millicent, whom Bella had privately nicknamed Maleficent. She had dreaded the thought of visiting her mother-in-law, let alone moving into her immaculate condo, but she and Max had no other family.

Eight hours into their road trip, they had come across a nearly identical pregnant tabby. They'd brought her to nearby Lakeview Animal Hospital, where veterinarian Drew Bailey had scanned a microchip. It revealed that her name was Chance the Cat and she belonged to Valley View Manor's innkeeper, Leona Gatto. With a nasty storm brewing, they detoured to return their feline friend to Lily Dale.

By the time Bella discovered that the village was populated by spiritualists and that Leona had been murdered, the weather and car trouble had stranded them here.

Coincidence?

No such thing, according to the friendly medium next door. Both Odelia Lauder and Max believe Chance is the same stray they'd left behind in Bedford. She bears such an uncanny resemblance that some days, Bella is almost willing to believe it. Most days, being a logical former science teacher, she tries not to.

"What are you watching on TV, Max?" she asks.

"It's a show called *Rudolph*. It's about this little reindeer. All the other reindeers laugh at him because his nose is red. Even Santa is not that nice to him."

"Yeah, I thought the same thing when I was your age," Bella admits.

"You saw *Rudolph*?"

"Every year . . ."

With my dad.

For Max's sake, she swallows the rest of the memory. She had always watched *Rudolph* with her father, snuggled on the couch together. Later, they'd graduated to Hallmark Christmas tearjerkers. Dad always blamed his sniffles on nonexistent allergies. Now that Bella, too, is widowed, she's just as prone to emotional blindsides and to protecting her child from reminders of a tragic loss.

"Don't worry, Max," she says. "I'm sure the real Santa is much nicer to Rudolph than the TV one."

"Kevin Beamer says there's no real Santa."

"*What?*"

They're having this conversation *now*? When she's exhausted and busy and . . .

3

Now, right before Christmas?

Now, when Sam isn't here to help her figure out how to handle it?

"Why would he say a thing like that?"

"Because he's never seen him. He asked me if I've ever seen him and I said, 'Nope, but just because you can't see something doesn't mean it's not there. Like Spirit.'"

"That was a good answer, Max." Bella changes the subject. "I wonder how the TV suddenly started showing *Rudolph* instead of PBS."

"I wonder that, too."

Bella bites a smile, wondering how to handle Single-Mom Disciplinary Action Challenge number . . . she's lost count today.

Lying is a serious offense, and she censors Max's viewing because he's experienced enough darkness already without stumbling across nightmare-inducing TV programming. Which *Rudolph* isn't, she reminds herself. The ferocious Bumble might be scary for other six-year-olds, but hers has met more than his share of real-life villains.

"Maybe Chance or Spidey bumped the remote, Mom."

"I don't think so." Bella points at the cats curled up in snoozy balls on the back doormat. Spidey was the runt of Chance's large litter, and Max hadn't been able to let him go.

"Well, maybe it was Nadine."

Nadine is Valley View's resident Spirit prankster, according to their neighbor Odelia. Even if Bella believed in that sort of thing, she's certain Max changed the channel, just as she knows that Max, and not Nadine, ate the gumdrops she was saving for the gingerbread men that he's been wanting her to bake ever since he started reading "The Gingerbread Man" story in school last week.

"Is dinner ready, Mom?"

She glances at the caulk gun, then at her son. "I'm sorry, sweetie. I lost track of time, and I forgot to make it."

"It's okay. We can order pizza."

If only.

Pizza delivery is a forbidden luxury if she's going to give Max the holiday he should have had last year, with decorations and a heap of presents under the tree. With only twelve shopping days till Christmas, she still can't afford even one small extravagance.

Max sneezes—once, twice, three times, just as Sam always did.

"Bless you. Are you feeling okay?"

"No. I'm feeling starving."

She grabs a clean kettle from the drying rack. "How about some spaghetti?"

"With meatballs? And cheese? The kind in the green can? That's what they had on TV."

"We don't have cheese or meatballs."

"Did you look in the freezer? Because there's a lot of stuff in there. I even found all that trick-or-treat chocolate we lost."

She sighs. "What were you doing in the freezer, Max?"

"Getting ice cubes for my milk."

"Milk doesn't need ice cubes."

"Yes, it does. Warm milk is disgusting. It makes people barf."

"Bet I can guess who told you that."

"Who?"

"Jiffy Arden."

"You're a good guesser, Mom. Jiffy says ice makes the milk nice and cold. What else can you guess?"

"I can guess that you like spaghetti with butter, right? Because that's what I'm making for dinner."

Maternal guilt assuaged by a cheerful "Yep," Bella doesn't tell him to turn the channel back to PBS as he skips back to the television.

Maybe she'll even let him eat in there while she finishes caulking the backsplash. She'll gobble some pasta later, unless she collapses into bed without dinner again.

That happens a lot now that Valley View's owner has decided to spruce up his newly inherited property rather than sell it.

As manager, Bella is grateful that the leaky, needs-to-be-replaced three-story Victorian roof will remain over her head for the foreseeable future—which, here in Lily Dale, is basically infinite. This old house is home, cracks, leaks, scars, and all. When Grant Everard told her about the renovation, she eagerly volunteered to help.

"Do you have any home repair experience?" he'd asked.

"A little. I can make curtains, and—"

He'd cut her off, sounding amused. "I'm going to hire professionals to do the work, Bella, but I appreciate the offer."

"No, really, let me help," she insisted. "What else am I going to do with myself all day every day while Max is in school?"

"How about relax?"

"No way." Relaxing gave a person too much time to think, and when a person thought—when *she* thought, anyway—it was often about everything she'd lost.

Standing at the sink, she scrubs her hands. She was never one of those women who considered her fingernails more accessory than tool, but these days, they're perpetually ragged. Her hands are dry and chapped, gold wedding and engagement rings conspicuously missing. She'd taken them off to paint the other day and had forgotten to put them back on. Though she remembered the next morning, she left them stashed in her jewelry box alongside her special tourmaline necklace. She told herself it was only because she was doing so much work around the house, but maybe that wasn't the whole truth.

She changes the tap to cold. As she waits for the kettle to fill for the pasta, she rubs her aching shoulders and realizes that she's ravenous. She'd love to call it a night right now, but . . .

"In for a penny, in for a pound," Sam used to say.

This time, it really is about pennies, so to speak. Grant pays her extra for the renovation work she's been doing. She can't bill him for the backsplash until the job is completed, and she needs the extra cash before Christmas.

She sets the pan on the burner and turns on the flame.

Can she caulk the seams while she waits for it to boil?

That way, she can catch the end of *Rudolph* and eat dinner with Max, e-mail an invoice to Grant, and get to bed with a full belly at a decent hour.

You can do anything you set your mind to. You're the most capable woman in the world, Bella Blue.

Sam's pet name for her. Sam's words, last December, and they came back to haunt her after he was gone.

Her husband, who'd been right about everything, had been wrong about her. She couldn't do anything, not without him. She was barely capable of dragging herself out of bed most mornings.

But look at you now, Bella Blue. Look what you can do. Look what you've done.

She turns away from the stove, and her gaze falls on the new white subway tiles.

A year ago, she wouldn't have known a wet saw from a see-saw, and she's pretty sure Sam wouldn't have either. He was a lot of things—a businessman, a poetry lover, a loyal husband, a loving son, and a devoted father. But he was no Mr. Fixit.

Bella, however, has transformed herself into . . .

Not *Miss* Fixit, and she's never been a fan of *Ms.* She always enjoyed being a *Mrs.*, but that no longer applies.

Guess that makes me the Widow Fixit.

I'd rather be Bella Blue.

When she first came to town, Pandora Feeney, a local medium, had told her that her aura was blue indeed.

"My what is what?" Bella had asked, thinking she must have misunderstood the woman's English accent.

"Your aura, luv. It's a bioenergy field that surrounds you. We all have them. As we move through our lives and our circumstances change, our auras change. Yours is the most smashing shade of blue."

"What does that even mean?"

"You're bloody logical. Stubborn. Intuitive and serene. You feel deeply, but you refuse to allow your emotions to impact your decisions. You guard them quite fiercely. You don't wear your heart on your sleeve. It takes you yonks to let someone in."

"Yonks?"

Pandora laughed. "That's a long, long time. But when they're in, they're in for yonks. You're true blue, darling."

Unnerved that a relative stranger had just described her to a T, Bella had asked Pandora what color her own aura was.

"What color do you think?"

"I have no clue."

"Come, now, give it a try. You're intuitive."

Bella had studied her, if only to prove to herself that aura reading was complete and utter BS. There were only so many colors to choose from, and she had a feeling that no matter what she guessed, Pandora would say she was correct.

They were in Melrose Park at the time, surrounded by lush, verdant foliage. Pandora, a gawky woman with plain, angular features, had a sickly complexion that made Bella want to say *green*.

But that might have seemed insulting. Green was the color of nausea, jealousy, mold, the Grinch . . .

"Pink?" she guessed instead. It was, after all, the color of Pandora's floral print sundress and matching ribbons at the end of her long salt-and-pepper braid. Her cottage, too, though Bella hadn't known that then.

"Brilliant guess, luv. *Brilliant!*"

"So I'm right?" Surprise, surprise.

"No! I do understand why you might think pink. I *am* utterly loving and generous. But these days, my aura is primarily green. Healthy, vibrant, creative, in tune with nature. That's me, tra-la!"

Remembering the conversation, Bella catches her own smile reflected in the window—along with something unexpected.

For a moment, she thinks the glint of light is coming from behind her in the kitchen. But when she leans into the glass, she sees that it's out there, piercing the darkness beyond the bare ginkgo tree branches.

The glimmer isn't in the broad backyard that lies between Valley View and this narrow swath of Cassadaga Lake. Nor is it in the rolling hills on the opposite shore one hundred and fifty, maybe two hundred yards away.

It's out on the water. Maybe it's a floating chunk of ice catching moonbeams, or . . .

Can it be a boat? Any other time of year, Bella wouldn't be surprised to see a night fisherman, but now?

Last week at the hardware store, she'd overheard a couple of avid anglers discussing how the unseasonably warm weather would keep the lake from freezing any time soon.

"Too bad I dry-docked my boat," the owner, Mitch, had said. "Then again, there's nothing out there now but a whole lot of puny perch."

"Muskies, too, if you know where to find 'em," his friend Virgil Barbor claimed. "Ten, fifteen pounders."

"Illegal in December."

Virgil merely shrugged.

Is he out there tonight, sneaking muskies?

Or did Bella imagine the light in her exhaustion?

That's more likely because there's no sign of it now.

She turns away from the window, picks up the caulk gun, takes aim, and presses the trigger.

*　*　*

He's no saint, but he's never shot anyone before, unless you count a squirrel with a BB gun. He sure as hell hasn't killed anyone. Not with a BB gun and not—until tonight—with the real one tucked into the glove compartment of his car.

He'll dump the weapon elsewhere. "First, I need to get rid of you," he tells the tarped bundle lying in the bottom of the rowboat.

He almost expects a reply. Around here, people talk to the dead, and the dead talk back.

But he hears only his splashing oars, his own wheezing breath in the chilly night air, and the gunshot that echoes in his head even now.

Most people who own a pistol might expect to use it sooner or later, but he never did. He bought it years ago because his idol collected guns—just like he eats fried peanut butter, bacon, and banana sandwiches because they were his idol's favorite food.

But there's no satisfaction in waving a sandwich around when you find yourself in a bad neighborhood or bad mood. A sandwich is only loaded with calories and fat, and they take years to kill someone, while a bullet . . .

Again, the gunshot reverberates in his head.

He still can't quite grasp that he pulled the trigger.

This wasn't target practice. He didn't shoot for sport, or by accident, or even in self-defense. He wasn't trying to scare off a predator. His life wasn't at stake. It wasn't about that.

"Don't you ever let anyone take what's yours, boy."

His father's voice floats back to him.

He'd been talking about the new Star Wars lunchbox snatched by a couple of third grade bullies.

"You go back to school tomorrow, and you get it back."

"How?"

"That's up to you. Come home without it, and you'll be sorry."

He had, and he was.

He'd cried himself to sleep that night, lying on his stomach because of the painful welts on his sides and back.

His father had put them there, and smashed him in the head so hard his skull had felt as though it would never be the same. After that, his father methodically handed over his nebulizer mask. *"Here, breathe. Guess you learned your lesson. Next time someone tries to take something from you, you'll make sure it doesn't happen."*

Yes. Tonight, he'd taken careful aim, and he'd shot to kill.

The experience has left him oddly emotionless, as if the frigid air has numbed his brain along with the rest of him. His only regret is that he isn't sitting by a roaring fire with a glass of single malt scotch.

Reaching the center of the lake, he stops rowing and checks his phone again. He'd silenced it when he got out of the truck in case someone had been lurking along the wooded path to the shore. But the spot was deserted, as he'd anticipated. He's the only fool out on the lake tonight, and all is quiet on the opposite shore.

When it stirs to life again, he'll be a world away. Lily Dale is a summer community. He'd spent miserable childhood Julys in bat- and bug-infested cabins nearby, shuttled off to sleepaway camp by parents who couldn't be bothered with him.

The screen glares in the darkness, its light catching on the thick, bejeweled gold bands stacked in pairs on both of his ring fingers. Still no texts or missed calls, but he's expecting to hear from her any second now. When he does, he'll act as though everything is status quo. By the time she figures out what happened, he'll be long gone—*with* his priceless bounty.

He puts the phone back into his pocket. He should have worn gloves, and not just to keep from leaving prints on the oars. His fingers are so cold that they seem to have shrunk a size or two. He can't have the rings slipping off out here. He musters the breath to blow on his frozen hands, wishing he'd grabbed his inhaler from the console of his truck parked back on Glasgow Road.

Wishing, too, that he'd picked up heavier rocks to weigh down the corpse. He'd been worried about sinking this barely seaworthy vessel, borrowed from a row of upended fishing dinghies on the opposite shore, but he should have been more concerned with sinking his hefty cargo. Dead men *do* tell tales, and he needs to make sure this one won't surface before the lake freezes over to entomb it till spring.

He sets aside the oars. A stiff wind ripples the water, piercing his parka and his lungs. Even the exertion of rowing can't warm him in this weather, and it sure as hell isn't helping his asthma. At this moment, he's pretty sure there's no other place on earth as cold as Cassadaga Lake.

Eager to dispatch his passenger, he bends over to grab the bundle and hoist it onto the seat, where he can weigh it down with the rocks before sending it into the water.

The movement is too quick; the little boat swoops starboard. Icy water sloshes in, swamping his ankles. With a yowl, he hurls himself back. The hefty bundle comes with him. He clenches the tarp in an effort to keep the rings from sliding off his slick, cold-constricted fingers as the boat undulates like a carnival funhouse, now dipping low on the port side. Doused in a mighty arctic splash, he cries out, falling backward with the corpse atop him.

For a long, terrifying moment, he seems to hang suspended upside down over the water, certain he's about to be washed overboard. He can't breathe, crushed by the dead weight on his chest. At last he relinquishes his grip, and gravity pulls his dead companion over the edge with a tremendous splash.

The boat bobs wildly, and he braces himself for the inevitable. But when it rights itself, he's still on board.

He attempts to inflate his aching lungs, drawing in the cold with a keening whistle. He checks for the rings. One, two on his left hand; one, two on his right. Yes. Good. *Good.*

Terror subsiding, he sucks another frigid breath, wiping slushy droplets from his face and hair. The tarp is rapidly drifting away on churning black water. Should he retrieve it and attempt to weigh it down as planned?

It will sink eventually, won't it?

What if it doesn't?

What if someone heard him cry out and comes to investigate? Voices carry across the water at night, and not every cottage on the eastern shore is dark and deserted. He sees lights in a couple of homes, and . . .

Is that a person?

Yes. In the window of the largest house, he can make out a human silhouette.

Valley View Manor is easily recognizable. Its turreted Victorian roofline towers over the others along Cottage Row.

As he watches, the light is extinguished. But someone is still there, looking out over the lake.

Mouth set grimly, he grabs the oars and rows toward the Dale, chilly detachment giving way to a heated rush of anger.

*　　*　　*

Bella turns away from the wall switch. With the kitchen dark and the glare eliminated, she has a better view of the lake. There's no sign of the flicker she spotted a few minutes ago, but she'd heard a distant shout just as she set the kettle on the stove.

She didn't imagine it. Chance and Spidey stirred from slumber. The little black kitten went right back to sleep, but Chance is alert, ears rotating like antennae trying to catch a signal.

As Bella searches the dark waterscape, another shout reaches her ears. Max, in the front room.

"Mom! Someone's here!"

"What do you mean?" Frowning, she turns away from the window.

"There's a car out front."

There shouldn't be. She's not expecting guests to check in until the day after tomorrow.

What if she got the date wrong?

She could swear that Lauri Wierzbicki, the woman who made the phone reservation last week, said she and her friend Dawn Tracy were coming on Friday afternoon. How could Bella have mistaken that for Wednesday night? Exhaustion must have gotten the better of her again. She really needs to start getting more rest. She hasn't yet made up the rooms upstairs, and the first floor is a shambles.

She can only hope Max is mistaken. Maybe someone is visiting Odelia, or the Ardens, who live two doors down, or—

The doorbell rings, and she groans. No such luck.

"Hey, it's Dr. Drew!" Max shouts. "Can I open the door?"

"Oh, no!" An unexpected visit from Drew Bailey is even more disastrous than unanticipated overnight guests—not because the place is a mess, but because she is.

"No?" Max sounds puzzled.

"I mean, yes. Go ahead. Let him in."

She quickly flips on the light, checks her reflection in the window, and groans again.

"I didn't know you were coming over!" she hears Max say and then, "Hey, are you a pizza guy now?"

Drew's chuckle drifts in from the hall, along with the mouthwatering aroma of fresh-baked crust and molten mozzarella.

"Nope, I'm not a pizza guy."

"Then why are you delivering it? Mom is making spaghetti without meatballs and cheese, and I didn't want that. I wanted pizza. Well, first I wanted spaghetti with meatballs and cheese, but then I wanted pizza."

"Guess I read your mind, then."

"Are you a medium?"

"Not a medium either."

No, Drew is a veterinarian by day and . . .

All right, maybe he's slightly more than a friend by night, though Bella keeps reminding herself—and Drew—that she can't possibly consider dating anyone so soon.

Still, she'd prefer that he didn't see her with her long brown hair tucked up beneath Sam's old Yankees cap, wearing a grout-smeared baggy sweat shirt and even baggier jeans. They fit a little too snugly in the waist after Thanksgiving, but she's since lost five pounds she needed to and another five she did not. This morning, pulling her belt in another notch, she'd seen in the mirror that her face looks gaunt with dark circles under her eyes.

Oh, well. This is me. I'm not trying to impress anyone.

13

She takes off the cap and leans toward the window, finger-combing her hair and making sure she didn't smear caulk on her nose.

"Hey, Bella."

She turns to see Drew standing in the doorway, holding a large white box. He could have stepped out of a sportsman's catalog, square-jawed, handsome, and wearing a waxed cotton khaki field coat over an untucked red flannel shirt, jeans, and work boots.

"Oh, hi!" she says a little too brightly.

Chance strolls over to greet him, affectionately rubbing against his legs, her tail straight up and hooked at the tip.

"There's that candy cane tail Max talks about. Guess she likes me."

"She loves you," Bella assures him. "If it weren't for you, she and her babies wouldn't have survived."

He flashes a rare smile.

When they first met last June, Bella had mistaken his stern demeanor for hard-heartedness. Watching him gently examine Chance in his office, she'd quickly amended her first impression. Drew Bailey may not be easygoing, but he's one of the kindest men she's ever known, with a passionate concern for all living beings.

"So what are you doing here? Not that I'm not thrilled to see you," she adds, lest he feel unwelcome. Then not wanting him to get the wrong idea, she tacks on, "I mean, I'm not *thrilled*, I'm, uh . . ."

"Surprised?"

"Very." She resists the urge to pat her hair into place. "Surprised. Definitely."

"Guess you didn't get my message again."

"Message?"

Balancing the box on his hip with one hand, he bends to stroke Chance's striped tabby fur with the other. "I texted that I was going to drop by with a pizza."

"I didn't get it. My phone is so old the battery keeps draining." Ordinarily she'd have connected it to the charger that she keeps plugged into the outlet above the countertop, but she'd moved it to install the backsplash. "Sorry. Everything is such a mess around here."

One night last week, Drew had popped in unexpectedly with a bottle of wine, a Scrabble set, and red-frosted donuts with green sprinkles for Max. He told Bella he'd sent a text and left her a voice mail to say he was coming, but she'd never got them. She was a lot more presentable that night than she is on this one.

"I figured you'd be too busy with the backsplash to cook a decent meal," he tells her, "and you've been wasting away with all you've got going on here."

She's as touched by his kindness as she is disconcerted that he noticed her weight loss. Embarrassed that he caught her primping, she points at the window behind her. "I was just . . . I, uh . . . I thought I saw something out there."

Which is true.

"And I heard a scream, too. So did the cats."

Also true—and unnerving.

Drew nods. "I heard one, too."

"You did?"

"Yes. Not here but back at home. It's that time of year."

"What do you mean?"

"It was a great horned owl. Courting season starts about a month before nesting. On cold, clear December nights, the males and females hoot at each other."

"Sounds romantic." She smothers a yawn, looking around for a place where he can set the pizza box. The counter is cluttered with backsplash supplies, the table with everything that usually sits on the counter.

"Actually, it *is* romantic. Great horned owls are a monogamous species."

"Unlike cats. According to Pandora Feeney, Chance was quite the trollop back in the day."

"You mean eight kittens weren't a virgin birth? Good thing I spayed you, huh, girl?"

The cat purrs and butts her face against his hand.

"Don't feel bad, Chance. You aren't the only trollop in town." Bella pushes the toaster, coffeemaker, and canisters into a corner of the table. "Pandora blames her ex-husband for destroying their marriage with his affairs, but she was just as guilty of cheating—according to Odelia, anyway."

"Odelia enjoys airing other people's dirty laundry, doesn't she?"

"Only Pandora's. Sorry, go on. You were talking about . . . owl monogamy, was it?"

"Right. They're among the few species that mate for life unless something happens to one of the pair. When it does, the survivor finds another long-term partner."

At that, Bella fumbles a ceramic canister. The lid falls off, and sugar spills onto the table. Face flaming, she reminds herself that Drew was talking about owls and not . . .

Well, he can't be thinking that *she* wants to find another long-term mate, can he? She doesn't even want pizza. She just wants to finish the damned backsplash, crawl into bed, and pull the covers over her head.

She wipes up the sugar as he chatters on about their fine feathered friends.

"They can swivel their heads almost all the way around, and they have excellent vision in the dark, although they're farsighted. They can see a great distance ahead, but they have a hard time with things that are close up."

Hmm. Kind of reminds Bella of Odelia and some of her cronies. Sometimes they're so caught up in channeling that they miss details right under their noses.

Yes, and sometimes Bella won't allow herself to see anything beyond the here and now.

When you've lost just about everything and everyone you ever cared about, that's the only way to get through a day. You live moment by moment, not looking back at the good times, not looking ahead to a life devoid of them.

". . . strikingly beautiful," Drew is saying as he sets the pizza box on the section of table she's finally managed to clear.

"Pardon?"

"Great horned owls."

Of course. Great horned owls.

"Powerful, too. They can attack prey several times their own weight and swoop it away in their talons. And they're enormous.

16

Their wingspan is almost five feet across. You'd know one if you saw one, but I bet you haven't. They're nocturnal creatures."

"Lately, so am I. Only I'm not out looking for owls," she adds around another yawn.

"Sorry—am I boring you?"

"No! Not at all. I'm just tired."

"You look it. When was the last time you got a decent night's sleep?"

Two summers ago, when she was living contentedly in the New York suburbs teaching middle school science, and she and her husband were raising their son.

Drew reaches out to push some strands of hair back from her eyes.

Unnerved, she blurts, "Tell me more about the owls."

"They live in the woods. Some night when the moon is bright, we'll go for a walk."

"I'd love that. I mean, you know, because I'd love to see one. An owl."

"Really? At least someone around here doesn't buy into ridiculous folklore."

"Wait, what?" Caught up in imagining herself and Drew in the moonlit woods, she must have missed something again.

"Haven't you ever heard the superstitions?"

"About what?"

"Great horned owls."

"No."

He shrugs. "Some people believe they're harbingers of doom and death."

*   *   *

Coughing, lungs whistling with the effort to breathe, he drags the dinghy onto the grassy shore. He's careful to keep his icy fingers bent, gold rings in place. The light is on again at Valley View Manor, and whoever was in the window has vanished.

The logical part of his brain keeps insisting that he flee, in case whoever it was called the cops. There's no way he can outrun them, especially without a shot of albuterol.

17

But he's propelled toward the house by some vengeful instinct, a relic of a hard, painful lesson in a hard, painful childhood. It's the same compulsion that spurred his finger on the trigger.

Trying to muffle a cough into his shoulder, he slinks through the darkness, fists clenched in his pockets. What will he do if he peeks in a window and finds someone looking back at him? If only he hadn't left the gun—and his inhaler—in the glove compartment on Glasgow Road.

Stealthily approaching the nearest window, he sees something dart across his path. Realizing what it is, he stops short.

Really? A black cat? Now?

Bad luck is the last thing he needs.

"Hey, Sanchez, where'd you go?" a child's voice calls from a few yards over.

He attempts to swallow another fit of wheezing coughs.

"Sanchez! You have to come inside with me and Albie. Come on!"

He hears footsteps. Before he can react, a little boy appears a few yards away. He's freckle-faced with unruly red hair, wearing a dark green ski jacket and pajamas tucked into snow boots.

"Hey, Mister, did you see a black cat? Wow, are you okay?" he adds, as the violent cough catapults forth.

Infuriated—by the cough, the inquisitive kid, the black cat—he shakes his head.

"You're not okay, or you didn't see him?"

"Didn't . . . see him." His voice is strangled amid another spasm.

"Some people can't, but Spirit can."

As he digests that cryptic, matter-of-fact comment, the brat adds, "By the way, you're s'posed to cover your mouth when you cough."

He clenches his fists harder, and not because he's trying to keep the rings on his fingers.

Who needs a gun? He can just—

Somewhere in the night, a door squeaks open, and a woman's voice calls, "Jiffy! What are you doing out there?"

The boy turns toward the house next door. "It's okay, Odelia! I'm just looking for something."

"Well, whatever it is can wait until morning. Get back home before your mother comes looking for you."

He steps deeper into the shadows, certain that if the neighbor is hidden from his view, then he's hidden from hers.

"She never comes looking for me. She doesn't know I need to be looked for," the kid calls back to the woman.

"Home, Jiffy," she says firmly. "Right now. Let's go."

He waits for the kid to tell her there's a strange man lurking out here, but Jiffy seems to take that in stride, reluctantly turning toward home.

Before he disappears around the corner of the house, the boy turns back. "By the way, if you see a black cat, he belongs to my friend Albie. Do you know Albie?"

He shakes his head, seized by another sputtering spell as the effort to breathe burns his clogged airways.

"Who are you talking to out there, Jiffy?" the woman calls.

"Just Spirit. Hey, Odelia, have you seen Sanchez?"

Heart pounding, chest constricting, he stands utterly still until the voices fade away and he hears two doors close firmly after them.

Now what?

Torn, he looks again at Valley View, then at the dinghy. The water is lapping at it, about to snatch it away.

With a curse, he moves toward it. For now, the best thing to do is get out of here, back to the truck.

After a few tortured steps, he halts, lungs aching fiercely. He struggles to inflate them, doubled over, hands splayed on his thighs.

He just has to calm down. He can't panic. Anxiety causes his chest to constrict even further. He sinks to the cold ground, hands cupped over his mouth to warm the air forced into his crippled lungs.

When he's finally certain he isn't going to die, he looks up.

Sure enough, the boat has left the shore without him, already too far out for wading.

He bolts toward the shore but stops short of the water. In his condition, an icy swim would leave him floating facedown alongside his tarp-wrapped friend.

Stranded on the wrong side of the lake, he can only watch his transportation drift away. He'll have to head back toward Glasgow Road on foot and find a place to rest—overnight, if need be. He's of no use to anyone if he keels over.

Anyone?

There is no more anyone, *dude. You're on your own now. Fresh start, remember? Moving on. Just not tonight like you planned.*

Fine. When he's warm and dry and breathing again, armed with his inhaler and pistol, he'll decide what to do about the kid, the neighbor, and whoever might have been watching him from the window at Valley View.

It isn't until he's covered nearly a mile to the base of Glasgow Road that he realizes the priceless rings have slipped from his hands.

Chapter Two

"Zip your bag, Max," Bella tells him as he grabs his yellow backpack, the same bright shade as the freshly sharpened pencils threatening to spill from the pocket. "And your coat."

"You just said it's not going to be cold out today."

"It's still December. Don't forget your social studies project. Come on, let's go; we're running late."

Her fault. She took extra time to blow-dry her hair after her shower and put on some light makeup.

Max grabs the rolled, rubber-banded poster board and opens the front door as Bella pokes among the jackets draped over the vintage wooden coat tree. Lily Dale's fickle seasons demand an array of easily accessible outerwear—down parkas, Windbreakers, sweaters, slickers, hats, scarves, umbrellas . . .

"Wait for me," she calls, moving aside a heavy parka as her son races down the front steps.

"Jiffy's out there. See you later, Mom!"

"Wait! I'm coming, too!"

Bella recently learned that it's not cool for a mom to escort a big first grader to and from the bus stop. Max had pleaded his case with help from Jiffy.

"Name one Mom who goes down there. Can you name one? *Can* you?" Jiffy challenged and looked pointedly at Max.

"I can!" her son had said on cue. "Her name is Bella Jordan."

"You're the only one, Bella." Jiffy, who would make a fine lawyer someday, had solemnly shaken his gingery head. "It's bad for Max."

"Yeah, it's bad for me, Mom."

Yet another moment when she'd wondered what Sam would tell her to do. That time, she'd known.

Now she watches from the porch every morning as Max meets Jiffy in front of his house and they head down Cottage Row together. As soon as they disappear around the bend, she knows, they're swallowed into a gaggle of older kids gathered at the bus stop just outside the gate.

She gives up on finding a light sweater or fleece and looks around for a pair of shoes to throw on. Figures that this is the one day she didn't leave any by the door. She hurries out onto the porch in her socks. "Max! I'm coming with you today! Didn't you hear me?"

He must have. That would explain why he's already sprinted to the Ardens' cottage two doors down, where Jiffy seizes upon the poster board.

"Hey, a pirate spyglass! Can I carry it?"

"Where's *your* project?"

"In my pocket."

"It's s'posed to be on giant paper."

"My mom didn't have time to get me some. Ahoy, mateys!"

They're off, leaving Bella standing helplessly in her socks.

It'll be fine, she tells herself. *It's fine every day. Today is no different. That scream last night was just an owl, like Drew said.*

Hugging herself in the brisk breeze that tinkles the wind chimes overhead, she watches the boys meander down the sun-splashed lane. The spyglass has transformed into a sword, a swashbuckling Jiffy climbing upon a stump to battle imaginary enemies.

"Careful!" Bella calls, hands cupped around her mouth. "And get moving or you'll miss the bus, guys!"

She always waits on the porch until she hears it rumbling to a stop, obscured by trees and houses but only about a tenth of a mile away. Afternoons, she returns to the porch and listens for it again. Even if Max and Jiffy take their time meandering back up the street, they appear within a minute or so.

She doesn't always breathe easily during that minute, but life seems a little less precarious every time she spots them at the foot of the lane.

Now, as they disappear from view, she looks around as if she, like Jiffy, might find unseen enemies lurking. Or just a great horned owl.

She'd forgotten all about the scream in the night until Drew had left and she was climbing into bed. Lying there in the dark, she'd reminded herself that she's not the least bit superstitious. Somehow, that was easier to believe last night, on the verge of plummeting into a deep, dreamless sleep, than it is today in broad daylight.

"Bella! I thought I heard you out here." Odelia Lauder pokes her curly orange head out her front door. She's wrapped in a fuzzy robe that's also orange, though it somehow clashes violently with her hair as well as with her hot pink suede slippers and her pinkish-orange painted house.

"Sorry, did I wake you?"

"No, I was up. Just running a bubble bath. I have an early client this morning. Is everything all right?"

"Yes, the boys just left for the bus, and I was trying to get them to wait for me."

"Didn't I tell you it's perfectly fine for them to walk down alone? The kids all look out for each other, Bella. You know that's how things are here."

She nods. The locals are in tune not only with the rhythm of small-town life but, ostensibly, with powerful unseen energy. They sense when something is amiss.

Right now, though, Bella is the one who's feeling that something is . . . *off.*

Odelia steps onto her own porch and peers at her from across the railings. "Ah, but today is different, isn't it?"

Her heart skips. "Different how?" Does Odelia know something she doesn't? "Is Spirit warning you about Max?"

"What?"

"You said today is different. Did you mean—?"

"I meant you're all fancy, so I figured you must be going some-place special. Or . . . perhaps seeing someone special?" she adds, and Bella feels her face grow hot.

"Fancy? I'm just wearing jeans, same as always."

On an ordinary morning, she'd be wearing them with a T-shirt, hoodie, maybe a fleece—or maybe all three in layers. Today, she has on a delicate silk blouse. It's a frosty shade of blue that lies somewhere between her cobalt eyes and the pale December sky—aura blue, perhaps, she'd thought with a smile when she'd dug it out of her closet earlier.

"And you're all made up," Odelia continues.

"All made up?" she snorts, as if that's the most ridiculous thing she's ever heard. As if she isn't wearing mascara, eyeliner, and a touch of lipstick. "I was just trying to cover these darned circles under my eyes."

"You need to get more sleep."

"Can't. I have way too much going on right now."

Odelia appears to consider arguing, then changes her mind. "Do you have any tea? Not the leaf kind that ridiculous woman is always prattling on about," she adds, casting a dark glance across Melrose Park at Pandora Feeney's cottage.

"Yes, but coffee is stronger, and I've already had three cups."

"I don't want you to drink it. I want you to put a couple of tea bags into the freezer and use them as a cold compress around your eyes tonight. It won't work miracles, but it'll help you look a little less like Dracula."

"Gee, thanks, Odelia. Way to make a gal feel pretty."

"You're a beautiful girl, Bella. You just need to take better care of yourself," she says as a cold gust clangs the wind chimes on both porches. "Brr. It feels like that snow is coming today instead of tomorrow."

"It isn't," Bella says. "Today is going to be warm and sunny. Tomorrow, we're getting three inches of snow."

"Six to eight."

"I just checked the forecast fifteen minutes ago."

"I checked it five minutes ago. Things change by the second around here, Bella."

Don't I know it.

She hears squeaking air brakes down by the gate.

"There's the bus. I'd better get moving, Odelia. Now that Max and Jiffy aren't around to 'help,' I can finally get some painting done."

Odelia smiles, well aware that a few days ago, the boys had managed to apply a lovely shade called Silken Taupe to everything—and everyone—in the third-floor bathroom.

"Well, I'm guessing you have more than enough help today," she tells Bella with a wink. "Tell him I said hello."

"Uh . . . Hugo? He's not scheduled today." Electrician Hugo Munson is a regular presence at Valley View, replacing the scary snap-crackle-and-pop wiring.

"No, Drew Bailey." Odelia waves and disappears inside.

How the heck did she know . . . ?

Her gaze falls on the bracketed sign hanging from a porch pillar. *Odelia Lauder, Registered Medium.*

She shakes her head, retreating into her own house. She pauses to reach for the thermostat on the wall beside the coat tree, adjusting it downward in anticipation of the warm day ahead. Then she grabs a hooded sweat shirt to put on over her silk blouse.

There. So much for fancy, Odelia.

In the kitchen, she admires the finished backsplash as she opens the dishwasher and loads it with Max's cereal bowl, spoon, and juice glass. Turning to the sink, she sees two mugs with soggy tea bags in the bottom and smiles.

Last night, after reading Max a bedtime story and tucking him in, she'd come back downstairs to find the leftover pizza put away, dishes washed, and box recycled. The tea kettle rattled on the stove, preparing to whistle, and Drew was leaning over the counter with the caulking gun.

"Put your feet up with a cup of chamomile while I finish this for you," he'd said.

"No way! I can do it."

"I know you can, but I'm already doing it, and I want to see it through."

"That's crazy! Why would you want to do it?"

"In for a penny," he'd said with a shrug, and her jaw dropped.

Sam's favorite old saying. "*Wh-what* did you say?"

"In for a penny, in for a pound. It means you finish what you've started."

"No, I know, I just . . ."

She'd just wondered why Drew Bailey was sounding so much like Sam. Acting like him, too, when he talked on over Bella's protests. "You take on too much. You have to let people help you."

"I do let people help me. Max took out the garbage just yesterday, and Odelia always—"

"I'm talking about *me*, Bella. You have to let me help you."

"Why?"

"Because that's what friends are for."

In that moment, *friends* was the perfect word choice, alleviating her reluctance to be alone with him. She'd sat sipping tea and chatting with him as he finished sealing the tiles. She can't even remember what they had talked about, but it hadn't been Sam, and it hadn't been owls.

She puts the cups into the dishwasher and, after a moment's hesitation, the tea bags into the freezer.

Beyond the window, a breeze sways the graceful bare branches of the ginkgo tree, and sunlight shimmers on the rippling blue lake. *So picturesque*, she thinks and then notices something lying at the water's edge.

Looks like a bag of garbage washed up, or maybe someone dumped it there. Or maybe, depending on how heavy it is, it had gone airborne on a strong west wind. A few weeks ago, a painted plywood reindeer had taken off in a storm from Mitch's Hardware Store a few miles outside the gate and landed beside the Mediums' League building in the Dale. That was front-page news around here, accompanied by the folksy photo caption, *Yes, Virginia, Reindeer Can Fly.*

Bella had better go move the garbage bag before an animal tears into it and scatters it across the lawn. She finds her sneakers by the back door and shoves her feet into them.

Before she can step out the door, the house phone rings—unusual during the off-season. Who can it be?

Who? the great horned owl seems to hoot ominously as she snatches it up.

"Valley View Manor."

"Bella, it's Drew. I've been trying to text you, but you haven't answered, and I wanted to make sure you saw."

"I didn't." She feels her back pockets for her cell phone. She must have left it upstairs in her haste to get Max ready for school and make herself—as Odelia put it—"all fancy."

Before Drew had left last night, she'd accepted with gratitude his offer to come help her paint today.

That's what friends are for.

Friends.

"I hate to do this, but I can't get over there this morning."

"It's okay," she says quickly. "I know you're busy. I should have told you not to—"

"No, I really wanted to help. But I got a call about an injured dog out on Route 60, and it sounds like she's pregnant and may be in labor."

"Oh, no. Poor thing. How badly is she hurt?"

"It doesn't sound good."

"Are the puppies going to survive?"

"Hard to say until I get there. I'm on my way now. Sorry to leave you on your own."

"Don't be silly. I'm fine on my own. I know your work comes first."

"It's . . . it's not . . . like *that*. I wish I could be there, but—"

"No, I just . . . I meant . . ."

She falters, as another conversation with her *friend* dissolves into awkward territory.

She didn't mean anything other than what she said. If it weren't for Drew's dedication to his veterinary practice, Chance and her eight kittens wouldn't be thriving today. They've been such an important part of Bella and Max's life here in Lily Dale . . .

As has Drew himself.

And so many others, she reminds herself after hanging up and heading outside toward the water's edge. Odelia, her granddaughter Calla, Jiffy, even Pandora, and—

She stops short.

Now that she's closer to the bag of garbage, she can see that it isn't a bag of garbage at all.

It's . . . something wrapped in a tarp, something that looks . . .

Human.

* * *

"Is this Mrs. Starr?"

Technically, she's Mrs. Arden. But here in Lily Dale, she goes by the name painted on the sign out front.

Misty Starr, Registered Medium.

"Yes, this is Misty Starr," she tells the male voice on the phone and hurries toward the parlor to find her appointment book and a pen. She trips over the mud-covered red sneaker she'd told Jiffy to leave out on the porch after he lost the other one out in the rain. "How can I help you, sir? Are you looking for spiritual guidance?"

"No. I'm looking for my December rent."

Misty stops in her tracks. "Is this . . . ?"

"It's Virgil Barbor," her landlord confirms, and she curses under her breath, wishing she hadn't answered the phone. "When I stopped by to fix the washing machine, you said you'd have it for me by last Saturday. I've been trying to let this slide, but it's over two weeks late now, and with the holidays coming, January rent will be due before you know it."

"I know. I'm sorry, but the washing machine is broken again."

"It is? Why didn't you tell me?"

Because I knew it would remind you that the rent is overdue.

"Okay," Virgil says, "I'll come take another look this afternoon. That way you can give me the rent check, save a stamp."

"I . . . today isn't good. I have back-to-back appointments all day."

It's not true. She has one, a new client who called over the weekend and is due here any second.

"Tomorrow morning will be better," she tells the landlord. She has no appointments scheduled, so she'll just make sure she isn't home when he arrives. She'll leave a note on the door saying she was called away on urgent business. That should hold him off for a while.

He hangs up with a promise to stop by around noon. Misty writes his name in her appointment book and circles it in red, a reminder that she needs to get out of here before that. She'll take her heaping pile of laundry to the laundromat. She and Jiffy have sparse winter wardrobes, having recently moved here from the blazing hot Southwest, and they're both out of clean clothing.

With that settled, Misty goes into her meditation room to prepare for her visitor.

Paneled in whitewashed bead board, it had once served as a storm porch off the kitchen. Sometime in the last century, the resident spiritualist medium had converted it, covering the creaky wooden floor in blue indoor-outdoor carpeting, installing baseboard heating, and turning the exterior door into a window. The top three sides of the trim match, but the sill is conspicuously no-frills. Viewed from outside, a crumbling stone stairway rises from the weedy foundation to a clumsily patched rectangle of clapboards that aren't quite the right shade of mustard yellow.

Just another little quirk in a quirky little house in a quirky little town.

As Misty reaches to close the drapes, she glimpses someone in the side yard that separates her cottage from Odelia Lauder's. He's stooped over the patch of ground cover alongside the house. *Probably a handyman winterizing the flowerbeds or whatever it is gardeners do,* Misty concludes, her knowledge of plant life restricted to the white sage she burns to cleanse the place of lingering energy.

She hears tires crunching up the street out front.

So does the handyman, who isn't a handyman at all. He's . . .

Elvis Presley?

She blinks, and he's gone.

Huh. Just when she thought she'd learned to distinguish an apparition from a living person.

A car door slams. Must be her client, Priscilla Galante.

Misty yanks the curtains closed, lights the candle on the table, and silences her cell phone. Time to earn her keep. She can't avoid Virgil Barbor forever, and there's no way Mike will help her pay the rent. Not when she and their son are supposed to be living in perfectly perfect—*unquirky*—housing back on the Arizona military base.

She opens the door to see a turquoise Mustang parked at the curb and a pert-looking, pretty brunette on the porch.

"My husband would go nuts for that car," Misty says, "especially with those Pennsylvania license plates. Where are you from?"

"Less than an hour from here. Erie."

"Mike grew up near Allentown." She doesn't mention that he's been estranged from his family there as long as she's known him, stemming from a silly argument that escalated after his mother passed away. She's never met his father or brothers. For all she knows, they aren't even aware that she and Jiffy exist.

Her visitor clears her throat. "Anyway . . . I'm Priscilla Galante. Are you Misty Starr?"

Shifting her attention from the car to her new client, Misty is struck by a fierce flash of recognition.

"We've met before."

"Um, I don't think so. I've never been here, and unless you've been in Erie . . . ?"

"No. That's not it."

Studying her more closely, Misty notes that her aura is black—not necessarily an indication of questionable character. She's here for a reason, and it might be that she's entrenched in grief, or anger, or depression. Any of those emotions might cast a dark pall over her energy.

"Well . . ." Shifting her weight and looking anxiously back at her car, Priscilla says, "I guess I just have one of those familiar faces. People tell me that I look like Anne Hathaway."

"Who?"

"The actress—after she cut her hair for the movie *Les Mis*. She—"

"I don't even know who she is. Must have met you in a past life."

At that, Priscilla looks again at her car, this time as though she's going to jump back into it and flee. Misty rests a hand on her shoulder, and she jumps as if she's been burned.

"Try to relax. Is this your first reading?"

"Yes. Sorry, I'm a little nervous."

Stress and uncertainty—a few more possible reasons her aura is showing black.

"Come on inside, and I'll explain how it works. Careful, don't trip." She kicks a Lego contraption out of their path as she closes the door and sighs when the pieces scatter. Jiffy isn't going to like that. He spent a long time building it.

"You have a son?" Priscilla asks.

"How did you know?"

"Just, uh, you know . . . the Legos."

"Girls play with them, too, you know."

"No, I know. Sorry, I shouldn't have assumed."

"That's all right. My son loves Legos. But so did I at his age. I don't believe in gender-specific playthings," she says with a forced smile.

Mike practically had a heart attack a few years back when she told him she'd bought their son a Barbie doll.

"Why would you do that?"

"Because he wanted it."

"That doesn't mean he should have it."

"If you don't approve of my decisions, maybe you should hang around long enough to make some."

"I'm serving our country!"

"You said you'd only be in the Middle East for a year. It's three going on four."

"I'm doing what I have to do," he'd said tightly.

Misty had decided it was time she did the same. She'd begun her mediumship studies back in Arizona, joining a Spiritualist Assembly not far from the military base where they'd lived until last spring.

Mike hadn't quite given his blessing—far from it. But he seemed to consider it a harmless hobby, like other spouses dabbling in scrapbooking or organizing weekly potlucks.

He hadn't been as accepting last spring when she'd rented a cottage in Lily Dale, where she'd spent childhood summers, and carted their kid and most indispensable possessions over two thousand miles. She'd told Mike that it was just for the summer, but she'd known they wouldn't be going back to Arizona when autumn came.

Mike had to have known as well, though he'd seemed flabbergasted when she'd enrolled their son in school here in September.

"How dare you make a decision like that without consulting me."

"If you're going to live halfway around the world, why do you care where we are? What difference does it make whether we're on the base in Arizona or in Lily Dale?"

"There's a difference, and you know it. He's my son, too."

Jiffy might look like his dad, but he's inherited something far more relevant from his mom. That was obvious as soon as he was old enough to hold what might have appeared to be a one-sided toddler conversation but was clearly—to her, anyway—something more.

Fearing for his future if he didn't embrace his gift, Misty had decided to embrace hers. It might not be paying the bills yet, and maybe it never would, but at least she's finally living an authentic life.

She leads Priscilla to her dimly lit meditation room and closes the door behind them, tuning out troubling thoughts about her marriage and the faint sound of a siren in the distance.

*   *   *

Waiting on the porch, Bella immediately recognizes the uniformed officer who steps out of the police car at the curb. Lieutenant John Grange showed up at Valley View back in July when one of her guests was pulled from the lake barely alive. That near tragedy, like Leona Gatto's drowning, hadn't been an accident.

Bella had found him thoroughly intimidating on that awful day. He'll probably be much nicer now that she's not a murder suspect.

"I'm Bella Jordan," she says as he flashes a badge and reintroduces himself. "I'm the one who called."

"I know."

He knows she's the one who dialed 9-1-1, or he remembers her name from that awful day last summer? Both, probably. Finding someone in the lake—dead or near dead—is probably pretty memorable. Although perhaps not as uncommon as one might expect in a town this size.

Grange fixes her with that unnerving gaze of his. "So you found something in the lake."

"Yes, I—"

"What's going on down there?"

She looks up to see Odelia leaning out of her bathroom window. She isn't wearing a stitch of clothing on the part of her that's visible, which is considerably more than Bella is comfortable seeing. Judging by Grange's pained grunt, it's far too much for him.

"Just here to check out some debris that washed up, Mrs. Lauder," he calls back, averting his eyes. "Nothing to worry about."

"Are you sure? Bella?"

32

"It's fine, Odelia. Don't worry. You go back to your bubble bath."

"Well, you'll have to come fetch me if you need anything. I was about to plug in my monks, and I won't hear a thing." She holds up a pair of headphones, revealing even more of her fleshy, freckled self.

Grange winces. "Plug in her monks? What does that mean?"

"She likes to listen to Tibetan chants while she's in the tub. They relax her," Bella explains, then calls to Odelia, "It's fine, go ahead. If we need you, we'll come get you."

"I'll leave that to you. Not that we'll need her," Grange mutters as the window slams shut overhead. "Show me what you found."

Bella leads him around the house. The shoreline is deserted, aside from a pair of Canadian geese bobbing in the lake and a few more honking overhead.

"There." Bella points to the large black object in the shallow water, mired by mossy rocks. "See it?"

"Yeah."

"Do you think it's—?"

"No way of knowing from here, is there?" he snaps.

She bites her lower lip to keep from reminding him that she's not a suspect but a good citizen reporting something out of the ordinary.

"How long has it been there, Ms. Jordan?"

"I don't know. It wasn't there yesterday afternoon."

"So it's been there less than twenty-four hours, correct?"

"I guess. I probably would have seen it when I was watching my son put out the garbage after school."

His eye goes to the rolling can alongside the shed that sits half-way between the house and the water. "You watch your son put out the garbage?"

"It was getting dark. He's only six. Anyway, I saw a boat out on the water last night," she goes on, "and I heard . . . something. I thought it was a scream, but my, uh . . . *friend* said it was an owl."

"She heard it, too?"

Bella shakes her head. No need to explain that the friend isn't a *she*.

"About what time was that?"

"After seven. Almost eight. Maybe after eight," she realizes, "because *Rudolph* was on."

"Excuse me?"

"My son was watching *Rudolph the Red-Nosed Reindeer* on TV at the time, so whatever time that aired . . . it was sometime in there."

Grange pulls out a notebook and jots that down. "Anything else you want to tell me before I go take a look?"

She hesitates and shakes her head, feeling like a suspect again.

He tucks the notebook back into his pocket and strides to the water.

She can't help but feel a guilty prickle of satisfaction as he skids in the muck at the shore, arms windmilling before he regains his balance with a curse. This endeavor is more suitable for waders than those shiny black shoes, and he doesn't seem like the kind of guy who'd want to get his feet wet and dirty.

However, not only does he proceed through the mud to get a better look at the tarp, but after leaning in, he takes a few steps into the water. Ankle deep, he reaches into his pocket and takes out a pair of gloves. Bella swallows a lump of trepidation as he puts them on.

He probes at the tarp, and she looks away, afraid of what she might glimpse. She spots a large black bird soaring against the clear blue sky. An owl?

No, a crow. It lands with a flapping of wings in the ginkgo branches and caws ominously. She turns to see Grange gingerly wading back to dry ground.

"Lieutenant? What is it?"

He doesn't answer her question, holding up a finger as he speaks into his phone.

"Yeah, I need backup at Valley View in the Dale . . . Yeah . . . Yeah. And the medical examiner. I've got a DOA here."

Chapter Three

"Any questions before we begin?" Misty asks Priscilla.

"Questions for you or for the ghosts?"

"For me. Not *Spirit*." Misty emphasizes the proper terminology.

"No, no questions."

"All right, good."

Misty rubs her hands together, preparing to shift her awareness away from this small room filled with shadows and flickering candles. Drawn navy blue draperies obscure the shoreline view and muffle the faint cries of gulls. She does her best to tune them out and tries, too, not to speculate about Priscilla's place in her past—recent or ancient. Someday, it will probably come to her. Her mediumship training has taught her that soul recognition is quite common, especially in romantic relationships.

"With more experience," her Lily Dale mentor, Pandora Feeney, had told her, "you'll be able to grasp the significance of various familiar strangers you meet."

So far, she's only grasped the significance of one: her husband.

She'd experienced an undeniable connection to Mike the first time she spotted him at the Cedar Point amusement park back in Sandusky. Misty had never been a fan of rides, and Mike hated crowds, and neither of them had ever visited the theme park before. Dragged along by pals, they were destined to find each other there on that blistering, humid summer day.

That is, destined to find each other *again*.

She and Mike have been together in countless lifetimes, not always as husband and wife. Some might call them soul mates, in

35

that they're repeatedly drawn to each other. But Pandora had told her that a connection as powerful as theirs isn't irrevocable in this lifetime or in any other.

"As long as you have unfinished business, you'll be together. When you've learned all the lessons you're meant to learn from each other, you'll evolve."

Misty doesn't like to think about that.

"Wait," Priscilla says, "I do have a question. Aren't you going to use tarot cards, or tea leaves, or . . . something?"

"No. Every medium works differently. I'm very visual. I pass along whatever Spirit shows me. Sometimes it'll be a symbol, and I interpret it the best I can."

"What do you mean?"

"Let's say I see white lace. It might mean a wedding, it might mean you have white lace curtains in your house, or it might mean, I don't know, Karen Carpenter is coming through again."

"Karen Carpenter?"

"You know, the singer? She sang that song, 'We've Only Just Begun,' about white lace and promises . . ."

Priscilla looks blank.

"Oh, well, anyway, she passed years ago, but she pops in once in a while. A lot of musicians do."

"Anyone I've heard of?"

"Sean Von Vogel touched in with me this morning." Seeing Priscilla's eyes widen, Misty goes on, "And just before you got here, Elvis Presley materialized outside."

"Wow. What were they doing here?"

"Hard to tell. I felt as though Von Vogel might have a message, but I'm not sure yet what it is. And Elvis . . . well, that was different."

"Different how?"

"Different energy. Spirit doesn't always manifest in a physical form, but I saw him clear as day."

"That's pretty cool. Do you see anyone now?"

"Only you." Misty flashes a smile. "Hold out your hands toward me."

"Like this?"

"No, palms up."

Priscilla obliges, a little shakily.

"Try to relax." Above her outstretched hands, Misty holds her own, face down, rife with hangnails and chapped from dishwater and cold.

She inhales deeply through her nose. Pungent cottage mildew mingles with freshly burnt white sage. She closes her eyes, visually surrounding the room in protective white light, and invites her spirit guides and other positive energy.

Hmm.

She's getting . . .

Nothing.

People with black auras can be difficult for even a seasoned medium to read. Maybe emotional anxiety is blocking Spirit. Or the person is just not as open-minded as he or she claims to be.

Peace . . . Light . . . Breathe.

In. Out.

In. Out.

An image appears in her mind's eye.

It's a bus. A big yellow school bus.

"A child," she murmurs, more to herself than to her visitor, whose chair creaks as she sits up a little straighter.

"What about a child? Is it a ghost child? Who is it?"

"Shhh . . ."

Misty silently asks her guides to enlighten her.

A bus . . .

A bus.

That's all she's getting. Not a figure, not a voice. Just a bus, likely meant to symbolize a child, just as Spirit sometimes shows her a cradle when bringing forth an infant.

"I'm seeing a bus. Yellow . . . black letters and numbers painted on the side, but . . . no, I can't read them."

"Wait a minute, are you seeing a school bus, or a ghost child, or both?"

"Just a bus. Spirit might be using it to represent a school-aged child. But sometimes a bus is just a bus."

"I don't get it."

"The message might become clear in time," Misty reminds her, eyes still closed.

"But a bus isn't a message unless . . . Is it a talking bus? Is the bus saying something?"

"No, it isn't a talking bus."

"Are you sure it's not a little turquoise car?"

Oh, for the love of . . .

"It's a *bus*. Big. Yellow."

"Is it parked or moving? Where is it going? Is a ghost driving it? What does it mean?"

Misty ignores the rapid-fire questions like a bloodhound tracking a fox amid a tennis ball barrage.

Peace . . . Light . . . Breathe . . .

The bus, no longer empty, rolls slowly against a bleak, snow-flurried landscape. Misty picks out silhouettes of passengers and a few of the black letters on the side of the bus. There's an *L* and an *I . . .*

Snow falls harder. The bus goes faster. Misty is breathless, as though she's running alongside it.

Faces press against the windows. They should be blurrier as heavy snow whirls in the wind and the bus picks up speed, yet somehow the features are sharpening into focus.

There's Katie Harmon, bedraggled and drenched as always, reddish braids tied with soggy blue ribbons. And towheaded Billy Buell, a neighborhood kid she'd known in Cleveland. And DeQuann Jones, bald and missing eyelashes and brows—she met him while doing volunteer work on the children's cancer ward.

Every child on that bus is on the Other Side.

"Excuse me?" Priscilla's voice echoes across a yawning chasm. "What are you seeing? Do you have a message for me?"

Now she can read the words on the side of the bus: *LILY DALE SCHOOL DISTRICT.*

Another familiar face appears in the window of the careening bus, and Misty realizes that the message isn't meant for Priscilla after all.

It's for *her*.

In the ominous moment before the bus vanishes into the blizzard, she recognizes the fourth child: her own son.

* * *

"And you've lived here how long?" Lieutenant Grange asks Bella, standing at the curb beside his parked police car. He's holding a clipboard, writing down her answers to so many questions you'd think she's guilty of something other than dialing 9-1-1.

"Six months. We got here at the end of June."

"And—"

At the sound of an approaching vehicle, they both look expectantly at the end of the street.

Another squad car appears, trailed by the medical examiner's white van.

"No sirens," Bella murmurs, glad her nearest neighbors remain oblivious to the unfolding drama. Odelia is soaking and listening to her monks. At the Ardens' house, an unfamiliar turquoise Mustang with Pennsylvania plates sits parked in the spot reserved for Misty's clients. Across the way, Pandora Feeney's driveway is empty. She, too, must be out.

Odelia's granddaughter, Calla Delaney, is probably home at the cottage she's been renting since Halloween, when she broke up with her longtime live-in boyfriend, Jacy Bly. But she's a novelist who retreats most days into her fictional world, tuning out the real one so effectively she might as well live on an island.

A female police officer steps out of the car, greets Grange, and nods at Bella. He doesn't introduce her. A pleasant-looking man in a suitcoat steps out of the van and flashes Bella a brief, professional smile.

"Wait right here," Grange tells her and disappears into the yard with the others. All in a day's work for them.

Not so for Bella, left alone to ponder the situation. Better than sharing the curb with gossipy gawkers. Not that there are many of those around the Dale at this time of year.

Still, a corpse in the lake behind Valley View isn't good for business, especially . . .

Especially one that didn't wrap itself in a tarp.

The thought that she's been trying hard to ignore roars in like a blizzard gust, chased by the realization that whoever disposed of the body might be nearby.

She scrutinizes the dense shrubbery along Odelia's property line and sees nothing unusual. Yet a chill permeates from within the fleece hoodie zipped over her silk blouse. She can almost feel some-one lurking there, watching her.

Gossipy gawkers might be better than standing here alone, even in broad daylight with armed officers within shouting distance.

As if summoned by the thought, someone emerges from the Arden cottage two doors down. Bella turns to see a young brunette descending the porch steps. The woman starts toward the Mustang parked at the curb, then spots the police cars, and Bella.

"Um . . . is everything okay over there?"

When Bella hesitates, uncertain how to answer that, the woman approaches.

"Ma'am? Are you all right?"

Ma'am? Bella's only thirty. But she feels frumpy and world-weary as she takes in the woman's heeled black leather boots and chic white wool winter coat, decidedly dressy for Lily Dale on a weekday morn-ing. She has a sleek short haircut that accentuates her big brown eyes and could only be flattering on someone with such finely sculpted facial features.

"I'm fine."

"Isn't that the medical examiner's van?"

"Oh. Yes, it is. There's, um . . . there's something out back in the lake."

"Something . . . ?"

"*Someone*," she admits, and the woman raises her perfectly arched, pencil-darkened brows.

"Who is it?"

"I'm not sure."

"Did they drown?"

"I'm . . ." Thinking of the tarp, she can only shrug.

"Guess it wouldn't be the first time, hmm?"

"What do you mean?"

"Didn't the woman who used to own this place drown last summer?"

"That happened before my time." Bella isn't in the mood to dis-cuss Leona Gatto's death—hardly an accidental drowning—with a stranger.

"What do you mean?"

"I wasn't living here when it happened. I took over Valley View after Leona . . . passed."

"Then you're Bella."

"I am." She tilts her head, taken aback. "How do you know that?"

"Oh, I . . . Misty must have mentioned it."

Really? Sometimes Bella wonders if Jiffy's mother even knows her name. She can't imagine why she might bring it up to a visitor.

"Are you a friend of Misty's?"

"I just had a reading with her. I mean, she *tried* to read me, but she was having some trouble today, she said."

"What kind of trouble?"

"I don't know. She said her concentration was off, and she kept getting some weird message about a school bus."

"What *about* a school bus?"

"I don't know. She said it was probably for someone else. She wouldn't let me pay her. She told me to come back tomorrow, and she'll try again."

Bella nods uneasily, worried anew about Max.

"Do you think whatever happened back there"—the woman gestures at the lake—"is the reason Misty was blocked today?"

"I don't really know much about it."

What if the message was for *her*? What if Max didn't make it to school? What if the bus—?

"Do you do readings?"

"Me? No! I'm not . . . I don't . . . I'm—I just run Valley View. That's it."

"You're a regular person then?" The woman smiles faintly. "I didn't know there were any around here."

Bella knows what she means, having come to the same conclusion herself as a newcomer to the Dale. But now that she's lived here for six months and considers the locals friends—even family—she bristles at the comment.

"Everyone I've met around here is a regular person."

The smile fades, and the woman fishes for a set of car keys in her oversized black leather bag. "Well, I hope everything works out all right with . . ." She nods toward the squad cars and van and heads toward the Mustang with an incongruous, "Have a good day."

Bella doesn't reply or watch her go. She hurries into the house, looks up the phone number for the elementary school, and dials it with a jittery hand.

Surely they'd have called by now if anything went wrong with the bus.

"Good morning, this is—"

"Christine, this is Bella Jordan," she interrupts the secretary's pleasant greeting. "I'm just checking to make sure Max is there today."

"That he's *here* today?"

"Yes, you know . . . that he isn't absent. Jiffy Arden, too."

Through the window, she sees Lieutenant Grange and the others stooped over the object in the shallows. She quickly turns away as Christine informs her that Jiffy happens to be in with the principal, Mr. Comanda, at this very moment.

"He is? Why?"

"Oh, Mrs. Schmidt sent him down first thing for something or other. He's what we call a frequent flier," she adds with a chuckle.

Hardly surprised that Jiffy is no stranger to the principal's office, Bella asks again about Max.

"Let me check attendance." A pause. "He's here."

She exhales in relief. "Oh, good."

"Is everything all right, Mrs. Jordan?"

"Yes, I just wanted to make sure the boys didn't . . ."

"Wander off?" Christine supplies with a chuckle.

"Exactly."

"No worries. Ed Johansen, the bus driver, always takes attendance and gives us the list. If Max was absent and you hadn't called him in sick, our policy is to contact you right away."

"That's what I thought."

She thanks the woman and hangs up with another glance at the unsettling scene beyond the window, not entirely reassured.

Then again, secondhand information from a stranger about a psychic's vision involving a school bus isn't exactly cause for alarm, is it?

Earlier, she'd been preparing to paint the parlor, with or without Drew Bailey's help. *Might as well proceed with that plan*, she decides and heads for the cellar stairs to collect her supplies.

* * *

"Welcome back," Mrs. Schmidt says as Jiffy walks back into the classroom. "Did you bring your listening ears with you this time?"

"I think I forgot them in the principal's office." He pats the sides of his head and grins when everyone laughs.

Everyone but Mrs. Schmidt. She tells him to take his seat.

He does, disappointed to see that they're doing social studies. He was hoping he missed it while he was down in Mr. Comanda's office, explaining why he was saying something other than the Pledge of Allegiance this morning.

"I *was* saying the pledge," he'd explained, "but then my friend was talking to me, and I had to tell him to be quiet and leave me alone because it was pledge time."

"Mrs. Schmidt said you were the only one talking. She said all your friends were saying the pledge."

That's because Mrs. Schmidt couldn't see the friend who wasn't. Only Jiffy could see him. He didn't bother to explain that to Mr. Comanda, who can't even see Pete, the boy who hangs around his office. Pete was Mr. Comanda's big brother when he was a baby, but he'd made Jiffy promise not to tell him because it might scare him.

Jiffy said he was sorry about the pledge and that he would try harder, and Mr. Comanda said, "All right, Michael. You can go back to class now. Just try to behave for the rest of the day."

He, like Mrs. Schmidt, always calls Jiffy by his real first name instead of the nickname he got a long time ago because he used to eat only peanut butter.

Now that he's almost seven, he eats some other stuff, too. Like hot dogs, ice cream, and spaghetti and curly French fries with cheese. Not mixed together.

"Please open your text to page forty-five, Michael," Mrs. Schmidt tells him.

"Is it about pilgrims? Because I saw a real live one yesterday at Mitch's Hardware Store."

"There's no such thing as pilgrims!" Kevin Beamer says.

"Yes there are! Right, Mrs. Schmidt? We read about them. They came on the Mayflower."

"Yes, but does anyone remember when that happened?"

"1620!" Jiffy speaks up before someone can steal his spotlight. "And this guy at Mitch's was wearing a black pilgrim suit and black pilgrim hat, and he had a big bushy pilgrim beard, and he parked a horse and buggy out front."

"So?" Kevin says.

"So everyone knows pilgrims don't drive cars. And Mrs. Schmidt said some of the Mayflower people had crazy names, like Remember and Humility and Oceanus, and this guy had the crazy name of Joe Yo, so—"

"So that doesn't mean he's a pilgrim! He's—"

"Boys!" Mrs. Schmidt cuts in. "Let's settle down. We can revisit this if we have time at the end of the lesson."

"But—"

"Listening ears, please, Michael. Page forty-five."

Jiffy mouths, *"It was a pilgrim"* at Kevin, who sticks out his tongue.

Mrs. Schmidt goes on talking about a guy named William Penn. From the sounds of it, he invented Pennsylvania.

"I've been there!" Jiffy informs her to prove that his listening ears are working just fine. "I ate curly French Fries with cheese in Pennsylvania with my mom last summer when we were—"

"Michael, did you forget something?"

No, but Mrs. Schmidt has forgotten her manners. Max's mom, Bella, says it isn't polite to interrupt.

"I never forget stuff," Jiffy tells the teacher. "I remember everything. The name of the restaurant was called the Couch Potato, and they had a couch and a lot of potatoes and no fish pretending to be roller skates, and I was glad about that because this one time when I was—"

"Michael." Mrs. Schmidt looks and sounds like she's really, really tired, but then she remembers her manners and says, "Please."

Jiffy waits for her to say what she wants, so that he can give it to her and politely say, "Thank You," but she just goes back to talking about William Penn.

He leafs through his social studies textbook, looking for page forty-five. When he finds it, he sees a familiar face looking back at him. He starts to shout out but remembers to raise his hand.

Mrs. Schmidt, reading from the text, doesn't see him.

He waves it harder, trying to contain his excitement. "Oh, oh, oh, Mrs. Schmidt!"

She looks up and seems even more tired than last time. "Yes, Michael?"

"Is this guy in the picture William Penn?"

"Yes, it is."

"Guess what? He didn't just invent Pennsylvania! He invented oatmeal, too. We have a round box at home in the cupboard, and I saw this same picture on it. My mom likes oatmeal, but I don't. I don't like kale either because that's a disgusting vegetable. So is *crudité*, even though it sounds like a delicious French dessert with whipped cream and chocolate sauce and sprink—"

"Michael! Do you want to visit Mr. Comanda again so soon?"

He considers that.

There were a lot of papers on Mr. Comanda's desk today, and his phone kept ringing. "I think he's pro'lly too busy for more company right now."

"So do I. Please hold your thought until later and listen to the lesson."

Jiffy tries, but instead he finds himself thinking about how much he hates vegetables.

He hates them almost as much as he hates poached skate with braised daikon and charred scallion jam in a lemon confit-kimchi broth. He'd never heard of any of that until last May, when he and Mom drove cross country to New York City. Dad flew there on leave, and they all had dinner at a dark, tiny restaurant full of candles and disappointment.

Mom had told Dad that they were spending the summer in Lily Dale. "I need to get away from the heat, and Jiffy needs a change of scenery."

"Jiffy is fine with heat. He likes heat. Right, Jiff?" Dad had asked.

"Yep, and I like scenery, too. Me and Mom saw a lot when we were driving, right, Mom?"

Mom hadn't said, *Right, Jiff.*

She'd said, "I don't want him to waste his childhood in those cookie-cutter houses on the base. He needs to spend a summer in a lakeside gingerbread cottage, like I did."

Intrigued, Jiffy tried to ask Mom whether base houses were made with a gigantic cookie cutter and whether he would be allowed to take bites of the gingerbread cottage whenever he wanted dessert.

But she hadn't been talking to him, and when he used his outdoor voice so she'd hear him, the fancy people at the next table got mad and shushed him, and then the waiter showed up with their food.

Having ordered the "skate special," Jiffy had been looking forward to eating a blade or wheels and then bragging about it to people later. But his skate hadn't been an ice skate or a roller skate. When he'd seen that it was just a stupid piece of fish, he'd accidentally shouted a little bit. That time, the shushy strangers talked to the restaurant guy in the bowtie. He came over and told Dad that he would appreciate it if the young gentleman would remain silent for the rest of the meal.

Jiffy always hates remaining silent, but Dad bet him five dollars that he couldn't, and of course he *could*, so he had. He'd gotten five dollars and a fancy chocolate dessert with whipped cream and sprinkles.

He'd forgotten all about gingerbread until they got to Lily Dale, which was not full of disappointment even though their cottage wasn't really made out of gingerbread, and it didn't have frosting on the roof, just plain old shingles.

At first, he'd thought that only old people lived there because of all the grandma ladies he met the first day. But there are kids, too. They just don't come knocking on the door bringing food and telling you "Welcome to town" and "If you need anything, just call."

Not all the kids who live there are even alive. Some are Spirit, and they don't have moms or rules like Max Jordan, the only alive Lily Dale kid who's Jiffy's age. His mom, Bella, is nice, but she doesn't let Max do most of Jiffy's fun ideas, and she likes to keep an eye on people when they do stuff like walk home from the bus stop. Especially Max, but also Jiffy.

Except for Max and Bella, the alive people who live in Lily Dale can talk to the dead ones. No one thinks Jiffy just has an active imagination, like they did back on the base, just because he had friends no one else could see. Around here, everyone has invisible friends, only they're called Spirit.

Spirit is everywhere, if you pay attention. It used to be harder for Jiffy to tell if someone was dead or alive, but he's getting better at it.

Like, at first he'd thought the pilgrim guy might have been dead because this wasn't 1620, but Mitch couldn't see Spirit, and he'd said, "Joe Yo, how have you been?"

When Mitch had gone to get the man's order, Jiffy told Pilgrim Joe Yo that he liked his name, and Joe Yo had thanked him with a smile in his beard.

"Did you get your name because it rhymes with yo-yo?"

"No."

"Well, I once had a yo-yo, but only for a few minutes because I bopped a lady on the head by accident, and my mom took it away, and then she lost it. By the way, I'm learning all about you guys from my teacher. Say cheese," he'd added and snapped a picture with his new cell phone to show Mrs. Schmidt.

To his shock, Pilgrim Joe Yo had started yelling at him and tried to grab the phone. Jiffy ran away so fast he'd left his bike behind, parked by the horse. He didn't go get it until after his mother had gone to bed that night.

Even though he's super brave, he'd thought he might be afraid out there alone in the dark. But it turned out that he hadn't been alone, because his friend Albie and his little black cat, Sanchez, had tagged along to keep him company.

They're both Spirit. Albie likes to whistle, and he smells like vanilla pipe tobacco. He wears a suit with a skinny black tie and a brimmed hat. Sanchez is a little black guy with eyes that are round and green like Granny Smith apples, and he meows a lot more than a regular cat. Sometimes it seems like he's trying to say something important. Too bad Jiffy doesn't speak cat.

He enjoys chatting with Sanchez anyway. With people, too, including alive ones, although Bella says talking to strangers is dangerous.

Jiffy has yet to meet a dangerous stranger.

He thinks about the coughing man he met in the bushes behind Valley View last night when he was outside looking for Sanchez.

Jiffy hadn't gotten the feeling that he was Spirit at first. But why else would a guy have been out there alone in the dark? For a minute,

Jiffy worried that he might be a kidnapper. But then he'd gotten a closer look, recognized him, and known he was wrong.

The coughing man wasn't a kidnapper, and he wasn't alive.

He was Elvis Presley.

*　　*　　*

The cellar is Bella's least favorite spot in the house, and not just because it's damp, musty, and full of mice, spiders, centipedes, and who knows what else. Last summer, Leona Gatto's killer imprisoned Max and Jiffy down here.

Bella pushes that from her mind now, along with thoughts of Misty's school bus vision and the corpse in the lake. Keeping an eye out for creepy critters, she crosses the dirt floor, stepping around household castoffs from Leona Gatto's time and likely long before.

When she first moved in, she'd imagined antique treasures hidden in plain sight down here. She's long since lost interest in pillaging the tangle of outdated small appliances, pottery, and rusted garden tools. But as she reaches for the stepladder, a handwritten label jumps out at her from a row of dusty boxes on a shelf behind it.

CHRISTMAS LIGHTS

When she and Max left Bedford back in June, they'd taken only what they could fit in the car. Christmas lights and ornaments were the least of what she was forced to leave behind in the move. She'd kept only the stockings she'd made of quilted calico after Max was born, embroidered with three names. She has yet to hang them because she isn't sure whether to put up two or three. She can't bear to think of leaving Sam's packed away. Yet nor can she stand the thought of it displayed, empty, another reminder of what might have been.

Forgetting to worry about creepy-crawlies, she tugs the box from the shelf and peeks inside. There are, indeed, lights. They're packed in vintage cardboard boxes and have opaque, elongated bulbs in deep colored hues, just like the ones in the old movies that she used to watch with her father.

Another box on the shelf is labeled *CHRISTMAS DECORATIONS*. Opening it, she finds spools of tinsel garlands, ornaments covered in jewel-toned satin thread, and the most delicate gold filigree tree-topper star she's ever seen.

She leaves the ladder behind for now and carries both cartons up to the kitchen table. Avoiding the window, she removes her white cell phone charger from the outlet and grabs one of the light strings.

"Three . . . two . . . one." She plugs it in gingerly, braced for a zap. The only shock is that it still works perfectly well. So do the others, with only a few burned-out bulbs that she can easily replace with extras from the bottom of the box.

There are enough strings for a Christmas tree and the front porch. Imagine Max's delight if he comes home to find the place bathed in a merry glow. She just needs to get some extension cords and—

Hearing a knock on the back door, she looks up to see Lieutenant Grange through the glass.

Her Christmas cheer disappears like prey snatched by a great horned owl's talons. She opens the door and sees a couple more police officers out back. One is setting up a camera on a tripod.

"We need to finish our conversation," Grange tells Bella, gesturing with the clipboard in his hand. "Mind if I come in?"

She shakes her head and steps back.

"Has he—or she?—been out in the lake for a long time, do you think?"

"The DOA?"

"Yes."

"Twelve, maybe fifteen hours tops."

So much for her theory that it's an old cold case. She gulps. "Do you know who it is?"

"We have a pretty good idea."

"Someone local?"

"Local? You mean someone you might know? No."

"What happened to him? Or . . . her?"

"Him."

"Did he drown?"

He levels a look at her, and she shrugs. Yes, she's well aware that drowning victims aren't delivered to shore neatly bundled in tarps, but doesn't she deserve to know what happened?

Apparently not. Grange goes back to questioning her, far more interested in what she saw and heard the other night than in sharing information about the case. Again, he asks for details about the flash of light on the water and the scream.

"And you thought it was an owl because . . ."

"My friend said that's what it sounded like. I described what I'd heard and *he*"—she stumbles over the word and feels her face grow warm like a middle schooler with a crush—"uh, he said it was probably an owl because they're nocturnal, and it's . . . I don't know, I guess it's mating season?"

Ignoring that and—mercifully—the fact that she's blushing, he asks what her friend's name is.

"Wait, why? Are you going to question him?"

"If necessary."

"He wasn't even here when it happened."

"What time did he arrive?"

"Later."

"How much later?"

"I don't know, five, maybe ten minutes?" For some reason, that feels like incriminating information.

Pen poised, he repeats, "And his name?"

She tells him, reluctantly, also forced to supply Drew's occupation, address, and phone number. "But you probably won't get a hold of him this morning. He has a medical emergency."

"Oh?"

Resenting his raised eyebrows and the lack of compassion in his expression, she explains about the injured dog in labor. "He's trying to save her and her babies."

He nods disinterestedly and moves on to a new question. Ten minutes later, she's left alone in the kitchen with her Christmas decorations and the chilling awareness that she might have heard someone's dying scream last night.

Chapter Four

It's been a few hours since Bella watched from the porch as the medical examiner's van pulled away, corpse on board. Odelia, hair still damp from her bath, had stood with a snug arm around Bella's shoulders, shaking her head sadly.

"Do you have any idea who it might have been?" Bella had asked her. "Or how he died?"

"No, but my guides are making me feel as though it was an act of violence. This was not a natural death."

Bella doesn't have guides, but her trusty gut instinct is making her feel the same way.

This was, in all likelihood, a homicide. With the tarp, Grange asking so many questions, yellow crime scene tape stretched along the shore, the CSI team snapping photos and taking measurements, a sheriff's boat trolling the lake . . .

It's still out there now, blue lights flashing, divers in the water. Bella can see it through the kitchen window as she washes her untouched lunch down the garbage disposal.

Odelia, whose "early" client had been scheduled at noon, insisted on bringing her a hot sandwich.

Bella peeled back the foil. "What is it?"

"Macaroni and cheese croquette on French toast. Now I know what you're thinking . . ."

"I don't think you do."

"You can stand to put on a few pounds, my dear, and anyway, it's not *that* fattening. I used hummus instead of mayo."

Bella had thanked her and sent her on her way, then brewed some coffee and went back to waiting for either Drew or Luther Ragland to return her texts. To both, she'd simply written, *Can you please give me a call when you have a chance?*

At one, Drew texted back that he was prepping to do a C-section on the injured dog and would call her shortly. He asked if everything was okay.

Max and I are fine, Bella responded, not wanting to go into detail. *How about the poor mama dog?*

Touch and go.

At that sad news, Bella told him not to worry about getting back to her. A stranger's body in Cassadaga Lake is the least of Drew's problems.

Luther's, too. But the retired detective is her go-to person at times like this.

Bella met him last summer through Odelia, whom he'd befriended years ago when she'd given him an unsolicited tip on a case. He'd been skeptical, but it panned out, and he's used her psychic assistance on investigations over the years.

Luther had helped Bella solve Leona Gatto's murder last summer and the Maynard case last fall. He maintains local law enforcement connections, and she has a feeling he might be able to shed some light on the latest crime to strike uncomfortably close to home.

As she washes the last flecks of deep-fried macaroni and cheese down the drain, she hears someone try to open the front door.

It's probably Hugo Munson. The electrician was tied up today with another job, but maybe he finished early and came back to work on the wiring. Or it might be Odelia again. She's still not used to finding the front door locked.

A few months back, Bella had hosted a destination wedding here at the guesthouse. Sadly, the bride had been targeted for murder and wasn't meant to live happily ever after with her groom. After that, Grant Everard had upgraded the security at Valley View. He'd had a locksmith install electronic keypads on all the guest rooms and a combination box on the exterior doors. Now Bella gives guests and workmen a code to open it.

"No more worrying about duplicated keys floating around out there," Grant had told Bella. "You can change the combination every night if you want."

She doesn't. Now that the Maynard-Langley wedding fiasco has fallen into the past, she doesn't always even bother to keep the doors locked during the day.

Today, however, has jarred her back to vulnerable reality.

She hurries into the hall and sees a familiar figure through the glass door. Not Hugo, or Odelia, or even Drew.

She throws the door open, so relieved to see Luther Ragland that she wants to throw her arms around him. "I can't believe you're here! I was trying to reach you."

"I saw." He indicates the cell phone in his hand. "And I had a good idea why. Figured I'd better come right over."

"I'm really glad you did. Come on in and have a cup of coffee."

"I won't argue with that. Late night last night."

Finally, something to make her smile. "All your nights are late nights. Out with a lady friend?"

"A gentleman never tells."

Luther Ragland is movie-star handsome. His skin is the same rich mahogany as the grandfather clock ticking beside the grand stairway, his presence even more commanding. No sweat pants and five-o'clock shadow for this retiree. He's clean-shaven, wearing dark jeans and a tweed sport coat over an open-collared dress shirt.

In the kitchen, Bella pours him a cup of coffee and refreshes her own.

"This place is really shaping up," he says, running his fingertips over the new subway tiles she'd installed. "You did a great job with this."

"Thanks. Once I got used to the wet saw, it wasn't as difficult as a lot of other stuff I've been doing around here."

Like getting out of bed every morning for the past year. She still doesn't have the hang of that, but somehow she's made it through 359 days without Sam.

A year ago, she couldn't imagine ever smiling again, let alone laughing or . . . *living*. She'd clung to him that last day in the hospital, terrified of losing him, of being alone.

"You have Max. You have . . . me," he'd reassured her with every bit of strength left in his failing body. *"I'll be with you, even when . . . Promise me you'll . . . stay . . . strong . . ."*

"I promise."

Those were the last two words she'd ever said to him.

Somehow, she's kept that final promise.

She *is* strong.

And she isn't alone. Not here in Lily Dale. Far from it.

She sits across from Luther. "So you know what happened?"

He nods. "Heard it on the scanner earlier, and I called my buddy Fred right away to see what was going on."

"Is he the one who works for the sheriff's office?"

"Yes, Fred Donohue. He's with the forensics investigation team."

"So it's . . . it's a homicide, right?"

"Right. They've got an ID on the victim. He had some identifying tattoos."

"Do I know him?"

"Not unless you're dabbling in organized crime on the side. His real name is Yuri Moroskov."

"*Real* name?"

"Guys like him like to use aliases."

"So he's, what—a mobster of some sort?"

"Of the worst sort."

Mobsters have families, too, though. She thinks of Yuri Moroskov's loved ones, how they're going to get a terrible phone call, how they'll have to learn how to go on without him.

"Does his family know yet?"

"No family. Not the kind you're thinking, anyway."

"What was he doing in the lake here?"

"Floating." He smirks a little, then sees her face and stops. "Sorry. But Bella, this is not what you think it is."

"A human being wasn't murdered?"

"We're not talking about another Leona Gatto here, okay? Yuri Moroskov was not a nice guy. In fact, he was a pretty lousy guy."

"You knew him?"

"I knew *of* him. He's part of the Amur Leopard, an international organized crime network. They're involved in smuggling, money laundering, illegal gambling, jewel theft, art forgery, you name it . . . all kinds of fun stuff. This guy was trouble, Bella." He pauses, allowing that to sink in.

He wants her to see this his way, but *she* isn't a retired detective hardened after dealing with a career's worth of corpses. Nor is she a medium who chats daily with the dearly and not-so-dearly departed.

To her, death is harsh and tragic and permanent and yes, dead is dead.

"Luther, look, I know this is all black and white to you. A dead good guy is bad. A dead bad guy is good."

"Death is never *good*."

"But sometimes you take it so lightly. Not just you. All of you around here, and I just . . . can't."

"I don't take it lightly, I promise you. And I'm sorry if it seems that way," Luther says gruffly. He sets down his coffee mug, and his sturdy hand closes over her chapped, scraped, ragged-nailed, bare-ring-fingered one.

She swallows hard. "Some days are just still really . . ."

"I know."

She sighs and looks up at him. "Tell me about this guy."

"He's been wanted for a while."

"By the police?"

"This is bigger. The FBI and Interpol, too. Anyway, he's got some very distinctive tattoos that allowed him to be identified pretty quickly at a glance. Do you remember the Easter Egg Heist five, maybe seven years ago?"

"Someone stole an Easter egg?"

"Moroskov did. A priceless one from a private collection in Moscow. You may have heard of imperial eggs?"

"You mean Fabergé eggs?"

"Yes. That's why it was such big news. Moroskov murdered a few innocent people during the heist, but they couldn't pin anything on him. After he walked, he had a replica of the egg's design and color scheme tattooed on his arm, along with the date. That's how the ME was able to ID him so quickly."

"Why would anyone want to wear the evidence of a crime he got away with?"

"Sheer hubris. Fred said the guy's covered in ink drawings of prominent stolen artwork, precious jewels, rare artifacts—he's a walking tapestry."

"Guess he figured he'd never get caught, but it doesn't seem very smart to . . . you know, wear the evidence on your sleeve, so to speak."

"Yeah, well, we're not talking about a cunning criminal king-pin. Moroskov's just one piece of a very large, complicated operation based in Europe and New York." He steeples his hands under his chin and changes the subject. "Fred said you're a witness—that you saw something or heard something out on the lake last night?"

"A scream." She shudders, remembering the eerie cry echoing across the lake, and explains the situation to Luther.

"If it makes you feel any better," he says, "the ME thinks Moroskov had been dead for at least an hour before he hit the water. So far there's no evidence that he was killed nearby. And I'm sure whoever did it is long gone. Like I said, these guys are pros."

"You think it was a hit?"

"Something like that, if I had to guess."

"Do you think we're in danger here, Luther?" she asks, thinking of Max and of Misty's school bus vision.

"No. I honestly don't think the killer is wandering around the Dale or even has any ties to the immediate area. He was probably just looking for a remote spot to dump the body. I don't even think that was a scream last night. I've heard the owls' mating cries around here at this time of year. That's probably all it was."

She nods, trying to summon relief.

Nothing but a great horned owl.

Yep, that's all.

Just a big old legendary harbinger of death and doom.

*   *   *

This morning, after Priscilla Galante had left, Misty spotted a commotion at the end of the street. Her first thought was that it might have something to do with her unsettling vision about Jiffy on the school bus.

But Odelia Lauder, watching the action from her porch, said some guy had drowned in the lake—something like that. Whatever. Misty has too many problems of her own to worry about a tragedy that doesn't involve her.

She goes back inside and drifts aimlessly around the house, wondering about the vision and worrying about how to pay the rent. Odelia had mentioned that she'd referred someone to Misty because she herself didn't have an open slot, but who knows if that will pan out?

At least Priscilla will be back tomorrow. When Misty had invited her to return for a do-over, she'd never expected her to agree.

But she'd said, "Sure. What time?"

"What time is good for you? I mean, it's a weekday, and you must be working."

"I'm off this week."

If Misty hadn't been so rattled at the time, she might have wondered if that was really the case. The remark had seemed a little forced. But what does it matter? If she comes back, Misty will earn some sorely needed cash.

As long as I can read her next time.

She looks out the front window to see if Pandora Feeney's car is parked at her cottage across Melrose Park. Yesterday, she'd mentioned that she was heading to Buffalo to meet a friend and wouldn't be back until midafternoon.

It's past two now, but she still hasn't returned, and Misty's patience is wearing thin. She really wants to discuss her vision with someone, and Pandora is the only person she'd dare tell around here. Everyone else, even Odelia, seems critical of Misty's parenting skills. It's not that they say anything, but judgment radiates whenever someone mentions that they saw Jiffy here or there or he did this or that. They'd probably interpret her vision as a warning to keep Jiffy on a shorter leash.

She's doing her best, struggling along on her own here with an energetic kid who tests her patience along with his boundaries every minute of every day. She hadn't given him this much freedom back in Arizona and not just because he had been younger. Things were different there. *That* had felt like the real world.

Sometimes Lily Dale doesn't. It's a throwback to a simpler, safer era, an old-fashioned community where people look out for each other. Here, she can loosen the reins and allow him to explore the way she did when she was a child, spending summers here with her great-aunt Ellen.

She turns away from the window and considers calling Mike. Not to tell him about the vision, necessarily. But they still haven't discussed specifics for his upcoming visit for Christmas, and anyway . . .

Maybe she needs to feel connected to someone right now. Someone who isn't on the Other Side.

Someone who's supposed to be on *her* side.

Her soul mate.

She thinks about that day seven years ago, when she first spotted him at the amusement park, about to take his turn at the snow cone stand. She grabbed her friend's arm and pointed. "See that guy? He's the one."

"What are you talking about? Wait, where are you going? What are you doing?"

She was marching over to the snow cone stand, stepping up beside Mike as he placed his order.

"I'll have cherry, please," she'd said when the cashier asked him if that was all.

"Excuse me?" Mike turned to gape at her.

She didn't look into his eyes as much as she *melted* into them, her soul fusing with his.

"Did you say cherry?" the cashier had asked, and she recovered her voice.

"Yeah. Cherry. Extra syrup."

Mike bought her the snow cone. Their first date had been the following night. On their second, she'd slipped and mentioned that he was going to marry her someday. That had scared him off for a while, but he'd drifted back, just as Spirit had promised he would.

They were meant to be.

Still are, though he's a world away from her now and somehow seemed even more remote than when she saw him in New York City last May.

But I still love him. And need him.

She finds her cell phone, still silenced from her session with Priscilla. She's missed a call from an unfamiliar number, and there's a message, but it'll keep.

It's almost midnight where Mike is stationed and costly to call him there. She dials his number anyway.

It rings a few times before he picks up, sounding groggy.

"Hey, babe," she says, "it's me."

"Sorry, I feel asleep. How'd it go?"

"How'd *what* go?"

A pause. "Mary Ellen?"

"Yes," she says, born Mary Ellen Grzeszkiewicz twenty-four years ago. "Who did you think it was?"

"Oh . . . one of the guys was supposed to call me back about something."

"About what?"

"It's not important. What's going on? Why are you calling me so late?"

"It's not late here. And I needed to talk to you."

"Why? Is something wrong?"

He sounds concerned. Good. He should be.

"Yes, something's wrong."

"What is it? Is Michael okay?"

"He is now, but . . ."

"You're scaring me. What's going on?"

"I had a premonition."

He exhales audibly. Not, she realizes when he speaks again, in relief.

"What was it this time?" he asks, and she can see him rolling his eyes at her.

"You really want me to tell you?"

"If you want to."

She doesn't. Not anymore. "I'm just worried about him now."

"About Michael?"

"Jiffy. Yes."

"Then keep an eye on him."

"I always do."

He says nothing to that, just asks around a yawn, "Is that it, then? You called about the premonition?"

In other words, *Can I hang up and go back to bed?*

"No. I called about Christmas."

"We need to talk about that right this second?"

"You didn't answer my text about which day you're coming."

"My leave starts on the twenty-second."

"Okay . . . so are you getting a connecting flight from JFK to Buffalo? Or renting a car in New York and driving here?"

Silence.

"Mike? Which is it?"

"Neither."

"Neither?"

"I don't want to spend Christmas in Lily Dale. I hate everything about that place. It's creepy and crowded and—"

"That was during the season. The crowds, I mean." She bites her tongue to keep from insisting that it isn't creepy. He was only here once, years ago. "It's different now. There's no gate fee, no crowd. It's peaceful and relaxing. You'll see."

"I don't want to see. You guys can meet me in New York City for the holidays. Michael would love all those store windows, and we can go skating by the tree in Rockefeller Center and see Santa at Macy's . . ."

"Are you serious?"

"He loved New York last May."

"And it cost us a fortune to spend one night there then. How would we afford Christmas?"

"Okay, then we'll spend it with your mom in Cleveland."

"You're kidding, right?"

A decade ago, her widowed mother married a man who had three young sons from his first marriage, and they've since had two daughters together. There's barely room for lunch guests in their tiny house overrun with children, clutter, and chaos, let alone long-term visitors.

"Jiffy and I spent the night there last May when we were driving east. We slept in sleeping bags on the floor in the hallway. *With* the dog. I promised myself never again."

"I had a feeling you might say that. But I have another idea. How about Bethlehem? It's not that far away, and—"

"Maybe not far for *you*, but Jiffy and I can't fly to the Middle East, Mike."

"Not *that* Bethlehem. My hometown!"

Flabbergasted, she says, "But you haven't spoken to your father in years!"

"That's long enough. Life is too short to hold grudges. I think I'm ready to mend the fences. Wouldn't it be nice for Jiffy to have a grandpa? And an uncle? I'd like to show you and Jiffy where I grew up."

They've already seen it, last May when they were driving from her mother's in Cleveland to meet Mike in New York. They'd stopped for lunch in Allentown at a little café called the Couch Potato. Unaware that he was a stone's throw from his father's hometown, Jiffy had gobbled curly fries smothered in melted cheese and bacon as Misty scrutinized every man in the place, searching for a resemblance to Mike.

She'd opted not to tell him about it when they got to New York, thinking it might upset him and ruin the fleeting time they had together. He's never liked to discuss his past. So why the sudden change?

"It's great that you want to reconcile with your family, Mike. But we can't just show up there for Christmas after all these years."

"Why not?"

"Because . . . because it's crazy, that's why not."

"Any crazier than spending it in a wacky town full of people who talk to ghosts?"

Mike doesn't know that Jiffy has a gift. It isn't something she wants to tell him over the phone or via text. She'd thought it could wait until Christmas, when she could show him how happy they are here.

Now he's not coming.

And suddenly, this conversation isn't just about the holiday. It's about where, and with whom, she's going to spend the rest of her life—this one and those to come.

"My son is going to wake up on Christmas morning in his own bed."

"Well then, I guess that means you're going to be driving *our* son to Arizona. I'll change my plane ticket to Phoenix.'"

"Feel free. But Jiffy and I will be in Lily Dale for Christmas. If you want to see us, you know where to find us," she says and hangs up, shaking.

Chapter Five

Beyond a pair of French doors in Valley View's parlor lies a small room with creamy yellow walls and a built-in window seat with blue-and-white floral cushions. Leona Gatto had used it as a meditation room, but for Bella, it's a pleasant little study. It's just big enough for a desk that holds the computer where she sits now, typing *Amur Leopard* into a search engine.

It returns plenty of hits, first and foremost about the animal itself. It's an endangered species in Russia, recognized—and hunted—for its distinctive, exquisitely patterned skin.

Kind of like Yuri Moroskov himself, Bella notes, and she types his name instead.

How, she's been wondering, did an internationally notorious mobster find his way into Cassadaga Lake?

The search returns a long list of links to news about the Amur Leopard gang and the Easter Egg Heist that Luther mentioned. It had been front page news around the world, but there's a good reason Bella doesn't remember it. She was in labor with Max that Easter. International crime headlines were the last thing on her mind.

According to the online accounts, the Fabergé eggs were made for the Russian tsars back in the late 1800s through early 1900s. There are only about fifty of them in the world, and seven have been lost over the years. Those that remain are priceless.

On Easter Sunday, the most important day of the Russian Orthodox calendar, a brazen thief had slipped into a private home in Moscow, murdered the elderly resident and her household staff, and stolen the egg known as the Budding Crocus.

It's encrusted with alexandrite, one of the most precious gemstones in the world, known for its startling ability to change colors. In some lights, it tends to appear green, in others, red or purple. Thus, the floral design cleverly depicts buds giving way to blossoms.

The egg has never been recovered. Moroskov was indeed a suspect, but as Luther said, the lack of evidence set him free.

From there, he made his way to the United States, where he has used a number of aliases and was thought to be linked to many more thefts of priceless gems, artwork, and rare artifacts stolen overseas, smuggled to Canada, and then into this country.

This is starting to make more sense to Bella now. The Canadian border is a little over an hour north of Lily Dale. And now Moroskov has been murdered—by whom? Should it matter? The man has no connection to Bella or Valley View or Lily Dale.

Still . . .

This is one day she's going down to the bus stop, no matter what Max and Jiffy have to say about it.

* * *

Misty was sure Mike would call back immediately to apologize. But when immediately gave way to ten minutes, and now half an hour, she realizes it's not going to happen.

Maybe he fell asleep.

Or maybe he's busy talking to the someone-else whose call he was expecting.

How'd it go?

Misty seethes, pacing the master bedroom that she has never shared with Mike and, according to him, never will.

How'd *what* go?

He said it wasn't important. Said it was one of the guys, but . . .

Things are adding up.

They used to be good at the long-distance relationship thing. She'd felt connected to him even when he was overseas. Now she probably wouldn't even if they were sharing a bed.

Hey, babe, it's me, she'd said when he picked up the phone.

He'd mistaken *that* for one of the guys?

She curses and looks around for something satisfyingly fragile to hurtle across the room. Her gaze lands on the bedside clock.

Jiffy will be coming home from school soon. What the heck is she supposed to tell him about Christmas?

Remembering her vision, she's tempted to crawl into her rumpled, lonely bed and pull the sheets over her head. She might, if they'd been changed more recently. They're stale, smeared with chocolate from the morning Jiffy brought her "breakfast" in bed, and belong in the mountain of dirty clothing and linens she should be sorting for tomorrow's avoid-the-landlord trip to the laundromat because, oh, yeah, she can't pay her rent.

Beneath her bedroom window, she hears a car coming down Cottage Row, driving much too quickly to be Pandora—or, fortunately, Virgil. The driver can't possibly be familiar with the Dale's potholes.

Her doorbell rings a minute later.

Frowning, she goes to the window. A black luxury SUV sits parked in the spot reserved for her clients.

She checks her reflection in the bureau mirror. Her haywire hair is as out of control as her emotions. She picks up a brush, then sets it down again. Why bother? Yesterday's coffee dribble is prominently featured on the purple sweater she picked up from the floor this morning. It's tighter than it was when she bought it a few months ago and not because it shrunk. She's never been particularly svelte, but she's been eating—and all right, maybe drinking—more than she used to and picked up some extra pounds.

She gives up on her appearance and heads downstairs, hoping that whoever is at the door is looking for a reading and that she'll be able to deliver this time.

The buxom middle-aged redhead on her porch starts talking before she can say a word. "I tried calling you this morning for an appointment. Your neighbor Ophelia gave me your number because she was booked. She said you take walk-ins, so I'm walking in."

"*Odelia.*"

"What?"

"Her name is Odelia, not Ophelia."

"Okay. *Odelia.*"

She's wearing an insincere smile, several gaudy rings with massive diamonds, and what appears to be a genuine leopard fur coat, unzipped to bare generous cleavage in a low-cut V neck. She reeks of stale cigarette smoke. Her long nails are probably as fake as the rest of her, polished in glittery scarlet, the same shade as her aura.

A red aura signifies passion, adventure, and a competitive spirit, but with her, Misty gets plenty of conflict and perhaps greed.

"Well?" she asks. "Can you read me?"

Good question.

When the timing isn't right, the energy isn't there, or Misty just doesn't like someone, she prefers not to waste the sitter's time and her own. But in desolate December, she can't afford to turn down business.

Maybe if she meditates alone first to get her focus back where it belongs . . .

"Are you in a rush? Because I have something I have to do first. But it shouldn't take long," she adds quickly as the woman checks her watch, a jewel-encrusted gold clunker.

"Yeah, I guess I can wait for a little while."

"Okay, great. I'm Misty, by the way."

"I figured. I'm Barbara."

Yeah, sure you are.

Some visitors choose anonymity because they're not entirely comfortable with what goes on here. Others, because they're skeptical and "testing" the process.

Odelia once tried to explain the reasoning. "They think that if they provide us with legitimate information, even a first name, it's giving away too much and they won't get a genuine reading."

Ironic, considering that the very foundation of Spiritualism is to deliver truth.

Even if that truth is unwelcome, she thinks, with Mike's "one of the guys" echoing in her head as she closes the door behind the stranger.

*　　*　　*

Heading down Cottage Row toward the gate, Bella runs into Calla Delaney coming up. Wearing jeans, sneakers, and a hooded sweat shirt embroidered with the name of a writer's retreat, she's effortlessly pretty without a trace of makeup, her long brown hair in a ponytail.

"I just heard what happened. Are you okay, Bella?"

She nods and tells her side of the story, which Odelia apparently already shared.

"What happened is pretty awful," Calla says, "but at least it doesn't sound like we need to worry that it has anything to do with Lily Dale."

"Maybe not, but I'm still going down to the bus stop to get the boys."

"I don't blame you. I'm on my way over to Gammy's. She's having a Crock-Pot emergency."

"What happened?"

"Hers broke a while back, and she's been trying to replace it, only no one carries it anymore. So now she wants me to help her try to order it online. You know how she is."

Bella nods. Odelia is hopeless when it comes to online shopping—or online anything.

"How about you?" Calla asks. "Have you finished your Christmas shopping yet?"

"I haven't even started it yet."

"Too busy?"

"Too busy, too broke, too confused."

"Confused about what?"

Bella glances at the Ardens' cottage nearby, making sure Misty isn't out on her porch. She's spotted Jiffy's mom sitting there only once, before the weather turned. Bella herself was perched nearby on the steps at Valley View, watching the boys ride scooters along the deserted lane.

Given the size of the glass in Misty's hand, Bella had assumed it must be soda or juice. But she'd overheard a thirsty Jiffy asking his mom for a sip.

"This is my wine," she'd said. "Run inside and get yourself some water."

Confirming that the porch is vacant today, Bella sees a black SUV with Ontario license plates parked out front. She must have a client.

Still, Bella lowers her voice as she explains to Calla that Jiffy wants a snowboard, so naturally Max wants a snowboard.

"Are you going to buy him one?"

"How can I? Kids under seven aren't even allowed to take snowboarding lessons. I can't have him careening down the side of a mountain."

Calla flicks a gaze at the rolling slopes on the far side of the lake. Okay, they aren't exactly mountains, but still.

"Maybe you can show him how to use it on the sledding hill. It's not steep."

"I wish I could. Except I don't know how to snowboard. I've never skied. I've barely been on a sled. Winter sports aren't exactly my thing."

"Mine either," Calla says, "but if Jiffy gets a snowboard for Christmas and Max doesn't, you'll hear about it every moment of every day from now until Mother's Day."

"Why Mother's Day?"

"That's pretty much when it stops snowing for the year. If we're lucky."

"Terrific. And I'm sure I'll never hear the end of the cell phone."

"Max wants a cell phone for Christmas, too?"

She nods. "Jiffy has a cell phone."

"That's ridiculous. They're first graders. Have you talked to his mom about all this?"

"I don't talk much with Misty. Anyway, I really can't relate to her. She's young. Jiffy said she just turned twenty-four."

"That's only six years younger than you. You've breached that same massive generation gap with Drew. He's thirty-six, right?"

"That's different. Drew seems younger than he is, or maybe I just feel older than I am after everything I've been through. But we're not talking about Drew and me."

"I wish you would. I think it's time that you—"

"By the way, I installed that backsplash."

"'By the way'—now you sound like Jiffy. How'd it come out?"

"Let's just say it's far from perfect."

"Perfect is boring."

"I love you, Calla," Bella says with a smile and checks her watch. "I've got to get to the bus stop. Good luck with Odelia."

"Good luck with the snowboard situation."

Too bad that's the least of my problems right now, Bella thinks as she continues down the lane, keeping an eye out for strangers lying in wait.

*　*　*

Jiffy notes a sudden swirl of snow in the air.

It isn't really there.

The sky is brilliant blue, and the late afternoon sun is as bright yellow as the empty school bus disappearing around the bend. The breeze is so warm that he's not even wearing a coat, mostly because he left it on the bus. The other kids' jackets are unzipped, and they're not hurrying toward home, heads bent against the wind, the way they usually do on December days.

Only Jiffy can see the white flakes, and he knows what it means: snow, real snow, is coming soon.

Back in the Arizona desert where he used to live, interesting weather never happened.

Too bad he can't be excited about his first big snowstorm on account of the kidnappers.

"Hey, how come your mom is here?" Jiffy asks Max, spotting Bella up ahead.

"I don't know. She's s'posed to wait on the porch at home."

"Maybe something happened. She's worried."

"She doesn't look worried."

Jiffy peers at her. She doesn't, but he feels like she is. *Really* worried.

"Hi, boys," she calls, smiling and waving. "Hey, Jiffy, where's your jacket? Did you lose it?"

"Nope. I know 'xactly where it is."

"Where?"

"On the bus, smushed on the floor in front of the third seat on the right."

"You're not s'posed to meet the bus, Mom!"

"Oh, I know I'm not," she tells Max. "I had to come down here to check something at the gatehouse."

Jiffy looks at the little white hut. Someone works in there during the season, collecting money from the cars that come through. "What are you checking? Do you have a key? Can me and Max check with you? Because I want to go in there and see what it's like."

"Actually, I . . . already checked it. Now I'm going home."

"Well, don't go home next to me," Max says, "because people will think I'm a baby."

Jiffy nods. "And me, too, because I'm his best friend. You should stay here for a while."

"I can't, but I won't walk with you, okay? I'll stay way behind. I promise."

As Jiffy and Max hurry to catch up to the older kids, he smells vanilla pipe tobacco. Somewhere nearby, Albie is whistling "Santa Claus Is Coming to Town."

You better watch out, Jiffy sings along inside his head.

He can't whistle because he fell off the monkey bars one day and knocked out one of his front teeth. The tooth fairy didn't even come because he forgot to find the tooth in the dirt to put under his pillow. He was too busy bleeding and crying just a little and looking for his mom because she said she'd meet him at the playground. She'd forgotten, but that was okay, because the Spirit kids were there. They said he was going to be just fine, and they were right, except for the tooth fairy part and the whistling part.

And the snow, he thinks, looking at the flakes dancing all around them like glitter dust.

No one is paying any attention to it, other than the girl who slipped into their group as they got off the bus.

She isn't wearing a backpack like everyone else. She's carrying her books in both arms, flat against her chest. Her face is almost as freckly as Jiffy's, and her long hair is reddish orange like his, except hers hangs in braids tied with blue ribbons, and it's always wet. The hem of her blue dress almost reaches the little white socks folded down above her shiny black shoes with silver buckles. Her clothes, too, are always drenched, and sometimes she smells like the lake.

Jiffy sees her look up at the snow swirling down from the sky and hold out her hand as if to catch the flakes. She turns to Jiffy, and her eyes are big and wide like she's scared.

He glances back at Bella. She doesn't seem to see the snow, but she's scared, too. She's just acting like she's not.

"She can't hear us now. She's way back there," Max says, checking over his shoulder.

"Yep."

"Then how come you're not talking?"

"'Cause I'm being quiet."

"Why? Does your throat hurt? Mine does."

"No, I'm being quiet 'cause I'm thinking."

"You're hardly ever thinking," Max observes.

"I know. But I am right now."

"About what?"

"Snow. I think it's going to snow a lot tomorrow or the next day, so—"

"That stinks. We won't have our snowboards from Santa till Christmas morning, and that's over a week away."

Jiffy ponders that. It does stink because if he's not kidnapped after all, he'd like to enjoy the storm on the sledding hill.

"Wait, I know! We can borrow your mom's ironing board. I bet that would work awesome."

"I don't think my mom would let us," Max says. "Wait, I know! We can borrow *your* mom's ironing board instead. That would work just as awesome."

"She doesn't have one, and she doesn't even have a washing machine right now! We won't tell your mom. We'll put it back 'xactly where we found it, and she'll never know."

"She knows everything."

"Not like my mom."

"Well, she's not psychic like your mom, but she knows a lot."

That's true. Bella's good at figuring stuff out even though Spirit doesn't tell it to her.

A terrible thought strikes him. "Uh-oh. What if your mom stays up late on Christmas Eve and says something to Santa?"

"About what?"

"About stuff she knows! Like when we're sleeping and when we're awake, and whether we've been good for goodness' sake."

"I have," Max says.

"Me, too. I try not to pout, and I never cry."

"Me either. Only babies cry."

"Right. But sometimes, good behavior is not always that easy."

Like the other day, he didn't mean to draw a giant Sharpie picture of a ninja zombie on the living room wall. Well, he did mean to draw it, and it turned out to be his best artwork ever.

But he was so busy thinking that the boring white wall needed something interesting that he forgot all about how you shouldn't draw stuff on rental cottage walls. Or probably any walls. Except whiteboards at school. But not in Sharpie there either, even if you know the answer to *2+2* and you want to make sure Kevin Beamer doesn't erase your name next to the *4* and write his instead.

Jiffy glances back at Bella, wondering if Mrs. Schmidt told her about that. Or maybe the janitor did, after he had to hang up the new whiteboard. Or maybe she just knows, like she knows all that other stuff.

"By the way, Max, you need to give your mom a really super great Christmas present."

"I'm going to. I have the handprint."

"The one we made in school?" Jiffy shakes his head. "You need to give her something way better so that she won't tell Santa on us."

"You mean on me."

"Or me. Get her a beautiful golden present like I'm giving my mom."

"Okay. Where'd you get it?"

Jiffy considers telling Max he bought it at a fancy store. But Max might not believe him, so he decides on the truth. Sort of.

"It's buried pirate treasure I found by the lake. Only it wasn't buried, and it wasn't in a chest. But it's very golden."

"Doubloons?"

"Rings. I can give you one for your mom because I have four."

"Can I have two? My mom used to wear two golden rings, but I think she lost them."

"Okay, two."

"Good." He holds out his hand, palm up.

"I don't have them now. I hid them."

"Where?"

"In a secret spot. I'll go get them later."

"Thanks. My mom will be happy."

"Plus Santa will bring us snowboards for sure, as long as . . ." He glances back at Bella again. She smiles at him. He smiles back even though he doesn't feel like it.

"As long as *what*?"

"*The kidnapper is coming*," he whispers, turning back to Max.

* * *

He should have known better than to hang around this crazy place after the black cat crossed his path last night. He *did* know better, but there's no way he's leaving without his missing rings.

He felt lucky just to be alive this morning, after an asthma attack so crippling that he hadn't been able to make it all the way back to his truck. He'd spent a sleepless night huddled in a chilly barn that smelled of manure, which didn't help his irritated airways or his mood.

When the sun finally rose, he debated whether to backtrack for the rings on foot or get the truck and move it closer. He opted to head back toward the Dale, retracing his steps. A risky move in broad daylight, but with luck, he thought, the rings will quickly turn up glinting in his path, and he'll be on his way.

He doesn't find them along the stretch of road outside the gates and weighs the wisdom of reentering the private community. But there isn't a soul in sight, and anyway, it's not like he is conspicuously costumed this morning. He has on street clothes like someone out for a nice morning walk.

Besides, he reminds himself as he enters the Dale, it's not as if he has no experience with hiding in plain sight. Isn't that his job?

Emboldened by the solitude, he heads back up Cottage Row, subtly panning the ground all the way. He's careful to focus on breathing slowly to keep his asthma in check, relieved the air is warmer today.

He can feel panic edging in when he reaches Valley View and hasn't found the rings, but he reminds himself that they'd most likely slipped off his hands while he was distracted by the chatty kid and black cat. They'll be somewhere in the grass behind the guesthouse and the cottage next door.

That's where he is, combing the lawn between Valley View Manor and the cottage next door, when he hears a commotion. Doors opening, voices shouting . . .

"See you later, Mom!"

"Wait! I'm coming, too!"

He lunges into the bushes and stays there, heart pounding. When at last things have quieted and he dares to emerge, he spots a jarring sight at the edge of the lake.

His pal Yuri has come ashore like a vengeful ghost. He is staring in horror, wondering what to do, when the back door opens and a brown-haired woman steps outside.

Again he dives for cover, heart pounding, lungs crushed.

There is no way she'll spot the tarp.

She *can't.*

If she does, he'll have to—

She does.

As he crouches there, fighting to draw a breath of air, she looks toward the lake, and he knows it is all over. For him, for now.

But soon, for her, too. For good.

She takes a closer look, then hurries back inside, and he knows she's calling the cops.

He bolts and is panting in the shadows alongside the gate by the time the squad car arrives. If he ever gets his hands on that cursed creature, or the kid, or the lady snitch over at Valley View . . .

Still, he's not going anywhere without reclaiming what belongs to him. No, he'll stick around and kill some time before he kills . . .

Anything else.

*   *   *

For a while now, Jiffy has been dreaming about being kidnapped on a snowy day. In the dream, it's snowing so much that he can't see the kidnapper's face. It hasn't snowed that hard here yet, but when—not *if*—it does, he's going to get kidnapped. That makes it hard to look forward to a big snowstorm.

"It might not happen," Max tells him. "Like, last night, I dreamed my dad came back alive today."

"Did he?"

"Nope."

Until Jiffy met Max, he'd thought the worst thing was to have a soldier dad in the Middle East. Now he knows there are worse things. Way worse.

"Jiffy, just because you dream about something doesn't mean it's going to happen, even though I wish it did for me."

"Guess I won't get kidnapped then," he says, even though he doesn't believe it. His own dreams usually do come true.

"Well, that's good."

"Yep. By the way, if I *do* get kidnapped, I'll run away as fast as I can, like the Gingerbread Man. No one ever catches him."

"What if the kidnapper does?"

"Then I'll escape and run, run as fast as I can. Plus, I'll be famous. You'll see me on TV. You might be a little famous, too, because you'll be on TV saying you hope the police find me soon because I am a great kid. And super brave. Make sure you mention that."

"Super brave. Right, I will. But won't you be afraid?"

"Nah," Jiffy lies.

People should never be afraid. His Dad isn't, and he has the scariest job in the world except for whatever you call those guys who study sharks from underwater cages. Oh, and ninjas.

"If you get kidnapped," Max says, "I can save you, and then we'll both be super brave. And famous."

Hmm. *Two* super brave and famous guys might be one too many for a little town like this.

"How would you save me exactly? In a helicopter?" Jiffy has always wanted to ride in one. His dad does sometimes.

"I guess. By the way, where would I get it? And who would drive it?"

"You'll have to get an army guy."

"Okay. Your dad?"

"He just rides in helicopters. He doesn't drive them."

"Well, maybe I can find you the regular way. Like, you could call and tell me where the kidnappers are hiding you."

"You don't have a cell phone, by the way."

"Maybe my mom will give me one. Or Santa."

"You better give her the golden present before Christmas, because if you don't get a phone, I won't be able to call and tell you where the kidnappers are hiding me."

"Wait, I know! Maybe you can tell Spirit to tell your mom or Odelia or someone, and then they can tell me and I can rescue you."

Jiffy shrugs, rapidly losing interest in the rescue if there aren't going to be helicopters. Anyway, they've reached his house.

"See you later, Jiffy," Bella calls, and he turns to see that she's almost caught up to them.

"Hey, are you doing another little painting project today? Because me and Max can help you again."

"Not today."

"Are you sure? Because me and Max loved painting, and this time we can be more careful not to get it on the rug and the cats and the toilet."

"Oh, I'm positive, but thanks anyway, Jiffy. Max and I have to run an errand."

"But me and Jiffy are going to ride scooters," Max protests.

"Jiffy and I," Bella corrects him. "You can do that when we get back. We have to go to the hardware store."

"Can I come? I go over there all the time to visit my friend Mitch."

"By yourself?" Max asks, impressed.

"Yep."

Bella tilts her head at him. "That's a long way to ride your bike, Jiffy."

"I know. That's why I want to ride in your car this time."

"Well, I think Max and I will just go on our own today because you'd need your mom's permission. Looks like she's busy with clients, and I know you're not allowed to interrupt her readings." Bella points to the big black SUV parked in front of Jiffy's house.

"She won't care if I go. Please? I love it there. Mitch has cool stuff like metal detectors and peanuts in a barrel, and—"

Mean pilgrims, he remembers.

"Never mind, I'll stay here," he tells Bella. "How many minutes will you be gone?"

"Maybe fifteen."

"That's how long it takes to sing 'The Twelve Days of Christmas' five times."

"How do you know that?"

"'Cause my phone has a stopwatch app, and I like timing stuff. So when I sing it five times, you'll be back. By the way, Bella, what's your phone number?"

"Why?"

"So I can call you and tell you fifteen minutes are up if you forget."

Smiling, she rattles it off. "Don't you want to write that down?"

"Nope," he says, "I got a great memory. See you in fifteen minutes. Then me and Max can ride our scooters. I mean, Max and *me*."

"You mean I," Max says.

"I mean *I* and Max." Hoping Bella will mention his good manners if she does talk to Santa, Jiffy scampers into the house, singing. "On the first day of Christmas . . ."

A lady is sitting on the padded bench by the stairway. "Hello," she greets Jiffy.

He stops singing, wondering if she's a regular person or Spirit.

"Are you waiting for my mom?"

"Is your mom Misty Starr?"

"Yep."

"Then yes, I am."

If she's here for a reading, then she's not Spirit. She's trying to talk to Spirit or maybe just find out what's going to happen in her future. Mom sometimes knows that, too.

The door to Mom's meditation room cracks open, and she peers out. "Hey, you're home already? I lost track of time. Go watch TV until I'm done here, okay?"

On a regular, not warm and sunny day, that would sound like a great idea to Jiffy. Not today.

"I want to ride my scooter."

"But you can't be out there alone."

Surprised, Jiffy asks, "How come? I'm always out there alone."

"Not today. Okay?"

"But Max is riding scooters, too, and Bella is watching us."

Mom looks relieved. "Okay, then. I'll come find you when I'm finished here. Sorry, Barbara. I just need a little more time," she adds and shuts the door again.

The lady makes a loud breathing sound and leans her head back.

"Hey, can you move your butt?" Jiffy asks her and remembers to add, "Please?"

"Excuse me?"

"Bella says I need my helmet, and you're sitting on it."

Her eyebrows rise, but so does she.

Jiffy opens the hinged bench top and peers inside. No helmet, but hey, there's his red sneaker. He thought he left it outside in the rain one day when he took off his shoes to see how mud felt squishing on bare toes. He found out it feels pretty good.

He digs through the stuff, tossing some of it over his shoulder—last week's science project, a folder full of papers that scatter all over the floor, an empty soda bottle with a folded straw in it, a remote control without batteries, some Sharpies, which he's been looking for ever since the ninja on the wall incident, and . . .

"Hey, my hockey puck!" He hasn't seen it since the day his hand accidentally dropped it into a bowl of tomato soup that stained his yellow shirt and Mom's white one.

"Do you like the Sabres?" asks the lady.

"When they're not stinky," he says as he checks to see if his yo-yo might be in the bench, too.

"They've been winning all week."

"You like hockey?"

"I love it," she says. "But my team is the Maple Leafs. They're playing the Sabres tonight."

"Don't worry. Your team is going to win eleven to zero."

"Eleven to zero? I don't think so, kiddo."

"I do think so."

"Why?"

"I just know."

Unable to find a helmet or a yo-yo, he plunks the bench top down again and pats the cushion. "There you go. Thanks for moving out of my way."

"You're very welcome . . . what's your name, again?"

"I didn't tell it to you yet."

"You're pretty sharp, aren't you, kiddo?"

"Yep. And I'm named Michael J. Arden the third."

"Is that what your friends call you?"

"No, they call me Jiffy. But you and me are not 'xactly friends, since I'm a kiddo"—her phrase, and he follows it with a tactful one of his own—"and you're a kind of older lady."

"True, but we're going to be friends anyway."

"Can you predict stuff, too?"

"Not nearly as well as you can. See you later, Jiffy."

Chapter Six

"Wait, did they just say three *feet* of snow?" Bella asks, gaping across the counter at Mitch and then at the plate glass window. It's hard to imagine any snow at all dropping from that blue sky by this time tomorrow.

But the store's speakers are tuned to WDOE, the local radio station, and the forecaster just said . . .

"Three feet," Virgil Barbor confirms from the corner by the woodstove. "That's what they said, all right."

A strapping grape farmer with a full dark beard, he grew up in the Dale and still maintains several properties there, now choosing to live nearby in his sprawling farmhouse with acres of vineyard. He wasn't around much during the harvest season but seems to be here whenever Bella visits the store lately—not necessarily to shop, but to shoot the breeze with Mitch and whoever wanders in the door.

"Wow," Bella says. "I heard we were only going to get six to eight inches. Although, back where I come from, we wouldn't say 'only' for that much snow."

"Where I come from, that's nothing." Mitch, who comes from *here*, grins at her. In his midseventies, he has thick white hair and warm brown eyes in a pleasantly weathered face. Like Virgil, he's wearing a flannel shirt, well-worn dungarees, and thick-soled Timberland work boots.

WDOE goes back to playing Christmas carols in the background. Mitch hums along with "Do You Hear What I Hear?" as he rings up the nails, bolts, and screws that Bella had selected from open bins, along with joint compound and spreaders, more drop cloths, another can of Sylvan Mist latex, rollers, brushes . . .

"Mitch, I almost forgot—do you have any paint remover that's safe to use on a kitten?" she asks, remembering that little Spidey's black fur still bears Max- and Jiffy-sized Silken Taupe fingerprints.

"A kitten? You'd better check with your vet about that. But if you need to remove paint from anything else . . ."

"I do. A shower curtain. Oh, and a toilet seat."

"Had some help painting the bathroom, did you?" Mitch chuckles and nods toward Max, who's busily shelling peanuts from a barrel. "Let me see what I can find."

Humming, he heads toward the shelves, past a garland-draped endcap display and beneath a hand-lettered sign.

50% Off Gifts for Everyone on Your List

There's only one person on Bella's list.

The Christmas music in the background is a reminder that her shopping days are dwindling. If she finds something Max might like, she can ask Mitch to put it aside for her now so that at least she'd have one surefire gift for him.

Too bad a six-year-old has no use for a Crock-Pot, though she wonders if this one might suit Odelia's purposes. Nor would a little boy like jumper cables, a toaster oven, a power screwdriver, a—

No, wait, there's an idea—a metal detector. Over the summer, Max and Jiffy had enjoyed playing pirate and digging for buried treasure along the lakeshore.

"A star, a star," she sings along in her head, picking up the box. A metal detector might not turn up gold doubloons, but there might be some interesting relics out there, and at least it would distract them from digging in the lawn.

"I hope you've got a good, strong snow shovel," Virgil comments, watching her browse.

"I hope your weatherman was wrong."

"Hard to be right or wrong in lake effect country. It all depends on wind direction, air temperature, the temperature of Lake Erie . . ."

As a science teacher—*former* science teacher—she's familiar with basic meteorology. As a busy, broke innkeeper with guests due tomorrow, the last thing she needs is a massive storm.

"I've driven through a blizzard to find it dry and clear a half mile up the road," Virgil goes on. "But around here, we don't let a little bit of snow stop us."

"What about Santa Claus?" Max asks. "Does it stop him?"

"No, see, he's from the North Pole. People up north are even more used to it than we are."

"Good, because Lauri and Dawn are also from up north," Bella comments.

"The North Pole?"

"Buffalo."

"Some people might have a tough time telling the difference. Who *are* Lauri and Dawn?" Virgil asks.

"Guests who have reserved two rooms for three nights—unless they're snowbound and don't show up."

"Must be nice to have the place all to yourself, though."

"I'd rather have guests."

"Get spooked there alone at night, do you?"

She thinks of Yuri Moroskov, murdered and dumped in the lake. Luther said his killer is long gone, but who knows?

She pushes the troubling thought from her head and explains that she gets a commission on off-season reservations, and they've been scarce lately.

"I wish visitors were scarce on my farm. Had a squatter in the hayloft overnight. Animals were all riled up this morning, and I saw footprints in the mud by the barn door. Now it's got me thinking about what happened in the lake this morning. Did you hear? They found—"

Bella puts a finger to her lips with a nod at Max.

"What? What did they find?"

"Nothing," Virgil tells him and mutters to Bella, "Maybe I should sit out in the hayloft with my shotgun tonight."

"You have a shotgun?"

"Sure do," Virgil tells Max and shakes his head at Bella. "Kid has sharp ears."

"Why do you have a shotgun?"

"For hunting."

"What do you hunt?"

"Deer, mostly."

"And squatters?"

"Not yet. You sure don't miss a trick." Virgil laughs.

"What *is* a squatter?"

"An unwelcome guest."

Mitch returns with a small rectangular can. Noticing the box in Bella's hand, he asks if she's taking the metal detector, too.

"Not today," she says quietly with a nod toward Max. "I'll come back."

"I'll put one aside, just in case. They're selling like hot cakes this year." At Virgil's doubtful expression, he insists, "I sold one just before you came in. Fellow was a quite a character. Takes all kinds."

"Was he a squatter?" Max asks, and Mitch grins.

"I don't think he was, no."

"Do *we* have squatters, Mom?"

"No, our guests are definitely welcome. I just hope they can get here."

"Don't you worry," Mitch says. "It takes a lot more than three feet of snow for western New Yorkers to be snowbound."

"How much more can there be?"

"We had seven feet in one storm a few years back."

"*Seven?*" Max is delighted.

"Yes sirree, Bob."

"My name is not Bob."

"That's just a saying. But do you know whose name really *is* Bob?"

"No."

"Mine. But my nickname's been Mitch for years, ever since I bought this place from the original owner."

"Was *his* name Mitch?"

"It was, but everyone called him Pookie."

"That's a crazy nickname! Got any other ones?"

"Oh, sure, let's see, there's Big Joe Yo and Little Joe Yo. They're both named Josef Yoder, and they live on the same road, so that's how we tell them apart."

"Are they a father and son?"

"I don't even think they're related," Virgil comments. "Are they, Mitch?"

"No, Yoder is a popular Amish name around here."

Naturally, Max wants to know what Amish means.

"I'll tell you later. Let's let Mitch work, Max." Bella usually appreciates Lily Dale's unhurried pace, but at this rate, they'll be here until bedtime.

"I *am* letting him work. What other nicknames do you know, Mitch?"

"Boxer, Frenchie, Alley Cat . . ."

"Frenchie!" Virgil echoes from the woodstove corner. "Now there's a name I haven't heard in a while. Whatever happened to him? Or do I not want to know?"

"Probably not."

From Max, "I want to know."

"Trust me, you don't."

"Well, what about Alley Cat? Is he a guy or a cat?"

"He's a guy. Lives over on Glasgow Road on the farm next to Virgil."

"What's his real name?"

"Alan Katz."

"I know a town called Allentown. My friend Jiffy went there and—" Max breaks off to sneeze, one, two, three times.

"*Gesundheit* times three."

"Huh?"

"It means 'God bless you' in German."

"Hey, Mrs. Schmidt is teaching us to sing 'Silent Night' in German," Max informs Mitch, squirming as Bella feels his forehead.

"Are you coming down with something?"

"Yep. I better stay home from school tomorrow."

His prompt reply earns hearty laughs from Mitch and Virgil and a "Don't count on it" from Bella.

Max frowns. "Well, school will probably be canceled anyway because of all the snow."

"Don't count on that either," Mitch says.

"What *can* I count on?"

"In this world, kid?" Virgil shakes his head. "Nothin' at all."

"Oh, I'd say a white Christmas would be a safe bet." Mitch slides Bella's bags across the counter. "Should I put this on the Valley View account?"

"Everything except the extension cords." She fishes in her purse for her wallet. "Max and I are going to decorate. I found some old light strings in the basement."

"Need some new ones? We have a whole bunch on that display over there."

"That reminds me," Virgil says. "I need to get some new ones to hang around my pond next month."

"Well, I like my old ones just fine," Bella tells Mitch. "They'll cheer up the guesthouse for the holidays."

"Sounds like a business expense to me."

"No, it's personal." Bella hands him her last ten dollar bill.

Mitch hands it back. "Extension cords are on the house."

"Since when?"

"Store policy."

"But—"

"Merry Christmas, Bella. You, too, Max."

Virgil meanders over to hold the door for them, opening it with a silvery tinkle of sleigh bells attached to the handle. They step out onto the low porch in front of the store. White Christmas lights twinkle from the eaves, and the pillars are wrapped in more lights and green garlands.

Dusk isn't far off, and the air seems to have grown a little sharper already. Bella reminds Max to put on his mittens and wishes she'd put on her gloves before grabbing her bags.

As they make the short drive along the country road back to the Dale, Elvis sings about a blue Christmas, and Bella thinks about Sam.

Jiffy greets them, coasting along Cottage Row on his scooter, bare-headed, phone in hand.

"That was longer than fifteen minutes!"

"How many times did you sing 'The Twelve Days of Christmas'?" Max asks.

"A lot. The timer went off a long time ago, and I've been waiting and waiting and waiting and"—he pauses to take a breath—"waiting and waiting and—"

"Where's your helmet, Jiffy?" Bella asks.

"Dunno."

"Why was I sure you were going to say that? Max has an extra one you can borrow."

"My mom says I shouldn't borrow stuff because I lose everything. I lost a boring book the other day."

"And your jacket," Max reminds him.

"Things that are on the bus don't count."

Bella wonders why, if he loses everything, Jiffy is allowed to have an expensive cell phone. He got it last month, and naturally, Max has been asking for one ever since. When she pointed out that her own phone is so old it barely holds a charge, he'd suggested she ask Santa to bring her a new one.

"We'll make sure you don't lose Max's extra helmet," she assures Jiffy, though it isn't really extra. She bought it for Jiffy to use whenever his own is MIA.

She turns off the car, curtailing the last sad line of "Blue Christmas," and ushers the boys to the porch. Unlocking the front door using the new code, she tells them to go up to Max's room for a few minutes until she's ready.

"Ready for what?"

"Ready to watch you ride scooters," she tells Jiffy, who looks like he's about to argue, then appears to think better of it.

"All right," he says agreeably. "And you're very welcome."

"Welcome for what?" Max asks as he and Jiffy head inside, leaving the door wide open behind them.

"It's good manners to say stuff like that."

Max emits another trio of sneezes. "Well, it's good manners to tell me *gesundheit,* too. That's German, by the way. Like '*stille nacht, heilige nacht,*'" he sings through a stuffy nose.

"I like 'The Twelve Days of Christmas' better because it has golden rings in it."

"Shhhhh! It's a surprise!"

"I know! She can't hear us!"

"Maybe she can," Max says. "She has the best listening ears in the whole wide world! Just sing and don't say any more words about golden rings!"

Smiling and shaking her head, Bella deposits the first load of bags in the house. As she returns to the car for the rest, she wonders about Drew and the puppies. Maybe she'll have time to give him a quick call before the boys start pestering to ride scooters.

Hurrying back up the porch steps with another armload, she loses her grip on a bag. Its contents—all the metal hardware—spill across the floor.

Terrific.

With a groan, she puts the intact bags inside and goes back out to scoop up loose nails. Crawling along the porch, wary of splinters, she hears an abrupt creak-bang from down the street. The Dale is full of antique hinges that loudly protest movement. After a while, you recognize the distinct sound of each one.

This particular creak-bang belongs to the Arden household.

Footsteps descend to the gravely street, and one of Misty Starr's clients comes strolling past Valley View in the midst of a one-sided conversation.

Just about anywhere else, Bella might assume she's on the phone. Here, it's just as likely she's talking to Spirit.

"Yeah, I got tired of waiting so I stepped outside to have a cigarette," Bella hears the female voice say, followed by the flick of a lighter. Seconds later, a tendril of smoke wafts to the porch.

"Nah, it's so nice out I left my coat inside," the woman chatters on, strolling and smoking. "Yeah, it's safe. There's no one around to steal it unless the spooks wear fur."

It's one thing for Bella to harbor doubts about what goes on in the Dale but quite another for this cavalier, sarcastic stranger to refer to Spirit as spooks.

The woman laughs into the phone. "Well if he *is* around, I'll hear him choking his brains out. Smoke him right out!"

She listens again. "Yeah, I think he bolted, too, but—yeah, she's supposed to be good . . . Right. Let's hope she picks up on where he is and not the rest of it . . . I know . . . No, I'm just worried that she'll—hey, I *am* open to it. Believe me, I want them back as much as you do . . . I hope so, too, but if not, then we'll do whatever we have to do to . . . Illegal? What, are you kidding?"

Phew. For a moment there, Bella thought she was about to over-hear incriminating evidence from Moroskov's killer.

"Of *course* it will be illegal. Desperate times call for desperate measures, my dear."

Heart pounding, Bella leans closer to the railing to get a look at the woman. She's of medium height and build with teased red hair and is wearing a tight, low-cut sweater that reveals an ample bosom.

"Listen, I'd better get back in there. My turn with Ms. Misty Starr is coming up . . . what? Please, does it *sound* like a real name? . . . What, are you kidding me? No, I didn't . . . Yeah, *Barbara.*" She laughs. "Sure, call me Babs. I'll let you know how it goes. Bye."

Heart racing, Bella watches the woman pocket her cell phone and stride back up the lane, leaving a trail of smoke in her wake.

*   *   *

The attempt at meditation doesn't leave Misty feeling any more capable of summoning Spirit for her walk-in client, but she's done a whole lot of thinking about her money woes and her marriage.

She's put aside her earlier concerns about Jiffy for now. As long as he's with Max's mom, he won't be boarding a school bus to . . .

Well, anywhere. Not even school.

Misty can never remember Max's mother's name, but it makes her think of a Disney princess. Elsa? Ariel?

Anyway, she's the kind of person who keeps a close eye on her own kid and other people's kids whether she needs to or not. Most days she doesn't, but today Misty is grateful. She'll thank her later, after she's finished with Barbara-who-probably-isn't-Barbara.

"Come on in," she says, sticking her head out into the hall. "Thanks for waiting."

"No problem," Barbara says in a tone that indicates it really was a problem.

"Have a seat. Ever had a reading before?"

"Never."

Two for two in the novice department today, Misty thinks, and she asks Barbara what brought her to Lily Dale.

"I have something specific I need to know. I'm trying to get in touch with a certain . . . *friend.*"

Isn't everyone?

"There's no guarantee that someone specific is going to come through."

Or, for that matter, that anyone will.

Misty rhythmically rubs her hands. "When I'm not sure how to interpret an image, I just let you know what I see. If you don't understand right away, keep an open mind. Got it?"

"I guess."

"Let's get started and see what happens."

She closes her eyes.

Breathe . . .

Breathe . . .

There's the careening school bus again.

Breathe . . .

Aware that message is meant for her and not the sitter, she accepts it and puts it aside, rubbing her palms against each other and focusing her energy intently on Barbara.

Breathe.

Something about finances.

A troubled relationship.

Not unusual. Love and money—the vast majority of her clients, at one time or another, are concerned about those things, either separately or together.

Breathe.

An image flashes in her brain. Stacks of cash, bills rubber-banded together.

Symbolic or real? She still isn't getting a clear read on what that might have to do with Barbara, or if it's even related.

Maybe it's the just the pressure she's putting on herself to continue this reading due to her own financial need.

Focus . . .

She sees the bag of dirty clothes she left in the mudroom—another reminder that she's in dire straits.

Stop thinking about your own problems. You need to focus on Barbara . . .

Breathe . . .

Barbara . . .

Breathe . . .

At last, something else begins to take shape.

She's getting a word, maybe ranger or ninja or . . .

No, it's *ginger*. She can see it spelled out in her mind's eye: *G-I-N-G-E-R . . .*

A blur of other letters follow, indicating that there's more to the word or that the word was the first part of a phrase.

"Are you getting anything?" Barbara asks.

She hesitates, on shaky ground, eyes squeezed shut as she searches for the rest. *Gingersnap? Gingerroot? Ginger and Mary Ann?*

Maybe it's just her own desire to make the reading worthwhile, projecting the word into her subconscious mind. *Hey, look, a redhead. Bet* ginger *means something to her.* Or maybe it is a message, but meant for Misty, like the school bus.

Barbara makes an impatient sound.

Misty keeps rubbing her hands, keeps trying to channel something else, keeps getting only ginger.

"Sorry," she says at last. "I don't know if this is supposed to be the spice or the color or what, but I'm getting something about ginger."

She hears a slight gasp, and then, "Ginger?"

"Yes."

"What about it?"

"I don't know. Ginger is the first part of a word or maybe a phrase. *Ginger* . . . something. Is it relevant to you?"

"No, not . . . not at all."

She's lying.

Misty opens her eyes to see that Barbara's aura has flared a bright shade of scarlet. She's angry. Yet her voice is calm as she asks, "Is that the only thing you're getting?"

Should she mention the money? People don't always react well to that. When she asked her very first Lily Dale client if he was worried about his finances, he shut her down on the spot, retorting, "Who isn't?"

"I'm sorry," she tells Barbara. "If you'd like to stop . . . ?"

"No. Keep trying."

She closes her eyes and rubs her hands together again.

There's the school bus.

Once again, it's rolling Jiffy away from her with a bunch of dead kids.

Katie Harmon.

She was Great-Aunt Ellen's childhood friend, drowned in Cassadaga Lake decades before Misty was born.

Billy Buell.

His fifth-grade locker was right next to Misty's before he was killed in a car accident.

DeQuann Jones.

He lost his battle with cancer back in March.

This time, Misty gets a good look at the driver.

Her father.

Chapter Seven

True to Mitch's prediction, the snow that began falling last night has already topped a foot and is expected to grow heavier as the day wears on. Also true to his prediction, neither Bella's inbound guests nor the local school district have canceled due to weather.

Nor has Hugo Munson. When Bella answers his knock, the electrician blows into the guesthouse on a bitter gust of wet, white wind that slams the door hard behind him.

"You locked me out," he says, stomping his feet on the mat. "Trying to tell me something?"

"Yes, that I didn't expect you to come on a day like this!"

"I'd come through worse to be here," he tells Bella with a wink. "The wife was after me to help her wrap a huge pile of presents for the grandkids."

"There are worse things in the world."

She's thinking of her own meager shopping budget, but Hugo's smile dims.

"Yeah, I heard what happened over here yesterday morning. If you hadn't already changed the keypad code, I'd have told you to do it. You all shook up about it, Bella?"

"*Should* I be?" she asks, thinking that depends on how one defines *all shook up*.

Hugo shrugs. "Just be careful and keep your doors locked."

Drew had said the same thing when she finally reached him last night and told him what had happened. "I don't like the sound of this. Are the police still around there keeping an eye on things?"

"I'm sure they would be if they thought there was any threat, but they've moved on."

"Because they don't want to hang around outside in crappy weather?"

"Luther says they're pretty sure there's no connection to the Dale. Looks like the body was dumped on the other side of the lake."

"Still spitting distance. I feel like I should come over to Valley View and make sure everything's okay."

"Everything's fine! You have your hands full there with that precious doggy family." She knew he couldn't leave the three fragile newborn puppies and their valiant mama. They'd all made it through the night and appear to have a fighting chance, according to Drew's latest text.

Bella had stayed up late baking peanut butter blossom cookies, cleaning for the guests, and prepping the parlor for painting. It was after midnight when she finally got to bed, so exhausted she forgot to set the alarm.

She dreamed that a man-sized Easter Bunny wearing a gun holster slid down the chimney on Christmas Eve and filled the stockings with stolen Fabergé eggs. Max had appeared in pajamas shouting, "Hey, you're not Santa! It's not Easter! What are you doing?"

"I'm a fence!" the sinister rabbit had said and turned into a ferocious leopard, claws and fangs bared . . .

She'd awakened to find the room filled with grainy morning light. Rattled by the nightmare, she realized she'd overslept and Max had missed the bus. When she'd gone to wake him, she'd found his cheeks flushed with fever. No school for him. He's spent the morning asleep with Spidey curled beside him and Chance the Cat keeping watch over both from the foot of the bed.

Bella spends most of it preparing for her guests. Hoping to greet them with a cheerful holiday display, she braves the storm to hang several light strings along the porch eaves. There are hooks from years past, so it doesn't take long to get them up.

But the wind is ferocious, and she's too chilled to run the extension cords to the outdoor outlet in the side yard. Chilled, too, by the corpse in the lake and the prospect, no matter how remote, that his killer might still be in the vicinity.

She'll ask Hugo to give her a hand outside before he leaves later. For now, she's comforted to hear him working in the basement as she balances on the second-to-top tread of the wobbly stepladder, using a putty knife and joint compound to cover a network of ceiling cracks.

Scoop, spread, repeat.

She thinks about Yuri Moroskov as she smooths globs of joint compound overhead and about last night's dream. It hasn't faded as the day goes on, the way dreams often do. This one lingers, almost seeming to make sense in that wacky, illogical dream-logic.

In the midst of her brooding about the crime—and *scooping, spreading, repeating*—she hears footsteps on the porch and then a knock on the door.

Please don't let it be Grange, she thinks, descending the ladder. She has a feeling she hasn't seen the last of him.

She's relieved to find Calla on her doorstep. She, too, is covered in white powder, but it isn't sanded spackle. Her long brown hair and puffy blue parka are flecked with fat flakes, and her pretty face is ruddy from the cold.

"I'm here to see the backsplash and to deliver this to Max, from Gammy." She holds up a mason jar wrapped in a dish towel. "It's still hot."

"What is it?"

"Lime and ginger pho soup. She said to tell you it would have been better if her Crock-Pot was working, but she did the best she could on the stove. Oh, and she says it's the best cold remedy, and she hopes he feels better soon."

"How does she know he's sick?"

"You didn't tell her?"

"I don't think so."

Calla shrugs, handing over the jar of soup. "It's Lily Dale."

Ah, yes, Lily Dale—not merely a typical small town where everyone knows everyone else's business, but an atypical small town whose psychic residents seem to know . . . well, everything. Maybe that's why Bella seems to be the only one around here with a nagging concern over the body in the lake.

"Luther's coming over later to help Gammy set up her Christmas tree, so she's cooking up a storm. She wants you and Max to come over, too."

"Unless he has a miracle recovery by dinnertime, we'll have to pass," Bella says, leading the way toward the back of the house.

After the dusty, drop-cloth-shrouded parlor, she appreciates the wallpapered dining room with its formal furniture, vintage etched-glass sconces, and built-in cabinetry filled with delicate china and crystal.

Through an archway, the adjacent breakfast room is especially cozy this morning, snow flying past the wide, unadorned windows that sit between the white-washed bead board ceiling and lower wall.

Ball jar vases on the small café tables hold evergreen sprigs and red berry twigs that Bella cut from the backyard. A vintage sideboard holds a larger jar filled with mini candy canes and small baskets of assorted tea bags and hot cocoa mixes. Tomorrow morning, Bella will be up at dawn to start the coffee and bake cranberry orange muffins for her guests' breakfast, *if* Lauri and Dawn manage to get through the snow.

In the kitchen, Bella puts the jar of soup into the refrigerator as Calla helps herself to a peanut butter blossom from the plastic-wrapped plate on the table.

"Amazing," she pronounces around a mouthful of cookie, checking out the gleaming white subway tiles behind the countertops.

"The cookie or the backsplash?"

"Both. I knew you could bake, but I can't believe you installed this yourself. I'm taking a picture to show Gammy."

She brushes crumbs from her hands over the sink and pulls her cell phone from her pocket. She snaps a couple of photos, texts them to Odelia, and gestures at the white charger cord. "Mind if I plug my phone in for a few minutes? My battery's about to die."

"Welcome to the club. Mine won't stay charged."

"Maybe Santa will bring you a new phone," Calla says, plugging her phone into the charger. "I can't believe how much work you've done around this place. Is Grant pushing you?"

"Grant is in Madrid this week on business, and then he's heading to the Holy Land for Christmas, London for Boxing Day, skiing in St. Moritz, and St. Bart's for New Year's. Or is it the other way around?"

"*Which* other way around?"

"Good question. I can't keep track of Grant and his world travels. The point is, Valley View is the last thing on his mind. But I need the extra money, so full speed ahead."

"I see Nadine is lending a hand." Calla points at the basement door. It's ajar with the light on and an electric drill whirring below.

"That's Hugo. But Nadine is more than welcome to pitch in with the rewiring. Her rates might be more affordable than his."

"Probably, and I bet she learned her electrical skills from Thomas Edison himself."

Bella smiles. Then her gaze falls on the window above the sink.

All is peaceful this morning. Drifts drape like drop cloths over the lakeside Adirondack chairs where she spent many a summer sunset. Evergreens and the towering ginkgo tree sway in the wind, prettily flocked in white. Whooshing snow obscures all but the edge of the lake.

"I know you're worried."

Bella turns to see that she, too, is looking outside.

"It's just that I heard a scream the other night, right around the same time I saw someone on the lake in a boat. I wondered if someone was in trouble, but Drew convinced me it was a great horned owl."

"It's the right time of year for them. They're trying to lure their mates."

"That's what he said."

"Maybe he and the great horned owl have a little something in common."

Bella ignores that. "He told me that some people consider them a bad omen."

"That's true, but Jacy believes the opposite."

"He thinks the owl's scream is good luck?"

"I wouldn't go that far, but he does say that they're highly intelligent and spiritual creatures and that they seek out beings who share similar qualities."

"And you think that's true?"

"Jacy's the most brilliant, sensitive man I've ever met, so . . . yes."

Bella is pretty sure that she spots a fleeting wistfulness in her eyes before she turns back to the window, staring out.

"Calla, I don't want to overstep, but . . . it sounds like you still love him."

"Oh, I do. I always will."

"Then do you ever think about getting back tog—"

"No. No way. Sometimes love isn't enough. He's so busy with his residency and volunteer work and training for the next marathon and saving the world . . . there's nothing left over for me. I got tired of spending so much time alone. And let me tell you, lonely stinks."

"Yeah. It does."

"I'm so sorry." Calla hugs her. "I'm glad you have Max and the kitties. Thanks to you, I have Li'l Chap, and thanks to him, I have Blue."

The Russian Blue kitten had turned up at Valley View while Calla was visiting back in October, having just broken up with Jacy. She believes it was a sign that she was meant to reconcile with Blue Slayton. Her former high school sweetheart lives beyond the gate in what would pass for a mansion anywhere but around here is a palace.

"Anyway, Bella, getting back to the owl . . . if one visits you, I really think you should consider it an honor and a blessing, not a curse."

"I'll try, but . . . I just wish I hadn't been so quick to dismiss the scream. I should have called the police."

"If it's any consolation, it was already too late for Moroskov. He was dead before he hit the water, and I'm sure whoever did it is long gone."

Luther's words, spoken with Luther's confidence.

If only Bella felt the same.

If only this hadn't happened, especially now when she's trying so hard to make up for the Christmas Max didn't have last year.

If only Sam were here to remind her that they're safe in their new home and that she's strong enough to handle anything that comes their way and that—

"Hey, do you hear that?" Calla asks.

"The drilling? That's Hugo."

"No, the music."

"What music?"

"Shh." She holds up a finger, head cocked, eyes closed. "'Blue Christmas.' Elvis. Hear it?"

Bella's eyes widen. "I heard it the other day on the car radio. But I don't hear it now."

"Then it must be Spirit."

"You mean you can't tell?"

"Not always. Sometimes I hear something or see something, and I'm not sure if I'm the only one. If I am, it's Spirit."

"But . . . why is Spirit playing 'Blue Christmas'?"

"Why do you think?"

Merry Christmas, Bella Blue . . .

Your aura is very blue . . . true blue . . .

Is this a message from Sam?

Calla dispels that theory before she can voice it. "Guess Spirit approves of my *Blue* Christmas."

Swallowing her own disappointment, Bella asks, "Your new kitten or your new love life?"

"Both. I just put up a tree in honor of my fresh start with them. It's a blue spruce, and guess what color the lights are?"

"Purple?" Bella asks, deadpan.

"Funny. You know what I'm getting at here."

"Spirit likes your holiday decorations?"

"*Blue . . . Blue . . . Blue Christmas.* Hard to miss the meaning in that, right?"

Privately, Bella thinks interpreting the song as a message that Spirit approves of Calla's rekindled romance is a bit of a stretch. She's usually one of the more level-headed people around here, but she's only human. Maybe she's looking for meaning where it might not exist. When it comes to Blue Slayton, especially, she sometimes sees what she wants to see.

Then again, maybe you do the same thing, Bella Blue.

Calla decides she'd better get back over to her grandmother's and heads out into the storm, leaving Bella to return to her ladder. With luck, she'll be able to patch and sand the San Andreas ceiling and make the room—and herself—presentable before Lauri and Dawn check in. Painting can wait another day.

Scoop, spread, repeat.

Her cell phone buzzes in her pocket. It's a text alert from the local school district, dismissing the students immediately due to inclement weather.

Her first reaction is relief that she doesn't have to venture out in the storm to get Max.

Her next is, *What about Jiffy?*

When she'd locked the door after Calla, she'd seen the aqua-colored Mustang parked in front of the Arden home again. Yesterday, the well-dressed young woman had said Misty had asked her to come back another time; that she'd been distracted by *"some weird message about a school bus."*

Regardless of whether Bella believes in that stuff, Jiffy shouldn't be out there alone in this storm, especially on the heels of yesterday's murder investigation.

I'll go meet him, she decides. *It'll only take a few minutes.*

The trick is figuring out which minutes, since the bus isn't running on its usual schedule.

It's eleven twenty-five now, and the bus can't possibly arrive for another fifteen minutes. At eleven forty, she'll ask Hugo to keep an eye on Max while she goes down to fetch Jiffy. The boy won't be thrilled, but she'll ease the humiliation by bringing him cookies.

Last time she made peanut butter blossoms, she'd left them to cool on the counter, and Jiffy had plucked the chocolate kisses from most of them. He was genuinely contrite when she confronted him with a tray of cookies that had gaping holes in the centers. "Sorry, Bella. I love chocolate. I guess you need to put two kisses in every cookie from now on so they won't be ruined by me."

Smiling at the memory, she moves her ladder back to where she began spackling this morning. Her shoulders, arms, and neck ache as she sands the dried compound. The gritty rhythm mingles with Hugo's hammering below. He's whistling a Christmassy tune that's much jauntier than "Blue Christmas," and Bella sings along in her head.

You better watch out . . . you better not cry . . .

* * *

Cash poor or not, Misty had been hoping Priscilla Galante wouldn't show up for her appointment this morning, given the weather. But she arrived right on schedule, wearing a smart tweed coat over a beige cashmere sweater, trim brown velvet pants, and suede boots with a cozy sherpa lining.

Sitting across from her, feeling most inadequate, Misty asks if she has any questions before they begin.

"Not really."

"Try to relax, okay?"

"I am, but I'm a little freaked out about the guy in the lake."

"What?"

"You know . . . that man they found out here yesterday. I saw it on the news when I got home."

"The drowning victim? Did you know him?"

"No. He didn't drown," Priscilla adds. "Someone killed him. Didn't you hear?"

"No, I, uh . . . I guess I didn't. What happened?"

"I'm not really sure, but I thought it was safe around here."

"It is."

Priscilla gives her a dubious look.

Heart pounding, Misty tells her it's time to begin. She bows her head and rubs her palms against each other, attempting to quiet her brain.

It's been in overdrive ever since the skittish sitter, Barbara, left yesterday. The scary school bus transporting Jiffy and the dead children had stayed with Misty to fester overnight, as did the sense of foreboding and her troubling phone conversation with Mike. Before going to bed, she'd texted him that he'd better call her today.

He had, while she was brooding over coffee and Jiffy was chomping his way through a bowl of cereal, chattering nonstop as usual.

The conversation with her husband didn't start well.

"You told me to call you back," he said flatly, "so I am."

Their discussion erupted in curses and accusations and ended abruptly, just before Jiffy ran out the door with his backpack. She isn't sure if he fled because he was late for the bus or because he'd figured out that his dad isn't coming for Christmas.

It's beginning to look as though her son is going to grow up father-less, just as she had. She was Jiffy's age when hers drank himself to death. The night he passed, before she found out he was gone, he came into her room and sat on her bed. She smelled the liquor even before she heard his voice and felt the weight of his hand on her shoulder. He wasn't slurring the way he usually did when he staggered in to say good night—and he wasn't saying good night. He was saying good-bye.

"You're going to be just fine, little girl. I can help you more from here than I ever could there," he'd said and apologized for not being a good daddy.

She hadn't argued. Of course she loved him, and he'd shown glimmers of affection and good humor over the years. But he'd spent his scant six years of fatherhood as an unhappily married, often unemployed drunk.

Misty had thought that final encounter was just a dream until she'd woken up to her mother sobbing the terrible news.

"I know, Mommy. I know he's gone." She'd known for a long time, somewhere deep inside, that her father wouldn't live to see her grow up. But how could she have known he was going to die?

How could she have seen him after he had?

She hadn't yet known about Spirit, or Lily Dale, or—

The young woman sitting across from her makes a huffy sound. Soft, but decidedly impatient.

Misty opens her eyes. "I'm sorry. I just don't know if I can get anything. Today is . . . tough."

"Because of what happened yesterday?"

"Because of a lot of things," Misty shoots back. Least of all that. Yes, it's troubling, but it's not as if she knew the man.

"Can you try again?"

I wasn't really trying before, Misty thinks. *I was worried about my own problems, not yours.*

Does Priscilla have problems? From where Misty sits, the attractive young woman, with her sophisticated clothing and fancy car, must be pretty carefree. But then, she's still surrounded by that dark aura, and she doesn't seem as edgy today.

"Take your time," she tells Misty.

If only she had that luxury. Virgil Barbor is going to turn up at noon looking for his rent. It would be nice if Misty could get out of here before then as she'd planned. Nicer still if she could hand him enough cash to hold him off for a while longer.

Like the other mediums here in the Dale, she earns a modest fee—considered a donation—for her readings. Back in Arizona, she'd heard about mediums who charged a hundred times more for an hour's session.

Unlike other first-timers, Priscilla didn't ask about cost. Maybe Misty should charge her double. Triple, maybe, or a little more—nothing crazy. But she seems to have money to burn, and Misty only needs enough to make this time, on a very stressful day, worth her while.

Pushing aside another twinge of guilt, along with the strange trepidation that's dogged her since yesterday, she bows her head and closes her eyes again.

*   *   *

Turns out metal detectors don't work in snow.

At least, this one doesn't, despite what the old coot told him back at the hardware store yesterday.

"It'll do the job," he'd said, "as long as you can swing it. Snow gets too deep, and that'll be hard. Got snowshoes?"

Snowshoes? He has only the clothes on his back and the ones he changed out of after work the other day before . . .

Yuri.

The gun.

Everything.

Now some old guy—Mitch? Was that his name, Mitch?—wanted to sell him snowshoes?

That's the *last* thing he'll need where he's going after this. Someplace where the sun shines year round and the breeze is balmy, a place with tropical trees and warm clear turquoise water . . .

Mexico? The Caribbean?

But that would involve a passport and leave a trail.

Now that Yuri's body has been discovered, both sides of the law are going to be looking for him.

Fine. He'd be bored at the beach anyway. He needs some action. *Vegas.*

It's out in the desert, and deserts are hot, right? Plus, the Strip will be crowded with the holidays looming. He can lose himself there for a while. No borders to cross, no planes to board.

There's no way he can go back to his old existence even if he wanted to. His future—his very life—depends on finding those rings.

He can only hope he didn't lose them back on the road outside the gate. It was a lot easier to swing the metal detector on plowed pavement, but he's pretty sure he'd have found the rings yesterday if they were lying in the road. If he missed them there, it's too late—they're now buried in grungy mountains along the shoulder.

It's far more likely that he dropped them here, inside the Dale. He concentrates his snowy search in the yards and fields he crossed the other night in his haste to escape.

The longer he trudges through the snow, the harder it is to breathe. The harder it is to breathe, the more frustrated he becomes.

A ferocious wind howls off the water and bites through his coat as he plods along a small clearing near the gate. He can barely feel the wand in his gloved hand, let alone sway the device as instructed, back and forth above the rapidly deepening snow.

Earlier, when the thing was emitting an occasional blast of beeps, he would stop to dig doggedly through the snow. At least he hadn't had to hack into the frozen earth, but he'd found only bottle caps, hardware, coins . . .

Pennies, mostly. It would have been nice to find rare antique ones. Or any jewelry—say, someone's long-lost engagement ring he could hock just in case he doesn't find his gold rings.

His.

"Don't you ever let anyone take what's yours, boy."

His father tops the growing list of those to blame for this situation: Mitch, the cat, the kid, the woman who called the cops . . .

Especially her.

If he were to run into her now, after what she did—

Why wait to run into her? He knows where to find her. She's a sitting duck in this weather. When he finds his rings, he'll detour over to Valley View and see that she pays the price.

When . . . or *if*?

Reality is beginning to set in. This task, under these circumstances, is nearly impossible.

Maybe he should go back to the hardware store and buy some snowshoes. Or—the hell with that—go back, throw this piece of useless garbage at the old coot, and demand his money back.

But he's afraid he might not stop at that. And after what happened to Yuri and then again last night . . .

He isn't a cold-blooded killer, though. He's just like anyone else. As long as he keeps his temper under control, everything is—

Hearing a vehicle approaching out on the road, he ducks into a stand of trees.

It's bigger, more cumbersome than a car. Salt truck, maybe, or another plow.

When it rumbles into view, he sees that it's a yellow school bus, the kind he used to ride when he was a kid. He'd boarded last, too late to sit up front by the driver. He'd been forced to make his way down the aisle crowded with leering kids who poked and tripped him, kids who stole what was his—his lunchbox, his homework, his dignity, his childhood.

He clenches the metal detector like a weapon as this bus brakes squeakily, and he thinks about the gun. It's in his pocket because you never know . . .

The doors fold open. Little brats waddle off one by one, swaddled like mummies in layers of down.

All, that is, except the last kid, the smallest of the crew. He's not wearing a thick winter coat, gloves, hat, or boots. He's not wearing any of those things at all, just a light sweat shirt and sneakers, head bare—and face recognizable.

"Jiffy! Your coat!" the driver calls after him.

"I forgot it at school, Mr. Johansen!"

"Then you run straight home, you hear me? It's too nasty out there to lag."

The bus pulls away, its dispatched passengers chattering excitedly the way kids do when a school day is unexpectedly curtailed. He remembers that.

He remembers a lot of things. Everything.

He watches through narrowed eyes as the vast majority of the group branches off to the right at the fork, scattering toward houses there.

Only one—a shivering, yet visibly ebullient Jiffy—walks alone toward Cottage Row.

*　*　*

Bella is still high atop the ladder when Hugo's whistling and hammering is joined by the antique clock chiming in the hall.

Uh-oh—noon?

Her sock-clad foot slips from the rung. The ladder pitches wildly, threatening to toss her headfirst onto the nearest object—a marble table draped in an old, paint-stained sheet—before it rights itself.

Shaken by her near miss, she hurriedly descends to the drop cloth–covered floor. Lost in thought about stolen treasures and murdered corpses, she'd forgotten all about meeting Jiffy at the bus. She'll head out now. If she doesn't find him safely at home, she'll keep going down to the gate and wait.

She shudders at her reflection in the vast hall mirror. She's covered in dust, with a clump of white gunk in her ponytail, which pokes out from beneath her backward baseball cap. If shampoo doesn't get it out, she'll have to grab the nail scissors and treat herself to a hasty hack job. A few spackle-hardened strands are a small sacrifice in the grand scheme of renovating the Valley View Manor to its former magnificence.

Hurrying to the coat tree, she lifts Max's backpack, packed and ready for school, to grab the insulated hooded parka beneath it. She pulls it on and looks to the mat for the boots she left there this morning after she shoveled the walk.

At least, she thought she did. Either her tired brain was playing tricks on her, or Nadine is, because the boots are nowhere to be seen.

Bella heads upstairs to find them, pausing to open her son's bedroom door a crack.

Max is not the kind of boy who spends his waking hours idly.

She expects to find him drowsy and flipping through a picture book or playing with Legos or even the handheld video game he's not allowed to have in bed.

Instead, he's just lying there, staring up at the ceiling, with Spidey curled up asleep beside him. Chance has moved over to the windowsill, fixated on the snow outside in the way she used to watch the gulls last summer when Max tossed them stale bread.

"Max? You awake?"

"Yep."

"Feeling better?"

"Nope." It comes out *dope*, and she remembers he's past due another dose of decongestant.

She steps into the room, pausing to give Chance a little pat. Ordinarily, when she hasn't eaten in a few hours, the mere sound of Bella's voice triggers her to come running. Today Chance doesn't even turn her head, ignoring the hand that feeds her.

Bella turns to Max. His fingertips are pressed against his temples.

"Is it your head, sweetie?"

"Yes."

She touches his forehead. "No fever. It hurts?"

"Not outside. Inside."

She reaches for the medicine she left on the nightstand. "That's sinus pressure. You're all clogged up. This will help the pain go away."

"No, not like that. It's not hurting . . . it just feels bad."

"How does it feel bad?"

"My thoughts just hurt inside my head."

"Did something happen to make you feel bad?"

"Not yet."

He looks toward the window. Chilled, Bella follows his gaze.

Chance still hasn't moved. From where she's sitting, there's a view of the backyard and the lake.

With a shaky hand, Bella pours purple liquid into the little plastic cup and hands it to her son. He dutifully swallows.

"Are you worried about something? Want to tell me about it?"

"No."

"No, you're not worried? Or no, you don't want to tell me?"

"I don't know." He hands back the cup and lies down, turning his head to the side. "I just want to go back to sleep."

She wants to say something else, ask something else.

He's got a cold. Of course he's feeling lousy, inside and out. It has nothing to do with . . .

Anything.

"Odelia sent soup if you're hungry," she tells him.

"What kind?"

"Lime and Ginger Pho."

"Does it taste like chicken noodle?"

"I'm sure it's delicious, but if you want chicken noodle, I'll make it for you. Anything you want."

He shakes his head and snuggles into the pillow. "I'm not hungry."

Bella kisses his cheek and walks back over to the window. Again, she rests a hand on Chance's furry back. The feline doesn't respond, tail twitching, intent on the action beyond the glass.

Through the white squall, Bella can see Calla out by the lake. She's talking to an agitated Misty Starr, who appears to be frantically searching the churning blue-black water for something . . .

Or someone.

Chapter Eight

"Jiffy!" Misty howls above the wind. "Where are you? Jiffy!"

She closes her eyes, shutting out the desolate tundra, begging her guides to show her where her child is now. But all she sees in her mind's eye is the same ferocious white storm that surrounds her.

While Misty was tied up in a futile effort to channel Spirit for her client, the school had sent an early dismissal notice.

Priscilla had finally left in a bit of a huff. Misty, no wealthier than she'd been an hour before, watched glumly through the window as she brushed snow from her car and saw her dodge something . . .

A snowball?

For a moment, Misty thought one of her own guides might have tossed it—slightly satisfying payback for the wasted time.

Then she'd seen that it was one of the Miller twins. They're a few years older than Jiffy and live across the Dale.

Why, oh why, hadn't she gone to find out why he was home from school already? Why had she assumed the kid was playing hooky?

At least fifteen, maybe twenty minutes had gone by as she prepared for her escape to the laundromat. It wasn't until she grabbed her car keys and phone that Misty had spotted the text and found out about early dismissal.

Jiffy should have been home by then. By now.

If only she'd canceled Priscilla's appointment or curtailed it when she should have. Why did she have to keep trying—or pretending to try? Had she really thought the woman would fork over enough money to cover the rent when Virgil showed up?

Now she's being punished for her greed. For thinking she could evade the landlord and her problems. For not making sure her son got safely off the bus.

Oh, the bus.

Is it possible that the vision had nothing to do with Jiffy? Maybe it was just some random image.

But why those passengers?

And why that driver?

Her father's spirit never touches in with her. Why was she seeing him now with her son?

"Please," she whispers. "Please let him be okay."

She feels a hand on her shoulder. Calla Delaney. She'd come running out of Odelia's house a minute ago when Misty came back here to check the lake.

"Tell me what happened."

Opening her eyes again, Misty snaps, "What do you think? I can't find my son."

"When did you last see him?"

"When he left for school this morning."

"Well, I'm sure he's still there. It's barely noon and—"

"They let the kids go because of the storm. He isn't there. He isn't anywhere!"

Thinking of the man in the lake—the one Priscilla said was murdered, not drowned—she combs the shoreline for a sign of Jiffy.

Something is terribly wrong.

She knows it with the same certainty she knew he was in trouble two other times in his short life. Once, before he was even born, when she knew something was wrong long before her obstetrician discovered that the cord was wrapped twice around her baby's neck. And again, when Spirit told her to check on Jiffy, and she found him choking on a jawbreaker. She was lucky she'd been there to give him the Heimlich.

If only she'd been there this time, when . . .

What happened? What could have happened?

"Please," she whispers, staring at the water. "Please let him be okay."

She can't bear to think of him out there in the lake, and she's almost certain that he isn't. But there must be a reason her guides drew her here.

"Jiffy!" she shouts into the emptiness. *"Jiiiii-fffffy!"*

* * *

Bella closes Max's bedroom door behind her, hurries down the hall, and shrieks as Yuri Moroskov's killer leaps out at her.

No. It's just Hugo, poking out of one of the guest rooms.

"Sorry, didn't mean to scare you. Everything okay?"

"I thought you were in the basement!"

"I came up here to see if that ceiling fan is working yet. It isn't."

"But . . . it's not ceiling fan weather."

"I need to troubleshoot this line before I can get on with the rest. Going somewhere?" he adds, seeing her coat.

"I just have to run outside for a few minutes. Can you keep an ear out for Max?"

"No problem."

Bella's worst fears chase her back downstairs, where she takes another quick look around for her boots before jamming her feet into a pair of sneakers.

Opening the back door, she finds the steps buried in a downy drift. She hesitates only a second before wading in. The knee-deep snow soaks her legs and cakes inside her sneakers as she makes her way toward Calla and Misty.

Jiffy's mother is wearing pink sweat pants and yellow rubber rain boots. The rest of her is wrapped in a crocheted poncho. Her curly, straw-colored hair looks as though it wasn't neatly combed even before it became matted with snow.

"Have you seen him?" she calls, spotting Bella.

"Jiffy?" she asks, praying it's a wrong guess. Maybe she's looking for Rudolph Valentino, John Lennon, or one of the other recognizable—even to Bella—spirits reportedly spotted around the Dale lately.

At Calla's slight nod, Bella musters optimism. "Maybe the bus is delayed. I'm sure the roads are treacherous, so they're probably crawling along. You can call the school and—"

"I tried to call the school! No answer."

"Well, maybe—"

"The bus already came."

"How do you know?"

"Because a kid tried to hit my client with a snowball!"

"By accident," Calla quickly explains. "It was the Miller twins. They told Misty that Jiffy got off the bus with them, but they don't know where he went from there."

Why, oh why, hadn't Bella gone outside at eleven thirty? She should have set a reminder on her phone or—

"Jiffy has a phone," she remembers. "Have you called it?"

"Of course I've called it! He's not answering."

"Maybe he has it silenced. Did you text him?"

"He can't *read*!" Misty, the mother who gave a six-year-old a cell phone, gapes as if Bella is the crazy one here. "I mean, he can read 'cat' and 'dog' and whatever the heck he's learning in kindergarten, but . . ."

"You mean first grade," Bella corrects her, though perhaps not as gently as she'd intended.

"*What?*"

"Your son! He's in first grade, not kindergarten."

"I know that! Geez! I'm his mother!"

A mother who doesn't keep a close enough eye on her child. Bella bites her tongue to keep from saying it.

Misty shoves strands of soggy hair out of her eyes. The wind whips it right back into them. "Sorry," she mutters. "I'm just, like, so worried."

And you're just, like, so young.

"It's okay. I'd be going crazy if I were you." Wrong thing to say. "But I'm sure he's fine." Also wrong. She isn't sure of that at all. "Maybe his phone battery is dead."

"Maybe."

"Does it have a locator on it?"

"I have no idea. My husband is the one who got it for him, and I can't get a hold of him right now either."

"Maybe Jiffy's with your husband," Bella says. "He's been so excited that he's coming home for Christmas, so maybe his dad decided to surprise—"

"Trust me, he didn't." Misty's tone is curt, her expression desolate.

Bella casts a fearful glance at the black and choppy lake, its opposite shore obscured behind a veil of white. She turns back toward the street, hoping to see Jiffy riding his scooter through the storm. There's only a plow truck beeping and scraping along, yellow lights flashing.

"Do you really think he would have come out here in this weather, though?" she asks Misty. "I mean, I don't see any footprints, so . . ."

If they were here, they'd long since have been blown over. Bella's trail from the house is already nearly obliterated.

Yet she goes on, "This is his first real snowstorm. He was probably so excited that he stopped to play in it like the other kids. I mean, it wouldn't be the first time he got sidetracked on the way home."

"No, but this is different, because of . . . yesterday."

"I know," Bella says, "but you can't dwell on that."

"Wait, dwell on what?"

She and Calla exchange a glance. It's hard to imagine Yuri Moroskov's demise could have escaped her in a town this size.

"Just . . . in the lake, yesterday . . ." Calla falters and looks at Bella.

"There was . . . the police were . . ."

Misty dismisses them with impatience. "I'm not talking about that. I'm talking about a vision I had yesterday."

"About the school bus?" Bella asks, remembering, and Misty's jaw drops.

"How did you know that?"

"I saw your client—the one who drives the Mustang, right? She mentioned you'd had a premonition. What was it, exactly?"

"Spirit warned that something might happen to Jiffy on the way home from school. I saw a bus. He was on it. There were other kids . . . they'd all passed." Misty presses both hands to her mouth.

At a loss for words, Bella looks around, expecting to spot a great horned owl on a branch overhead. Nothing but a bruise-colored sky and bare ginkgo branches creaking in the wind.

They listen to the silence for a long time until Misty breaks it again.

"I don't like the lake."

Calla and Bella exchange a worried glance.

"What do you mean?" Bella asks, and she shrugs.

"I always like it, but not today."

The simple explanation makes perfect sense. Not in a good way.

Misty cups her hands to her mouth and shouts again for her son. They listen for a reply, hearing nothing in the hush but wind and the distant rumble of a plow.

Bella touches Misty's arm. "I bet he's home by now. He's probably soaked and chilled to the bone and ready for hot chocolate."

"Bella's right," Calla agrees, though not wholeheartedly. "Let's go check. I'm sure he's wondering where you are."

"He isn't there. If he was, I'd feel it here." Misty thumps the spot beneath her left collarbone.

Bella thinks of Max, who had a "bad feeling," though he didn't tell her what it was about.

Odelia claims everyone has innate psychic ability. She says that children, too young to have learned skepticism, are more likely than adults to embrace it.

Bella would embrace it if she believed it. She's reasonably certain that no one in the entire history of the world has ever longed to connect with a lost loved one as much as she does with her late husband.

And that attitude will never get you anywhere, a disapproving voice—her own—tells her. Everyone experiences their share of heartache.

There's no way she'd trade places with Misty Starr right now.

"Have you checked with any of the other kids who got off the bus with the Miller kids?" she asks.

"No. I don't really know them."

"I do. I'll make some calls if we don't find him waiting inside. Come on." Calla thrusts her hands deep into her jacket pockets, shoulders hunched against the icy wind as she turns away from the lake.

Bella walks with them around to the front of Valley View. Across the lane, a stand of ancient maple tree trunks are dotted with lopsided smiley faces, courtesy of ill-aimed snowballs.

She wants to think Jiffy did it, but Misty tells her it was the Miller twins, aiming for the trees when they hit Priscilla. Hugging herself, Misty starts toward her house, head bent against the cold. Calla hurries to catch up to her.

Bella calls after them, "Let me know when you find him."

When—not *if.*

Jiffy has to be someplace around here. He always is.

Bella makes her way up the snowy stair slope and hesitates, wondering if she should get back inside to Max. But he's sleeping, and Hugo is puttering around working. He's grandfatherly and familiar.

She grabs the shovel she left propped on the porch. Her sneakered feet and lower legs are cold and wet, her bare hands numb even clenched inside her pockets.

If Jiffy lost track of time, he won't stay outside indefinitely. Sooner or later, he'll be uncomfortable enough to go inside and warm up.

But what if he can't find inside?

Visibility is lousy. Bella turns toward Pandora Feeney's place a mere hundred yards across the way.

The cottage—like its owner—was the bane of Odelia's existence even before Pandora installed a vast Christmas light display.

"She copied my paint colors right down to the trim," Odelia had grumbled to Bella.

"Think of it as an homage."

"I think of it as an abomination."

Pandora's house is hard to miss now that it screams "Hallelujah" with flashing LEDs plugged in around the clock.

"Across the pond, we call them 'fairy lights,'" she told Bella and Odelia, after summoning them to admire her handiwork the weekend after Thanksgiving. "Spot on, wouldn't you say?"

"I'd say you must have obnoxious, big-arse fairies across the pond," Odelia muttered.

In this whiteout, Bella can make out only a faint blur at Pandora's. Jiffy might have gotten disoriented and headed in the wrong direction. He could be wandering, lost in the storm.

"Jiffy!" she shouts. "Jiffy!"

He wouldn't hear her over the wind, even if he were nearby. Calla and Misty don't seem to, and they're still in her sightline just a few doors down.

She watches for him as she clears the steps and a path to the street. Still no sign. *Wherever he is, he's just fine,* she assures herself, pushing the last bit of snow off the steps and propping the shovel against the door again. Of course he is, because . . .

Because he just has to be, and that's that. Because the doom and gloom are behind her and Max at last. Because . . .

Because the Dale is home, and Odelia made soup, and the old light strings still work.

Because the puppies lived, and Drew is caring for them and cares for Bella, too, and Max, and . . .

Because it's Christmastime, and they're going to celebrate this year, and—

You better watch out . . . you better not cry . . .

Hearing the whistling nearby, Bella looks toward the electrician's van, parked across the street. "Hugo? Hugo?"

No reply, and no break in the whistling.

He sees you when you're sleeping . . .

Blowing on her raw red hands, she looks up at the Christmas bulbs she'd strung along the porch eaves. She should go grab the extension cord and light them. At least her guests will be greeted by a welcoming exterior before they set foot into the less than festive interior.

Yes, and if Jiffy really is out there in the storm, the lights might help guide him home like . . .

Like Rudolph's nose?

Like the star guiding the wise men to the stable?

"A star, a star . . ."

Humming "Do You Hear What I Hear?," she steps inside and kicks off her sodden sneakers by the door. No time to finish the parlor now. She'll find her hardware store purchases from yesterday, run back out to plug in the lights, then take a quick hot shower and—

She cries out, spotting a figure standing on the stairs.

"Sorry!"

Hugo again. Thank goodness.

"You're jumpy today," he observes. "I don't blame you. Finally got that ceiling fan working."

"I thought you were outside."

"Why would you think that?"

"Because I heard you whistling by the van, and—"

"Whistling? Me?" Hugo laughs as he descends the stairs, shaking his bald head. "Never have, never will. My brother teased me about it when we were kids, but my mother said it was just the way my mouth was shaped."

"So you're saying you weren't whistling 'Santa Claus Is Coming to Town' a minute ago?"

"Wasn't, and *can't*. Can't roll my tongue either, see?"

She gapes at him as he sticks it out. If he wasn't whistling, then who was?

No time to answer that troubling question now, Bella decides, finding the new extension cord in a bag she'd left on the registration desk.

"What's that for?" Hugo asks.

"Lights on the porch. The cord didn't reach the socket. I'm going to run back out and plug them in."

Hugo looks down at her wet socks, then at his own work boots, and he holds out a hand, palm up. "Give it here, Mrs. Jordan. I'll take care of that for you."

"You don't have to—"

"Least I can do for the cookies."

"What cookies?"

He grins. "The cookies you're going to bake me for plugging in your Christmas lights. I'm still dreaming about those snickerdoodles you made last week."

It must be nice, Bella thinks as she watches him amble out onto the porch, *not to feel stressed and overwhelmed by every day's obligations*. What's it like to live in Hugo's world, with ceiling fans that can wait till summer and Christmas gift-wrapping that can't but will get done anyway?

He's back too quickly, still holding the cord and shaking his gray head. "Where'd you get those old lights?"

"They came with the house."

"If I were you, I'd go out and buy myself some new ones."

"I wish that was in my budget this month, but it's not."

"Well, you'd better be careful with these, or the whole place is going to go up in smoke. Geez, that would be a real shame," he adds in his understated way.

A real shame? That would be a *disaster.*

"They were working yesterday. What's wrong?"

"I plugged in one string, and nothing happened. They were all dead."

"Dead! How can that be?"

"You mean because there's no such thing in Lily Dale?" he asks with a smirk.

Ah, but there is.

Yuri Moroskov, Leona Gatto, and so many others—dead. Gone. *In the lake.*

"Plugged in another string," Hugo is saying, "and it blew out. Got a nasty shock. Can't say I'm surprised."

"But they were fine when I tried them."

"Not fine now. Want me to throw them away for you?"

She ponders that. What is she going to tell Max? He was looking forward to decorations, and those old lights are their only options. If he sees them in the garbage can, he'll be upset. She'll wait to toss them until she can figure out how to replace them.

"Just leave them for now, Hugo. But I'll bake you a double batch of cookies if you'll do me another favor?"

"Name it."

"I need take a quick shower, and I have guests on their way. Just keep an eye out for them and holler if they arrive, okay?"

"Sure. In the meantime, I'll change out those bulbs for you." He points at the antique fixture high overhead, hanging from a plaster medallion, where two of the four lights have been burnt out for months.

"You don't have to do that, Hugo. I'll get to it. You'd need a ladder."

"I see one handy." He nods at her spackly mess in the parlor. "Go take your shower."

Upstairs, she smiles as she turns on the tap, thinking about all the friends she's made in Lily Dale. Sam would be glad to know so many people are looking out for her and Max.

He *does* know, if you believe the locals.

Her smile fades as she thinks of Jiffy out there in the storm, Misty's premonition, the body in the lake, and the great horned owl.

Chapter Nine

Staring into the bathroom mirror, Bella runs a blow-dryer over her damp hair. She sees only Misty Starr's frozen, straggly strands and the dread in her eyes.

How many times in the last six months has Bella criticized her parenting skills? She can justify her concern for the largely unsupervised Jiffy, but today, seeing the vulnerability in the woman's face . . .

She turns off the dryer, tightens the belt on her robe, and hurries back down the hall to the Rose Room.

When she first crossed the threshold six months ago, she thought she could have designed the space herself—charming antique decor, vintage architectural details, splashy reddish-pink color scheme, even the quirky layout with a window nook, angled wall, and gabled ceiling.

She couldn't help but compare it to the monochromatic rectangular guest room she'd expected to inhabit for the summer or beyond. She may have made peace with her mother-in-law, but Millicent's sleek condo in a Chicago skyscraper would never have felt like home. Not like the Rose Room and Valley View do, and did, from that first night.

She checks her cell phone, left charging on the bedside table. No texts or messages. That doesn't mean Jiffy's not home by now, Bella assures herself as she throws on jeans and a sweater. Calla probably just forgot to let her know, and it's not as if Misty Starr is going to pick up the phone to share the news.

When this is resolved, she'll invite Misty and Jiffy over to dinner. She probably should have done it long before now since the boys are inseparable. She can't imagine that she and Jiffy's mom will ever become the best of friends, but they can at least get to know each other better.

She texts Calla, *Is he back?*

When Calla doesn't immediately reply, Bella leaves her phone on the charger and looks in on Max. He's asleep with his arms around a snoozing Spidey, whose paws clasp Max's sleeve. She expects to see Chance still keeping vigil over the landscape below, but there's no sign of her.

Bella lifts the comforter to see if she's under the bed, one of her favorite hiding spots. Nothing there but dust bunnies and a stray sock. Grabbing it, she tosses it into the hamper beneath the window and looks out at the yard and lake.

Was Chance aware, as she roosted in this vantage point, that something was amiss? Bella may not believe in everything her Spiritualist friends do, but even she wouldn't argue against animal instinct. Or maternal instinct, for that matter.

"If you can accept the idea that cats and mothers are intuitive," Odelia had once said, "then why is it so hard for you to take it a step further?"

"It's not exactly a step, Odelia."

More like a leap across a yawning chasm.

They'd dropped the subject that day, but the conversation pops into Bella's head whenever she experiences something inexplicable . . . like the phantom whistler.

Back downstairs, she finds the foyer brightly lit, all four bulbs intact. The ladder is back in the parlor with the electrician atop it, sanding the ceiling.

"Hugo! What are you doing?"

"Lending a hand. Yours are full."

"But you don't have to do that."

"It's a nice change of pace, and I want to make those cookies worth your while."

Before she can protest, the front door opens, and a pair of women blow into the house on a gust of snow and laughter. Both are wearing floor-length faux fur coats, furry Eskimo boots, and Santa hats. They tug two enormous wheeled suitcases over the threshold and introduce themselves as Lauri and Dawn.

"But some people still call us Fire and Ice," Lauri tells Bella. She's the shorter of the two with a perky smile and red hair falling past her shoulders. "Those were our nicknames when we worked at Ponderosa together back in high school."

"I'm sure you can guess which is which," Dawn adds. Her hair is ash blond and cut above her shoulders in a similarly layered style.

"You must be Ice. Speaking of ice, how was your trip?"

"Slippery. We were in a whiteout pretty much the whole time after we left Buffalo," Dawn says cheerfully, "but we're used to it, so no biggie, right, Laur?"

"Not for us, but we passed a lot of accidents. Nothing serious. People just don't know how to drive in this."

"Right," Dawn agrees. "They try to go too fast and end up in a ditch. Like that little green car that came flying past us on the road in."

"It was blue."

"It was green!"

"Blue-green," Lauri says with a shrug.

"Speaking of colors, Bella, as soon as we came up the street, I said my girls would love the lavender paint, right, Laur?"

"She did. And I said, 'I know, it's just too cute!'" Lauri gives a vigorous nod, her hat's white pom-pom bouncing around her shoulders. "Lisa was right. This place is so *us*!"

Lisa Koellner is a friend of theirs who had spent the night at Valley View last summer. As she checked out, she'd told Bella, "This place is super cute. I'm going to send everyone I know here!"

"To Lily Dale?"

"To Valley View!" she said with a laugh. "I wouldn't call Lily Dale super cute."

Bella wouldn't necessarily call Valley View super cute either, but she's grateful for the business.

A whirlwind of conversation yields that both women grew up together and are married. Dawn has three daughters. Lauri has one and a son. He and Dawn's twins are eighteen, and both their older girls are twenty-one. They ask in turn about Bella's family.

"I have a son. He's six."

"That's such a great age, isn't it, Dawn?"

"Six is *a-dor-able*!"

Sometimes, Bella thinks, *it's even super cute.*

And super vulnerable. Jiffy, momentarily forgotten, somersaults back into her mind.

She reaches to close the door, but Lauri stops her. "We still have to go get the rest of our stuff."

"Let's go now," Dawn says, "before the car is plowed in like the ones down the road."

They disappear out the door.

Bella eyes their oversized luggage. They're only staying two nights. How much more stuff can there be?

"Well, *they* seem like a couple of festive gals. Just what the doctor ordered for you, Mrs. Jordan," Hugo pronounces from the ladder in the parlor.

She'd forgotten all about him.

"You need to stop sanding, Hugo. Please. I'll finish it later or tomorrow. I know you're used to driving in this, but I'll feel awful if you don't get home before the roads are even more dangerous."

"My truck has gotten me home through a lot worse."

"But you're parked at the edge of the road. Next time the plow comes by, your truck is going to be buried like those cars they were just talking about."

She imagines an enormous truck pushing a mountain of dirty snow up ice-slicked Cottage Row, heedless of objects in its path. What if a little boy had slipped and fallen on his way home from the bus? He could have lost consciousness or broken a limb. If the truck came along and didn't spot him in the whiteout . . .

The front door blasts open, curtailing her ugly speculation.

Lauri and Dawn are back. This time, they have a large framed poster, a plastic tub labeled *craft supplies,* and a large canvas tote bag. It's overstuffed, with a few items poking out the top: a board game, a bottle of top-shelf gin, and two pairs of white ice skates tied with fuzzy pink pom-poms and little silver bells.

Dawn follows Bella's gaze. "We like to keep busy when we do girls' weekends."

"And have fun," Lauri adds. "Do you like to play games?"

"Games? You mean like Scrabble?"

She and Sam had been avid players. When Max's birth impaired their social life, they'd kept a Scrabble board on the coffee table and played every night. Then Max had started toddling, tiny hands grasping for the tiles, and that was the end of Scrabble.

Until Drew Bailey showed up at her door with the Scrabble set one night last week.

She'd wanted to ask how he knew, but of course, he couldn't have known. She'd never told anyone about Sam and Scrabble. Yet oddly, she'd been thinking about it just that evening, imagining what she and Sam might have been doing on a blustery Saturday night like that one.

"Scrabble's fun, too," Lauri tells her now. "But did you ever play Catch Phrase? That's what we brought."

"I love Catch Phrase." That comes from Hugo in the doorway, denim overalls and bald head covered in dusty spackle. "My grand-kids got it last Christmas."

"Awesome! You'll have to play with us. We brought the eighties' music version. That's actually the whole reason we're here."

"To play Catch Phrase?" Bella asks.

"No! Because of him." Dawn turns the poster around, revealing a close-up of a shaggy-haired, bare-chested electric guitarist in black leather pants.

"Hey, Sean Von Vogel!" Hugo says.

"Yes! You know him?"

"Sure do. Saw him in concert at least half a dozen times."

"We're super fans," Lauri tells him. "We were front and center at the show in Buffalo last month."

"Last month?" Bella echoes. "But isn't Sean Von Vogel dead?"

"Von Vogel is the name of the band, too. They still tour without Sean. It's so sad."

"Speaking of so sad and Buffalo, did anyone catch the Sabres game last night?" Hugo asks.

Dawn shakes her head. "Don't remind me. My husband was hyperventilating."

Feeling lost, yet relieved for the distraction, Bella asks what happened.

Hugo cringes. "Blowout. They lost to the Maple Leafs eleven to nothing."

"How is that score even possible?" Lauri asks.

"I'd have said it isn't, but I saw it with my own eyes. Hopefully the Bills will do better tonight against the Dolphins."

"They'll squish the fish!" Dawn predicts.

"Let's hope so. The wife has my to-do list waiting, and the game starts at eight, so if you really don't mind my calling it a day, Bella . . ."

"Not at all."

"Nice meeting you ladies."

"You, too! You'll have to come back for gin and tonics and Catch Phrase while we're here," Dawn calls after him as he heads down to the basement to pack up his tools. "So nice to meet a fellow Von Vogel super fan, isn't it, Laur?"

"Yes! Especially on the ten-year anniversary."

"Of what?" Bella asks.

"The day the music died."

"Well," Lauri says, "ten years *tomorrow* since the day the music died."

"Wasn't that back in the fifties? Buddy Holly's plane crash?" Bella had heard all about that from Odelia, who claims that Buddy, Ritchie Valens, and the Big Bopper visit her regularly.

"That was way before our time. For our generation, the music died when we lost Sean Von Vogel, right, Dawn?"

"Right. It was the worst day of our lives."

Sean Von Vogel had been killed during a solo performance on a custom-built glass stage protruding high over Antelope River Canyon, Bella learned. The band's signature song had featured a sustained high C. When he'd hit it, the amplified note had fractured the glass, and he'd fallen to his death.

"That concert was our fortieth birthday gift to each other," Dawn tells Bella. "But we missed our connecting flight. There was a storm, and we were stuck in Denver for three days. That's probably when the trouble started. We were jinxed, right, Laur?"

"Right. Like I said, it's the reason we're here."

This, Bella notes, is how many conversations tend to go here in the Dale. She thinks she's following along, then stumbles into a gap that leaves her certain she must have nodded off and missed a sentence or two.

"I'm not sure I get it. *Why* are you here?"

"You know, because of Sean."

"Hopefully by tonight, we'll have the answer." Dawn squeezes her friend's hand. "Then everything will be back to normal again."

Lauri nods. So does Bella. By tonight, surely Jiffy will be accounted for, and everything will be back to normal—whatever that means here in Lily Dale.

She helps them lug their bags upstairs and leaves them to settle in. A quick peek into Max's room assures her that he's still asleep. She returns to her own to check text messages.

Still nothing from Calla.

Drew texted a photo of the injured dog's newborn puppies.

She responds with a heart emoji.

He sends a heart back, which gives her pause.

Then he writes, *All okay there? How's Max?*

Not great. Sleeping.

She hesitates, wondering if she should tell him about Jiffy, then hits send. She'll have to call him for that. But not until she knows more.

Poor guy, Drew texts back. *Show him puppies to cheer him up.*

About to reply with another heart, she changes it to a thumbs-up.

She heads back downstairs. It's been nearly an hour since Jiffy would have gotten off the bus.

She finds Chance perched on the window seat in the parlor, gazing out into billowing clouds of white.

"What is it, kitty?" Bella rests a hand on her fur. "Are you looking for Jiffy?"

For a long time, the two of them stare at the storm. Then she hears whistling again, somewhere in the house. It's that same Christmas song . . .

You better watch out, you better not cry . . .

Hugo must have been pulling her leg before when he claimed he doesn't know how to whistle.

Maybe Bella should ask him to stick around while she dashes down the street for a few minutes to see what's going on.

"Hugo? Hey, Hugo?"

No reply.

She checks the hall, then the kitchen. The door to the basement is now closed. She opens it and sees that the light is turned off.

"Hugo?"

Silence.

Puzzled, she returns to the hall. This time, she realizes that the electrician's canvas work jacket is no longer draped over the coat tree. Looking out into the street, she sees that his van is gone.

And her snow boots are sitting neatly on the mat beside her soaked sneakers.

Chapter Ten

Bella makes her way down the steps and onto snowy Cottage Row, glad her boots turned up, but wishing it had been Jiffy instead.

When they magically appeared exactly where she'd left them last night, she figured Hugo must have come across them and put them there before he departed. Yes, that would make perfect sense . . . had he known she was looking for them.

It makes no sense whatsoever to consider Nadine, so—

"Bella?" a voice calls, and she looks up to see Odelia on the porch next door. Today, her ample figure is wrapped in a zebra print housecoat, and her orange hair is stacked in a pillar of rollers high above her round face and cat-eye glasses. "Any news about Jiffy?"

"I don't know. Calla is down there with Misty, and I'm going to find out what's going on. I actually just tried to call you."

"Sorry, I was doing a phone reading with a client. Julius came through again."

"Caesar?"

"How many Juliuses do you know?" Odelia asks as if that—and not the fact that she's been chatting with a Roman politician who's been dead for a few thousand years—is the outlandish aspect of the conversation. "We always go overtime. You can't cut him off."

"I'm sure you can't," Bella agrees, "being a dictator and all."

"How is Max feeling?"

"He's asleep right now. Thank you for the soup. I was calling to see if you could keep an eye on him while I run over to the Ardens', but I found someone else."

Lauri and Dawn, busy unpacking their bags in their adjoining rooms down the hall, were happy to watch Max for a few minutes.

"He probably won't wake up," Bella told them, "but if he does, tell him I just had to check in on someone, and I'll be right back. Oh, and keep your distance. His cold might be contagious."

"Don't worry, we're moms," Lauri said as if that gave them some kind of super-immunity.

Certain she's left Max in capable hands, Bella wishes she felt the same confidence about Jiffy. Seeing Odelia's worried expression as she gazes out into the falling snow, Bella says, "You know Jiffy. He's probably building the world's biggest snowman somewhere out here."

"He isn't."

Bella nods. She doesn't think so either.

She tells Odelia what she found out about Yuri Moroskov. "I feel like what happened to him must have something to do with Jiffy."

Odelia is shaking her head before she's even finished the sentence. "I don't think so."

"What do you mean?"

"My guides aren't pointing me in that direction."

That's the trouble with Lily Dale. Occasionally, when something—or someone—is amiss, the locals rely heavily on Spirit for answers when they could be, in Bella's opinion, channeling their time and energy into more productive, logical pursuits.

Okay, maybe it isn't entirely fair to think that Odelia is illogical. Maybe Bella is being too hard on her. She has plenty of perfectly reasonable moments . . .

"I'd come over to the Ardens' with you, Bella, but I have a bun in the oven."

. . . and this just isn't one of them.

Seeing her expression, Odelia quickly explains that she isn't pregnant—as if that were a biological possibility. "It's a giant cinnamon sticky bun. You bake it in a round cake pan."

Ah. A bun. In the oven.

"It's Luther's favorite dessert," Odelia goes on. "He's coming for dinner."

If Bella hadn't already known that, the head full of rollers would have been a dead giveaway. Last time he joined them all for dinner, Odelia had set her hair and worn full makeup and a black velvet hostess gown with a plunging neckline. "Oh, this old thing?" she'd said when he complimented her, as if she'd just thrown it on, rhinestone sash, tiara, and all.

Bella heads on down the street, wanting to believe Odelia is right. But she's the one who claims there are no coincidences. When a child goes missing twenty-four hours after a murdered corpse turns up . . .

As she climbs the Ardens' snowy steps, she prays that Jiffy is back and she'll find him sharing his adventures over a cup of hot chocolate.

But Calla answers the door, cell phone in hand, wearing a grim expression.

"Still missing?" Bella asks needlessly, stepping into the house. She looks for a doormat, but there isn't one. She gingerly stomps her boots on the worn patch of hardwood, where melting snow is already pooling.

"Still missing," Calla confirms.

"I've been trying to text you. I was hoping you weren't answering because he was back at home and you were back at work."

"No, I forgot my phone at your house. This is Misty's. I've been using it to call around. Most of the local kids I talked to saw him get off the bus, but no one paid attention to where he went from the gate. I'm glad you came over."

She leads Bella through an entry hall that's far smaller than the one at Valley View. No hint of old-world elegance here. The ceilings are low, fixtures basic, moldings unembellished, hardwoods scuffed and scarred. A steep, narrow staircase leads to a shadowy second floor.

In the parlor, Bella sees far too much furniture for such a compact room. Rickety antiques mingle with seventies-style colonial pieces—1970s, not 1770s—and eighties' Victorian odds and ends—1980s, not 1880s.

On the white wall above the red sofa appears a child's artwork in black marker: a clumsy stick figure with black scribbles over the eyes. Bella recognizes Jiffy's depiction of a ninja zombie warrior.

Her gaze falls on a framed photo nearby. Jiffy beams between his mother and a young man with a short military haircut. They're posing against a familiar backdrop—Times Square, crowded with people, yellow taxi cabs, and neon signs.

Misty is wearing a floppy sun hat and a sleeveless dress covered in a colorful zigzag print, with turquoise and silver bracelets stacked along her fleshy arms. Jiffy's dad is wearing a collared dress shirt and perfectly creased khaki slacks. They don't seem to go together, Bella thinks. It isn't just fashion diversity or the fact that Misty is overweight and her husband lean and muscular.

Her smile is open and warm. His mouth is set beneath a pair of aviator sunglasses. Her posture is relaxed, his visibly rigid. The soldier and the free spirit.

Jiffy is his mother's son.

He often mentions the New York City weekend of last spring when they last saw his father. He's more cheerful than wistful, but that's his personality. He must miss his dad and surely Misty does, too. Heaven knows raising a little boy single-handedly is challenging even when you're surrounded by helpful friends.

Maybe Misty, like Bella, was at a crossroads when she stumbled across the Dale. Maybe there's a mysterious stray cat somewhere back in her story, too.

Bella turns away from the photo. "Where's Misty?"

"She's meditating."

"Shouldn't she be calling the police? Or out looking?"

"Blue organized a couple of people to search the Dale, and I called the police."

"What did they say?"

"The desk sergeant took down the information. They're sending someone over."

"Did he seem concerned?"

"He was a she. And she was until I mentioned Jiffy's name. She said she knows all about him and that he tends to wander. She's sure he'll turn up." Calla doesn't look any more convinced than Bella feels.

"Did you have a vision, too?"

"You mean like Misty? No. More just a feeling that something is wrong."

She breaks off as a door creaks open. They hear footsteps in the next room and then the refrigerator opening and closing. Through the doorway, Bella spots Misty clutching a bottle of water, still huddled in the crocheted poncho, hair bedraggled.

They join her in the kitchen. Like the rest of the cottage, it's seen better days. The cabinets are dark, the mustard-colored appliances dated, the stainless steel sink loaded with dirty dishes. Two upper cabinet doors are ajar, revealing crowded shelves. The countertop below is littered with packaged goods, as if they've jumped out to make a run for the back door.

It, too, is ajar. The outer storm door is closed but still wears its summer screen, allowing a wintry draft to permeate the room. No doormat here either, Bella notices. Just a puddle on the linoleum and wet tracks across the floor.

No wonder she always has to remind Jiffy to wipe his feet when he walks into Valley View. He doesn't know any better. Maybe Misty doesn't either, having come from arid Arizona, though you'd think common sense would tell her otherwise.

Then again, Bella has met plenty of people here in the Dale who pay little attention to their physical surroundings. Odelia frequently mentions that she's far more interested in channeling energy than she is in expending it on mundane household chores.

Misty is, too. Laundry, anyway. Dirty clothes spill from a tall, stuffed bag propped by the back door, with a container of detergent and a jar of quarters sitting on the floor alongside.

Last week, Jiffy wore the same stained sweat shirt four days in a row, unusual even for him. Bella hadn't commented, but Max had asked him why, and he'd mentioned that his mom's washing machine was broken. Why hadn't it occurred to Bella to make a phone call and offer hers?

You were too caught up in your own problems to worry about anyone else's.

"Have you heard anything?" Misty asks, fumbling to open her water bottle.

"The police are on their way," Calla tells her. "And my . . . uh, *friend*, Blue Slayton, has rounded up a couple of people to go door to door asking if anyone has seen him. He's already checked a few places where kids hang out."

"Like where?" Misty frowns, peering down at the bottle top. She attempts to twist it again.

"The gazebo, the playground, the parking lot over by Leolyn Wood, the skating pond . . ."

"Skating pond?" She looks up. "I didn't know there was one, but Jiffy's been asking if we can get ice skates this winter. Where is it?"

"On a farm off Glasgow Road. After it freezes, usually later in January, the guy who lives there hangs lights for night skating."

"Wait . . . is it Virgil Barbor's farm?" Bella asks, remembering what he'd said about buying new lights.

At Calla's nod, Misty makes a choking little sound.

"What's wrong?"

"Nothing, just . . . he's my landlord. I just remembered he was supposed to stop over here at noon. Maybe he won't because of the weather."

"I doubt that. I ran into him at Mitch's the other day, and he said the weather never keeps him from doing anything."

"Do you think Jiffy went over there to try to skate?"

Bella knows what she's thinking, and her own heart shivers as she imagines a little boy out there testing the ice alone.

"No. Blue said there were no footprints around the pond."

"There are no footprints anywhere! That doesn't mean anything! Why won't this stupid cap turn?" Misty hurtles the plastic bottle across the room. It ricochets off the wall and rolls into the puddle by the door.

Bella's head is starting to ache. The house, drafty a few minutes ago, now seems too close and warm as she wordlessly retrieves the bottle. She twists the cap to break the seal and hands it back to Misty.

"Thanks," she mutters and sips. "Sorry. My emotions are all over the place. Did your friend check the Stump, Calla?"

Inspiration Stump, Lily Dale's most sacred landmark, is located on a peaceful forest path in Leolyn Wood. The spot is said to be highly charged with spirit energy. During the season, mediums gather there to demonstrate their abilities at public readings. Year-round, they visit to meditate and channel Spirit.

"He did check. He said no one was out there. Why? Does Jiffy go there?"

"Not usually. But I just remembered that he mentioned it last night."

"What did he say?"

"He asked me if it's really full of secrets. I told him that when we first moved here. It's the same thing someone said to me when I was a little girl." She frowns. "You know what? I'm going to go over there now. If he's not there, I'll wait. Maybe he'll show up."

"You wouldn't stay long in this weather," Calla says. "You probably can't even get there in this deep snow. You need to stay warm and safe yourself. Just try to relax, and meditate. Maybe you'll get something."

"Or," Bella says, "maybe instead of trying to *get* something, maybe you should . . . I don't know . . ."

She can't bring herself to tell Misty to *do* something like go out and join the searchers or even just stop meditating—forget the spirit guides and the Stump and use common sense.

"What?" Misty snaps, turning to Bella, eyes gleaming. "What should I do?"

"I don't know."

"Well, I don't either!" Her voice breaks, and Bella realizes she's more distressed than irritated. "Tell me, and I'll do it."

"Maybe try to put yourself into Jiffy's shoes."

"What do you think I've been doing? I just told you, I can't channel him."

"Okay, well, he's been telling Max he wants a snowboard for Christmas. Maybe he's over at the sledding hill."

"Blue was headed there next," Calla says.

"But he doesn't have a snowboard yet. He doesn't even have a sled."

"Maybe he found one or borrowed one from a friend," Bella tells her as Jiffy's words echo in her head.

My mom says I shouldn't borrow stuff because I lose everything . . .

"I guess he might have done that. But I don't know who he'd get it from, other than your son . . ."

"Max," Bella says, when Misty trails off as if she doesn't remember his name.

"I *know*. Are you sure he's not over at Valley View with *Max*?"

"No, Max has been in bed, mostly asleep, all day. I'm pos—"

Wait a minute.

Is she positive Jiffy isn't at Valley View?

She did hear someone whistling.

"You thought of something. What is it?"

"Nothing, just . . ."

"*What?*"

"Jiffy and Max love to play hide-and-seek. Maybe that's what he's doing."

"At your house? By himself?"

"You never know with Jiffy. He's such a creative thinker, and he has all those imaginary friends."

"I can't believe you're saying that *here*! That's what our neighbors in Arizona used to say. They didn't understand about Spirit, but *you* . . . *You* live *here*. You know better."

Backtracking through her own comments, Bella pinpoints the offensive phrase. "Sorry, all I meant was, a lot of kids *do* have imaginary friends."

Bella wonders if Jiffy could have slipped into Valley View while she was busy in the parlor. Or maybe he sneaked in through one of the hidden tunnels. It wouldn't be the first time.

"Misty, does Jiffy know how to whistle?"

"Whistle?"

"Yes, I heard—" She breaks off at a loud knock on the door. "Do you want me to get that?"

Misty nods, shivering. She must be chilled through in those damp clothes. And terrified.

Calla puts a hand on her trembling shoulder as Bella goes into the entry hall.

"We meet again," Grange says. "Didn't expect to find you here."

He crosses the threshold, brushing white powder from his shoulders and reaching back to close the door. It slams behind him like a gunshot.

"Sorry about that," he says quickly, hand still on the knob. "It was the wind. Where's the boy's mother?"

Ah, yes. Mr. Warm and Fuzzy himself.

"Right here. I'm Misty Starr, and this is Odelia's granddaughter, Calla . . ."

"Delaney."

"Sorry," Misty says. "I'm not good with names."

"Misty Starr." Grange writes it down on his clipboard.

"Yes. Two *Rs*."

A star, a star, Bella hears in her head. Oh, if only this were Bethlehem and three wise men—or even one wise man—would guide Jiffy safely home.

"I saw the sign out front," Grange says. "What's your real name?"

Bella probably shouldn't be surprised by the question. Sometimes it seems as if no one around here is who they claim to be.

She's met more than her share of villains who used stolen identities or simply passed themselves off as ordinary people. And just the other day, she'd overheard Misty's client on her cell phone laughing about using a pseudonym for her reading.

Wait a minute.

That was the day an SUV with Ontario license plates was parked in front of Misty's house. The border is just over an hour away. In the season, Bella hosted nearly as many Canadian guests as Americans, and yet . . .

Yuri Moroskov was part of a money-laundering crime ring that smuggles contraband through Canada. Could Misty's client have been connected to the Amur Leopard, too?

Lily Dale's refrain echoes back to her.

There are no coincidences.

* * *

"So you're Mary Ellen Arden. Is that your maiden or married name?" Grange asks Misty.

"Married. My maiden name is Grzeszkiewicz, but I've never used it. Even when I was a kid, people just called me Meg."

"Meg? Not Mary Ellen."

"Yes. Mary Ellen. My initials were *M-E-G*. Meg is a lot easier than trying to say Grzeszkiewicz."

"Spell it," Grange commands.

"*G-R-Z* . . ." Misty begins, but she stops spelling, stops breathing, when the phone rings in Calla's hand.

"It's Blue."

Grange frowns. "What do you mean, blue?"

"Her boyfriend," Bella explains. "That's his name. Blue Slayton."

"Did you find him?" Calla is asking.

Misty closes her eyes. *Pleasepleasepleaseplease* . . .

"Okay, well, keep looking . . . yes . . . What? Where? . . . How long ago?"

"What is it? What happened?" Misty asks. "Did he find something?"

"Hang on," Calla says into the phone, then tells Misty, "No, he didn't."

"Mrs. Arden?" Grange prompts her, gesturing with his pen. "Your maiden name? You were spelling it for me."

"Oh. Right."

Calla turns away with her phone. It doesn't allow her any more privacy, because every word on her end is still audible, but they can't see her expression. Still, Misty can hear the trepidation in her voice.

"Are you sure? . . . Okay, well maybe it's not . . . No, I know . . . I just—"

"Mrs. Arden?" Grange says, waiting for her to finish spelling her name as she prays that the dismal-sounding phone call might miraculously transform to word that her son has been found.

"Uh, *Z-E-S*—"

"There are two *Z*s?"

"Three."

Grange scowls and clears his throat. "So it's *G-R-Z-Z-Z* . . ."

"What? No!" She turns back to listen to what Calla is saying.

"I know, Blue, but . . . Yes. I just can't—"

"Miss Delaney!" Grange barks. "Can you please chat with your boyfriend somewhere else?"

Calla looks up, startled. She mouths *sorry* and grabs her parka, draped over the newel-post. She puts it on and steps outside, phone still clasped to her ear.

Ignoring Misty's accusatory look, Grange commands, "Spell your maiden name again from the beginning, please."

Eyes narrowed, expression taut, she complies.

Grange writes it down and asks her a few more basic questions. Then he flicks his blue-gray gaze in Bella's direction and asks Misty if she'd like to continue the conversation privately.

"First you kick out Calla, and now you want Bella to go, too?"

"I didn't kick her out. Her phone conversation was interfering with my investigation."

"But her conversation was about my son!" Misty can see Calla through the window, out in the snowy street talking to a man who must be Blue. He's unrecognizable, his lean, muscular frame bundled in layers of down, his features and even gender obscured by a ski hat and scarf. Calla, in a thick parka, hugs herself against an icy wind.

How long will Jiffy last out there in this weather? What if he's lost?

She can't bear to think of it.

She should have been watching him more closely. She shouldn't have let him walk home alone.

Bella turns toward the door, zipping her own jacket to her chin.

Misty grabs her arm. "No, Bella, don't go! No matter what he says. I don't want to be alone right now."

"Try not to worry. I'm sure it's going to be all right. But I really need to—"

"You can stay," Grange cuts in. "I didn't mean to chase you out of here. Some people prefer not to involve outsiders in domestic matters."

Outsiders might be accurate police jargon, but if he knew anything about Lily Dale off-season, he'd realize that pretty much everyone still in town is an insider.

"My friend is here to help me find my son, Lieutenant, and I need all the help I can get."

Bella rests a supportive hand on Misty's shoulder. "I'll stay for a few more minutes if you need me to."

Misty wishes she didn't, but she doesn't want to be left alone with this man. He rubs her the wrong way. Maybe because his aura is yellow, like her husband's.

Yellows are smart, confident, independent, logical . . .

Yes, and that's why she knew from the moment she met Mike that he'd protect her, make her feel safe. For a long time, that was true. But when the wedding rings were on and the baby came along, something—everything?—began to change.

Within his yellow aura, there was also a tendency to put goals and work before personal relationships. She used to admire that strength and independence, the way he didn't want to lean on anyone. Now she believes he simply doesn't need anyone. He's been pulling away, and now, when she needs him most, he's not here.

To be fair, he doesn't yet know Jiffy is missing. She's afraid to tell him because—

"Mrs. Arden!"

"What?"

"I *said*, 'What was your son wearing when he left for school this morning?'"

"I don't remember."

Grange's eyes flicker with incredulity or maybe suspicion. "You did see him today, right?"

"Of course I saw him. I gave him breakfast and kissed him good-bye when he left for school, same as I do every morning."

"But you don't know what he had on?"

She closes her eyes and bows her head, trying to conjure her memory of Jiffy's wardrobe or her Spirit guides to help her navigate this nightmare.

"Mrs. Arden?"

Her eyes snap open. "*What?*"

"Was Michael wearing a coat?"

"No one ever calls him that!"

"Was your son wearing a coat?" he asks evenly.

"It's *December*. It's *snowing*. What do *you* think?"

"I know this is stressful, but let's try to be patient. Does he have more than one winter coat?"

"That fits? No."

"So he has one coat."

"Yes. I just said that."

"What color is it?"

"Dark green."

"Wait, didn't he leave that on the bus?" Bella asks.

Misty frowns. "Did he?"

"I think that's what he said."

"Then I guess he wasn't wearing it." She looks back at Grange, who writes something on the form, then asks for a recent photo of Jiffy.

She grabs a framed snapshot from a nearby table. "This was taken in May. Jiffy and I met his dad in New York City for the weekend."

"Oh, I know *him*. Curious, chatty little kid. He was over at Valley View Manor when I investigated the Leona Gatto case. Are you married to his father?"

"Yes, we're . . . yes." *But not for long* seems to dangle in the air as she toys with a frayed piece of yarn on her afghan wrap.

"Where is he?"

"Deployed in the Middle East."

"How long?"

"Years."

"You mean he's been there for years, or he'll be there for years?"

"Both, probably." She shrugs.

Grange writes on his clipboard. "When did you last see him?"

"He had a short leave in May. Before that, it was almost a year."

"And you last spoke with him . . . ?"

"This morning."

"About what?"

Misty looks over at Bella, reevaluating whether she wants her to hear this. No choice now.

"About Christmas."

"Do you want to share the details of that exchange, Mrs. Arden?"

No. I don't want to share them. I'd love to forget them.

"I was trying to get him to change his mind about coming home," she says flatly. "Well, not home—*here*."

"Meaning . . ."

"Meaning he doesn't consider Lily Dale home, and he isn't coming for the holidays. He says he never wants to come here again."

"I thought you said you moved here in June, and you haven't seen your husband since May."

"I haven't. He was here with me on our honeymoon seven years ago."

She was in her late teens then, already expecting Jiffy.

"You honeymooned in Lily Dale?"

"Niagara Falls."

"Where does Lily Dale come in?"

"I'm from Cleveland. We got married there, and Lily Dale was on the way to the Falls. We drove up in Mike's crappy truck. Some honeymoon. Just overnight, all we could afford back then. Can't afford even that now."

"So finances are tight?"

"Very. Always."

Money is the least of her worries right now.

Yet as Grange makes a note, she wonders why Virgil Barbor hasn't yet come over to collect his rent. It's long past noon. What if he shows up in the middle of this interrogation?

"Does your son know about this custody dispute, Mrs. Arden?" Grange asks.

"Custody dispute? I told you, we're married!"

"Sorry. Slip of the tongue. Is your son aware that you and your husband disagree over how and where the child will be spending the holidays?"

She hesitates. "Yes. He knows."

"You told him?"

"He was sitting here eating his cereal while Mike and I were arguing, and he asked what was going on, and I told him."

"So he was upset?" Grange asks.

"Jiffy doesn't get upset about that kind of thing. He's used to it."

"Used to what?"

"You know, me and Mike fighting. He's an easygoing kid." She looks at Bella. "That's how boys that age are, right? In one ear, out the other." When Bella fails to agree, she mutters, "Well, that's how *my* kid is."

Bella clears her throat. "Maybe that's what he wants you to think."

"What do you mean?"

"Maybe he doesn't want to make things harder on you. Whenever Max sees that I'm upset about losing his dad, he tries so hard to cheer me up."

"That's different. Your husband's dead. Mine's just a jerk."

"I think it's safe to assume that when your son left for school this morning, he might have been concerned about not seeing his father for Christmas," Grange decides. "Possibly resentful, too. If he was counting on his dad being here and now he won't be . . ."

"This is nothing new. His dad is never here."

"That doesn't mean your son doesn't resent him. Or you."

"Why would he resent *me*?"

"All kids resent their parents from time to time, Mrs. Arden."

"You may have met Jiffy, but you sure don't know him very well." She turns to Bella. "Right? Tell him! Jiffy hangs around at Valley View all the time. You know him."

"I do," she agrees. "He does. He and Max are good friends."

"And have you ever seen him angry or resentful?" Misty feels like a trial attorney doing cross-examination.

"No, I actually never have," Bella agrees, and Misty nods, satisfied.

Jiffy may be a handful, but he's the most agreeable kid in the world. Misty can't imagine him running away in a fit of anger, if that's what Grange suspects.

He turns to Bella. "Have you asked *your* son if he knows where his friend might be hiding, Ms. Jordan?"

"He doesn't even know Jiffy's missing yet. He's sick at home in bed, asleep."

"My son isn't hiding, Lieutenant!" Misty protests. "He's in danger!"

"What makes you think that?"

"For one thing, he hasn't picked up his phone."

"He has a phone?"

"Yes. And for another thing, I'm a medium."

Ignoring that, Grant says, "Tell me about the phone. Can you track it?"

"If I could track it, you wouldn't be here."

"So there's no locator on it?"

"There might be, but I wouldn't know. Mike bought the phone for him. I had nothing to do with it. I didn't even want him to have it."

"Why not?"

Misty ticks off the reasons on her fingers. "He's too young, too irresponsible, too distracted by it . . ."

"Most six-year-olds are. Why would your husband get it for him?"

"He spoils him with stuff because he's never here."

Grange asks for Jiffy's phone number, and for Mike's, and for a photo of Jiffy that he can take with him.

"A close-up headshot would be good."

"A headshot? He's not an actor. He's a kid."

"I mean like a school photo, something like that?"

"School pictures were taken back in September," Bella says. "And an order form came home in their backpacks."

"Guess I missed it," Misty murmurs and waits for a judgy look from Miss Perfect.

But Bella appears sympathetic, pulling out her cell phone. "I have a couple of good shots on my phone from the other day when the boys were helping me paint," she tells Grange. "I can send you one of Jiffy."

"Six-year-olds helped you paint?"

"It seemed like a good idea at the time." Scrolling through the photos, she finds several close-ups of Jiffy. He's in most of them, but she shows Grange one where he's relatively clean.

"Can I see?" Misty asks.

"Sure." Bella shows her the picture.

Misty stares down at a broadly grinning Jiffy, who appears to be covered in war paint. "What is he wearing here?" she asks, noting an oversized men's button-down with the sleeves rolled up.

"Oh, that's one of my husband's old shirts," she says with a bit of an ache in her voice. "I had to get rid of most of his stuff when we moved, but . . . these make good smocks for the boys. I figured you wouldn't be thrilled if Jiffy ruined his school clothes."

Even if the school clothes were probably a stained old sweat shirt that hadn't been washed in weeks.

Touched, Misty thanks her. "I didn't realize . . . thank you. It was nice of you to do that."

"Aw, it was nice of him to help me paint. He did a great job."

"Yeah, that's hard to believe, but thanks for keeping him busy. Sometimes I get caught up in what I'm working on, and I guess . . ." She glances at Grange. "I really was planning to keep a closer eye on him starting today."

"Why is that?"

"Because I had a vision yesterday that made me worry about him, and I—"

Grange's cell phone rings. He looks at it, holds up a finger, and answers the call.

"Grange here . . . yeah . . . where? . . . Do you know if . . . Okay, got it. On my way." He hangs up and tucks his pen into his pocket. "Sorry, but I have to go."

"Wait, what do you mean?"

"An officer needs backup, and I'm closest to the scene. I'll be back."

Misty notices that Grange, who tends to make unflinching eye contact, is avoiding it now. His job is to investigate, not provide reassurance, but you'd think Mr. Freeze could summon a smidgeon of compassion.

"But what about Jiffy?" Bella asks.

"I'll be back," he repeats, opens the door, and closes it behind him.

Misty mutters a choice word under her breath and looks at Bella. "Think he really will?"

She nods. "It's a small police force. They're probably short-handed and overwhelmed on a day like this."

Outside, a car engine starts up and so does the siren. Fluid red light falls through the window.

Misty looks out into the street as the squad car departs. "Hey, where's Calla?"

"I don't know. She was out there a few minutes ago, with—"

"Blue." She nods. "Bella—"

"Excuse me?" Bella whirls around to stare at her. "Did you just say *Bella Blue*?"

She didn't. Not in that order. And she was about to thank Bella for coming over and tell her she's free to leave, that she *should* leave, but . . .

Now there's an expectant look on her face. Misty studies her, taking in her aura. Earlier, she'd noted that it's blue. Now she finds the depth remarkable. She nods. It fits. *Bella Blue.*

"No wonder my kid is so drawn to you. You're peaceful. A survivor. And Jiffy is an indigo child."

"What, um . . . what does that mean?"

"You're compatible. He craves what you are, what you have to offer."

"I don't think that's the case at all." Bella smiles faintly. "He's not big on rules, helmets, boundaries, curfews . . ."

"No. But he needs them just the same." She shakes her head. "I'm a magenta, myself. I'm suited to yellows—my husband is a yellow—but then, he's not here either, is he? Looks like everyone's abandoning me." The words are meant to be light, but she chokes on what was supposed to be a chuckle.

Bella touches her hand. "Maybe you should call your husband before Grange does."

"He'll blame me or Lily Dale."

"You said you stopped here on the way to Niagara Falls for your honeymoon?"

"Yes. I used to spend summers here with my aunt, and I thought . . ." She gives a little laugh, shaking her head. "I don't know what I thought. I guess that Mike might like it. Boy, was I wrong. It was during the season, crowded, and we had to pay a gate fee. Long story short, Mike got the wrong idea about Lily Dale."

"Is that why he's not coming for Christmas? Because he doesn't like it here? Or because he can't afford to travel? Or is it that you're having marital difficulties?"

"D. All the above."

"Maybe you can spend Christmas with him someplace else."

"That's what *he* said. But there is no place else. The base is too far away. New York is too expensive. My family is in Cleveland, and well . . ." She makes a face, shaking her head. "They're difficult."

"What about *his* family?"

"Pennsylvania. Just outside of Allentown. I've never even met them. Mike hasn't spoken to them for years. Look, I need to go meditate. Maybe I can get something now. Make sure you keep a good eye on your kid, okay? And don't trust anyone, no matter who it is."

"I'm here if you need anything. And Jiffy's going to be all right. I know he is."

"Yeah? How do you know?"

Bella taps her coat, indicating her heart.

Yeah, well, she's not a medium.

Swallowing a lump in her throat, Misty allows Bella to give her a quick hug before she trudges back out into the blowing snow.

Chapter Eleven

The Dale is hushed, Cottage Row draped in fleecy white. Barren cottages are enveloped in drifts. Already, a robust west wind is attempting to obliterate Grange's tire tracks, and Bella hears the eerie echo of the fading siren.

The lieutenant reminds Bella of Sam's first oncologist. Dr. Stacey Fischer was highly regarded, but her bedside manner had left something to be desired.

Grange knows what he's doing, but he's so cold he makes people nervous.

She remembers the way he was watching Misty as if he doesn't trust her. That's his job, Bella knows. Luther once told her that when a child goes missing, the parents always fall under suspicion.

But he'd probably handle this investigation very differently. He knows Jiffy well and might even have some idea where to find him. He wouldn't dismiss Misty's concerns, her instincts, or even her psychic visions. Then again, he wouldn't rely on them either.

Bella doesn't know about meditation, but if her own son were lost, she'd be doing whatever it took to find him. Misty's introspection is unnerving, sitting around meditating and analyzing auras when she could be mobilizing search parties and combing the area, putting up posters, making calls . . .

That's not who Misty is, though. It's not what she does. She's magenta. Whatever the hell that means.

Magenta, a medium, mother, wife . . .

Friend.

Bella was surprised Misty used that word to describe her. But it did the trick, just like the other night with Drew. It made her stay.

That's what friends are for . . .

"Calla?" Bella calls. "Calla!"

Her friend, like Jiffy Arden, seems to have been swallowed by the maelstrom.

She looks toward Calla's rented cottage across Melrose Park. It's lost in the whiteout, but now that the wind has shifted, she can see Pandora Feeney's fairy lights. Flashing bulbs illuminate the tree in the window, outline the roof, and snake around pillars.

"It looks like Snoopy's damn doghouse in the Charlie Brown special," Odelia declared when Pandora first plugged them in.

"I think it's pretty."

"Just you wait. You're going to go crazy looking at that for the next six weeks."

Odelia was right, of course. Yet in this moment, Bella welcomes the garish blinking display, casting bright reassurance into this bleak afternoon.

"Calla! Blue! Where are you guys?"

Unnerved by the silence, Bella starts home. Valley View's third-story turrets are barely visible through the billowing snow.

What's happened to her warm and inviting little village? Does the Dale have a dangerous underbelly? Is it brimming with ominous secrets? Who killed Yuri Moroskov? Could he have had local ties? Could it have been someone here? Someone she knows?

She wonders if Misty heard the scream the other night out on the lake—the great horned owl's cry or Moroskov's. Either way, it was blood-curdling. Maybe that's what triggered the vision Grange so readily dismissed.

Bella may only be an amateur detective, but she understands the skepticism. She, too, relies on logic when it comes to solving a crime.

Still, what about maternal instinct? She'd known Max was coming down with something long before he had a fever or started sneezing. It wasn't about logic. Something just felt off about his energy the other night. So if Bella, who isn't the least bit psychic, can sense when something isn't right with her child, why wouldn't Misty have the same feeling about Jiffy?

Especially Misty.

Luther says that mediums tend to be in tune with other people's moods and emotions, regardless of whether you believe they're getting their information from Spirit guides. He, unlike Grange, is open-minded about using psychic assistance on a case and would probably have asked Misty for more detail.

And Bella can tell him about Barbara, Misty's client. She'd intended to tell Grange but hadn't been able to find the right opening before he blew out of there. She pulls off her glove and dials, praying Luther will pick up. He may be retired, but he never sits idly waiting for the phone to ring. He might be on an indoor tennis court, getting a massage, or at a matinee with one of his many female companions.

He answers with his full name as if he's still on the job.

"Hi, Luther."

"Bella? Is that you?"

"It's me."

"Good. I can't find my reading glasses so I took a chance picking up. I was hoping you weren't . . . oh, never mind."

"Who is she?" Bella asks, smiling as she pulls her glove on again.

"You don't know her. Everything okay?"

"Max and I are fine." That's not entirely true, but Max's flu bug is insignificant in this conversation. "But Jiffy's out there somewhere in the storm. We can't find him."

"Did he go out to build a snow fort and forget to come home?"

"I hope so, but . . . Misty's worried. She had a vision. And . . . the murder."

Luther expels a curse. "Tell me what happened."

Bella explains the situation as she trudges toward Valley View, her aching head bent against the wind as icy crystals encrust her hair.

"The good news is, kidnappings are extremely rare," Luther tells her. "Especially when you're talking about the ones committed by a stranger. When kids disappear, a lot of times, they turn out to be runaways. Or a parent or close relative is responsible. Especially a noncustodial parent."

"Jiffy's parents aren't divorced."

"I'm aware. And I am concerned."

"I keep wondering if he might be hiding in Valley View. This morning, I thought I heard . . . someone. Maybe it's him, hiding."

"Let's hope so. I'll be there as soon as I can shovel out."

"Luther, no. The roads are bad, and it's dangerous for you to be shoveling at . . . uh, you know."

"At my age? I may be an old coot, Bella, but I do it all the time. And I was coming to the Dale anyway."

"Right, I heard you have a date with Odelia."

"*Date?* Did she say that?"

"No, I did, just meaning that when two compatible, eligible adults get together, it's a date."

"So that would make you and Drew Bailey—"

"We're not talking about Drew and me!"

"We're not talking about Odelia and me either," Luther returns. "I'm on my way. Sit tight and stay positive."

"I will . . . and, Luther?"

"Yeah?"

"Do you think he's going to be okay? Or are you coming because you think this has something to do with what happened to that man?"

"Yuri Moroskov?" He hesitates. "All I know for sure is that in weather like this, all missing persons are considered endangered."

"I hate hearing that."

"I hate saying it. I'm going to make some calls and loop in a couple of old colleagues. We need as many people as possible aware that Jiffy's missing and trying to find him."

As she hangs up and pockets her phone, she hears a staticky snatch of familiar music.

Elvis Presley, singing "All Shook Up."

Not as fitting for the season as "Blue Christmas" but an apt choice for this particular moment. The world, beneath its hoary dome, looks like a violently shaken snow globe. Similarly jarred within, Bella looks toward Odelia's cottage. She often listens to golden old-ies' hour on WDOE, the music floating through her screens in the summer. Today, there are no screens, and right now WDOE is all

Christmas music, all the time. Anyway, Bella can no longer hear the song. It was just a blast of sound . . . in her own head?

Uneasily thinking of Calla and "Blue Christmas," Bella covers the last few yards to Valley View. She sees that the walkway and steps need shoveling again. That could take her ten or fifteen minutes, and the snow is coming down so fast it'll be buried again in no time.

It can wait. Her head is pounding, she needs to check on Max, and no, she doesn't like hearing music when she has no way of knowing if anyone else can hear it.

"All shook up . . ."

She hurries inside and pulls the door shut behind her. Leaning back against it, she closes her eyes and exhales. Yet as she relishes the warm, dry tranquility, the faint sound of a siren reaches her ears.

It's probably the police responding to a fender bender. That wouldn't be surprising in this weather. Or maybe it's a fire truck—could be a false alarm. Or an ambulance going to help an elderly person who slipped and fell.

Any of those explanations, while not entirely pleasant, would allow her to go on thinking that Jiffy is fine, wherever he is.

She hears a floorboard creak. Her eyes fly open, and she looks around to see who's lurking.

Jiffy?

Santa?

"Lauri!"

"Bella! You scared me!" The tiny redhead lowers her weapon—a hair-flattening iron brandished like a bayonet. "Geesh. I thought someone was trying to kidnap Max."

A thought—a memory?—dances at the edge of Bella's mind and is gone.

"Why would you think anyone would kidnap him?"

"Don't worry, it won't happen with me here. I'm a tough mama bear," Lauri says, though she looks like anything but. She's still wearing her Santa cap, plus fuzzy pink legwarmers and a red Christmas sweater with a green sequined tree across the front.

"Well, thanks for keeping an eye on him. Did he wake up?"

"Not at all. I looked in on him a few times. He's out cold."

Under the circumstances, the innocuous phrase strikes her as sinister. She hurries toward upstairs, still wearing her snowy boots, still hearing those sirens in the distance and Misty's parting words in her head.

Don't trust anyone . . .

"Hey, where are you going?"

"To check on Max. Can you hear sirens?"

"Yes."

"Good."

"Good?"

"How about fifties music? Can you hear that?"

"What? No. Why?"

"Never mind." Bella can't hear it either now.

She peeks into Max's room and sees that he is, indeed, out cold. Closing the door again with a quiet click, she turns to see Lauri in the hallway.

"Is everything okay with your neighbor?"

"It's . . . no. Not exactly. You didn't happen to see a little boy hanging around the house while I was gone, did you?"

"You mean Max?"

"No, his friend Jiffy. My neighbor's son. He got off the bus and never showed up at home. He's probably out playing somewhere."

Lauri follows her gaze to the raging white cloud beyond the window at the end of the hall. "In that?"

"It's a novelty for him. They just moved here from Arizona."

"Wait, is his mom Misty Starr?"

"How did you know?"

"Dawn and I booked appointments with her for tomorrow. We met her at a Stump session over the summer. She gave me a message from my Aunt Sassy, right, Dawn?"

Bella turns to see Dawn standing on the steps. She's still wearing her Santa hat, and there's another Santa etched in red and white sequins across her green sweater.

"Right," she says. "I hope Jiffy's okay."

"I'm sure he will be. He's a mischievous kid. I'm hoping he's just hiding somewhere right in this house."

Hiding, whistling, and maybe even pranking her by moving her boots around. By now, though, surely he'd have grown restless and made himself known by jumping out at her and shouting boo or something.

"Want us to help you look for him?" Lauri offers.

"That would be great. If you two can just check the rooms on the second and third floors, I'll look down here and in the basement."

She'll also peek into the secret passageways tucked behind walls and beneath old floorboards. If Jiffy's hiding, chances are that he's in one of those concealed cubbies.

She tells them not to bother looking in Max's room. Like most of the vintage Victorian bedrooms at Valley View, it lacks a closet. The only possible hiding place there is beneath the bed, and she'd already checked it when she was looking for Chance.

Downstairs in the parlor, she calls, "Jiffy? Are you here?"

No reply.

She can still hear that siren outdoors.

She checks beneath drop cloths and behind draperies. "Jiffy?"

Chance is still sitting on the window seat looking out at the storm.

Bella nudges her to the floor and moves the cushions aside to open the hinged top.

You never knew what you were going to find in Valley View's hidden compartments. Back in July, she lifted a stair tread and found a tourmaline necklace like the one Sam had meant to give her last Christmas.

Intellectually, she knows it's not the same necklace they'd seen while browsing in a gift shop the summer before. Even if he'd bought it for her that day, he couldn't have left it *here* for her. Not without anticipating the bizarre series of events that led her to Lily Dale and Valley View without him.

Sam was no psychic. He couldn't have imagined, in the middle of a typical happy, healthy summer, that he wouldn't live to see Christmas. Or that Bella would lose both her job and the apartment by spring, or that a stranger named Leona Gatto would be murdered in a faraway town they'd never heard of, or that Chance the Cat would turn up on their Bedford doorstep and a highway four hundred miles away, and . . .

But Chance didn't, Bella reminds herself. There were two identical cats, just as there were two identical tourmaline necklaces. Still, she likes to pretend that Sam left it for her here in the house. Every time she opens a hidden nook like this window seat cubby, she half expects another gift from heaven.

Today, she's keeping an eye out for a six-year-old boy as well, but finds only household clutter.

She replaces the cushions and pats one. "Sorry to disturb you, Chance. You can go back to doing whatever you were doing."

The cat leaps back onto the bench to perch in precisely the same spot, her green gaze again focused on the window. Maybe she's pondering the lacy white curtain that seems to billow on the wrong side of the glass. Or maybe she's looking for the missing child. Or she senses danger—Yuri Moroskov's murderer.

Bella turns away with a shudder.

Her gaze falls on the undisturbed spackle and paint supplies that Hugo had left neatly stacked near the ladder. Jiffy would be incapable of walking past any of it without dabbling, toppling, or climbing.

And there's no way he'd have passed up the peanut butter cookies, she thinks when she reaches the kitchen, hoping to find that someone has pillaged a few dozen chocolate kiss centers. But all the candies remain intact.

Trying to ignore the sirens outside, she opens the door to the basement. Everything is dark and still below.

"Jiffy? If you're down there, you need to let me know."

Silence. Bella flicks on a light. The bare bulb throws off a sickly yellow glow. She grasps the rickety railing tightly, the rough old wood clammy in her hand.

As she descends, she thinks of Max and Jiffy, imprisoned here last summer by Leona Gatto's killer. For every frantic moment her son was missing, Bella had endured a lifetime's burden of stress. Misty is going through the same thing now.

"Jiffy! Where are you?"

On the far side of the basement, she tugs the barely visible cast-iron ring from its groove in a wood panel embedded in the stone wall. The hidden door creaks toward her. Using her cell phone's glow, she illuminates the cobwebby opening and peers at the crude ladder that disappears into the shadows above.

"Jiffy?"

The whisper echoes around her, as does the rasp of wood against hard earth as she pushes the door closed.

Back on the main floor, she hears someone calling her from above. Hope sparks, and she hurries toward the front hall, flailing and nearly losing her balance as she skids through a melting patch of snow she'd tracked in across the hardwoods.

"Whoa, are you okay?"

She looks up to see Dawn alone on the stairway.

"I'm fine. When I heard you calling me, I was hoping you'd found him."

"No, but there's a cat crying in your room."

Bella turns toward the parlor. Though the archway, she can see Chance still on the window seat. Must have been Spidey.

"Our kitten was in Max's room. I guess he escaped. Did you or Lauri open the door by mistake?"

"No," Dawn says, following her up the stairs, where Bella sees that Max's door is indeed still closed. Opening it, she peeks in and finds both her son and Spidey still sleeping exactly as she'd left them.

"How many cats do you have?" Dawn asks as she pulls the door closed again, frowning.

"Just the two now that all the kittens have been adopted."

"Well, I definitely heard meowing in your room."

Bella looks toward her closed bedroom door. "Maybe it was Jiffy trying to sound like a cat. Or the wind. It makes strange sounds sometimes."

"Does it whistle Christmas carols?"

"Christmas carols?"

"I heard meowing, and someone was whistling."

"Which song?"

Bella knows the answer before Dawn confirms it. "'Santa Claus Is Coming to Town.' You know, 'You better watch out . . .'"

Yeah. She knows.

Bella scurries into the Rose Room.

"Jiffy! I know you're here!" Bella stoops to check under the bed. Dust bunnies. No Jiffy.

She yanks open the closet door.

Empty.

She moves aside the hangers, presses a release, and a section of wall swings toward her. It leads to the tunnel she'd just checked on the opposite end, down in the basement.

Dawn gasps. "A secret passageway!"

Not so secret anymore.

Bella leans in, using her cell phone's light to illuminate the wooden ladder leading into a cavernous hole.

"Come on, Jiffy. Stop fooling around right now! Are you down there?"

"I don't think he is," Dawn observes after a moment of silence. "Maybe it was a ghost, whistling and meowing. After all, this is Lily Dale."

Yes, it's Lily Dale, and Bella is the only person in town unwilling to accept a paranormal explanation for an invisible whistling cat.

It wasn't Nadine.

Nor, unfortunately, does it seem to have been the missing Jiffy Arden.

Time to find out who killed Yuri Moroskov, Bella decides with a sinking heart, because that mystery might hold the key to this one.

*   *   *

Sitting on Jiffy's bed, hugging his pillow, Misty stares out the window at the lake, trying to make sense of what's happened.

At first, she'd feared the strange vision meant Jiffy's school bus was going to crash, but that wasn't it. He'd made it safely off the bus. Something happened to him afterward.

She should have been there to see him home safely. If only school hadn't let out early. If only she'd received the text and gone to get him. If only she'd been a better mother. If only she weren't so alone here.

After Bella left, Misty went to call Mike, wanting to tell him about Jiffy before Grange does. Unfortunately, Calla had walked off with her cell phone. She picked up the landline phone in the kitchen. No dial tone. Of course not. She'd never bothered to hook it up.

Sooner or later, Calla will be back with her phone. If—God forbid—Jiffy still hasn't returned, she'll let Mike know what's going on then. It's not like he can help from where he is, and it would take him almost a full day to travel here.

So easy for him to judge her from the other side of the world. He has no idea how challenging it is to do what Misty does every day, channeling Spirit, earning a living, and running a household while keeping track of a six-year-old who's as likely to stay put as sand in a sieve.

It may be Mike's fault that he isn't here, that he doesn't share her gifts or beliefs or love of Lily Dale or parenting responsibilities. But it's hers that she wasn't doing what she should have been when it comes to their son—not just today, but all along.

She just hopes it's not too late to start.

She's been trying to envision Jiffy's surroundings, but all she sees in her mind's eye is a blizzard. Is it because that's what Jiffy is seeing? Is he lost in the storm? Or is the snow meant to be a symbol of . . . ?

Of what? The icy chill in her heart? Her own blindness?

She's can't count on Lieutenant Grange to focus on finding him and bringing him home. His aura told her everything she needed to know the moment she saw him. He's closed off and doesn't trust anyone, including Misty. He may even think she has something to do with this—not just inattentive parenting but something more sinister.

As if she could ever, *ever* knowingly or willingly harm her child.

She'd wanted to come right out and tell him to stop focusing on her, but that would have made things even worse.

Never declare your innocence, kid, unless someone challenges it.

Mike once said that to Jiffy after being met at the door with, "Hey, Dad, someone tried to play catch with your autographed Cole

Hamels ball, only it got lost, and I don't know who did it, but it wasn't me."

Like Mike, Grange didn't come right out and say he suspects her of lying. Unlike their son, the one-man toss team, Misty isn't guilty. But his flinty glare made her so fretful that she got his message loud and clear.

Men.

Why, she wonders, do they always complicate matters? Even the ones she loves have caused their share of problems in her life.

"Men are trouble," her mother has told her for as long as she can remember. "But it's the worthwhile kind."

Mom is no picnic herself. But with her, what you see is what you get. At least she's dependable. She doesn't drift or disappear. Misty knows exactly where to find her at any given moment of any given day. She knows what she should never say, ask, do in her mother's presence. She knows just how much her mother is capable of giving—which is often nothing at all. But somehow, that's okay. No expectations, no disappointments.

The same is true of her half sisters and grandmother—and of her late great-aunt Ellen, with one notable exception. She hadn't let Misty down until the summer she'd turned thirteen. Until then, from the time her father died, her aunt had been the most dependable person in her life.

Not long after his funeral, she'd invited Misty to spend the summer with her at Echo Grove, her rickety Lily Dale cottage.

"*Where* does she want me to go?" Misty had asked her mother.

"Lily Dale. It's not even three hours away. You'll love it."

Mom, who had considered the in-laws eccentric, had already been dating and needed a place to park Misty now that school was out. She'd talked up the Dale as if it were an all-inclusive beach resort with an elderly maiden aunt as activities director. The only thing she'd neglected to mention—or hadn't known—was that Great-Aunt Ellen was a registered medium and that Lily Dale had been colonized by them.

"It wasn't too horrible, was it?" she'd asked with a trace of guilt when Misty returned home on Labor Day.

"Not too horrible," she agreed and shared stories of fishing off the little pier, learning to swim, and making new friends. She just hadn't mentioned that some, like her pal Katie Harmon, weren't . . . *alive.*

Great-Aunt Ellen hadn't thought that was unusual. She hadn't batted an eye when Misty told her about the vision and visitation she'd experienced the night her father died.

"I guess it skipped a generation, my dear."

"What skipped a generation?"

"The gift," Aunt Ellen explained—sort of. "I have it and so did your great-grandmother and your grandfather, although he was a stubborn one, my brother. Denied it till the day he died. He changed his tune afterward, though, I'll tell you! He still pops in once in a while."

"What about my father?"

"He hasn't popped in at all."

"No, I mean the gift. Did he have it?"

She peered into Misty's face, but said only, "If he did, he never mentioned it."

The following summer, Mom had still been dating, working two jobs, and taking community college classes. She and Misty had both been thrilled when Aunt Ellen again extended her invitation, and Misty had spent another summer immersed in the unofficial family business—a tradition that continued for seven enlightening years.

The spring she'd turned thirteen, Aunt Ellen had done something Misty had never seen coming. Something so unexpectedly horrible that she's never managed to forgive her or get over it.

On a warm May afternoon, Aunt Ellen had crossed over to the Other Side. No warning, no wee-hour farewell. She hadn't even visited afterward.

Without her, Misty had been stuck in Cleveland learning to smoke cigarettes, drinking pilfered cinnamon schnapps, kissing older boys behind the IHOP, and wondering what to do about all the needy, noisy souls hanging around her.

Looking back, she suspects that just as the gift hadn't skipped her generation or her son's, it probably hadn't skipped the one before hers either. Her poor father had probably drunk to drown out the dead.

At thirteen, she, too, had learned to ignore the spirits with a little help from spirits. Not just cinnamon schnapps, but also vodka, whiskey, gin . . . whatever she could get her underaged hands on.

Now Misty can't imagine silencing the whispering voices in her head. Now, *especially now*, she needs their guidance. Spirit is all she has left.

She closes her eyes, hugging the pillow, breathing deeply, wanting to inhale her son's scent. Lord knows his sheets haven't been washed in weeks.

But she smells only her own sour, metallic fear.

Chapter Twelve

Bella stands over Max's bed, watching him sleep.

One night, when he had been just a newborn baby, Sam had deliberately woken him up. He'd just gotten off the commuter train after another long workday in the city and wanted to hold his son.

"Why on earth would you wake him up when he was sound asleep?" Bella had shouted over Max's incessant wailing in his father's arms.

"I wanted to play with him!"

"Play what, Scrabble? He's ten days old, Sam!"

"Well, I miss him all day. I miss everything. I never get to see him awake!"

"Well, this is him awake at midnight. Happy now?"

Bella and Sam rarely argued, but a fussy infant could try anyone's patience. They'd taken turns pacing the floor with Max that night, trying to settle him. In the wee hours, when the baby had finally fallen into an exhausted sleep, Sam apologized.

"You were right, Bella Blue," he whispered as they sank into their own bed and found their way into each other's arms. "We have to promise that we'll never, ever, *ever* wake up this kid again."

"Unless it's morning, and he's late for school."

"Or work," he added, and they'd laughed.

That night, they'd been dumbfounded by the thought of that tiny, diapered creature going out into the world one day, all grown up.

He isn't there yet—far from it—but he is on his way, and Sam's missing it all.

"Sorry I have to break our promise," she whispers to her late husband as she pulls the comforter away from Max's face. "But I have to wake him up and tell him, right?"

If only Sam were here. He'd know what to do.

Or even . . .

She finds herself thinking of Drew Bailey. She never answered his last text. Maybe she should let him know about Jiffy. Like Luther, he's fond of the boy, and he might have some ideas Bella hasn't yet considered.

But first, she really should tell Max. As Jiffy's closest confidante, he might know something.

Bella taps his shoulder gently. "Max? Hey, Max?"

No reaction from her son, but Spidey yawns and stretches into a sitting position. He begins grooming his black fur, watching Bella warily as if he, too, knows this is a bad idea.

She pats Max's arm. At last, his lashes flutter. "Max? Sorry, sweetie, but I need to talk to you."

His eyes, when they finally open and meet hers, are glassy. His cheeks are flushed.

"I already know. He told me," he murmurs and closes his eyes again.

Yes, just like his father.

Sam, too, used to talk in his sleep.

She feels Max's forehead. He doesn't seem feverish.

She strokes his head, pushing his hair away from his face. He needs a haircut. Before Jiffy, he never gave her a hard time about the barbershop. Now he wants whatever his new BFF has—shaggy hair, snowboard, cell phone, far too much freedom . . .

Darn that Misty Starr.

Bella wants to like her regardless of her permissive parenting style, but the woman has an edge that's as much a part of her as her red hair and green eyes. Maybe it's youth. Or maybe she's simply had a hard life.

Around here, who hasn't? The Dale draws people who are searching, hurting, or at a crossroads. Even those who provide truth by channeling Spirit for others are seeking answers to their own questions.

"Max? Come on, wake up."

"I am awake. I'm just thinking."

"Can you think with your eyes open while I tell you something?"

"Is it about Jiffy? Because I already know. He told me."

She stops stroking, her hand frozen on his tousled hair. "What are you talking about?"

"Everyone thinks he got lost. But he didn't."

"Why would you say that?"

"He *told* me," he repeats, opening his eyes to stare up at Bella.

"So he's here? In your room? Or maybe hiding somewhere in the house?"

"He's not hiding," Max shakes his head, takes a tissue from the box on his nightstand, and blows his nose. "Uh-oh. That's the last one. Do we have any more?"

"Yes, I'll get you another box, just . . . what do you mean about Jiffy not hiding?"

"He's not hiding. And he's not lost."

"Then where is he?"

"Kidnapped. He told me that he was going to get kidnapped in the snowstorm."

Kidnapped.

That's it. She remembers now. Jiffy had told her the same thing.

One night back in October, he'd asked if she was insisting on walking him home after dark because of kidnappers. When she'd assured him that there were no kidnappers around here, he told her he'd dreamed that there were.

"But don't worry," he'd gone on. "In the dream where I get kidnapped, it's cold and snowy, and it's Christmastime."

Jiffy says a lot of bizarre things, but that comment had resonated for its odd detail. He'd had other dreams that some people around here—the ones who don't believe in coincidence—might consider premonitions.

And what about Max? Earlier, he'd told her his head hurt from the inside and that something bad was about to happen. As much as Bella longs to take that with a grain of salt, she can't help but wonder if—

The doorbell rings below, curtailing the troubling idea.

Luther made it here in record time. Thank goodness.

"The TV guys!" Max shouts.

"TV guys?"

Ah, he's delirious with fever. That would explain a lot.

"Bella?" Dawn calls from below. "Want me to get that?"

"Would you? Thanks." She turns back to Max. "Why would it be TV guys?"

"They want me to tell them that Jiffy is a great kid and super brave. He'll be a lot famous then, and I'll be a little bit famous. I need to get dressed, because people don't wear their PJs on TV."

"Don't worry, it's not TV guys. It's Luther."

"How do you know? Are you psychic now?"

No, and neither are you.

"Has Jiffy said anything lately about his dad? Or running away?"

"His dad didn't run away. He's in the army."

"Right." And Max couldn't know about an argument that Jiffy's parents had this morning because he hasn't seen his friend since yesterday. "Max, does Jiffy ever whistle?"

"He can't, on account of the song."

"What song?"

"The one we learned in school about 'All I Want for Christmas Is My Two Front Teeth.' Jiffy only needs one front teeth, but he still can't whistle. Wait, I know! It was probably Albie! He's Jiffy's friend."

"Albie? Who is he?"

"I *told* you! Jiffy's friend. You better check your listening ears, Mom."

"I've just never heard you talk about Albie before. Is he a boy at school?"

"No, he's a man. Jiffy said he wears a suit and tie and he likes to whistle a lot."

There goes her smile. She's certain no one named Albie lives here in the Dale off-season.

"What else do you know about him, Max?"

Max shrugs.

Maybe he's someone who visited one of the mediums or perhaps someone whose path Jiffy crossed in his considerable wanderings beyond the gates. She's always warning him not to talk to strangers, and it never seems to sink in, and now . . .

"Bella?"

She looks up to see Calla standing in the doorway, wearing a troubled expression.

"Your guests let me in. Oh, hey, Max," she says with a little wave, attempting to smile. "Feeling any better?"

"Nope."

"Bummer. Can I talk to you for a second, Bella?" She jerks a thumb, pointing down the hall to indicate the need for privacy.

Fear clogs Bella's brain as she tells Max she'll be right back. She closes his door behind her and leads Calla down the hall to the Rose Room.

"Might want to close this door, too," Calla suggests, and Bella's hand trembles as she does.

"I'm all shook up . . ." The Elvis song is still playing in her head. She sits on the edge of the bed, steeling herself for whatever is coming.

"Listen, they found a body out by the skating pond, but . . ."

Bella lets out a strangled cry that drowns out the rest of the sentence.

"Bella!" Calla squeezes her arm. "I said it isn't Jiffy! It was a grown man. Not a little boy."

"Not Jiffy."

"No. And not Drew."

"Drew!" Fresh dread slams her like an iceberg.

She hadn't considered that it could have been him. She'd assumed that he was safe at the animal hospital, caring for the puppies and their stricken mama, thinking about owls, and perhaps wondering, in an offhand way, why he hasn't heard back from her.

That's how it happens. You're living your life, assuming the people you love will go right on living theirs, and then . . .

A horrific scenario zooms through her brain like a getaway car needlessly blowing red lights with no one giving chase. What if it *had* been Drew?

What would she tell Max? How would she face another loss, just when she was ready to . . . ?

No. This is why she wasn't ready. *Isn't* ready. Why she'll never be ready. If you don't love, you can't lose.

It wasn't her this time, but someone has lost. A grown man—maybe a husband, a father. Another family struck by tragedy so close to Christmas.

"What happened to him?" she asks Calla.

"I don't know. When Blue called me at Misty's, he said he'd just seen cops and paramedics heading up Glasgow road. We walked over there to see what we could find out. Lieutenant Grange showed up, too."

"He got a call and went running, and then I heard all the sirens. No wonder. I was so worried it was . . ."

"I know. Me, too. Do you know Al Katz?"

"Al Katz?" Mitch had mentioned him just the other day when he was telling Max about nicknames. Alley Cat. "I don't know him, but I know of him. Is . . . um, is he the one who . . . ?"

"No. But he's the one who found the body. He was out with his dog, and it went crazy and started digging. Al saw a hand sticking out of the snowbank and called the cops."

"You don't know who it was?"

"No, but Blue is still over there. He'll update me. I wanted to get back to Misty's."

"How is she doing?"

"She didn't answer when I knocked."

"Maybe she's channeling again."

"I don't think so. I went around back to see if she was out by the lake, and I could see right into her meditation room. She wasn't there—or outside either—but the back door was open, so I went in and called for her. She's not home."

"I hope she's okay. If she heard all those sirens, she might have panicked. Maybe she went to see what was going on."

"If she had, I'd have seen her out there or passed her on the way. I couldn't even call her because I have her phone and I left mine here. My head is spinning. I wish I could unsee that person lying in the snow."

"They just had him out there in the open?"

"No, he was covered up. I saw a lot of blood, and it didn't seem . . . nonviolent."

"Blood!"

Panic surges into her gut. Yuri Moroskov's killer *is* still here. She senses it. *Knows* it.

With a trembling hand, she opens her texts and sees that she has a new message. Not from Drew. She still hasn't replied to him about Max and the puppies. He's probably wondering if everything's okay. Then again, she hasn't heard from him, so he must be busy.

This text number is unfamiliar. The message consists only of an emoji. Enlarging the screen, she sees an image of a fountain pen followed by several trees.

"What is it?" Calla asks, leaning in to see.

"I don't know. And I have no idea who it's from."

"Must be a wrong number. That happened to Blue the other day. Some girl sent him a naked picture of herself. I know what you're thinking," she says quickly, seeing the look on Bella's face, "but he swears it was random, and I believe him."

Bella shrugs, knowing what Odelia would say about that. She doesn't approve of Calla's rekindled relationship with her childhood sweetheart. The son of prominent celebrity medium David Slayton, Blue broke Calla's heart more than once over the years.

Odelia disapproves of the way Blue's father exploits spiritualism through his television show, *Dead Isn't Dead*, and his recent book by the same title. But she has other, apparently valid, reasons for being wary of his son.

Bella closes the cryptic message and opens her contacts list. She'd saved Misty's number back when the boys first became friends, but she's never called her.

As she dials, she tries not to let her thoughts go to the dark place, tries not to think that the bloody man buried in the snow might have anything to do with Jiffy's disappearance.

The phone is ringing now—in Bella's ear *and* in the room.

Calla groans and reaches into her pocket. "I keep forgetting I still have her phone."

Bella disconnects the call, and the ringing stops. "Maybe she went over to your place to get it back."

"What should we do?"

"Just wait, I guess."

"For . . . ?"

"For . . . I don't know. For Misty to show up here. For Jiffy to appear. For Luther to come. I called him."

"Thank goodness."

"By any chance, do you sense any cat ghosts hanging around? I mean, cat *spirits*?"

"Not at the moment."

"How about whistling spirits?"

Calla raises her eyebrows. "I did hear someone whistling earlier."

"Did you recognize the song?"

"Yes . . ."

"'Santa Claus Is Coming to Town,' right?" Bella shudders. "I thought it was Hugo, but then he left, and—"

"Wait, that wasn't the song. It was 'O Little Town of Bethlehem.'"

"Earlier, I heard 'Santa Claus Is Coming to Town.' What do you think it means?"

"I guess Spirit has Christmas spirit. At least someone does right now." She sits heavily on the bed.

Bella sits beside her. "Are you, um, getting anything about it? You know, from your guides, about the man who died in the snow?"

"No, but when you experience something shocking, it can be hard to receive energy in the moment or in the aftermath."

"Like Misty? When she said she was blocked?"

Calla nods. "Her aura was cloudy when we were over there, and I'm sure mine is right now, too."

"I didn't know you can see auras."

"So can you. Ever see lightning strike? That flash of blue, yellow, white . . . It's energy, and so is your aura. Yours is deep blue."

"That's what Misty said. Pandora, too."

"Oh, Pandora." Calla rolls her eyes. "She's such a pain in the—but she does know her stuff, and I guess Misty does, too. You're a deep blue. Indigo."

"Someday, you can explain what that means."

"I can explain right now if you're interested."

Bella shakes her head. "I'm too worried about Jiffy. Misty, too."

Calla thrusts Misty's phone into her hand. "Do you want to see if she has any texts? She took off the password so that I could use it."

"It still seems wrong. Answering it if it rings is one thing, but . . . Let's just wait till Luther gets here. He'll know what to do."

"Okay." Calla wearily leans her head back onto the mattress, eyes closed. "I hate waiting."

Clutching Misty's phone, Bella flops back beside her. "Me, too."

She stares at the ceiling, tracing the familiar crack from the crown molding to the light fixture. How many hours has she spent lying here trying to avoid getting out of bed because she couldn't bear to face the day ahead?

They're fewer and farther between now, but last summer when she first arrived, reeling from fresh losses . . .

"Bella?"

"Yeah?"

"Do you really think everything is going to be okay?"

"I'm not the psychic. That's your department. What do *you* think?"

"Spirit is just saying, 'Things aren't what they seem.'"

"Well, what the heck does Spirit mean by that? Is it about Jiffy?"

"I'm not sure. Remember, mediumship isn't a perfect science."

It isn't really a science at all as far as Bella is concerned, but right now, it's all they've got.

*   *   *

Heading out to Inspiration Stump probably isn't the best idea Misty's ever had. In fact, it might be one of the worst.

But she needs to see for herself that her son isn't there.

"Is the Stump really full of secrets, Mom?"

She may not find Jiffy there, but she can sit and meditate. If Spirit can't reach her on that hallowed ground with its powerful energy vortex, it won't reach her anywhere.

That's where her father found her, years ago, on one of her first visits to the Stump. While Great-Aunt Ellen and the other mediums were busy channeling Spirit for the people gathered on the benches, Misty had spotted him standing in the woods. She'd felt his gaze before she'd seen him. He had been looking right at her as if he'd known exactly where to find her.

She hadn't been afraid or even particularly surprised. He'd motioned with his hand as if to ask if he could join her, and she'd nodded.

He'd sat down beside her and rested his arm around her shoulder, enveloping her in his familiar scent—aftershave that reminded her of limes and trees and mint mouthwash no longer accompanied by a stronger medicinal odor. Booze, she'd later come to recognize. That day at the Stump, the mouthwash hadn't been masking anything. It had just been there, a familiar part of him.

He had just been there—with her, for her.

He'd stayed until the message service was over.

She'd expected one of the mediums to notice as they took turns giving readings. Someone might have said, "I have someone here for the little girl in the third row . . . A father figure . . ."

But no one did. Even Aunt Ellen down front, channeling other people's loved ones, seemed oblivious to her nephew's presence.

Walking home along the forest path illuminated by a flashlight, Misty had told her about Dad.

"That stinker. It's about time he showed up. Figures it was at the Stump."

"Why?"

"Because it's mystical."

"What is mystical?"

"You know, full of secrets. The Stump is where things happen in the Dale."

"Good things?"

"*All* things. So he was there right under my nose." She'd laughed and shaken her head. "My nephew always did have a lot of gumption. So do you, young lady. That's why you'll always get through whatever is thrown at you in this life and those to come."

In that moment, as in this one, Misty hadn't been concerned about what her next incarnation might bring. Her father's unexpected visit had taken so much out of her that she had been able to think of nothing but crawling into bed.

That would be nice now, too.

But she has to find her son. Nothing else matters. The Stump is where she needs to be. Too bad she doesn't have snow shoes, hiking poles, a team of sled dogs . . .

A husband by her side?

Funny, in a not-funny-at-all way. After all these months—years—of wishing Mike would come back, she's no longer sure she wants him. He'll insist on returning to the base or making a fresh start on another one in some other place . . .

Any other place. Not here. He'd made that clear last spring, when she'd told him she was renting a cottage in the Dale.

"I don't want my son surrounded by . . . you know."

Yes. She knows.

Mike is the one who doesn't know.

Your son is embraced here. He belongs and so do I.

But she'd kept that to herself, saying instead, "When you go back to Arizona, I'll go back."

At the time, she'd meant it. Now . . .

Her husband's return would mean leaving the only place she's ever felt at home. It would mean going back to being an ordinary person with an extraordinary secret.

People in other places can't grasp what is accepted without question here in the Dale.

For a few months now, she's been wondering if their marriage will last. She used to think that it would be stronger if it hadn't been in a state of suspended animation all these years. *But it probably would have ended by now*, she thinks as she struggles along the path through Leolyn Wood.

Every bit of progress entails lifting her right foot out of nearly thigh-deep snow, plunking it back in about as far in front of her as it will stretch, then extracting her left to do the same. At this rate, it will take her days to get there.

But she has to keep moving, keep trying. She refuses to become her mother. She doesn't want her son to think of her as someone who has limits—someone who will only go so far, no matter how much she loves him.

No, Misty is better than that, stronger than that. She'll do anything for Jiffy. She's the only person in the world he can count on. Mike may not be on the Other Side, but he sure as hell isn't here, and—

Misty stops short, spotting something unusual just off the path ahead, barely visible beyond a wall of snow thick as fog.

As she stares, a tall, bulky shadow emerges from the trees.

A bear?

Her father?

No, and no.

Silhouetted by blowing powder, whoever it is seems to be staring right back at her. If only it were her son. But this isn't a child; it's an adult. From this distance, she can't tell if it's male or female, mortal or apparition. Given the locale, she'd be willing to bet on the latter.

She closes her eyes and bathes herself in white light, then attempts to tap into the energy. Having exerted so much effort to get here, she's depleted, and there's no sign of her guides.

She musters the strength to take a few more steps. Now she can make out dark clothing and some kind of . . . is that a cloak? A coat with a hood? She senses that it's a man and a living being. As much as she'd love to ask Spirit for help in finding her son right now, this person might provide greater assistance.

She sees him turn as if he's about to leave.

"Wait!" she calls above the wind. "Have you seen a little red-haired boy?"

No response, but he goes still, as if he's trying to hear her.

"I'm Misty Starr, and I live over on Cottage Place," she goes on. "I'm looking for my son. Please . . ."

He slowly turns back toward her. Did her words resonate?

"Sir? Have you seen him?"

He walks toward her, and her jaw drops in recognition.

Chapter Thirteen

Lying on her bed in the Rose Room, Bella continues to gaze at the ceiling crack she's stared at so many mornings as she musters the courage to face another challenging day.

When that happens—when she makes it through the day and it's over at last—she climbs back into bed. Somewhere above her, the crack is shrouded by darkness, and she drifts off to sleep knowing that everything turned out okay again.

That will happen again tonight. It has to.

She sits up and looks at Calla. Her eyes are closed, and she doesn't stir.

Is she meditating or sleeping?

No longer able to lie still waiting for something to happen, Bella heads down the hall and looks into her son's room.

Spidey, giving himself a bath, stops licking his fur to regard her as she walks into the room. Max does not. Staring at the ceiling, hands clasped beneath his head, he doesn't even blink.

"Feeling any better?" she asks.

"A little."

"What are you doing?"

"Thinking."

"About what?"

"Nothing."

"Are you sure?"

He doesn't answer the question.

Thinking of the bereft Misty Starr, Bella leans over to hug him. He squirms out of it.

"Hey, Mom, by the way, I sneezed six times while you were gone. Not in a row. Three plus three equals six, right?"

"Yes, it does, smarty pants. So *gesundheit* times six."

"How come Calla didn't want me to hear what she told you?"

"Oh, it was, um . . ."

"Was it about a Christmas present?"

She seizes that innocuous explanation. "Yes."

"You can't trick me, buster!" Max says with a grin. That's what Odelia tells him when he tries to get her to pick the Old Maid from his hand of cards.

"Can you give me a hint, Mom? Does it start with a *sssssss*? Not like the sound Chance makes at Jiffy, but, you know, a word that goes *sssssss*."

As in *ssssssssnowboard*, Bella thinks.

And *sssssorry, buster, but that's ssssssoooooooo not happening.*

"Just one hint? I can give you one about your present if you want. There are two, and they're golden and beautiful."

"I'm sure I'll love them."

Mrs. Schmidt must have covered the plaster-of-Paris handprints in gilt spray paint. She'll treasure it, just as her father had hers. She'd found it among his things after he passed away. And Sam's gilded plaster handprint still holds a place of honor in Millicent's otherwise stark Chicago condo.

"Listen, Max. When Calla showed up, you were telling me about Jiffy's friend, Albie. Remember?"

He nods.

"What's his full name? Do you know?"

"No, he's Jiffy's secret friend."

"Have you ever seen him here at our house? Maybe you did, and he wanted you to keep it a secret, like . . . you know."

"Like a Christmas present?"

"Right. Like that."

"No. I don't have any secrets with Albie. Just Jiffy does. Albie doesn't come to our house."

"Are you sure? You said he whistles, and I've been hearing some-one whistling around the house today. I keep looking around, and I can't find anyone here, so I thought maybe . . ."

She hesitates, not wanting to frighten Max.

But he doesn't seem the least bit concerned. In fact, he's grin-ning. "Mom! That's because *you* can't see Spirit!"

"Albie is Spirit?"

"Yep."

"You're sure?"

"Yep. And so is Sanchez."

"Tell me about Sanchez."

"Um . . . he's black."

"Like Luther?"

"Like Spidey. Right, Spidey?" Max pats the kitten's head.

"So is Sanchez another secret friend?"

"He's Albie's cat."

"He's a cat?"

"Yep, but don't worry. Jiffy says some people think black cats are bad luck, but Sanchez is good luck because Jiffy's dad isn't allergic to him, so he can come and stay for Christmas and not be sneezy. But if he is, I will say *gesundheit*."

"So Jiffy's really looking forward to seeing his dad for Christmas, hmm?"

Max nods vigorously. "I wish . . ."

Oh, could Bella's heart ache any more if he'd finished the thought? It's wrenching enough that he lets it dangle, incomplete.

"I know." She hugs him. This time, he lets her.

She gives his quilt a final tuck, then closes his door behind her and looks down at Misty's phone in her hand.

The screen is black. All she'd have to do is press a button, and she'd be able to see if there are any missed calls. Maybe Grange is trying to reach Misty with news. Or maybe her son is trying to call her for help.

Mind made up, she presses the button. The screen lights up. Sure enough, there's a missed call.

Her heart skips a beat. The number is familiar, and—

It's your number. You tried to call her upstairs, remember?

There are no other missed calls, and she's not going to look at any of her texts. Not until she talks to Luther. He should be here any second now.

She starts down the stairs and then freezes, hearing music below. Not whistling this time. Electric guitar, but it almost sounds like . . .

Yes, it is. Some discordant version of "O Little Town of Bethlehem."

Not a phantom message from the Great Beyond, though. She finds Lauri and Dawn in the breakfast room, stirring cups of instant hot cocoa with . . . oversized hot pink–striped candy canes?

The music is coming from the speakers of a phone sitting in the middle of the table. Spotting Bella in the doorway, Lauri grabs it and lowers the volume.

"Sorry. Too loud?"

"No, I . . . what is it?"

"It's Sean's album, *A Very Von Vogel Christmas*," Dawn says. "Have you ever heard his version of 'Blue Christmas'? It makes me cry every time."

"So does his version of 'Frosty the Snowman,'" Lauri says. "They all make you cry. Bella, do you want a candy cane? We brought tons of them."

"Oh . . . um, sure." She hasn't eaten since the cookies she'd gobbled for breakfast hours ago. No wonder her head is pounding.

Dawn reaches for a large leather purse sitting on a nearby chair. An even larger leather purse is on the opposite chair, and two fluffy white coats are draped over the backs.

"Looks like we got the last pink lemonade ones. Sorry. Do you want blueberry buckle or Bananas Foster?"

"I . . . surprise me."

"Blueberry buckle matches your outfit," Lauri says.

Bella looks down at the worn jeans and old navy cardigan that she'd never in a million years consider an "outfit."

Blue . . .

Bella Blue.

"You look tired. Why don't you sit down for a minute?"

She shouldn't, but she does, relieved to have found a logical explanation—this time—for the music. Maybe this is what Calla was hearing, instead of phantom strains from the Great Beyond—or a killer or kidnapped kid, whistling somewhere in the walls.

Dawn hands her a hefty blue-and-white-striped candy cane and mentions that they're leaving in a few minutes for an appointment with a medium.

"Who are you seeing?"

"Pandora Feeney," Dawn says. "Do you know her?"

"Oh, I know her."

"Is she any good?"

Frowning, Bella sets down the phone and concentrates on getting the wrapper off her candy cane. They're not asking about Pandora's personality, she reminds herself. They're asking about her mediumship.

The woman may be an insufferable busybody, but there's no denying that she's told Bella things about Sam that no one could have known.

"I've never had a reading myself, but everyone says Pandora's good."

"Maybe she'll be the one," Lauri tells Dawn.

"I hope so. Wouldn't it be great if we can find out before tomorrow?"

"What exactly are you trying to find out?" Bella asks.

"About Sean's hair," Dawn says.

"Sean's *hair*?"

"Years ago, we were in the front row at a Von Vogel concert, and he dove into the mosh pit, you know, like he used to do at every show?"

Bella nods as if she knows, picking the last bit of cellophane wrapper from her candy cane and thinking about the dead man in the snow.

"Long story short, we cut his hair with Dawn's nail scissors." Lauri makes a cheerful snipping motion with her fingers.

"But wasn't that . . ." Bella fishes in the vast adjective pool flooding her brain.

Bizarre . . .

Rude . . .

"It was awesome!" Dawn's word isn't the one Bella would have chosen. "But then everything went wrong."

"His security team grabbed you?"

"No, not then. I mean everything went wrong this year when we lost it."

"You lost . . . what?" Bella asks, feeling like everyone's "lost it" at this point, including herself.

"The locket with Sean's hair in it," Lauri explains—sort of. "We share it, and on the last day of every month, whoever has it gives it back to the other person. But we forgot this was leap year."

"Right, and we went to lunch on February twenty-eighth instead of the twenty-ninth, but then we realized Lauri could keep the locket an extra day, so she took it back home."

"We were going to meet the next day again, but then we all got that awful stomach bug in my house, so I told Dawn I'd just leave it in the mailbox for her. I sprayed it with Lysol so she wouldn't get germs."

"That was considerate," Bella murmurs.

"I told my daughter to pick it up," Dawn goes on, "but she forgot, so I said never mind, I'll just do it myself the next morning. But by that time, I had the stomach bug, too. Our friend Lisa said she'd go get it, but when she got there, the only thing in the mailbox was mail. At first we thought Brutus stole it, you know?"

Bella tilts her head, wearily licking her candy cane that really does taste like blueberries. "Um, Julius Caesar's assassin?"

"No, Dawn's mailman. But he passed the lie detector test."

"You gave the mailman a lie detector test?"

"He didn't mind. Lauri's neighbor has a polygraph machine. Her kids are kind of wild. She makes everyone take one."

"All of her kids?"

"Her kids, her husband, the neighbors . . . she doesn't believe anything anyone says. Anyway, Brutus didn't steal the locket—not that we thought he did. We love Brutus, right, Dawn?"

"We *love* Brutus."

"What about Lisa?"

"She loves Brutus, too. He's the best."

"I meant, did Lisa take a lie detector test, too?"

"No! She's our friend. We love her."

"*Love* her," Lauri echoes. "I mean, you know her, Bella. Don't you love her?"

"I don't know her that well, but she does seem like a nice—"

"She would *never* steal it. *Never*. She's not even a fan! Plus, I've never seen her wearing it. Have you, Dawn?"

"No, and that was ten months ago. Although I guess she wouldn't wear it around us. But still . . ."

They exchange a long look, and Bella can see the wheels turning.

"Maybe Lisa should take a lie detector test, Laur."

"Let's just see what Pandora Feeney thinks. We'd better get going. See you later, Bella!"

With that, Bella is left to digest too much sticky blueberry sugar along with the longest "long story short" she's ever heard—a momentary diversion from her concerns about Jiffy, Misty, and bloody corpses.

She goes to the kitchen and tosses the rest of the candy cane into the garbage. Her stomach suddenly hurts. Her head still does. Her brain, too, from working Jiffy's disappearance from every angle and circling back around to only one conclusion, if you accept that there are no coincidences.

The body count is rising around here, confirming that a killer remains in their midst, and Jiffy must have crossed paths with him.

*   *   *

So Misty was wrong about the figure in the woods.

He isn't a living person at all but an apparition—and an instantly recognizable one. Only this time, he's not there and gone in an instant.

He keeps coming closer, plodding through the snow. She hears him cough and wonders what it means. There is no illness on the Other Side. But sometimes Spirit uses it to convey a message.

Her apprehension escalates with every bit of ground he closes between them.

It's not just because the apparition is incredibly solid—no filmy edges and not a hint of transparency.

And it's not as if she's never seen a celebrity, dead or alive. Back in Arizona, one of the other wives on the base had once been a contestant on *The Bachelor.* And last summer, celebrity medium David Slayton had personalized a copy of his book for her.

But she's never met anyone on par with the King of Rock and Roll.

Is Elvis Presley here to tell her where her son is? Like a celebrity guardian angel appearing out of the mist?

Only he's not bathed in a white glow like others she's encountered, or even like Frankie Avalon's angel in *Grease.* His aura is a muddy shade of brown.

Nor is he wearing white like Frankie Avalon or like Elvis himself in Vegas in later years. He has on a black down jacket, jeans, and big, clunky, practical snow boots.

Still, he's easily recognizable, just as he was the other day when she spotted him out in the yard. His jet black hair is combed straight back from his forehead, and sideburns stretch all the way from the sides of his aviator glasses to his chin.

"Excuse me, um . . . Mr. Presley? Do you know where I can find Jiffy?"

He's only a few yards away now, and he must have heard her, but he doesn't reply.

"My son . . . he's been missing since he got off the school bus," Misty goes on, noticing that he's not nearly as good-looking as she'd thought he'd be.

That happens sometimes when you meet celebrities in real life. David Slayton, for instance—his eyes were every bit as blue as in his publicity photos, but he had a bit of a paunch.

Elvis does, too. It protrudes even in his thick winter coat. Plus, he has double chins that gray razor stubble can't camouflage, and his dark hairline is receding. She'd always thought Elvis had blue eyes, but close up, they're a pebbled gray that reminds her of a puddle on concrete. Talk about disillusionment.

When Misty meets celebrity spirits, they appear as they did in the most flattering era of their mortal lives. She'd have expected to see Elvis looking young and wearing a leather jacket like he did in his teen idol days.

Then he takes something out of his coat, and she stops wondering about his appearance and starts wondering why he has a gun.

* * *

Bella opens the door to find Luther standing on the porch looking dressed up even for Luther.

Seeing her take in his red-and-black cashmere scarf worn over a long cashmere overcoat dusted in snow, he says, "I wore my parka to shovel, and it was soaked, so I threw this on."

Remembering Odelia's *Oh, this old thing?* velvet and rhinestones ensemble, Bella asks, "Sure you're not trying to impress someone?"

"Are you impressed?"

"I wasn't talking about me. You're going to Odelia's for dinner, so I thought maybe—"

"You thought wrong." He takes off the coat, revealing jeans and a Buffalo Bills hoodie with ragged cuffs and a faint stain above the red emblem.

"Wow. You weren't kidding."

"This is my lucky Bills sweat shirt for the game tonight. I wear it every time we play Miami."

"Squish the fish."

"Spoken like a true western New Yorker. Where's Max?"

"Still in bed."

"Good."

The tree wobbles as she hangs his coat. She quickly moves it to the hook opposite Max's backpack and briefs him on what Max told her, that Misty has also gone missing, and that a dead man was found out on Glasgow Road.

"I heard. I spoke to Fred on the drive over. Bella, listen. Fred said that the victim out on Glasgow Road was shot."

"A hunting accident or suicide?"

"No. Homicide."

Just like Yuri Moroskov. Another noncoincidence.

"Did they identify him yet?" she asks Luther.

"Yes."

"Is it someone from the Dale?"

"No."

She exhales just a little. It probably isn't anyone she knows.

Then Luther says the victim's name, and her heart stops.

She was wrong.

Chapter Fourteen

Misty probably shouldn't have been surprised to find that Elvis isn't Elvis or even Spirit. He's just an overweight, middle-aged stranger posing as someone he's not, just like countless others she's encountered here in the Dale.

Including Misty who isn't Misty.

The nose of the gun propels her back along the trail over her own broken path, jabbing the spot between her shoulder blades even through the layers of her down parka and the fleece sweater beneath.

When he'd drawn the weapon, terror had flooded every crevice of her body, leaving no room for rationale, let alone Spirit.

He'd told her what to do, and she's doing it. Silently, without question, as quickly as she can through deep drifts of snow.

"Come on . . . come on," he says, coughing and panting along behind her with a pronounced wheeze, the kind an inhaler would dispel.

Maybe he doesn't have one. Or maybe he doesn't want to juggle the gun to use it.

"Let's . . . move it," he adds as if she's the one holding things up.

At last, she finds her voice. "Where are we going?"

There's a pause. Well aware that he's armed, she doesn't dare turn around, but she can hear him gasping, trying to catch his breath. This forced march is as hard on him as it is on her.

"Wherever I say we're going."

Caught off guard by his inane response, she perceives the slightest hint of a whine layered within the belligerence, like a petulant child wielding playground power.

Yet he is no child, and he's holding a gun on her back as they make a laborious journey to heaven knows where. Even if he has no intention of killing her, he might trip or slip and pull the trigger.

He doesn't want to, though.

The reassuring thought pokes through the dense fear clouding her brain.

This person is not evil like some she has encountered. His brown aura indicates tremendous stress and confusion. Something has gone terribly wrong in his life. He's mired in something deeper and more chilling than a few feet of new fallen snow.

If she could just have a moment's peace to channel, she might find some information she can use to get herself out of this.

She glances at the endless white path ahead. No obstacles. The trees are safely to her right and left. She just has to keep walking straight.

Closing her eyes, she breathes deeply, searching for her guides.

For a few moments, there's nothing.

Then she hears a coughing fit behind her.

On its heels comes a sudden flash of clarity.

Darth Vader?

She's never been a Star Wars fan, but even she recognizes the menacing black-helmeted figure looming in her mind's eye.

If she were at home and Elvis were sitting across from her in her study, she'd ask him if the image means anything to him. Under the circumstances, that's the last thing she's going to do.

There's something else, though . . . Spirit wants her to make a connection between Elvis and—

"*Move!*"

The gun nudges, hard.

She opens her eyes and trudges on.

*   *   *

Bella's heart is in a freefall as she struggles to absorb the shocking news, no more believable now than it was a few moments ago. She listens as Luther repeats it to Calla, who had joined them in the hall as if summoned by . . . well, Spirit.

Shaken, she stares at the railroad map on the wall, telling herself to get a grip. It's not as though she knew Virgil Barbor well enough to mourn him deeply. She had barely known him at all—the burly farmer who'd told Max that he couldn't count on anything in this world.

Sadly, he'd been right.

Now Bella—having spent the past year trying to forget that life can be precarious and capricious—needs to face reality and a fresh bout with dread.

"He was Misty's landlord," Bella tells Luther. "She said she was expecting him over there at noon to collect the rent."

"Did you tell Grange?"

"No, it didn't seem important until—no wonder he never showed. I can't believe this is happening."

Luther reaches for his coat. "We need to go over to the scene so that you can tell that to the team, Bella."

"But Max—"

"I'll stay with him," Calla tells her, giving her a quick squeeze. "Go."

She hesitates, remembering Misty's warning.

Don't trust anyone, no matter who it is.

But this is Calla. And she already left Max with Lauri and Dawn—though that now seems as reckless a maternal move as some of Misty's.

"Come on, Bella. The clock is ticking." Luther pulls a parka from the coat tree and holds it by the shoulders, lining toward her. "For Jiffy's sake."

"I'd never let anything happen to Max, Bella. I'll go guard him, sit right on his bed if you want, and lock the bedroom door. We'll play Old Maid."

"He'll love that. And he'll cheat," she says as she shrugs her arms into the sleeves and follows Luther out the door. She hesitates for a moment, thinking of Lauri and Dawn. It doesn't seem fair for her to lock them out, but Pandora's readings run long, and Calla is here to let them in if they return before Bella does.

The blizzard attacks like a guerilla as they battle their way toward the SUV, heads bent against the cold wind, snow drifting past their knees. Luther holds her arm, guiding her along, tall and protective beside her. She wonders if he's carrying a weapon and finds herself hoping he is.

The SUV is already cold and entombed in snow. Luther starts the engine, turns the vents on full blast, and presses the button for the seat heaters before grabbing the brush and scraper. Closed into the dark, she breathes in the scent of new leather and aftershave, teeth chattering as she assures herself that Max is safe with Calla.

But who's protecting Jiffy? And his mom?

When Misty had left the house, she hadn't known there was still an armed murderer in the area. Or maybe she'd sensed it, and that's what had sent her out into the storm alone on a desperate mission to find her child.

Luther gets behind the wheel and turns on the wipers. Top speed isn't fast enough to keep the windshield clear as he drives painstakingly toward the gate. Bella leans forward, scanning the narrow road as they go, looking for any sign of Jiffy, troubling lyrics echoing in her head.

A child, a child, shivers in the cold . . .

"Do you believe in coincidences, Luther?"

"Sometimes."

"So two homicide victims turn up in the same quiet, safe little corner of Chautauqua County, both shot . . ."

"By the same gun, they think," Luther puts in.

"And now Jiffy's missing. He must have . . ." She can't even say it aloud, sick at the thought of a vulnerable little boy swept into it all like a hatchling in a cyclone.

Gruff with emotion, Luther says, "Let's just hope and pray he didn't, and focus on what we know."

She nods, regaining her composure. Now is a time for logic and facts, not emotion.

"I saw Virgil at Mitch's yesterday afternoon. So he wasn't murdered the same night as Yuri Moroskov."

"Right."

"And it means Yuri didn't kill Virgil. And he didn't hurt Jiffy, either. But I keep going back to the Amur Leopard gang. They're involved in smuggling. I read about the Easter Egg Heist and how they operate. Could there have been a woman involved, maybe?"

"Of course. Anyone who has some street smarts and has no scruples about who's signing his—or *her*—paycheck. Why?"

"There was a woman the other day. She was here from Canada for a reading with Misty, but she was using a fake name, Barbara, and she talked about wanting to do something illegal in order to get something or find something."

"Wait, back up. *What* happened?"

Bella recounts the overheard cell phone conversation.

Luther nods thoughtfully. "If we can piece this thing together, we might be able figure out where Jiffy is."

"And Misty, too."

"What did she say, exactly, about Virgil?"

"Nothing other than that he was supposed to be coming over today. Do you think he was involved with the Amur Leopard somehow?"

She can't imagine that Virgil, in his flannel and denim, might be a mobster. But . . .

Things aren't what they seem.

"Doesn't seem to be anything professional about the killing," Luther says. "It sounds messy. Fred said there were multiple wounds."

"Overkill? Crime of passion?"

"More likely failed attempts to get that fatal shot. I'm guessing the killer is fairly inexperienced."

"Isn't it true that most first-time murderers seem perfectly ordinary leading up to it? Like, they come across to others as regular people until they just snap and lash out?"

"A lot of times that's true," Luther agrees as they roll past the gatehouse, tires crunching on the snow-covered road. "You know your stuff, Bella."

"When Sam was sick, we spent a lot of time watching TV. He liked crime dramas. Now I seem to live them."

"And solve them." He brakes as they reach the deserted intersection and glances over at her. "I see the wheels turning. What are you thinking?"

"That the best way to find a killer is to find the motive first."

"You're right. And the vast majority of murders come down to only a few."

She nods, ticking them off on her fingers. "Love, money, revenge . . ."

"Self-defense," he adds and something clicks in Bella's brain.

"Luther, when I saw Virgil yesterday, he was worried about a squatter. He thought someone had spent the night in his barn and riled up the livestock. He said if it happened again, he was going to get his shotgun."

"That sounds like him, but he's all talk. This is a lifelong bachelor who hangs lights so that the local kids can skate on his property at night. It's his neighbor, Al Katz, who used to yell at anyone cutting across his property to get to the pond."

"He's the guy they call Alley Cat, right? The one who found Virgil's body?"

"You know him?"

"No. Do you?"

"Everyone knows everyone around here."

"Then do you think Virgil knew the person who killed him?"

"Hard to say, but at this time of year, there aren't many people passing through."

Bella thinks of Jiffy's secret friend, Albie. Max said he's Spirit, but maybe he's mistaken or Jiffy was. If a seasoned medium like Calla can't always tell whether something she sees or hears is coming from the Other Side, a little boy must get it wrong sometimes, too.

Glasgow Road has been plowed more recently than the Dale, allowing Luther to drive a little faster. In a matter of minutes, they see flares on the road and law enforcement taillights and dome lights beyond—splotches of red piercing the swirling pristine backdrop like blood.

*　*　*

If the hike into Leolyn Wood had been a monumental task for Misty, the reverse trip is nearly impossible. Straining beneath sheer fatigue, shoved along by a gun in her back, she retraces her steps into the woods along with the ones that led to her son's disappearance.

If this man—this fake Elvis—is the missing piece to the puzzle, how on earth does he fit in?

"Hey! What are you doing? Walk!"

She hadn't realized she'd stopped.

"Give it to me!" he shouts, his voice so close and loud it's as if he's slipped into her brain like Spirit.

"Give what to you?"

"*What*?"

"You just said—"

"I *said*, walk! That's what I said! Do it, or you'll be sorry!"

This time, his voice shifts behind her again—until he adds, "I'll shoot you!"

Those three words thunder from the past and present, punctuated by a gunshot.

Her guides once told her that when a person leaves their physical body in a violent way, the soul is wrenched instantaneously to a place where there is no pain.

That isn't what's happened to her, though.

He didn't fire at her. The gunshot was a part of the vision, as was Elvis's voice inside her head. She's still standing in the frozen woods where everything aches—her body, her brain, her heart . . .

An image blasts into her head like a bullet.

Nighttime.

Dark. Cold. Outdoors.

Elvis and another man.

He's lanky with blond hair. His name is . . .

Harry? Maury? Rory? Something like that.

His sleeves are rolled up, and his forearms are covered in elaborate ink designs.

She sees the man crumple to the ground, a red stain spreading across his white dress shirt.

A voice roars at her—right here, right now, right behind her. "I *said*, let's go!"

The gun is no longer poking at her back. She feels it, cold and deadly, against the back of her head.

She starts moving again.

She needs to find her son. She can only hope this creep is leading her to him, one way or another.

* * *

Buffeted by the wild white wind, Bella stands in a clearing alongside a two-story farmhouse. It appears to have been enlarged several times over the years with no regard for architectural style or scale. On one side, neat rows of grapevines stretch into the snowy distance. A large gray barn sits behind the house. Somewhere beyond, a pond awaits January's hard freeze, neighborhood kids with skates, and new light strings Virgil Barbor had planned to hang in the old orchard trees surrounding it.

Bella thought she'd steeled herself to see what lies on the ground, surrounded by a wide perimeter of yellow crime scene tape, its ends flapping in the incessant wind.

But as she gazes down at Virgil's bloodied remains, it's all she can do to stay on her feet. Feeling herself sway a bit, she notes that she wouldn't have far to fall, keeling into deep snow that resembles a cushy featherbed. It wouldn't cradle her with comforting warmth, though. Quite the opposite.

She stares at Virgil, surrounded by vivid scarlet stains. His eyes gape in shock, jarred by the harsh, cold finality of this violent plunge into a snowy grave. Had he recognized his killer? Had the last face he ever glimpsed been a familiar one?

Cops, sheriff's deputies, and the forensics investigation team are busy all around her, voices calling out to each other above the howling gusts. Lieutenant Grange is off to one side, conferring with two other officers. He glances over at Bella and Luther, frowning, then focuses again on his conversation.

Luther introduces her to a middle-aged man with a bushy black mustache and very little hair poking from beneath his dark snow-dusted, broad-brimmed hat. "Bella Jordan, this is Officer Donohue. He's with FIT."

"That's the forensics investigation team," Fred explains, removing a rubber glove from his hand to shake hers, then gesturing down at his stocky frame. "As you can see, I'm not exactly fit in other ways—unlike God's gift to women here."

Bella likes him right away, appreciating the friendly jostle he gives Luther, who rolls his eyes, and the dose of self-deprecating humor that helps her breathe a little more easily.

"I've been looking forward to meeting you in person, Bella. I've heard good things about your deductive skills."

"From Luther?"

"From Luther, from the deputies, and the local force, too."

Surprised to hear that, she glances at Grange. Making brief eye contact, he all but glares at her. If the compliment came from him, then things *really* aren't as they seem.

"Bella has information that links Barbor to the missing boy," Luther says and asks her to tell Fred what she knows.

When she does, his eyes widen. He asks her a few more questions, none of which she can answer. She doesn't know about Misty's working relationship with Virgil or much of anything else, other than that he thought someone had trespassed in his barn the night of Yuri Moroskov's murder.

"They found some evidence that someone might have broken into the barn, so that makes sense."

Bella shudders and gazes at Virgil. "We have to find Jiffy, because if he crossed paths with the person who did that . . ."

Noticing something other than Virgil's expression of frozen horror and the frozen blood, she says, "He's not wearing a coat. Do you think he's been out there since before the storm started?"

"No. There's at least a foot and a half of snow underneath him," Fred tells her.

"And he died on this spot?"

"Yes."

"Well, there hasn't been a lull in the storm since it started. So if he didn't put on a coat, then he wasn't planning to leave the house for any amount of time."

"Not in these temperatures," Luther agrees, and Fred nods.

Bella thinks of Misty Starr, out by the lake wrapped in a poncho, frantically searching for her son.

"Something or someone must have lured him out here," she says, looking from the house to the barn located a hundred yards away at most. Virgil's corpse lies between the two, either struck down while crossing from one to the other—or perhaps while confronting someone who was doing just that.

She asks Fred if Virgil had been armed.

"No. Not carrying anything other than a handkerchief and a wallet."

"Is there money in it?"

"A couple of twenties."

"So the motive wasn't robbery," Luther notes. "The perp could have easily taken the wallet."

"Right, and then helped himself to whatever he wanted from the house," Fred says. "Back door was unlocked."

"Is anything missing?" Bella asks.

"A theft in a case like this where the victim lives alone can be hard to detect. It hasn't been ransacked. The place is neat as a pin."

"Maybe he looked out the window, saw someone in the yard, went out with his hunting rifle, and whoever it was got it away from him."

"No, he was shot with a pistol. Multiple times."

"Was there any evidence of a struggle?"

"Hard to tell. A sloppy kill leaves all kinds of trace evidence, but the weather wreaks havoc on a good day. It's almost impossible for our team to find anything outdoors on a day like this." Fred shakes his head. "The sheriff's in the house, and he's going to want to hear what you have to say, Bella. Come on in and talk to him."

"Go ahead," Luther tells Bella. "I'm going to have a word with Grange about Jiffy."

Grateful to leave the grisly death scene, she follows Fred through the swirling snow along a crudely shoveled path around the side of the house. Out front, the black wrought-iron railing is wrapped in shiny red and gold garlands. They climb snow-caked, boot-printed steps to a concrete stoop.

"We think Virgil came out the back way, so we're dusting that area for prints," Fred says, opening the door hung with an artificial pine wreath.

Inside, they're greeted by several uniformed officers with paper coffee cups and squawking phones and a whiff of mothballs that suggests elderly residents.

So does the outdated decor—blue floral wallpaper, drawn venetian blinds overlaid with sheer curtains, and furniture upholstered in a nubby-looking brown-and-navy-plaid fabric. Vinyl runners travel the wall-to-wall carpeting like boardwalks, leading from living room to dining room and kitchen beyond.

A framed photo sits on the mantel: Virgil clad in hunting camouflage, proudly holding a rifle and a slain buck. Its antlered head is mounted above the fireplace. The artificial eyes seem to regard Bella calmly, spared the eternal distress now reflected in those of its slain human hunter.

A small artificial tree sits in the corner by the window, decorated with tinsel, shiny gold balls, and multicolored pinprick lights. The coffee table holds outdoorsy magazines fanned just so, and an arrangement of fake red poinsettias in a white wicker sleigh.

In the background, she hears the radio—WDOE running down a list of cancellations and closures. In her head, she can hear Virgil: "Around here, we don't let a little bit of snow stop us."

Oh, Virgil.

"He was a bachelor, right?" she asks Fred, trying to blink away the image of him lying in the snow. "Virgil? Lived alone?"

"Yes, ever since his mother died a few years back." He gestures at a tall handsome man talking quietly on a cell phone. "That's the sheriff. We'll wait till he finishes his call, okay?"

Bella nods, wondering how long that will be.

Eager to get back to Max, she decides to check in with Calla and reaches into her pocket for her own phone.

Uh-oh. Did she remember to grab it before she left? She peels off her gloves, the knit fabric catching on her rough skin and a torn fingernail. Feeling around, her bare hands encounter only a crumpled old tissue and lint.

When she gets back outside, she'll borrow Luther's phone to call Valley View or text Calla. For now, acutely aware that her child is beyond her immediate reach, she tries not to dwell on the thought of an opportunistic killer prowling around the Dale with pistol.

Virgil may have been the kind of man who decorated his house for Christmas and hung lights by his pond, but that doesn't mean he hadn't been involved with the international gang of smuggling thieves.

That must have been what Spirit had been trying to tell Calla. Virgil had not been just some random citizen who was in the wrong place at the wrong time. There had to be a reason he had been targeted by the killer. Had to be because Bella needs to know that the same thing won't happen to Jiffy or his mom.

The house had felt warm and cozy after being out in the gale. Now the forced heat blasting from the baseboard vent seems suffocating. She steps away from it to stand beside a shelf lined with photos displayed in colorful frames. Each one is stamped with a year.

The bygone holidays aren't in chronological order, and the set isn't complete, discontinued a few years back. But at a glance, the pictures are identical: Virgil and an older couple, obviously his parents, posed in the corner beside the tree. It's the same backdrop year after year: same couch, wallpaper, curtains, perhaps even the same wiry tree with the same lights and decorations, and . . .

Bella leans closer, spotting a macabre addition to the festive tableau.

In every photo, a tall shotgun sits propped in the corner behind the tree.

Today, in a house frozen in time, with everything neatly in its place . . . the shotgun is missing.

*   *   *

Trudging through the woods where her father appeared to her years ago, Misty wonders whatever happened to the girl who'd inherited his gumption, the one who could get through—as Great-Aunt Ellen said—whatever any lifetime might throw at her.

Not even a third of the way through this one, she's nearly defeated, depleted, and—

Her foot turns on a rock buried deep in a drift, throwing her off balance. She topples into the snow. It isn't a long fall, cushioned by a downy drift, but it knocks the wind out of her.

Lying there, she closes her eyes, wet snowflakes falling down her face like teardrops.

I need to find my son.

In her mind's eye, she sees a schoolyard.

A child.

Not Jiffy.

The boy is small, dark-haired. He's wearing thick horn-rimmed glasses and shorts that are pulled up too high at the waist and cut so long they brush the tops of his knobby knees. They aren't bruised, scraped, scabbed, and scarred like Jiffy's knees are. And he's different. Timid. Frightened.

Wide-eyed, shoulders hunched, he clutches a metal lunchbox with both hands as a couple of oversized bullies try to grab it.

She hears Elvis, coughing above her, barking, "This isn't nap time! Come on; get up."

She opens her eyes. His fleshy face looms over her, eyes narrowed behind his glasses. The frames are golden aviator style, but the eyes are the same. He's still holding the gun, but with his other hand, he's fumbling in his pocket.

Misty takes a deep breath. "Someone hurt you. A long time ago. You were just a little boy."

He stops fumbling. The eyes are startled, then narrow. But in them, distress mingles with anger.

"A lot of . . ." He pauses, trying to catch his breath. "A lot of people . . . hurt little boys."

"I hope you're not one of them."

He coughs, long and hard, glaring at her and shaking his head. But why should she believe that he's not a child predator?

"I'm looking for my son, Jiffy Arden. Please. Red hair. Talks a lot. Huge Star Wars fan." The last part is a lie. She's not even certain Jiffy has ever seen the movie, though Mike is certainly a fan.

But it seems to resonate with Elvis.

If she only knew what it means to him, as well as the other thing she's supposed to be connecting to him, something about . . .

No, not Jiffy.

But right now, what else matters?

"Have you seen my son?"

193

"Yeah. I've . . ." More coughing. "I've seen him."

"Where is he?"

He shrugs, hacking away, his gloved hand back in his pocket.

"Please tell me. I'm so worried."

"Yeah? If you're so worried, such a great mom and all, then why's he walking around this place at all hours of the night alone? Why didn't you meet him at the bus stop? Why doesn't he wear a coat in a blizzard?"

The lengthy speech dissolves in a sputtering fit of violent coughs. Misty is as shaken by his words as he appears to be by his inability to catch his breath—and not just due to a rash of maternal regret.

"You saw him today," she says, trembling. "Where is he?"

He ignores her, wheezing, and takes out an inhaler at last.

If she weren't down here flat on her back, she could have made a grab for it. But that's why he waited until she was incapacitated. By the time she's back on her feet, his moment of weakness will have passed.

He starts to put the mouthpiece to his lips, is seized by a coughing spell, and fumbles it. The device drops to the ground and disappears into the snow inches from Misty's hand. She whips off her glove and plunges her bare hand into the icy spot before he can react. Making contact with the inhaler, she closes her fingers around it and looks up at him.

"Give . . ." He pauses, huffing, pressing his arms against his straining ribcage. "Give . . ."

"Give it to me!"

Elvis's voice, inside her head only, echoing words Spirit gave her earlier.

In this moment, staring into his frightened eyes in a flushed face, she can't imagine that *it* might have been anything more crucial than the inhaler clenched in her hand. But to him in that moment . . .

Someone had had something he'd desperately needed. Something that he would have killed for.

He tries again to speak. "Give . . ."

Misty sits up and glances at the gun in his trembling hand. Then she holds out her fist, turns it over, and opens it. He plucks the inhaler from her palm and sticks it into his mouth, gasping.

He presses the top, sucks the medication deeply into his lungs, and holds it there, eyes locked on hers.

"Please," she says. "I'm begging you to tell me where my son is."

He exhales slowly. She braces herself for the answer, expecting a lie. When it comes, she'll regret that she didn't hurtle the damned medication into the snowy woods.

"Tell me," she says again. "I want the truth."

"Truth, lady. I swear I have no idea," Elvis says, and with a sinking heart, she believes him.

Chapter Fifteen

As far as Bella is concerned, Virgil's missing rifle validates the squatter theory. He had probably spotted a trespasser through the window, grabbed the weapon, and gone out to confront him, not realizing he'd been dealing with an armed career criminal. His killer must have taken the shotgun.

"That does make sense," Fred agrees, leading her back outside to find Luther after speaking with the sheriff and a detective.

Both are concerned about Virgil's connection to the missing boy and his mother. She'd mentioned the car with Canadian plates that had been parked at her house yesterday, too, and the woman in the turquoise Mustang. They promised they would do everything possible to locate Jiffy and Misty.

Somehow, in the mothball-scented overheated house, she'd managed to forget that it's possible to be chilled to the bone or breathe too much fresh air. Enveloped in a bracing white whirlwind, she follows Fred over to Luther. He's standing to the side with Grange.

"Where do you think Mary Ellen Arden might have gone?" the lieutenant asks her without preamble.

"I have no idea. I left her house right after you did, and she was still there."

"Well, did she *say* anything?"

Make sure you keep a good eye on your kid . . .

"Say anything . . . like what?"

"Anything you think I should know," Grange replies. "Anything she might not *want* me to know."

"She's worried sick about her little boy, Lieutenant."

"And why would she give you her phone?"

"She didn't give it to me. Calla was using it to call for help because she left hers at Valley View. She accidentally left with it."

"Where is it now?"

"Valley View."

Along with ailing Max, innocent and worried about his friend.

"I need to get back to my son now," she says, mostly to Luther.

"I'd like to talk to him, Ms. Jordan."

"He's sick in bed."

"Bella, maybe he can tell Lieutenant Grange something that will help find Jiffy," Luther says, and she nods. She won't stand in the way of anything that could help.

"I'll be over as soon as I'm finished here. Just make sure you both stay put until I can get there."

"Darn. We were going to head out to the beach to build sandcastles."

His mouth quirks at her sarcastic comment. She wonders if it might go from *grim* to *grin*, but it doesn't.

"One more thing," she says. "Can you please send someone over to the Ardens'? Just in case Jiffy shows up and finds an empty house."

"Anything else you'd like me to do, Ms. Jordan?"

His turn for sarcasm.

"Nope, I'm good."

Back in the car with Luther, Bella borrows his phone to text Calla, who assures her that all is well and that Max gobbled two pieces of toast and an apple.

Now we're on game three of Candy Land. Guess who lost the first two?

That is punctuated with a googly eyed emoji that gave Bella another slight measure of relief. Reminded of the strange text message she received earlier, she tells Luther about it.

"It's not like it was a ransom note or anything," she says, "but the timing makes me wonder if it has something to do with all this. Especially now. If Virgil was going about his business and crossed paths with a psycho killer, then that means Jiffy could have . . ."

She shakes her head, staring at the bleak world beyond the sweeping windshield wipers, unable to voice her darkest fear.

"We're going to stay hopeful and do whatever we can to find him."

"And Misty."

"And Misty," Luther agrees, but Bella can tell by his expression that he isn't convinced she had nothing to do with her son's disappearance. He probably suspects that she was involved in Virgil's murder or is a part of the Amur Leopard.

Is she? Bella herself doesn't know for a fact that she's innocent. Why, then, is her instinct to defend her?

Back at Valley View, Luther accompanies her inside to make sure all is well. She can hear Max and Calla laughing behind his closed door, and a quick once-over ensures that the place is otherwise empty.

"I'd like to take a look at those messages on your phone," he says. "I'll run the number just in case."

"Good idea." Finding it, she sees a new text from Drew. Moving past it, she shows Luther the pen and tree emojis.

"I'm going to guess wrong number," he says, "since that doesn't seem to have anything to do with anything. But send me a screenshot, and I'll see what we can find out."

Headed back to the scene, he tells her he'll shovel the steps and walkway before he goes.

"No, I'll do that. You shouldn't be shoveling."

"Now you're getting on my nerves, kid," he says with a good-natured sigh and hugs her. "You just lock up and sit tight. Leave the shoveling to me and the case to law enforcement. I'll be a quick phone call away if you need me."

"Thanks, Luther. I hope Jiffy turns up soon."

She wants him to reassure her that he will. Instead, he says, "I hope so, too."

She doesn't like the look on his face any more than she likes the heaviness she's lugged home, like a clunky duffle filled with stuff she doesn't need but can't let go.

Left alone in the quiet house, Bella spots Chance on the window seat in the parlor. Her back paws are balanced on the cushion, front paws on the sill. Her whiskers twitch, and her tail is fat, swishing from side to side as she gazes outside.

"What do you see out there?" Bella crosses over and leans in to look out.

Nothing but falling snow and Luther with the shovel. Yet Chance seems riveted on something else.

Do you see what I see . . . ?

The lyrics echo in Bella's head. The carol is the perfect theme song for this place, where people are always seeing and hearing things that Bella cannot.

A star, a star . . .

Oh, if only there were a mystical star in Lily Dale as in Bethlehem to shine through the snow-blackened sky and guide Jiffy safely home.

That, she thinks, would be the kind of evidence she wouldn't be able to ignore. Maybe then she'd be able to believe in what goes on around here . . . or so her new friends claim.

Unsettled, she checks the locked door again, then heads upstairs to knock on Max's door. Calla unlocks it to reveal a happy but weary-looking Max sitting on his bed putting the game pieces back into the box.

"Mom, I won four times!"

"This kid is a Candy Land wiz," Calla says. "Our tournament wore me out! I just told Blue to head over to my place to feed Li'l Chap, so unless you need me here . . ."

"I don't," Bella says, "but Blue should walk you back home."

Seeing the look on her face, Calla nods and quickly texts him. "Okay, he'll be here in a minute. It was fun hanging out with you, Max."

"You, too," he says around a yawn, settling back into his pillows.

Bella walks Calla downstairs, briefing her on the scene at Virgil's and her suspicion that Moroskov's killer is still prowling the Dale. "I'm worried about your grandmother now, too."

"Blue and I will stop over there and tell her to be careful. But what about you, Bella?"

"I'm fine. Luther will be back soon, and Lauri and Dawn, too."

"We will, too, after we take care of the kitten. In the meantime, just let me know if you hear anything."

"I will."

"You should eat something. Gammy's soup is in the fridge. Max didn't want it, but it really is pretty good."

Bella promises she'll try it, locks the door after her, and watches her retreat along the freshly shoveled path toward Blue's waiting car.

She stands still, listening to herself breathe, the wind outside, and the scrape of Luther's shovel on concrete, a hint that she's not alone here.

Yet how secure is Valley View, really, with its network of secret tunnels? For all she knows, there might be an undiscovered passageway an armed killer could use to slip right past the dead bolts.

Or he might already be in, lurking.

She'd prefer to believe that Jiffy's ghostly pal, Albie, is hanging around the house whistling and that his cat, Sanchez, is responsible for the meows Dawn had heard behind her bedroom door.

Upstairs, she checks on Max again. He's already asleep.

In her own room, she sits on the bed, feeling shaky and a little nauseated. She should have eaten something. Depleted, she can't seem to sort through the barrage of information in her head. Facts keep flitting about like important papers scattered by a cold wind. Every time she grabs hold of one, another slips from her grasp.

She opens the text message from Drew.

All okay? Where are you?

Home, she types.

That answers the second question.

The first begs a difficult conversation. She dials his number quickly, longing to hear his voice.

And there it is.

"Drew Bailey."

He has caller ID. He always knows who's on the other end of the line. Yet he always answers efficiently and professionally, not just for her but for anyone who calls.

Once, she'd asked him why, and he'd seemed surprised.

"It's just what I do. Most of my calls are business."

She hadn't known whether to be dismayed for his sake or pleased that she has so little competition for his attention. He lives and breathes his veterinary work. He doesn't let many people in, but she and Max have managed to work their way into his life just as he has theirs.

"Hey," she says.

"Hi. What's going on over there?"

Where to begin? She looks at the ceiling and then the window. "Well, it's snowing."

"No way, really? Are you sure?"

Despite everything, she smiles. Stalls. Asks him how the new mama is faring.

"Carol? She's stable and nursing her puppies."

"Carol?"

She smiles. He always names the strays who find their way to him.

"As in Christmas."

"Christmas Carol. That's sweet."

"So is she."

"How about the babies?"

"They're perfect. Precious. Very . . . puppy-ish."

"Have you named them?"

"I'm going to let Max do that. Did he like the picture?"

"I haven't shown it to him yet." She sighs heavily. "Drew—"

"I know."

"You know?"

"You're worried that if he names them, he'll want to keep them. But I figured it would give him something fun to think about on a sick day. How's he feeling?"

"Better, but that's not what I was worried about. It's . . ." She pauses to gather her composure.

"If Max is better, I know he's okay. But obviously something isn't."

In this moment, she can't think of *anything* that is okay.

She tells him—about Misty, Jiffy, Virgil, the whole story.

He absorbs it quietly, then asks, "How can I help?"

"Those four words are a great start."

"I'm going to come over there."

"You can't! This is a full-blown blizzard and—"

"I've driven through worse than this for reasons that don't come close to comparing. My pickup truck has four-wheel drive, and I just grabbed my coat and keys. It might take me a while, but I'm on my way."

She should protest, insist that he not come. Somehow, though, she can't make herself do that. She needs him here, the way she needs Luther—another voice of reason, another pair of eyes, hands, legs.

And yet, not just the way she needs Luther—and has *needed* them all, the friends she's met here in Lily Dale.

Sam had believed that she was strong enough to do this alone, and for the most part, she has—with a little help from her friends. But needing and accepting help aren't quite the same thing as leaning on someone. Twelve months of balancing the weight of tremendous grief with the burden of single-handedly raising Max, working to keep a roof overhead, have left her wobbly.

Like the overladen Circassian walnut coat tree downstairs, she's fragile and desperately needs to lean against something—someone—sturdy, or she's going to collapse.

"Hang in there," Drew tells her, and she hears a car door slam and an engine start. "I'm coming."

She opens her mouth to reply, to say, *Don't*—or at least, *Drive safely* or *See you soon.*

All that comes out is a heartfelt, "Thanks."

She disconnects the call and goes back to her phantom text messages.

Now there are three more.

She turns the screen to enlarge them. The first is a church, the second a bridge, and it's followed by the church again.

Is it really coming from someone who misdialed? Or is it a message from . . . Spirit?

"Who is this?" she types and hits send, then heads down to the kitchen to heat up the soup.

Beyond the window, the white-frosted ginkgo tree sways in a wintry flurry. She half expects to see a great horned owl perched there staring back at her, but the branches are bare.

No bad omen. Nothing to explain the strange things going on in the house lately or the phantom texts. Yet no reassuring star either.

"Nadine? Was that you before? Are you texting? And whistling?"

She should probably feel foolish, whispering into an empty room, but she finds herself listening for an answer.

It doesn't come.

Of course it doesn't come. She's trying to be open-minded here, but she's pretty sure ghosts can't send text messages.

And yet . . .

"Albie? Was it you? Or Sanchez? Here, kitty, kitty . . ."

She's rewarded by the instantaneous jangle of a feline collar. A cat bounds into the room.

Chance.

Well, of course. Was Bella really expecting a ghost cat?

With a purry chirp of a greeting, Chance noses around Bella's ankles and circles her legs, rubbing her affectionate furry self against her shins.

"Good girl." She bends to pet her. "I bet you're hungry, huh? I've been ignoring you."

To be fair, Chance has also been ignoring Bella, preoccupied with staring out the windows all day. Whatever she was searching for—or watching—must have disappeared for now.

Bella dumps the food into a shallow metal bowl, fills another with water, and sets them on the mat for Chance. As the cat hungrily devours her dinner, Bella's phone *dings* with another text. Again, it's from the number that has her mistaken for someone else. Now, instead of emojis, she's looking at a photograph, and not a very good one.

A grainy white blur takes up most of the frame with parallel diagonal slashes across the middle. There's a rounded shadow in the lower left corner, and a faint hint of green breaking through the white—

Oh! That's snow, viewed through a window.

No, not a window. A *windshield*. The slashes are wiper blades.

The green is a highway sign in the distance.

The shadow is the back of someone's head—the driver's head.

The photo was taken from the back seat of a car.

* * *

Misty stares up at Elvis, trying to absorb the fact that his presence here has nothing to do with her son's disappearance.

It isn't that she doubts him. She can feel the truth in his words. He really doesn't know where Jiffy is. But she senses there's more to his story. Her son didn't wander off this time.

Spirit nudges her to remember something, dragging her out of this moment and back through the hours, back through the woods . . .

He pockets his inhaler. "Let's go."

"What aren't you telling me?"

"Huh?"

"Did you know where my son was, and then . . . I don't know—he got away, maybe?"

"Got away? What the hell, lady? I didn't kidnap your kid, if that's what you're thinking."

It is. Just one thing she's thinking and maybe not even the worst-case scenario. "But you said you've seen him. Just tell me where."

"I don't have to tell you anything."

Something snaps inside her. "Just like I didn't have to give you any-thing. But I did. I should have kept the inhaler and let you suffocate."

"I said, 'Let's go.'"

"Where are we going? Graceland?" Great-Aunt Ellen's gumption girl is back, more outraged than frightened.

He's wheezing again, and she can see that he's unnerved by this shift from helpless to sass.

Then he looks down at the gun in his hand as if he just remem-bered he has it. "Get up! I've got nothing to lose by shooting you."

"If you shoot me, I won't be able to get up."

"I've got no time for a wiseass. Move."

She squirms and struggles to her feet.

"Walk."

Her thoughts churn as they resume their march along the path through the woods.

"When did you see my son? This afternoon? This morning?"

"Did I *say* it was today?" He pokes her with the gun.

"It wasn't today?"

"Shut *up*!"

She does. For now.

But if Elvis isn't behind Jiffy's disappearance, who is?

*   *   *

Bella stares at the texted photo. Can it possibly be from Jiffy?

She'd rattled off her phone number when he'd asked for it the other day, and he had said he has a great memory, but he's six. How could he possibly have remembered it now, especially under duress? And if these texts really are from him . . . what do they mean?

She hurries toward the front of the house, hoping Luther is still out front, shoveling. Maybe he can trace the number, or—

Wait a minute. Jiffy's number would be in Misty's phone. She looks around, wondering where she left it and how she could have let it out of her sight at a time like this. But there's so much going on, too much—

Hearing a loud rap on the front door, she hurries to the hall and sees a small figure through the frosted glass. Not Luther. Calla?

No, there are two figures. Calla and Misty? Lauri and Dawn?

Opening it, she finds three people.

Lauri, Dawn, and . . .

"Hallo, luv!"

Pandora Feeney is recognizable even swaddled in a long, red hooded parka with a thick pink muffler wrapped around her face, leaving only the bridge of her nose and granny glasses visible.

"Sorry to bother you," Dawn says, "but our code didn't work."

"I must have given you the wrong one," Bella lies, peering over their shoulders. Luther's truck is still at the curb, and the walkway is cleared, but there's no sign of him. "Did you see my friend Luther out there, shoveling?"

"He's shoveling Odelia's steps," Pandora tells her. "I asked if he would mind doing mine next."

Bella is sure he said he wouldn't mind, and maybe he doesn't. But Pandora is the last person she wants involved in whatever is going on around here.

She follows Lauri and Dawn across the threshold with the same proprietary air that always accompanies her into Valley View, her home for many years. The woman has a knack for working her way into the house and under Bella's skin.

"You need to salt those steps, Isabella, or someone is going to go arse over teakettle. Speaking of which, it's teatime. Is the kettle on?"

"It's—no. It's not on."

"Time to light the flame, then." Pandora turns to Lauri and Dawn, stomping snow from their fuzzy boots. "There, now. Do mind the hardwoods. Shoes off!"

She's already plucked her own rubber Wellies from her feet and left them on the mat.

"I thought you were having a reading?" Bella looks from Lauri to Dawn.

"We were. Sean didn't come through. And when we mentioned what happened with your friend's son, Pandora was concerned, so we came back here."

"I wasn't even told he was missing, Isabella. I could have been helping in the search."

"In this weather? It's not safe out there, Pandora. The police are looking."

"I don't mean out there. But had I been told, I could have asked Spirit for guidance. And I might have known that certain things I've been sensing might have something to do with the lad."

"What? What are you sensing?"

"I'll explain once I'm situated." She strips off her wet parka and thrusts it into Bella's hands, saying, "There you go," as if Bella had requested it.

With a muttered, "Thanks," Bella hangs it on the overloaded coat tree that was well within Pandora's reach. She drapes it over a hook already holding two jackets and a wood-handled umbrella. The whole thing wobbles precariously.

"Do be careful, Isabella! That's a vintage piece carved from rare Circassian walnut! It's very fragile, as is the map!"

She's referring to the framed artwork on the wall between the thermostat and the coat tree. Earlier, trying to block out the news about Victor, Bella had stared at the yellowed Victorian railroad map of the region. A Rust Belt relic, it shows the main lines and connections between the steel and coal mining towns of New York, Pennsylvania, and Ohio.

The coat tree rights itself. She does value it, when she can actually see its lovely ornamentation. Right now the hooks, sculpted to depict cherubs' wings, are obscured by layers upon layers of garments along with the extension cords Hugo had left draped over the top.

She turns back to her visitors—welcome and not.

Had Pandora really had some kind of vision or premonition involving Jiffy? Or was that claim her ticket in the door, just as she had offered flowers from her garden and volunteered to sing at the wedding Bella had hosted in October? Having wrangled an invitation to the nuptials, she had been right in the thick of things when the bride collapsed.

What if—?

No. Pandora is a pain in the arse, as she might say, but she's not dangerous. She's the one who had provided key information that had helped Bella solve that case. If there's any chance she can do the same thing now . . .

She turns to see Pandora reaching for the thermostat, nudging it up a few degrees as if she's still the one paying the heating bills for this drafty old house.

"There," she says. "That's better. The place is an icebox. Now, what size are your shoes, Isabella?"

"Pardon?"

"My socks were soaked through on the walk over. I'll need to borrow some slippers while I'm here. What size are yours?"

Bella eyes the woman's enormous bare feet. Confident there's no way they'll fit into her slippers, she tells Pandora that she's an eight.

"Splendid. We're the same size. Off you go."

"Wait, what about Jiffy?"

"Do go fetch them before my chilblains set in again, and then we'll have a chat over a cuppa."

Having learned to take the path of least resistance with Pandora, Bella hurries up to her room to grab her slippers, thinking about the text.

One moment, it seems obvious that it came from Jiffy; the next, like a long shot.

If it was, he's in a car.

She'll find out what Pandora's vision involves, and then she'll go tell Luther.

Vowing to muster patience for her visitor, Bella finds her slippers under her bed and looks around for Misty's cell phone. No sign of it here.

Downstairs, she finds that the three women have moved into the drop cloth–shrouded parlor.

Pandora stands in the stepladder's shadow, perusing the label on a paint can.

"Sylvan Mist? What shade is this? Gray?"

"It's more of a green. You know, like your aura," Bella adds. "Sylvan means woods, and it's a nice forest gr—"

"I know what sylvan means, luv, but green isn't the proper hue for this room."

Pandora sits on the drop cloth–covered sofa to pull on Bella's well-worn imitation suede moccasins—at first daintily, then with the herculean effort of a Cinderella stepsister.

"Maybe you're not an eight anymore," Dawn suggests tactfully. "My feet got a half size larger every time I had a baby."

"I've certainly never had a baby! Isabella, are you an American eight or an English eight?"

"American eight. This *is*, you know . . . *America*."

"Well, that explains it." Pandora withdraws her foot and hands the slippers back to her with a harrumph. "These won't do. They're nearly three sizes too small. I won't stay long."

Ordinarily, Bella would seize the moment and show her to the door. Now she touches Pandora's arm and says, "Just please tell me if

Spirit has shown you anything about Jiffy. You said you've been sensing things . . . ?"

"The lad is quite all right for the time being." Her quiet, confident tone sends a ripple of relief through Bella until she adds, "It's his mum I'm concerned about."

"Misty? Why?"

"I sense rather a lot of trouble around her."

"What kind of trouble?"

"There's a man . . ."

"Her husband?"

"I'm not quite sure. I'll meditate over my cuppa." She gestures at the kitchen. "A watched pot won't boil, luv, but neither will one that isn't on the hot flame."

"That is so true," Lauri says, and Dawn nods.

Pleased by their appreciation of her wisdom, Pandora offers a sage smile. "There's nothing quite like a proper cup of tea to warm the cockles."

"We like to warm our cockles with gin and tonics," Dawn tells her. "Right, Laur?"

"Right. For us, teatime is happy hour."

"Ah, yes, the dear Queen Mother did love her gin as well," Pandora says fondly.

"Did you know her?" Lauri asks, impressed.

"Not until after she passed. She touches in from time to time. Most of the royals do."

"Well then you have to have a gin and tonic with us. We brought everything, even the limes," Dawn says. "I'll run upstairs and get it if you'll get the glasses and some ice, Bella?"

"Sure." With an inward sigh, she heads to the kitchen, trailed by Pandora and Lauri.

She yanks open a cupboard and takes down three glasses.

"Wait," Lauri says, "you have to have one, too."

"No, thank you." On her empty stomach, a cocktail is the last thing she needs.

"Are you okay? You're white as a . . ." Lauri glances at Pandora. "Um, spirit energy?"

Pandora chuckles and looks at the plate of peanut butter cookies on the countertop. "Those biscuits look scrumptious. May I?"

"Help yourself."

Pandora takes three as Bella opens the freezer to find that the ice trays are empty. Max, Jiffy, and their ice cubes in milk. Right now, Bella would give anything to have the boys here talking about warm milk and barfing or watching inappropriate television shows . . . even helping her paint.

She slams the freezer door shut. "Sorry. Out of ice."

"I noticed scads of icicles hanging from the roof," Pandora says, munching a cookie. "Have you had the shingles checked lately?"

"No, I haven't."

"Aren't you going to refill the trays, luv?"

"No."

"That's okay. Who needs ice cubes on a day like today?" Lauri says, and Bella shoots her a grateful glance.

Noticing the freezer door failed to close all the way, she gives it another push.

Still open.

She shoves harder, using her shoulder this time.

"You're going to tear the bloody thing off the hinges! Let's have a look." Pandora pads barefoot across the floor, popping the last bit of a cookie into her mouth.

Lauri offers Bella an apologetic little shake of her Santa cap.

"Oh, my. Frozen dinners? These aren't nutritious at all. Toss them into the bin. And . . . are these *tea bags*?" she asks as if she's just discovered human remains. She whirls to look at Bella, the plastic baggie containing Odelia's puffy-eye remedy dangling between her spindly thumb and forefinger.

"I was about to use them to brew your tea," Bella says darkly, well aware that Pandora only drinks "proper" tea—whole leaf, painstakingly brewed, and certainly not fresh from the freezer. "But since you've changed your mind . . ."

Relishing her flabbergasted expression, Bella plucks the bag from Pandora's hand, tosses it back into the freezer, and closes the door. This time, it stays closed. She gives a satisfied nod as Dawn returns, carrying a bottle of gin, one of tonic, a couple of limes, and the Catch Phrase game.

"What fun!" Pandora claps her bony hands. "I do love a musical challenge. I was a contestant on *Name That Tune* back in the eighties!"

"The game show?" Lauri asks. "I loved that! I wonder if I saw you?"

"Not unless you were watching the telly in England, darling. I was on the UK version."

"Did you win?"

"I very nearly did. Tripped up by 'Dirty Laundry' in the golden medley. Otherwise, I was *brilliant*!"

Pandora, tripped up by a song called "Dirty Laundry"? Talk about poetic justice.

"I have to get back upstairs to Max," Bella says. "But first, Pandora, I really need to know about Misty and Jiffy."

"There, now, don't be stingy with the gin, darling," Pandora tells Dawn as she begins mixing the drinks.

"Pandora—"

"Yes," she says, fixing Bella with a look. "I'm getting to that."

She closes her eyes and bows her head. After a long moment, she says, "She must tread carefully around him."

"Who?"

"Misty."

"But around who?"

"Whom."

Bella bites her tongue.

"Around this man."

"Where is he? And where is she? Is she with him?"

After a moment she nods as if listening to a voice only she can hear and murmurs, "Out in the cold."

"What do you mean?"

"That's what Spirit is saying. 'Out in the cold.'"

"Literally?"

"That isn't clear."

Bella looks toward the window, remembers the blue lights flashing as divers searched the lake. She swallows hard, tasting blueberry buckle and bile, and glances over at Lauri and Dawn. They're somber, arm in arm, listening to Pandora.

Misty had warned Bella not to trust anyone, and Calla had said things aren't what they seem. But when it comes to these two women, they aren't murderers. She's certain of that.

Nor is Pandora. She genuinely wants to help in her own way.

"Is Misty with Jiffy?" Bella asks.

"I don't feel as though she is. There's quite a good bit of distance between them. The lad is . . ." She inhales deeply through her nose and exhales out through her mouth for several breaths, nodding. "He's very peaceful. He may be asleep."

It shouldn't be an ominous message. Deep breaths could mean she's channeling someone in slumber.

"Is he asleep in a car, do you think?"

Pandora ignores the question, brows knit above her closed eyes as if squinting at something only she can see. "I see . . . golden . . ."

"The locket?" Lauri asks, and Dawn shushes her.

Pandora sways a bit as if in rhythm with music in her bowed head.

Then she sings, "Eight maids a milking . . ."

"The Twelve Days of Christmas!" Dawn shouts, as if they're playing *Name That Tune*, the Lily Dale version.

"Seven swans a swimming . . ."

Bella's thoughts whirl back to yesterday afternoon. Jiffy had told her it took fifteen minutes to sing "The Twelve Days of Christmas" five times.

"Six geese a laying . . ."

Pandora stops, brows furrowed.

Is that significant? The geese laying eggs? Is this some roundabout reference to the stolen Fabergé ones?

Pandora nods and sings on. "*Foooooour* golden rings . . ."

Wait, *four*?

"Five!" Lauri corrects.

Pandora looks up, eyes wide open, shaking her head. "Four. Four golden rings."

"No, it goes—" Dawn sings, "*Five golden rings.*"

"I'm not daft! I'm quite aware of how the song is written, but it's not what Spirit is telling me. There are *four* golden rings."

"But what does that mean?" Lauri asks.

"Hard to say, luv."

Thinking of her own wedding and engagement rings, tucked upstairs in her jewelry box, Bella asks, "Are you sure there are four? Not two?"

"Not two and not five. My goodness, Isabella, I'm—"

She breaks off, startled by a marimba tone coming from the next room. A cell phone is ringing.

Bella excuses herself and hurries to the breakfast room, remembering that she had had Misty's phone when she was talking to Lauri and Dawn there before they left for their appointment.

Sure enough, it's right on the table, lit up with a call.

And Bella intends to answer it.

Chapter Sixteen

The big black pickup truck with New York plates, parked in the snow-covered parking lot at the edge of the wood, is not what Misty expected.

"What, no big old Cadillac?"

He grunts something—probably telling her to shut up again. That's his favorite phrase, along with "Walk."

Oh, they've walked.

Now it appears they're going to be driving.

Misty is so cold, so exhausted, so numb that she almost welcomes the thought of getting into that truck. But she knows that if she allows that to happen, she may never get out of it again.

Not in her physical body anyway.

"Come on," Elvis says.

"I know, I know. Walk."

She walks. Her limbs ache with every step, her lungs with every frozen breath as they cover the last bit of ground toward the parking lot.

Jiffy rides his scooter here when it isn't covered with snow. It's not paved, but there are fewer ruts than on the roads. It's been plowed since the storm started. He wouldn't have been over here today, would he?

Could he have had a run-in with this man?

"You need to tell me about my little boy."

Elvis says nothing, perhaps because he can't muster the breath. He just pushes her along. It's faster going now that there's even ground beneath their feet.

Misty's physical body is here, moving forward. But Spirit propels her back to her blue-and-white meditation room, back to . . .

"Ginger."

She didn't mean to say the word aloud.

But when it slips out, Elvis stops in his tracks and turns to stare at her.

"*Ginger*? What about her?"

*   *   *

Grabbing Misty's ringing phone, Bella sees that the call is from "*Mike.*"

Misty's husband. Jiffy's father.

She hesitates only a moment before answering with a terse, "Hello?"

"Babe?"

"No, sorry, I—"

"Oops, wrong number."

"No! Wait, it's the right number!" She glances toward the doorway, expecting to see Pandora lured by her shout, but she remains in the kitchen, presumably still entranced.

"This is Misty Starr's phone," Bella goes on as she hurries to the study, yanking the French doors closed after her.

"*Misty*?" She hears a sigh on the other end of the line. "Misty Starr. Got it. Who is this?"

"I'm a friend of your wife's. My name is Bella."

"Max's mom."

"Yes. You know about Max?"

"My son talks about him. You said Bella, right?"

"Yes."

"And my wife is . . ."

She frowns. "Um . . . Misty?"

He gives a clipped little laugh. "Actually, I wasn't talking about her name. Which, for the record, is Mary Ellen. That's not what she calls herself these days, though, is it."

He isn't asking a question. If Bella hadn't already heard about the tension between the couple, she'd have quickly picked up on it now.

215

"I was just wondering where my wife is," he says, sounding close enough to be in the next room instead of in a desert on the other side of the globe. "I've texted her a few times. She usually answers pretty quickly, so I thought something might be wrong. Is she okay?"

"She's . . . I saw her a little while ago, and—"

"Where is she?"

"I'm not sure, to be honest," Bella says and waits for him to ask her to put Jiffy on the phone.

"Figures," he mutters instead.

"Excuse me?"

"Mary Ellen can be . . ." He clears his throat, shifts gears. "*Why* did you say you have her phone?"

"I didn't, but . . . I borrowed it."

"Why?"

Where the heck is Luther at a time like this? Or even Grange? Bella doesn't know how or if she should tell this man that his son is missing.

"My own phone is old," she says, "and the battery keeps dying, and I needed to make a few calls, and I walked away with it by accident, and . . ."

She's talking too much, saying nothing of substance. Lying, essentially. Stalling.

"So you were with my wife."

"Yes."

"At the house?"

"Yes."

"How long ago?"

"A few hours."

Does he know about Jiffy? There's something about the way he's questioning her, almost as if . . .

But if he knew, would he be doing it so calmly?

"And where are you now?"

"Me? I'm home."

"Valley View Manor," he says. "A few doors down from my wife and son."

"Yes."

"And you're not a medium, right?"

Taken aback, she says, "No. How did you—?"

"Jiffy likes to talk."

She forces a little laugh. "No kidding."

"He mentions you and your son a lot. He likes coming over to your house."

"We like having him. He and my son are good friends."

"I'm looking forward to meeting Max. You, too."

"Are you . . . visiting? Soon?"

"I'm sure I will. Eventually."

She doesn't know what to say.

Maybe he doesn't either. There's a long pause.

He sighs. "Will you ask Mary Ellen—*Misty*—to call me, please? Whenever she gets back or whenever you see her?"

She assures him that she will and hangs up the phone, pondering the conversation and revising her opinion.

Mike Arden obviously doesn't know Jiffy is missing. If he did, she'd hear a different kind of tension in his voice. But he wasn't relaxed, exactly. More like all business. The conversation was brisk and unemotional, and—

Wait a minute. Wouldn't it be natural, upon calling your wife's phone and having it answered by a stranger, to ensure your child's well-being?

But he only asked about Misty's whereabouts, Bella realizes with a chill. Not their son's.

*   *   *

"What about her?" Elvis asks again.

Her. Not *it.*

So "Ginger" wasn't gingerroot or gingerbread. It was a first name.

Misty's thoughts whirl back to the redheaded client in the leopard fur coat, the one who'd called herself Barbara.

"How do you know Ginger?" Elvis demands, grabbing her roughly by the shoulder with one hand and spinning her around.

"I . . . met her."

"Where?"

"My house. I gave her a reading."

"When?"

"Yesterday."

"What did you tell her?" he screams in her face, pointing the gun at her.

She weighs her answer, not wanting to lose leverage here—or, for that matter, her life.

"The details of her reading are private."

"They're *priv*—" The outraged echo transforms into a violent coughing fit.

He releases her, trying to control the spasms, yet never moving his eyes from her or relinquishing his aim.

When the spell passes, he shoves the pistol under her chin. "*Private*? Her reading was private?"

"Yes," she manages to say, neck arched back, eyes blinking against the snowflakes falling from the oppressive sky.

"You're kidding, right? Do you not see this gun?"

"Not from this angle." She swallows hard against the cold, unforgiving metal.

He jerks it away. His face is red, asthma kicking in again, and he glowers at her. She can hear the air whistling through his lungs, see it puffing white in the frigid air.

If it hurts her to breathe in the cold right now, it must be agony for him. He doesn't have much time before he'll have to use the inhaler again. This time, she's standing face-to-face with him, not lying helplessly on the ground.

He's still aiming the gun at her, but he won't use it as long as he thinks she has information he can use.

She rubs her gloved hands together, eyes closed.

"Hey! What are you doing?"

"Listening to my Spirit guides. They have messages for you."

"What kind of messages?"

"Shh!"

He falls silent, but not for long.

"What are they telling you? Is it about Ginger?"

"It's . . ." She opens her eyes. "It's about your blond friend. A man."

His jaw drops. "What . . . what about him?"

"Does Ginger know you killed him?" she blurts.

She's gone too far. Said too much.

She might have gotten it all wrong. There might be no blond man, or Elvis didn't shoot him . . .

Except, if she was wrong, he wouldn't appear fearful. Only furious.

She sees both emotions burning in his eyes. He starts to speak but is seized by another harsh coughing fit.

Time is running out, Misty knows.

For both of them and for her son.

* * *

Still clutching Misty's phone, Bella sits at the desk in her study, wondering about Mike Arden.

If parents are the primary suspects when kids go missing, and her gut tells her Misty isn't behind Jiffy's disappearance, then it stands to reason Mike might be guilty. Especially when she considers that the marriage is troubled, the holidays are coming, and they'd had a terrible argument this morning.

Troubling as it is to consider that Jiffy's father might have abducted him, it would at least rule out the possibility that he met foul play at the hands of a cold-blooded killer—regardless of the timing and what happened to Virgil.

Odelia might not believe in coincidence, but Bella wants to. *Needs* to.

An unwelcome thought barges into her brain, pushy as Pandora. *Things aren't what they seem.*

Is Mike Arden really an American soldier serving overseas? Or is that just what he tells his wife and son?

Or is it what his *wife* tells their son and the rest of the world?

What if he has ties to the Amur Leopard syndicate? What if he's the one who killed Yuri Moroskov and Virgil? What if he's a fence?

She considers what she read about the middlemen who accomplish what thieves themselves cannot—money laundering and trafficking stolen goods without attracting attention. They appear to be ordinary people going about their daily business.

Bella puts down Misty's phone and grabs the computer mouse, clicking the desktop to life.

It's still open to the web page she was reading—was it really only yesterday?—for information on the Easter Egg Heist.

She clicks the back button to the search window to replace Moroskov's name with *Michael J. Arden*, but pauses with her fingers on the keyboard as she spots a headline from the last results.

AMUR LEOPARD GANG SUSPECTED IN THEFT OF PRICELESS ARTIFACTS

She follows the link to an article about a brazen gunpoint theft at a British museum just over a month ago. Thieves made off with price-less jewels that had belonged to twelfth-century clergy—*including four sapphire-encrusted gold rings.*

Bella gasps.

Four golden rings.

This can't be a coincidence. There's no way.

As she sits staring at the screen, a sound reaches her ears.

Someone is whistling on the other side of the French doors, and it takes only a few bars for her to recognize the song.

"O Little Town of Bethlehem."

*   *   *

Misty can see that Elvis is spent from the latest coughing spell. Yet he's still armed, still dangerous. Even more so now that she's brought up the blond man and Ginger, whoever they are.

"What did you tell Ginger?" he asks, still fighting for breath.

"I didn't—"

"Did you tell her that I . . . you know."

Shot that man?

"No. I swear I didn't."

"Then what *did* you say to her?"

"Nothing!"

"I'm not . . ." He pauses to suck in air. ". . . not stupid."

"Look, it's the truth. She gave me a fake name, and she acted like she didn't know what I was talking about when I said 'ginger.'" Misty hadn't known what she was talking about either, but no need to tell him that.

"So then what did you do when she didn't say anything?"

She shrugs. "I dropped it."

"You dropped it."

He coughs, long and hard.

"What else did you see? Before that, after that?"

"Nothing. That's all I told her. *Ginger.*"

"I'm not talking about what you *told* her! I'm asking what you *saw*!"

Money. She saw money. Should she mention it?

"I saw a school bus," she tells him. "But it wasn't for her."

"How do you know?"

"My son was on it. He was—"

"Your son *again*?" He shakes his head. "I don't want to hear about him right now, lady! Tell me about Ginger. Tell me what you saw."

"I didn't see—"

"Yes, you did! What else?" he shouts.

She gulps. "Dirty clothes."

"*What?*"

"I saw a big bag of dirty clothes."

"What the hell are you talking about? Whose dirty clothes?"

"Mine and my son's. The washing machine is—"

"What part of *I don't want to hear about your kid* do you not understand?"

Misty clamps her mouth shut, watching him look down at the pistol. He fiddles with it, almost as if he's getting ready to use it.

"Money," she blurts.

His head jerks up. "Money?"

"Yes. I saw money."

"Anything else connected to the money?"

"Not unless it's laundry," she says, and something clicks in her brain.

Laundry . . . money.

Money . . . laundry.

Money . . . *laundering*.

No surprise that Ginger—and Elvis, too—are involved in something like that, but there's more to it.

Her thoughts fly like deft fingers working a jigsaw as he shouts, "I don't care about the damned laundry!"

"Spirit doesn't like it when you scream and curse at me."

He flinches, still belligerent, but his voice is lower. "What about something else? Something that might be lost?"

"Like what?"

"You're the psychic. You tell me."

Focus . . .

Breathe . . .

Did Ginger come looking for money?

Does Elvis know where it is, and he's hiding it from Ginger? Or is he, too, trying to find it?

No, wait . . .

It's not the money. It's something else. Something lost. Something . . .

Breathe . . .

Whatever it is—whatever they've lost—is somewhere nearby, here in the Dale. She can feel it.

"What do you see? You know where to look, right?" he asks, and she sees the hunger in his eyes, hears the plea in his voice, strangling as his lungs constrict.

Misty nods slowly, every molecule of her body taut.

He won't shoot her if he believes she has information he needs.

"So where are they?" His words are tight, airless.

They.

She closes her eyes.

An image sparks in her brain and is gone.

Gold.

Is it some kind of gold treasure? Gold coins, bars, doubloons, jewelry . . .

She listens to Elvis struggling to breathe. In her mind's eye, she sees the knobby-kneed, hunch-shouldered little boy in the schoolyard, clinging to his lunchbox, taunted by bullies.

A lot of people hurt little boys.

He coughs, hard and long, gasping. Deep within her, something taut begins to fray.

"Dude. You need your inhaler."

"I'm . . . fine."

"No, you aren't. I promise I won't try anything. Just get your medicine."

"Get . . . into the truck."

She stays rooted to the snowy ground.

"Go on." He gestures with the gun. "Get in."

"I thought you wanted to know about the money."

"I do . . . You're . . ." He stops to cough. "You're taking me there."

"Yes. I will. I promise. Just as soon as you tell me what you know about my son. Okay?"

He stares at her for a long time.

Then he nods. "Okay."

* * *

The whistling stops the instant Bella jerks open the French doors.

Stepping into the parlor, she spots Pandora standing in front of the open window seat cubby.

"What are you doing?"

"Buggering about memory lane whilst our chums mix the cocktails," she says cheerily, holding up a wall calendar. "Look what I've turned up! Truly spectacular photos of the Dale on every page. Oh, '99 was *such* a good year, wasn't it? 1999, that is," she adds with a merry laugh. "Although back in 17—"

"Were you whistling, though?" Bella cuts in before she can prattle on about some event that happened—ostensibly to Pandora herself—centuries ago.

"Whistling? Yes." She flips through the calendar. "Every date covered with appointments and engagements . . . What a marvelous whirlwind we were living, Orville and I. Pity he was such a wanker."

"Pandora! Please."

"Pardon my French. But he was."

"No, this isn't about your 'French.' I need to know why you were whistling *that song*."

"It just popped into my head."

"Because of the star, do you think?"

"Which star?"

"You know . . . Bethlehem. The star the wise men followed. I've been wishing there were one here to guide Jiffy home even though that's crazy in this weather."

"Well, Isabella, you should know that there are no—"

"Coincidences. I'm aware. Hey, Pandora, do you know Albie?"

She sniffs. "Not intimately, if that's what you mean."

Bella winces. "It isn't. What do you know about him?"

"He's a gentle soul. He protects the children."

"Jiffy, too?"

"Of course. All the children."

"Do you really think Jiffy is safe?"

"I do."

"And Misty?"

"She's gone off after him, has she?" Pandora sighs. "She's as cheeky as the lad. But good-hearted. I wish she'd understood that things aren't what they seem."

"Is Spirit saying that, Pandora? Because Calla said the same thing."

"Yes."

"What else is Spirit telling you? Please. This is so important."

Pandora sighs, sets aside the calendar, and closes her eyes.

Bella waits, listening to the ticking clock and the women chatting in the kitchen. No whistling to distract her, jumbling her thoughts. No odd bursts of WDOE oldies or carols. No "Twelve Days of Christmas" with only four golden rings.

Golden . . .

What had Max said earlier, about his Christmas gift for her?

"*They're golden and beautiful.*"

She'd assumed he was talking about the gilded plaster handprint, but wouldn't he have said, "*It's* golden and beautiful"?

And Jiffy . . .

"That's how long it takes to sing 'The Twelve Days of Christmas' five times."

He and Max were singing it as they went out to the shed after school yesterday.

"I like 'The Twelve Days of Christmas' better, because it has golden rings in it."

"Shhhhh! It's a surprise!"

"I know! She can't hear us!"

Who were they worried about?

As Bella runs through the possibilities—Mrs. Schmidt, Misty, Bella herself—Pandora murmurs something unintelligible.

"What is it, Pandora? What is Spirit saying?"

She's nodding intently as if listening to a response. Then she opens her eyes and looks right at Bella. "They're taking him home."

"What? Who? Who's taking who home?"

"Who's taking *whom*," Pandora corrects her. "I really don't know. But I feel that he's in good hands."

"All right, girls, the cocktails are mixed, and it's game time!" Lauri announces, sticking her head in from the breakfast room, holding a gin and tonic. "Want to play Catch Phrase, Bella?"

"No, thanks."

"But we need teams," Dawn tells her. "We can't play with three."

She apologizes, excuses herself, and hurries upstairs. She needs to find Luther and bring him up to date, but first things first. She peeks into Max's room. He's in bed, awake, expectant.

"Are the TV guys here?"

"No, they're not—" About to say *coming*, she leaves it at that. They're not here, but for all she knows, they *are* coming. Certainly, Grange is.

She sits on his bed and touches his forehead. No fever. "How are you feeling? Does your head still hurt?"

"Not really."

"Okay, good. That's good. Hey, Max, the other day, you and Jiffy were singing about 'The Twelve Days of Christmas,' remember?"

"Yep. We like to sing."

"What's your favorite part of the song?"

"What do you mean?"

"My favorite part is about the ten lords a leaping. What's yours?"

He hesitates just long enough for her to know that he isn't trying to decide. He's trying to come up with something other than the golden rings.

"Four turtle doves."

"Wait, are you sure it isn't four golden rings?"

"No! It's five!"

"I thought it went"—she sings—"'*four golden rings.*'"

"Nope. Five. But I don't want to talk about that."

"About what?"

"Golden rings."

"Why not?"

"Because it's a . . ." He clamps his mouth shut and shakes his head.

Surprise. That's what he was about to say.

What if her Christmas gift isn't a gilded handprint, but four golden rings?

She tells Max that she'll be back shortly and heads downstairs, not in the mood to face her guests or Pandora. She can hear voices chattering and electronic buzzing in the breakfast room, a lively game of Catch Phrase apparently under way.

How can they can laugh and play at a time like this? To be fair, Lauri and Dawn don't even know Jiffy. They're concerned, yet hoping for the best. As for Pandora . . .

She still thinks the dead are merely in the next room or some such nonsense. She doesn't grasp that at any given time, any given person can cease to exist. Bella has known that for a year now. Longer, if you count Sam's illness.

Remembering Virgil Barbor's horrible gaping eyes, Bella knows David Slayton is wrong. Dead *is* dead.

And Pandora is a fool.

She peers out the front window.

Midafternoon, and dusk is falling fast, along with the snow and her spirits. Luther's truck is nearly buried again out front, but she can no longer hear the shovel scraping against concrete here or next door.

Nerves on edge, she turns away, trying not to think that he might have run into danger. He's wary and probably armed.

He'll be back. He probably walked across the park to clear Pandora's walk. Stupid woman should have known better than to ask that of him, but she's always competing with Odelia.

She returns to the study to find Misty's phone where she left it on the desk beside the computer. She checks the call log, making sure she hasn't missed any since Jiffy disappeared. Then, feeling only vaguely guilty, she scans back over the past few days. One call jumps out at her.

It's from Ontario, Canada.

Heart pounding, Bella shifts over to Misty's text inbox.

There, she finds herself staring at the very same emojis and photograph she'd seen on her own phone. Only on Misty's, they aren't from an anonymous number. They're from one labeled "Jiffy."

Chapter Seventeen

The pickup truck is dark and cold, encased in a thick layer of snow. A shotgun sits propped against the passenger's seat. Elvis snatches it and tosses it out into the truck's bed, then orders Misty to climb into the seat.

Still holding the pistol on her, Elvis closes the door after her and begins to clear the windshield. She wedges her feet into the narrow spot between a duffel bag and a long-handled . . . tool? Weapon?

It doesn't look particularly lethal, she decides, eyeing the pole-like contraption that's propped from floor to seat. It appears to be electronic with a small windowed screen—a meter of some sort? There's a handle at the top end and an attachment at the bottom that almost looks like a steering wheel.

Snow brushed away at last, Elvis climbs into the driver's seat. Watching him juggle the gun to fasten his seat belt, she remembers to buckle her own.

Sometimes she forgets to do that. It drives Mike crazy. He's a stickler for rules. Okay, laws. He's always reminding her that it's as illegal to drive without a seat belt as it is to drive under the influence.

She'd never do that. She's not stupid or reckless. When she has a glass of wine or two, she stays home.

But her seat belt . . .

Yeah, she forgets. So sue her.

She thinks back to the day Mike had met her and Jiffy in New York after not having seen them for six months. Standing in the street alongside the car she'd just double-parked, he'd grabbed their son and hugged him hard, burying his face in Jiffy's red hair to breathe him in just as Misty had earlier in his bedroom, hugging his pillow.

"Hey, Dad, we drove almost all the way from sea to shining sea!" Jiffy had said, wriggling away. "Except there was a shining desert back there, and I haven't seen the shining sea over here yet."

"Did Mommy make you wear your seat belt?"

"Of course I did!" she'd snapped and hoped Jiffy wouldn't mention the few times she'd forgotten to remind him until they were well on their way. He didn't, happily distracted by the bustling city street.

Now she reconsiders buckling herself into Elvis's truck. Slippery roads are hardly the biggest threat to her safety right now. If she finds an opportunity to escape after he tells her what she needs to know, she doesn't need any obstacles.

As if he's read her mind, he presses a button and locks the doors with a click that sounds as ominous as the cocking of a revolver to Misty's ears.

*   *   *

Bella pokes her head into the breakfast room, where Pandora, Lauri, and Dawn are sitting around the table with cocktails and Catch Phrase.

"This is the song I sang to you that day at Ponderosa when you got that huge tip," Lauri is urgently telling Dawn.

"'She Works Hard for the Money' by Donna Summer."

"No! Geez, all you did was hand the guy a pat of butter, remember?"

"Oh! *That* huge tip! 'Money for Nothing' by Dire Straits!"

"Yes!"

As Lauri and Dawn fist bump, Bella says, "Sorry to interrupt, but I—"

"Ah, here she is. Now we can play." Pandora pats the vacant seat beside her. "Come, Isabella. We're chums, so you'll be on my team."

Any other time, Bella might pause to contemplate—or debate—that assumption. Now she says, "I need to step outside for a few minutes, to, uh, salt the walk."

"Splendid idea," Pandora tells her. "Cheerio, then!"

"Can you just listen for Max?"

"No need. Spirit is assuring me that he's safely asleep."

Bella detours upstairs, opens Max's door, and sees that Spirit and Pandora are indeed correct—about this, anyway.

With renewed hope that Jiffy, too, is merely dozing somewhere—in between sending texts—she returns to the front hall. As she grabs her parka, the coat tree falls forward. She catches it and pushes it back. It falls toward her again, and this time, the hard plastic end of the extension cord swings painfully into her shin like a nunchaku.

"Ouch! You . . ." She punches it back, rare Circassian wood, cherub wings, and all. It hits the wall. There she leaves it, precariously balanced, resting against the amber-and-brown brocade wallpaper. Relishing the thought of what Pandora would say, she pulls on a jacket, gloves, and boots and hurries out into the bracing air.

On the porch, she eyes the shovel propped by the door, then the faint indentations where the three women came up the walk.

The street is desolate, all but obscured by blowing snow that seems to devour people. One by one, they've vanished into the storm.

Jiffy . . . Misty . . . and now Luther.

She cups her hands around her mouth and shouts his name. Swept off into the wind, it brings no response. She calls again with growing apprehension, tethered to the porch like a penguin on an ice floe bobbing in a treacherous sea.

On the third try, his name is met with her own, shouted from the porch next door.

Odelia is there, shivering in the cold. Her hair, freed from its rollers, bounces about her head in loose coils that beg to be combed through. Her eyes are made up. Her mouth is not. She's wearing a pleated red chiffon skirt with black velvet heels and a pajama top.

"Have you heard from Luther?"

"He's inside on the phone."

Bella heaves a relieved sigh that he, at least, is accounted for.

"Is everything is all right over there, Odelia?"

"Nothing is right. Poor Virgil. And our sweet Jiffy, lost in this weather . . ."

"I know."

"And Misty, too." Odelia shakes her head, shivering.

"You don't think she was involved in this mess, do you?"

"I barely know the woman. Anything is possible. But if I were her, I'd be out looking for my son."

"That's what I thought."

"She left her car in the driveway, keys in the house, door unlocked."

"How do you know?"

"Earlier, Calla told me she was missing, so I was keeping an eye out for her."

Ah, the good old Lily Dale neighborhood watch—a little more omniscient than most and a little more hands-on as well.

"Interesting," Bella says, "that you could see that her door was unlocked from there."

"Yes, well, I might have . . . poked around a bit. Just to make sure there was nothing suspicious, no sign of a struggle, nothing like that because . . . oh, I don't want to worry you, Bella."

Already plenty worried, she asks what Odelia is talking about.

"My guides are concerned for Misty's safety."

Yes, aren't we all.

"Did you mention this to Luther?"

"Of course. He wasn't pleased that I'd gone over there, but I assured him that I didn't disturb a thing. Anyway, to me it looks like she just picked up and went out. I only hope she's careful. And you shouldn't be out here alone, Bella."

"I know. I just needed to tell Luther—" Misty's phone vibrates in her pocket. "Odelia, I'm going back inside. Just send him over as soon as he's free, all right? Please?"

Odelia promises that she will and tells Bella that she can come, too, if Bella needs anything at all.

Feeling as though she needs *everything*—other than inevitable conflict between Odelia and Pandora—Bella assures her that all is as well as it can be in this moment.

What she does need—what she craves now more than ever—is a partner in all this. Someone who will know what to do without being asked. Someone . . .

Like Drew.

He's not her partner, law enforcement, family, even a neighbor . . . Yet he's on his way.

Fortified by the knowledge, she steps back inside and locks the door. The coat tree is still precariously balanced against the wall, looking like a strong sigh will topple it any second. The extension cord weaves around the garments like a snake.

She leaves it that way and drapes her snow-soaked jacket over the newel post instead, ignoring the echo of an English-accented, "*Do mind the woodwork.*"

Reaching into her pocket, she pulls out Misty's phone. There's a new text from Jiffy, this time with a pair of emojis. She enlarges the screen.

A little sofa and some kind of round . . . is that a potato?

Stumped, she stares at the little pictures, wondering what they can possibly mean.

From the corner of her eye, she sees movement outside. Her heart stops and then reboots as she spies Luther coming up the front walk.

She opens the door before he can knock and holds a finger to her lips.

"What's wrong?"

"Pandora," she whispers. It doesn't exactly answer his question—and yet it does.

He rolls his eyes and shrugs out of his coat. Brushing past the overstuffed coat tree, he follows her up the stairs.

She peeks in on Max—still safely asleep in his bed. Then she slips into the Rose Room with Luther.

"Odelia told me you were looking for me. I was trying to get that number traced. It's—"

"It's Jiffy's. I know. That's what I came to tell you. He sent his mom the same messages that he sent me. There's a picture. Here, look, Luther. He's trying to tell us where he is." She hands over Misty's phone.

As he presses the screen with his thumb and peers at it, Bella goes on, "And her husband called. He was looking for her. He said he'd been texting her but she hadn't replied. He told me he was worried, but there was something . . . off about him."

He looks up sharply. "How so?"

"He didn't ask about Jiffy."

Luther tilts his head, mulling that. He isn't a father, Bella thinks. He doesn't get it.

"Maybe he was so distracted by the fact that someone else picked up his wife's phone that he—"

"Then wouldn't he be even more likely to make sure his son is okay? Sam would have."

Luther appears to weigh his words before saying, "Sam was one kind of father. Jiffy's dad might be another."

"Yes, but . . ." Bella trails off. He's right.

She peers at the photo over his shoulder, again noting that if Jiffy is in a car, then his mother isn't at the wheel. The silhouette of the back of the driver's head is barely in the picture. It isn't Misty. She has a wild pile of hair, as did her Canadian client. This person does not.

"Do you think that's a man or a woman?" she asks Luther.

"Hard to tell."

"Well, we have to respond to these texts and let that poor child know we're going to help him. He must be wondering why we're ignoring him."

"We can't do that, Bella. We don't know that he's the one sending these messages. Anyone could have his phone or even be spoofing the number."

Those words hit her like an extension cord nunchaku to the heart.

"But if he is sending them and if he's really been kidnapped," Luther goes on, "his captor probably doesn't know he has a phone. If we send a text and the notifications aren't silenced, the alert will give it away."

She swallows hard. "Okay. You're right. So what do we do?"

"I'm going to relay this to law enforcement to see if they can track the signal."

"But won't that take a while? Don't you have to go through a lot of red tape?"

"Unfortunately, it can be a complicated process, but—"

"Isabella!" a voice trills from downstairs.

Pandora.

"What is it?" she calls back through clenched teeth.

"You have a visitor!"

"That's Drew," she tells Luther, hurrying out into the hall. "He's coming to help us."

But when she looks down the stairs, she sees a snowy, stone-faced Lieutenant John Grange looking up at her.

*   *   *

Locked into Elvis's truck, Misty glances down at the small duffel bag by her feet. It's unzipped, the contents spilling out as if someone hastily put something in or took something out. She sees a swath of white fabric studded with sequins and crystal ornamentation.

This can't be the missing gold Spirit showed her. It isn't hidden, and it looks brassy even from this vantage.

An image drops into her brain, and she sees him on a stage, wearing a studded white jumpsuit.

She turns to Elvis, wheezing behind the wheel.

"So you're an Elvis impersonator."

He gasps—perhaps more in surprise than from his asthma—and fumbles with his inhaler, still aiming the gun at her.

He sucks the albuterol into his lungs, holds it there, exhales, and asks, "How'd you know that?"

From where he is, he can't see the open duffel on the floor. Maybe he's forgotten it's there.

Misty tilts her head and taps her temple. Let him think she's used her psychic abilities. No harm in maintaining some semblance of upper hand.

He starts the engine. The windshield wipers sway into action, and music blasts from the radio. Elvis Presley—the real Elvis—is singing "Jailhouse Rock."

The sound is deafening. He adjusts the volume.

Now as if from a great distance, she hears ringing slots, coins hitting a metal tray.

"You work in a casino."

Bingo. He says nothing, but she sees the answer on his fleshy face.

"It's in Canada," she goes on.

Right again. His eyebrows rise above the rims of his golden aviator glasses.

That part was a lucky guess based on Ginger.

"Your turn," she says. "Tell me about my son."

"Not yet. Tell me what else you know."

"About you?"

"About anything."

The truck begins to move toward the parking lot entrance, the road, and maybe a chance to escape. She can't count on anyone to come to her rescue, though. She's on her own, same as always. Better make the most of what she's got.

"You're smart," she tells Elvis. "You've had a hard life."

He shrugs. "Who hasn't?"

Yes, and who hasn't overcalculated their own intelligence? You tell someone they're smart, and they're going to agree, regardless of actual IQ.

"What else you got?"

"I know Ginger has a nasty temper," she tells him. "I know you don't trust her, and you shouldn't. She's not a good wife."

"*Wife?*"

Remembering Ginger's gaudy wedding ring, she'd thought it safe to assume she's somebody's wife. Apparently, not Elvis's.

"What do I care about what kind of wife she is? Anyway, I think you read that word wrong. You should have said widow. What else do you know about her?"

"She likes the finer things in life. She likes to spend money, you know? If it's other people's money, so much the better."

"It's *all* other people's money."

"She doesn't have much guilt over that, though. No guilty conscience for Ginger. She doesn't care who she hurts. Not like you," she adds. "You're a good person."

Smart move, appealing to his ego to head off suspicion that she's making it all up. No way he'd accuse her of that now that she's noted his noble efforts.

"I don't hurt anyone if I can help it," he agrees.

"That's why you and she will never see eye to eye. She doesn't respect you. You need to cut all ties. Get away from her. From all of this."

He's impressed. "That's what I'm doing."

"I know. That's why I'm saying it. This is the right decision. Time to get away, make a fresh start. Got it?"

"Got it."

"Good. Now it's your turn to tell me what I need to know. Tell me about my son. You saw him today. When? Where?"

He looks ahead at the snow-blown road. "Hey, I'm not the one who took him away, okay?"

That phrasing . . .

"Someone took him away?"

"Not me!"

"I know!" she shouts. "Did you see someone take my son?"

He shrugs. "Yeah. I did."

It's as if the asthma has seeped into Misty's body and sucked the air from her lungs.

"Who?" she manages to ask.

"I don't know. Some lady pulled him into her car and drove away."

Chapter Eighteen

Pandora, being Pandora, has trailed Grange to the stairs, peppering him with questions.

"Lieutenant, has something happened? Are we in danger here at Valley View? Are you looking into the missing lad? Are you here to make an arrest?"

On the top step, he turns to level a look at her, down on the landing. "No."

"To which question?"

"All of them. Would you mind waiting downstairs, please, Ms. Feeney, while I speak with Ms. Jordan and her son?"

"If you're here about the lad, I may have pertinent information for you."

He turns to Bella as though Pandora has conveniently evaporated. "Which information is she talking about?"

"She had a vision about—"

"Thank you, Ms. Feeney, but not right now."

"Lieutenant, this is urgent. I keep hearing 'O Little Town of Bethlehem' in my head."

"I appreciate your sharing that, and I'll get back to you when I'm finished up here, or"—he lowers his voice—"sometime. Or never. I don't have time for this."

Bella looks at Luther, standing in the doorway of the Rose Room.

"I do," he says. "You can tell me about it, Pandora. Hold that thought for a few minutes, and I'll come down and talk to you."

"Is that you, Luther? I didn't realize you were back. How delightful. Were you able to shovel my path?"

"Not just yet," he calls, then quietly tells Grange, "I'll go keep her occupied, Lieutenant, while you take care of business."

That isn't quite the case, Bella knows. Luther isn't so quick to write off Pandora and her visions.

"Thanks, pal. Remind me to take a bullet for *you* some day."

Luther flashes a mirthless grin. "First I need to show you something. Mind stepping in here before you talk to Max?"

Bella excuses herself as Luther leads Grange into the Rose Room to show him Jiffy's text messages.

She finds Max awake now, kneeling in front of the window just as Chance had earlier, staring out at the lake.

"What are you doing, Max?"

"Just thinking about a golden treasure."

"What about it? Did you find one?"

"No, Jiffy did. It was right here in our yard, and—" Max clasps a hand over his mouth. "Never mind."

"Sweetie, I need to know about the treasure."

"I can't tell you. It's a secret."

"Did Jiffy ask you to keep it?"

He shrugs.

"Right now," she says, "it's not a good idea to keep any secrets for Jiffy."

"But it's about a Christmas present."

"I still need to know."

"Nope. You can't trick *me*, buster!"

"This is different, Max. It's serious."

"You can't trick *me*, buster!" he repeats and presses his lips together.

Okay. For now, anyway. Bella grabs his bathrobe, hanging from a hook behind the door.

"Here, put this on."

"Why?"

"Because the house is drafty," she tells him, feeling the chill despite Pandora's tweak on the thermostat downstairs.

Max shakes his head. "I'm too hot."

Maybe he does have a fever. He should be tucked into bed resting without another care in the world. But if he can share anything that might help locate his friend . . .

She convinces him to wear his robe and hands him his slippers.

As he pulls them on, she thinks of Pandora downstairs, trying to jam her oversized foot into Bella's own slipper. What, she wonders, will Luther make of her revelations?

Four golden rings . . .

"O Little Town of Bethlehem" . . .

A man in trouble . . .

"Hey, a guy," Max announces, and for a moment, Bella thinks he's gone Lily Dale on her at last. Then she realizes he's looking behind her and turns to see Grange standing in the doorway.

"Are you Max?" The question isn't quite as point-blank as his usual style, perhaps softened by the sight of a small, runny-nosed boy in robe and slippers. "I'm Lieutenant Grange."

Grange holds out his hand just as Max sneezes three times into his own and quickly retracts the handshake.

"Gesundheit, gesundheit, gesundheit."

"Good job, Mom." Max wipes his nose on his sleeve and looks at the holster at Grange's hip. "You're that good guy with the real gun. You met me and Jiffy when the bad guy locked us in the cellar, remember?"

Grange nods. "I always remember brave little boys."

"We were little *then*, but now we're both almost seven. Jiffy will be seven first, then me. How old are you?"

"I'm, uh . . . older."

"How old, by the way?"

"*Old*. Listen, about Jiffy . . ." He pauses to look at Bella. "Can Max and I talk for a few minutes?"

"Sure. But I'm staying."

Resigned, he turns back to Max. "Do you have any idea where Jiffy might have run off to?"

"Well, he didn't run off. He was kidnapped."

"What makes you say that?"

"My brain makes me say it."

Grange glances over at Bella.

She keeps her expression neutral. You get what you deserve when you insert yourself into a six-year-old's bedroom and start firing questions.

"So you think Jiffy was kidnapped?" He pulls out a pad and pen.

"No."

Grange looks up. "*No?*"

"I *know* he was."

"How?"

"He told me."

"When?"

"A long time ago. Plus also yesterday."

"I don't understand."

Max explains about Jiffy's vision that he was going to be kidnapped during a snowstorm. Grange writes it down.

"So it sounds like Jiffy was planning this for a while, right, Max?"

"I guess so."

Bella's heart sinks. Two homicides, a raging storm, and he's going to believe it's some kind of prank?

"So Jiffy told you about his plans. Who else did he—?"

"They weren't *his* plans!" she cuts in. "Right, Max?"

"Right, they were the kidnapper's plans."

Grange writes on his pad.

Max sniffles, reaches for a tissue, and finds the box empty. "Can I go get some more tissues and have Lucky Charms and watch *Ninja Zombie Battle*?"

"Soon."

"I can watch *Ninja Zombie Battle* soon?"

Bella sighs. "We'll see."

"But—"

"Max," Grange says firmly, "did Jiffy tell you anything else about the kidnappers?"

"Like what?"

"Names."

"How would he know their names? Kidnappers are strangers."

"Not always."

"Do you know any?"

"Personally? No. Do you?"

"Nope."

"Who else did Jiffy tell about the kidnapper 'dream'?" Grange might as well gesture air quotes around the word.

"I don't know. Pro'lly not his mom."

"Why not?"

"She thinks that when you dream stuff it comes true because she's a medium. But that doesn't always happen. Like, if you dream your dead dad comes back alive, sometimes he doesn't."

Oh, Max. Longing to gather him into her arms, Bella stands and rests her hands on his shoulders.

"Moms don't want their boys to be kidnapped," he goes on, "even if they can be famous."

"What do you mean?" Lieutenant Grange asks a little too casually.

"Like, when the TV guys come to talk about how Jiffy got kidnapped, all the people who tell them he's a really great kid will get to be famous, but not as famous as Jiffy. Oh, and he's super brave, too. He said not to forget that part."

"Guess your pal thought this through pretty well. He sounds like the kind of guy who enjoys the spotlight, huh, Max?"

"You mean flashlights? He can make shadows on the wall with his hands like a duck and a dog. I can't make a dog, but I can show you the duck if you want. My mom has a flashlight, but she doesn't like us to use it because it's so heavy we might kill each other if we bump ourselves in the head."

"Do you think Jiffy wanted everyone to think he'd been kidnapped?"

"I don't *think* he's kidnapped. I *know* he is." He sniffles and turns pleading eyes to Bella. "Can we go downstairs now?"

"Max isn't feeling well, Lieutenant. Can we please take a break?"

He holds up a finger. "In a minute. Let's look at this from a different angle, Max."

"Look at your finger?"

Grange doesn't catch, or isn't charmed by, the impish glint in Max's eye. "At the *situation*. Where does Jiffy like to go after school?"

"My house."

"But you didn't see him today?"

"I'm sick so I can't have playdates, and Jiffy's kidnapped so he can't either."

"But did you *see* him?"

"No. I'm sick and that's why I need to get a Kleenex and—"

"Got it." Grange's jaw muscles clench. "What does Jiffy say about his dad?"

"He says he's in the army. And one time, they went way to the top of the Empire State Building together."

"Anything else?"

Max puffs his cheeks, juts his lower lip, and exhales heavily. "Can I be done now?"

"I need you to help me find Jiffy, Max. Okay?"

"Well, I can't. He said he would text me where he is if my mom let me have a phone, but she won't. Can you tell her to?"

"Turns out Jiffy's mom didn't let him have a phone either, Max," Bella says. "His dad gave it to him, probably so that they can stay in touch."

The moment those last words leave her mouth, she regrets them. Max would give *anything*—not for a cell phone, but to have his dad back, even on the other side of the world.

"Does Jiffy call and text his father a lot?" Grange asks Max.

"I don't know."

"What about his mom? Does he call and text her?"

"She lives in his house, so pro'lly not."

"What kind of mom is she?"

"Busy." Max shrugs. "And she lets him do stuff."

"Like what?"

"Like *everything*. Fun stuff."

Bella, on the receiving end of Max's pointed look, remembers the snowboard situation that was, just yesterday, her biggest concern.

"I think it's time to take a break and eat something, Max. Let's go downstairs, and I'll get you a bowl of Lucky Charms, and Lieutenant Grange and I can talk to the others while you eat it."

"Which others?"

"Luther, our guests and Pandora, and . . ."

Drew.

Drew will be here soon, she promises herself, looking toward the blinding powdery gales beyond the window.

*   *   *

How could someone have abducted her son right out from under Misty's nose? It's impossible to fathom, and yet . . .

It wasn't *right under your nose.*

Your nose is right under your eyes, and they weren't watching Jiffy.

"Who was the woman?" she asks Elvis, her voice rising shrilly above the real Elvis singing on the radio about suspicious minds.

"How should I know? What do you think, we were standing around shaking hands and exchanging phone numbers?"

Driving with one hand on the wheel and the other on the gun, Elvis shakes his sideburned, slicked-back, greasy, balding head at her perceived stupidity.

"Okay, then what—?"

"Oh, no, you don't. It's my turn. Tell me more about—"

"Oh, no it's not!" Misty's hands curl into fists. "I need to know when this happened, where it happened, how it happened."

He opens his mouth to argue. She fixes him with a glare, and he shrugs, guiding the truck along a road that hasn't seen a plow in a little too long. Even with four wheel drive, the vehicle is struggling.

"It happened this morning. Afternoon, maybe."

"You don't know?"

"Noon. Say noon."

"*You* say noon," she snaps, "if that's what you mean."

"Around then. I saw the kid."

"Where?"

"Outside."

"Where outside?"

"Hanging around down where the road branches off from the gate."

"What was he doing?"

"What do kids do? He was playing. Jumping around, shaking tree branches so the snow would come pouring down, making snow angels, throwing snowballs."

"At other kids? Were there other kids?"

"At trees. He was alone."

"And where were you?"

"I was back there in the trees when I spotted him."

"Lurking? Hiding?"

"No!"

Yes. She feels sick. "Did you say something to my kid? Did you—?"

"No!" He flinches and hits the brakes. The truck goes into a skid, sliding sideways along the road, toward a stand of trees.

Misty watches it unfold as if she's slipped out of her body. As if her own physical well-being weren't at stake here.

Watching him struggle with the wheel, she notes that he's going to have to let go of the gun. When he does, she'll grab it if she can, or jump out and run, or—

No. Somehow, he manages to regain control with one hand.

"You better not upset me," he says, breathing hard and fast as the wipers, "or you're going to get us both killed!"

"Okay, I'm sorry." Resigned—for now—Misty stares through the windshield as the truck rolls slowly on down the road at the edge of the Dale, past one deserted cottage after another.

If she were to get out and run, where would she even go? No one is around to answer a frantic knock on the door or hear her scream and call the police.

The real Elvis sings; the fake Elvis coughs.

"Please . . ." Misty swallows hard and looks out the passenger's side window. "You were there. So you didn't talk to my son. Yet you were lurking in the woods, and—"

"Not lurking! Don't upset—"

"I won't! It's just that I need your help! You were the only one who saw what happened. We can help each other, if you'll just . . ."

She trails off as his asthma attacks with a vengeance. Under cover of the music and his coughing fit, she moves her hand a few inches to flip the unlock button on the car doors. The click sounds deafening to her ears, but he doesn't seem to have heard it.

At last, the coughing subsides. None the wiser, he inhales. Exhales.

"Are you okay?" she asks, infusing her voice with concern. "Can I help?"

He shakes his head, breathing, driving.

After a minute, he says, "He was lying there making snow angels, you know?"

"What?"

"It's where you swing your arms and legs up so—"

"I know what snow angels are! I just didn't realize you were talking about Jiffy. What happened? He was making snow angels and . . . what?"

"I was going to go over and talk to him, you know? Real friendly-like. I just wanted to ask him a question, and I was going to say, 'Hey, kid, you shouldn't do that there.'"

"Do what where?"

"He was lying in the street, but I don't think he realized it because it was covered in snow."

Oh, Jiffy. Oh, no.

"So then the car came along . . ." Elvis stops to cough.

Jiffy, lying in the street. A car comes along.

The bitter self-loathing in Misty's gut threatens to surge into her throat. How could she have allowed this to happen? How could she have spent a single minute of her life not watching over her child?

"The lady hit the brakes, and the car went sliding, you know, because the road was icy. The kid didn't see it coming till the last minute."

"And you just stood there watching?" It takes every ounce of self-control for her to keep from screaming the words.

"What do you think I am, a monster? I yelled for him to move. I saved your kid's life, lady. He rolled over, and she just missed him."

He pauses—this time not to cough but waiting for her to congratulate him on his heroics.

"Thank you," she manages.

"You're welcome. Look, I like kids. I *was* a kid."

A kid in short pants with a lunch box, tormented by schoolyard bullies and asthma and who knows what else.

"What," she asks evenly, "did the woman do after you saved my son?"

"She stopped the car and opened the door, you know, like she was making sure he was all right. The next thing I knew, she had him in the back seat. She took off driving pretty fast."

Her breath catches in her throat. "Which direction?"

"Right out the gate."

"What kind of car was it?"

"Turquoise Mustang."

Chapter Nineteen

There's no sign of Luther and Pandora downstairs, but Bella can hear Lauri and Dawn's voices in the breakfast room. She leads Max and Grange into the kitchen, pours Max a bowl of cereal, and sends him off to the television room with it.

"Can I watch *Ninja*—"

"You can watch *Admiral Dee*. Go ahead."

"But—"

"*Admiral Dee*," she says, "or no TV."

At that, he hurries into the other room. She turns back to Grange, who is regarding her without expression.

"Would you like some coffee?"

"No, thanks."

"Tea? Cocoa?" She nods at the fridge. "I might have a juice box in there somewhere."

It's a quip.

Dead serious, he says, "Just ice water would be good, if you have it."

If she *has* it?

She reaches for the freezer, then remembers.

Who needs ice on a day like today? Lauri had asked.

Mr. Freeze, that's who.

"Sorry . . . I have the water part."

"Bottled?"

"Tap."

"No, thank you."

She fills a glass for herself and gulps most of it down. Her challenges are mounting like stanzas in "The Twelve Days of Christmas"—overtired, undernourished, stressed, worried, *and* dehydrated.

Where is Drew? And . . .

"Where are Pandora and Luther?" Grange asks.

"I know as much as you do. I was upstairs with you until a minute ago, remember?"

"Well, then, maybe you know who's talking in the other room?"

"Those are my guests."

She quickly explains about Lauri and Dawn.

"I'd like to speak to them." He heads for the breakfast room, and Bella hurries after him.

Lauri and Dawn are sitting at a table with their cocktails, flipping pages of what appears to be a scrapbook. Before she can make introductions, Grange flashes his badge, introduces himself, takes down their names, and asks where Luther and Pandora went.

"They're over at Misty Starr's house," Dawn tells him.

"Why? Did something happen?"

"No, Luther thought someone should be there in case Jiffy comes home, and Pandora wanted to channel Jiffy's energy," Lauri says. "She thought it might help if she could be around his stuff. So we decided to do the same thing."

"That's Jiffy's scrapbook?"

"No, it's mine," Dawn tells Bella. "It's all the clippings about Sean's last concert and the tragedy."

About to turn away, Bella notices something in one of the photos. Is that . . . ?

She leans in.

Maybe. Probably.

Bella looks up, about to tell Lauri and Dawn, but Grange is in her face.

"Who," he asks, "is Sean?"

"Sean Von Vogel."

"*Who?*"

"The rock star," Lauri explains. "We're doing what Pandora is doing. She says anyone can do it."

"Do what?" Grange asks.

"Channel Spirit. We're trying to soak up Sean's energy from the scrapbooks so that he can tell us where our locket is."

"And maybe just hang out with us," Dawn adds, "if we're lucky. Pandora says you never know."

Grange stares at them, sitting there in their Santa hats, then at Bella. "What am I missing?"

Ordinarily, she'd relate to the question.

Today, she merely shrugs. "To each his own. Listen, Lauri, Dawn, I just—"

"Not when they're violating a crime scene."

Bella's jaw drops, and she forgets all about the scrapbook photo.

"Wait, this is a crime scene?" Dawn asks, wide-eyed.

"No, I'm talking about Pandora Feeney, down the street trying to do whatever she calls this frivolous nonsense."

"She's trying to help," Bella tells Grange. "She doesn't believe Jiffy just ran away to get attention, and neither should you."

"There are investigative procedures to follow, and there's a lot going on around here today, and—"

"I know, but I'm trying—we're all trying—to make sure this missing child doesn't get lost in the chaos. Jiffy has to be your priority. Please." She clamps her mouth shut, realizing she might burst into tears at any moment.

"Look, the last thing I need right now is a mentally unstable woman interfering with this investigation, so—"

"Mentally unstable?" Dawn is on her feet, indignant. "How can you say something like that right to someone's face?"

Lauri rises beside her. "Bella is one of the sweetest people I've ever known!"

"I didn't mean—"

"And she's smart and reasonable, right, Laur?" Dawn cuts him off.

"Right," Lauri agrees, "and if she says Spirit is whistling and meowing in the secret passageways, then I believe her!"

Terrific.

Grange looks at Bella, as if deciding that she might have just earned herself a mentally unstable assessment after all.

"Actually, *I* said that," Dawn tells Lauri, "and Pandora said it was Spirit."

"Pandora," Grange says. "Again. Secret passageways, Ms. Jordan?"

Bella sighs. "This is an old house. It has some quirks."

"Which would make for a good game of hide-and-seek. Even if there's only one person playing."

No! You're wrong! Bella wants to shout. But Grange is all about facts and evidence, just as she herself tends to be. *Now is not the time to give him anything more than what he's asking for.*

Unfortunately, Dawn missed the memo. "We've all heard someone whistling Christmas carols and meowing," she tells Grange, "and we were worried that it might be the kidnapper."

"In my experience, kidnappers don't whistle and meow. Six-year-old boys, though," Grange says, thrumming his pen on the tabletop. "That's a different story."

"You have experience with six-year-old boys?" Bella asks.

"I used to be one. They're mischievous. I'm going to guess that someone was pulling your leg. Either your son or his friend." He turns back to Lauri and Dawn. "I'd like to just ask you a few quick questions so that we can move on."

"Wait, are we suspects for something?" Lauri asks. "Because I'll take a lie detector test if you want."

"Me, too," Dawn volunteers.

"That won't be necessary right now," Grange says tautly. He takes down their addresses and a few other cursory details, then asks what brought them to Lily Dale on this stormy day.

"We're looking for our locket with Sean's hair in it, and we thought the mediums could help us find it."

Not bothering to write that down, Grange seems to have had enough. He turns abruptly to Bella. "Mind if I take a good look around?"

"We already did," Lauri speaks up.

Ignoring her, Grange asks Bella if Jiffy knows about the secret tunnels. At her nod, he asks, "Who else knows?"

"We do," Lauri says, indicating herself and Dawn. "And Pandora does, too. Did you know that she used to own Valley View?"

"And she told us there's a spirit named Nadine who's been hanging around here for over a hundred years!"

"I'm sure she did," he mutters, writing something down.

"Pandora really knows what she's talking about," Dawn goes on, "and I'm sure Misty does, too. She nailed Lauri's Aunt Sassy."

"She . . . what?"

"She brought Aunt Sassy through to me last summer," Lauri says. "Talked about her spinach pie and everything!"

"It was the best spinach pie you've ever had," Dawn says. "*Fabulous.*"

Grange looks at his watch and then at Bella. "Can we wrap this up in private, please?"

Dawn jumps to her feet. "We were just about to go upstairs for a few minutes anyway. Come on, Laur."

She gives Bella's arm a quick squeeze as she passes. Lauri pats her shoulder, and they're gone, leaving their scrapbook open on the table.

Later, Bella thinks. *I'll tell them what I saw in that photo.*

It might not mean anything, but she suspects—

"Have a seat, Ms. Jordan." It's more a command than invitation.

"Not here. I need to be where I can keep an eye on Max, especially with . . ." All this talk of abduction and the reminder that she really did believe someone was lurking in the passageways.

She heads toward the front of the house with Grange on her heels. In the parlor, he eyes the renovation disarray, every horizontal surface draped in paint-stained, plaster-dusted canvas. "Maybe there's a better spot?"

"Not where I can keep an eye on Max." She grabs the edge of a drop cloth, yanks it to reveal a patch of velvet sofa, and sinks down onto it.

She peeks through the doorway into the TV room. Max is munching his cereal, transfixed by Admiral Dee buzzing around in her yellow-and-black-striped uniform, singing seafaring nouns that begin with the "Letter of the Day."

"*Salt . . . Ship . . . Starboard . . .*"

Bella can think of a few of her own as she imagines Jiffy out there in a car with a stranger. *Snow. Storm. Scared.*

She turns back to Grange. "You saw those texts. Jiffy isn't in this house. He's in the back seat of a car somewhere, scared out of his mind."

"Based on . . ."

"Based on the picture he sent. From the car."

"We don't know when it was taken or who took—"

"This isn't hide-and-seek! Two men were murdered here in the last few days!"

"I'm aware, and that's why I'm taking this situation seriously, Ms. Jordan. I want to find the Arden boy as much as you do."

Bella just shakes her head, swallowing a dismal lump of dread as she stares out the window at the storm.

* * *

A turquoise Mustang. Like the car her client Priscilla drove. Why in the world—this world, any world—would Priscilla Galante abduct Misty's son?

It makes no sense.

She wants to believe Elvis made it up, but her instincts tell her he didn't. Just as her instincts had told her there was something familiar about Priscilla the first time she showed up at the door.

"Have we met?"

"I don't think so. I've never been here before . . ."

Since it hadn't been in this life, Misty had been so certain it must have been in a past one. Souls connected somehow, destined to connect again like her own and Mike's.

But what if she had been wrong? What if she'd felt that flicker of recognition because of what lay ahead? Not Priscilla as a client but in a much darker role, one involving Jiffy's welfare.

"With more experience, you'll be able to grasp the significance of various familiar strangers you meet." So said Pandora.

Misty's tide of self-loathing begins to surge again.

Priscilla, a stranger, in her house. Getting to know her—and maybe Jiffy, too, in passing.

She should have been more careful! She should have sensed that there was something dangerous about her!

But . . .

Was there? Wouldn't Spirit have found a way to warn her that this person meant to harm her child? She did get the school bus vision, but if Priscilla was the danger, why wasn't she driving it?

"So there you go," Elvis is saying. "Happy now?"

Dazed, Misty looks over at him.

"I answered your question. Hell, I answered way more than your question. Now you can answer mine."

"Wait a minute, you have to tell me—"

"I've told you everything! I don't know anything else."

"Okay, then please, you have to let me go. I need to tell the police so that they can look for her, the car, my son—"

"No police. No way."

Too late, he's realized he shouldn't have told her any of this information. The wheezing is back—and so is the dangerous glint in his eye, reminding her that he isn't just some asthmatic Elvis wannabe with superhero fantasies. He's an armed killer, and Misty is his hostage.

He's not going to let her go. When she tells him what he wants to know, he's going to kill her.

She can't let that happen.

If she doesn't save herself, she won't be able to save her son. He belongs here, in his earthly body, just as Misty does. Every incarnation comes with lessons that must be learned. She has yet to master hers for this lifetime.

"I won't go to the police," she tells Elvis.

"You already did."

"What do you mean?"

"I saw the squad car parked in front of your house."

"You were at my house?"

"I was around it."

"Why?"

"Looking for something."

"Outside? In the snow?"

He nods, glancing at the long-handled instrument beside her. An image flashes in her head—he's outside, holding it out in front of him like a divining rod, and she understands what it is.

"You were out there with the metal detector," she says. "Right? You were using it to look for the gold."

"For the . . ." He swallows, and his breath whistles in his lungs. Perspiration beads on his forehead. "Gold. Yes. Right."

"But you didn't find anything there."

"I might have if that damned cop hadn't shown up."

"No, you wouldn't have."

"How do you know?"

"Because it isn't there."

She looks back through the rear window at the path into the woods. He was out at the Stump, but he didn't have the metal detector with him. Why not?

Because, for whatever reason, he knows it isn't there.

"So when Lieutenant Grange showed up," she says, "you left and came out here? Why?"

"Why do you think?" He manages a little laugh. "Because that's where the ghosts hang out, isn't it? It's where you people go when you need to ask them a favor. I figured they could tell me where the rings are. Too bad you showed up before they could answer me. Guess you'll just have to tell me instead since you claim to know."

"I do know."

"Where are they?"

Misty takes a deep breath and does the very opposite of what every medium is trained to do.

She delivers a big, fat lie.

*   *   *

"Are you tracking Jiffy's phone?" Bella asks Grange, turning away from the stormy window to face him again.

"We've put the process into motion. It doesn't happen instantaneously. There are certain procedures we have to follow."

"But every second counts."

"And that's why you need to trust that I'm doing my job and minimize the distractions."

Her temper flares. "What do you mean by that?"

"Let's face it, Ms. Jordan—it's difficult to accomplish anything when you've got someone telling you she's hearing Christmas carols in her head, someone else saying she had a vision of her child in danger but she lets him roam around anyway, and yet another person saying a kid had a dream, so that means he's been kidnapped . . ."

"He's six!"

"Mary Ellen Arden isn't."

"Her son is gone. She's beside herself."

"And what's Pandora Feeney's excuse?"

Admiral Dee cheerily fills the silence. "*Sail . . . Seashell . . . Shore . . .*"

Lieutenant Grange checks his watch. "I need to get down to the Arden house before it's contaminated."

"I don't think Luther would let that happen."

Something shifts in his eyes. "I know you and he have both been involved in a couple of cases here over the past couple of months, but I should remind you that law enforcement is experienced in handling this sort of thing."

"That's what I meant. Luther is law enforcement."

"You mean he *was*. With all due respect."

"*Steerage,*" Admiral Dee sings. "*Stowaway . . .*"

Smug, Bella thinks, watching Grange head for the foyer. *Soulless.*

Someone has righted the leaning coat tree again. Probably Pandora, worried about marring the vintage wallpaper. As she watches, Grange snatches his jacket from it and opens the door.

Off kilter, the coat tree sways.

As he steps out over the threshold, it crashes down behind him. On its heels, the bang of a slammed door.

"Mom?"

"It's okay, Max. Just the wind."

Through the window, Bella watches Grange retreat, accompanied by one last choice *S* phrase that begins with the word "son" and ends with something she doesn't dare utter in front of hers.

* * *

Misty holds her breath, hoping Elvis bought her lie.

"Wait . . . my rings are at *Valley View*?" he echoes.

"Uh-huh."

He turns back to focus on the stormy world beyond the windshield, seeming to mull it over. His breath comes with effort, while she holds hers, waiting, praying.

Please believe me.

Please.

"You're wrong."

At last, she inhales. To her, it sounds like a desperate gasp. To him, most likely . . . normalcy.

"Valley View is where I last *saw* the rings," Elvis says. "It's not where they are now."

"How can you be so sure?"

"Because I searched every square inch of that property with the metal detector. Every inch!"

"When did you search?"

"Middle of the night."

"You were prowling around inside Valley View with Bella and Max there?"

"No. Outside. Don't worry, I checked your yard, too. Retraced every step I took between Valley View and Glasgow Road that night. That's why I blew up when you said Ginger was here. I thought she must have figured out about Yuri . . ."

Yuri! That's it. The blond man. The one whose name she'd been hearing as Rory, Harry . . . He's Yuri, dead but not drowned in the lake the other night.

He goes on, "I thought she might just be pretending to believe that story I fed her . . . you know the story, right? From Spirit?"

"The story? Right." She begins ticking off her fingers, hoping to convince him that she's reciting a list she knows by heart, not making it up as she goes along. "I know you didn't tell Ginger you lost the rings. You didn't tell her Yuri is dead. You didn't tell her you shot him. You didn't tell her where you really are . . ."

She pauses, watching him shove his inhaler into his mouth again.

"You want me to keep going?" she asks after he puffs. She hopes not because she's out of ideas.

"Nothing else?"

The way he says it . . .

There must be something else. Something big.

She closes her eyes. Again, the gun goes off. A man falls.

The same man?

No.

She wishes that he would start driving again, but she opens her eyes just in time to see him put the car in park.

"You're the real deal, aren't you?" He's staring at her.

"Sure am."

"So if you say the rings are over at Valley View . . ."

"It's not coming from *me*. It's Spirit."

Let's just be clear on that in case you decide to wave that gun around again.

"Yeah? Does Spirit get confused?"

"Never. Not about the rings and not about the other guy you shot."

He narrows his eyes. "The one from the hardware store?"

She nods, her thoughts flying to gray-haired old Mitch, the proprietor. Jiffy talks about him a lot.

Now imagining that her son could have had a run in with the likes of this creep there, or anywhere in the area, including their own backyard . . .

Could have and did. And it's all Misty's fault.

If she's blessed in this lifetime with a second chance—at motherhood and marriage—she's going to do things very differently. She'll never again be so reckless.

"When I saw who he was, I felt bad," Elvis is saying with a shrug. "But he came barreling out there with a shotgun, and all I was doing was looking for what was mine. You never let anyone take what belongs to you. Never!"

Having gone from contrite to belligerent in a nanosecond, he releases the steering wheel to clasp the gun in both hands. His shoulders are hunched as if he's surrounded by bullies who want to take away the weapon.

"I need those rings back. Now."

"I told you where they are."

He glares at Misty. "Are you sure the spirits aren't lying? I searched that place."

"*Spirit*, not *spirits*. And you didn't look inside Valley View. You said that yourself."

"How would they get inside when I lost them outside?"

"Maybe someone found them and brought them in."

He blinks those watery gray eyes. "Who? The kid? The one who lives there?"

Her heart pounds. "Max? He's barely allowed outside. No, it wasn't him."

"*Your* kid?"

"My son didn't find the rings," she lies, though she can see him in her mind's eye, doing exactly that.

Finding them . . .

Keeping them . . .

Hiding them.

"Okay," he says.

"Okay, what?"

"We're going to go get my rings back from her. She saw me out the window with Yuri, so I've been planning to get back over there and take care of her anyway."

"Take care of who?"

"Who do you think?" He twirls the gun back into one hand, uses it to shift the car back into drive, and steps on the gas pedal. "Bella. That's what you said, right? We're going back to Valley View. Only this time, I'm going inside, thanks to you."

* * *

"Make one move," Elvis tells Misty, keeping the pistol trained on her as he drives slowly up Cottage Row, "and you'll regret it."

"I'm not moving. Don't worry."

Through the falling snow, she can see Grange's car parked in front of her house and a few others along the street.

"Looks like you have company."

He's right. As they roll past, Misty can see people silhouetted in the front windows of her cottage. What does it mean? Has Jiffy been safely returned?

Or has something happened to him?

No. No way. She'd have sensed it, the way she knew she was carrying him in her womb long before there was biological evidence. The way she knew Mike was her soulmate from the moment they met.

The way she knows Elvis isn't going to leave anyone alive at Valley View when he fails to find his gold rings hidden there as she had promised they are.

What happens to her, Bella and her little boy, and whoever else is caught in the crossfire, will be her own fault.

Wheezing again, Elvis pulls the truck all the way up to the top of the street, past the guesthouse. There are no more houses after Valley View, just the waterfront area and a small pier. He turns the truck around, aiming back down the street for a seamless getaway. Coughing, he turns off the truck, but the music is still playing.

"It's now or never," the real Elvis sings, and he's right.

Now.

In one swift movement, Misty opens the door and hurtles herself out into the snow.

*   *   *

Bella dumps an armful of jackets, umbrellas, hats, and Max's book bag on the hardwood floor beside the empty coat tree. Not pretty, but one quick way to ensure that it won't topple again.

Shaping one of the extension cords into a neat coil, she looks out the window for any sign of Drew. Or, for that matter, Jiffy.

Pandora had mentioned something about Jiffy being on his way home.

So you believe her, then? You believe in this stuff?

In all Bella's months at Lily Dale, she's never wanted so badly to subscribe to Spiritualism and its focus on instinct and the unseen. But hand in hand, she knows, goes an unwillingness to accept coincidence, so . . .

Two murders.

A connection between Virgil and Misty.

Now she's gone missing as well.

Bella can't ignore coincidence nor logic. Not with a pair of homicides. There's no way Jiffy simply ran away because his parents argued this morning and his father said he's not coming for Christmas after all. No way, after all this time and all that's gone on, that he's hiding here at Valley View.

All right, then.

She has to look at the facts, the clues . . .

The emojis.

If Jiffy sent those texts, then maybe they were meant to be clues to his location. Like an electronic version of those pirate treasure maps he and Max were so obsessed with.

What might they mean?

A pen and some trees.

Is he in the woods?

Churches and a bridge. And what about the picture he'd sent? The one that had made Bella think he was in the back seat of a car?

Again, she thinks of Yuri and Virgil.

Dead in the lake.

Dead in the snow.

Bella shivers.

Reaching for the thermostat on the wall, she finds herself looking at the framed vintage regional railroad map beside it.

A word jumps out at her so flagrantly that it might as well be illuminated.

Bethlehem.

* * *

Misty heaves herself through a wall of wet, blowing snow, away from the pickup truck's headlights.

The drifts are deep, and she can't move well. She's leaving a trail as she goes, but she has to try to escape.

She hears the driver's side door open and Elvis cursing and coughing over the sound of real Elvis singing on the radio.

It's now or never.

Never was not an option. And neither, she realizes, is heading toward Valley View with this armed lunatic on her trail.

She might be able to get away. How far can he possibly follow her?

She can hear him wheezing heavily somewhere behind her, coughing hard. Weaving in an effort to throw him off, she pushes on into the tempest, into the darkness.

* * *

"Pennsylvania. Just outside of Allentown . . ."

Bella stares at the antique map, hearing Misty's voice, telling her where her husband grew up, seeing the emojis of a pen and some trees.

Pen . . .

Sylvania.

Just this week, Max had brought home first-grade homework about the colony's establishment and William Penn.

What if . . . ?

"Hey, Max?"

No answer.

"Max?"

Still no answer.

"Max!" she shouts, whirling around. In the little room beyond the parlor, she can see that the TV is still on, but if someone were lurking in the house, he could have snatched her child in an instant.

She rushes toward the room.

There he is, remote control in hand, mesmerized by the television. Admiral Dee has been replaced by a ninja zombie.

The rush of relief at finding him safe is accompanied by the knowledge that she had just experienced a mere shred of what Misty is going through.

"Max?"

He looks up and hastily tucks the remote control under a couch pillow. "What's that?"

"What?" She looks down and finds that she's still holding the extension cord. "It's for the Christmas lights on the porch."

"Yay! Are you turning them on?"

"I . . ." She shrugs. Maybe she should.

After all, there are no mystical stars to light the night. And Drew is coming, and so is Christmas, and . . .

Hope. That's what Bella needs right now. For Max.

"Yes," she tells him. "I'm going to try to get them to work."

"Can I help?"

"No, it will only take two seconds, and it's nasty out there. But listen, Max, did Jiffy ever tell you where his dad's hometown is?"

"Nope." He turns back to the TV.

"Is it in Pennsylvania? Bethlehem, maybe?"

"Bethlehem is where the baby Jesus was born."

"Not that Bethlehem. Did Jiffy ever mention Pennsylvania?"

"Yep. And so did Mrs. Schmidt. She said that William Penn—"

"Max, what did *Jiffy* say about Pennsylvania?"

"He said he went to a restaurant there where they have the best French fries in the world. It's in a place called Allentown. Like Alan Katz. Do you know where it is?"

"Yes."

Allentown. Bethlehem.

"Good, because I want to go to that restaurant. It's called Couch Potato. And by the way, people shouldn't interrupt."

"No, they shouldn't. I'm sorry," she murmurs.

Couch . . .

Potato . . .

Those were the emojis he sent on the text messages.

Heart racing, Bella grabs her phone from her pocket, wondering if she should call Grange or Luther.

Luther's number is programmed into the phone. Grange's is not. And Luther will believe her. Grange will not.

"Bella?" he answers. "Everything okay?"

She blurts out her theory that Jiffy's father has taken him and is on his way to his hometown. He listens.

"Do you know where in Bethlehem his father's family lives?"

"No, but Jiffy is Michael J. Arden the third, so his grandfather would have the same first name. Maybe you can look him up."

"Thanks. I'm on it."

He hangs up.

"Mom? Are you going to plug in the Christmas lights?"

She looks from Max's hopeful face to the extension cord in her hands. He deserves some good news.

She nods. "I'll be back in two seconds."

*   *   *

Elvis was right behind her, so near that Misty was certain he was closing in. She could hear him coughing and gasping for air and then . . .

Nothing.

She moves doggedly on but not straight ahead. She veers to the right and then to the left—for all she knows, running in circles or heading straight for Valley View, the last thing she wanted. But she's running blind.

Running? If only.

She's wading blind through drifts up to her thighs.

A voice reaches her ears.

"Help! Please!"

Elvis.

Nearby. Closer than she thought.

"Can't . . . breathe . . . Please . . ."

Misty stops.

"Afraid . . . to . . . die . . . here. Please . . ."

The voice is muffled, coming from below. He's on the ground. Gasping. Perhaps dying.

This is her chance to escape. All she has to do to save herself is . . .

"Please."

Save herself? What about him? A man is begging for his life. She's been selfish her whole life—this is her chance to change.

She turns back, torn.

Every muscle in her body is urging her to keep going. Spirit, too, seems to be urging her forward.

But how can she leave a human being to die alone out here? The snow will bury him alive.

She takes a deep breath, something the struggling man can't do. Might never do again.

"Okay," she calls to him. "I'm coming. Hang on."

*   *   *

The bitter wind steals Bella's breath as she drags the stepladder from the parlor out onto the porch. She has a flashlight weighing down her deep front pocket and the extension cord draped around her neck.

Dusk has fallen out on the street. Now she can see scattered lampposts, lower thirds buried, bathed in a swirling grainy glow. No sign of Drew, although he should be here by now.

She looks up at the light strings stretching along the eaves as she sets up the ladder. She'd told Max that this would only take two seconds, but who was she kidding? There's no way she's going to attach an extension cord to the nearest plug, stick it into an outlet, and *voilà* . . . Christmas.

No, she's going to have to disconnect everything and start from scratch.

She sighs, drags the ladder over to the railing, and takes the white extension cord from around her neck, preparing to ascend. Worried that she'll lose it if she tosses it onto the snow-covered porch floor, she fumbles with numb fingers to attach it to the end of the connected light strings.

First things first—she'd better make sure it will even reach the outlet. If not, this task will have to wait.

She has to pull it taut for the prongs to reach the outlet, but it will probably work. Maybe she should try it, just to make sure it isn't a hair too short.

She plugs it in.

Not only does it reach, but the porch is bathed in vibrant light.

She looks up, stunned. Every string is lit. Every *bulb* is lit.

How could the electrician have been so wrong?

How could *she* have gotten it so right?

It's Lily Dale. That's how. Simple as that.

As she gazes at the lights, she hears a voice calling out in the night.

A man's voice in the clearing up at the end of the street.

"Help! . . . Please!"

Looking toward it, she can barely make out the headlights of a pickup truck parked there.

Drew. Drew is in trouble.

*   *   *

Misty was right. Up ahead she sees a human form slumped on the ground.

"Help!" Elvis gasps. "Please . . ."

She makes her way toward him, breathing hard herself. "It's going to be okay," she pants, reaching Elvis. "You need your inhaler. You need . . ."

She stops short.

He's wheezing, yes, but he's not in distress.

He's holding the gun.

Aiming it at her and smiling a cunning smile.

*   *   *

Bella starts toward the pickup truck.

It's off the road, mired in deep snow. Did Drew slide on the ice? Was he stricken while trying to push it back onto the road? Pulled muscle, back spasm, heart attack . . . ?

Or is it something else, something far more menacing?

About to call out to him, she thinks of Virgil Barbor and the man in the lake.

She stops, standing in the snowy lane, weighing her options.

Maybe she should go back for help. Get Grange and Luther. But that might be too late.

She starts moving again. The road hasn't been plowed recently enough, but it's easier going than what lies beyond. She wades into the deep snow as quietly as she can, toward the headlights and the voice . . .

Voices.

A man . . .

Not Drew.

And a woman. Misty.

"Don't do this," she's saying. "You're a good guy, remember?"

"You're wrong. I'm not a good guy at all. I'm a bad guy. Maybe not as bad as my pal Yuri, but you'll see what happens to people who try to take what's mine."

"I didn't take anything."

"You took my rings."

He—whoever he is—pauses to cough. He's breathing hard, gasping a little bit.

"I didn't take your rings," Misty protests. "I told you, I know where they are, but I—"

"You know where they are because you found them, and you could tell right away they're not lousy costume jewelry, right? Not like those customs idiots who wave me back and forth across the border every damn day. They can't tell the difference between a gold pendant from the party store's King of Rock and Roll costume and a priceless medallion that belonged to a sixteenth-century king."

His laugh dissolves into another coughing fit.

Bella creeps closer and crouches behind the truck. From here, she can see them standing a few yards away. Misty is cowering before a man who has his back to the truck.

Bella's icy hand reaches for the flashlight in her coat pocket. The one she doesn't let Max and Jiffy use because it's heavy enough to crush a skull.

"Look, I didn't find your rings, but I'll tell you where they are."

"Yeah, sure you will. They're not at Valley View."

"No, they aren't."

"Where are they?"

"Out at the Stump. They're hidden at the Stump. I'll show you, just—what are you doing?"

The man has shifted his position.

Now Bella can see that he's holding a gun. Raised with both hands.

"Please," Misty wails, "I just want to be with my son! Please don't do this!"

"Oh, you'll be with your son," he says. "According to you people, no one ever dies. Our families are always with us. Isn't that right?"

Bella steals toward them, step by painstaking step.

"I mean . . ." He gives a bitter, gasping laugh. "That would explain a lot. Maybe it's my old man hanging around me. I cut him out of my life while he was alive, and everything was great. I was on a roll. Singing, playing the tables, winning big. Then he kicks the bucket, and everything starts to go wrong. My luck turns. He's making my life miserable again. You know what, I bet?"

He pauses to cough again.

"I bet Yuri's haunting Ginger. Him and all those dead kings looking for their stolen jewels. What do you think?"

Bella hears an unmistakable click.

"Cat got your tongue, Misty Starr?" He wheezes. "This place is nothing but bad luck. I'm going to get my rings and get out of here for good. Don't even think about trying to catch me. You won't be able to do that from the Other Side."

He's about to pull the trigger.

Bella lunges forward, swinging the flashlight with all her might. It catches him in the back of the head.

The gun flies from his fingers and disappears into a powdery snowbank as he drops to his knees, then keels over.

Misty, too, is on the ground, crying.

Bella dials 9-1-1, blurts a plea for help, and then sinks down beside her. "It's going to be okay, Misty."

"No, it isn't," she wails. "Priscilla . . ."

She's in shock, confused. Bella wraps her arms around her. "No, sweetie, it's me. Bella."

"I know! I mean she took him! She took my boy!"

"Who?"

"Priscilla! She's a kidnapper! You were right."

Confused, Bella says, "Right about what? I never said—"

"You didn't have to say it. I could hear it in your head. Every time you looked at me, you were thinking I should have been taking better care of Jiffy. Watching him, the way you did. But . . ."

it's not easy for me. I'm all alone, and it's so hard, Bella! It's just so hard!"

"I know," Bella says, holding her tightly as she sobs, feeling tears slipping from her own eyes. "I know."

She had wanted to believe that Misty was different—an inattentive, lax mother who could have prevented Jiffy's disappearance. But they have so much in common, beginning with two little boys who love them and each other.

Could Misty improve her parenting skills? Yes. But no parent could fully ensure a child's safety. You could make him wear a helmet, but you couldn't encase him in protective bulletproof glass. You could keep an eye on him, but you couldn't guard him 24-7. You could be wary of strangers, but you couldn't prevent them from ever crossing his path.

"If I can just get him back," Misty says as Bella strokes her hair like a child's, "I swear I'll never take my eyes off him again! I'll never let anything happen to him. I'll spend every minute the rest of my life keeping him safe, just like you do."

"Misty, don't beat yourself up. I do what I can to keep Max safe. But the older he gets, the more he wants me to let go, and the more I"—she pauses to swallow—"the more I have to."

"But that's not right. If you let go, he might—"

"I know. He might. So I can hope that he'll be safe from harm forever, and I can pray that he has a guardian angel watching over him when I can't, but there's no guarantee. You can't blame yourself every time something—"

"No, I can. I should have listened."

"To what?"

"Spirit. I had that vision, and I knew someone was trying to tell me something. My father was driving that bus! I'm so afraid it means—"

She breaks off as Bella's phone rings in her hand.

"Oh, no," she says, and clutches Bella's arm. "I'm afraid. What if—?"

"It's going to be okay, Misty."

"You don't know—"

"I know this! I do. I know," she lies and answers the phone.

Luther.

It has to be good news. It has to be.

"Bella, you were right."

"I was . . ." She tries to keep breathing, tries to keep her voice steady for Misty's sake. "Right about what?"

"They just found him."

Scarcely daring to breathe, she manages to ask, "Is he—?"

"What is it?" Misty asks, voice drenched in terror. "What?"

"He's safe and sound at the grandfather's house," Luther is saying, and Bella exhales, closing her eyes in a silent, thankful prayer as he goes on.

"Bella? Is Jiffy . . . ?" Misty chokes on her son's name.

Jiffy is . . .

Troubled. Complicated. Hurting. The whole family is hurting. There are so many mistakes all around . . .

But in this moment, only one thing matters.

Bella kneels beside the terrified woman and gently delivers the greatest gift a mother's heart desires.

"Jiffy is safe."

"He is? He's—?"

"Yes. They've found him."

"Oh, thank you . . . thank you!" Misty collapses into her arms.

"What happened?" she asks Luther. "How did he get there?"

"Long story, and they're still sorting it out, but sounds like Mike Arden's been back in touch with an old girlfriend for a while. Guess he told her he was worried about his wife's mental state, so either he asked her to check on things out here or she took it upon herself. Sounds like she's the one who has a few screws loose. She's saying she took Jiffy with her to keep him safe. Claims Arden told her to take him back to Bethlehem and that he'd let Misty know."

"Where is he now?"

"On a plane headed back to the states, and the girlfriend is in custody."

"How's Jiffy?"

"I didn't talk to him," Luther says, "but they say he's put in a takeout request for curly fries with cheese and bacon, so it sounds like he's just fine."

269

Bella hangs up and half laughs, half cries as she relays it all to Misty.

"I need to get to him, Bella. I need—he needs me," she amends.

"Luther's on his way here, and we'll figure out how to make that happen. For now, just be thankful that . . . that . . ." Bella can't go on, searching the heavens with teary eyes.

This time, it has to be there.

A star, a star . . .

One bright star that will answer her own most fervent question. One bright, shining, mystical star . . .

She finds only an endless night sky and falling flakes that dust her face, melting into teardrops.

Of course it isn't there. This isn't a *Hallmark* Christmas movie. This is real life, and reality is marred by mishaps and bad guys, by meteorology and science and logic . . .

"The bus!" Misty says. "I get it!"

"What bus? Get what?"

"My vision . . . my dad, driving Jiffy on the bus . . . he was trying to let me know that he was trying to protect him, even if I couldn't. Like you said."

"Like I said?"

"Yeah. Like some kind of, you know . . . guardian angel." Misty lets out a choked little laugh. "Funny, since he was no angel when he was here on earth. I guess we all have our moment sooner or later, right?"

Bella smiles, too. And somewhere out there in this colossal storm, she hears someone whistling a familiar carol.

Ah, the Lily Dale theme song, with lyrical questions that Bella answers silently.

No, I don't hear what you hear! And I don't see what you see! I want to, but I can't because . . . because if I believe in meteorology and in logic and in science, then I can't possibly believe—

She hears something else. In her head. Not, as far as she knows, the way her medium friends hear Spirit—*claim* to hear Spirit. Not the way she herself hears the imaginary whistler or her own voice, coaching her back down to earth where she belongs.

She hears Max, longing to believe in Santa: *"Just because you can't see something doesn't mean it's not there."*

Smart boy, her son.

Our son.

Again, she tilts her head back.

Good old science and logic.

Somewhere up there, beyond the stormy sky . . .

Beyond what she can see in this moment or in this realm . . .

There *is* a star.

Millions of stars, shining brightly.

Epilogue

A lifetime—or a season, at least—seems to have passed since the blizzard that ultimately dumped not three, but more than four feet of snow on Lily Dale.

It's been just over a week, though. A week of climbing temperatures that melted mountainous drifts into slushy heaps and rivers running along rutted lanes. Now they're reduced to a smattering of shallow puddles, glinting in unseasonable sunshine.

So much for a white Christmas—Mitch's "safe bet" back when Max had asked him what in this world he could count on. Today's temperature is expected to rival the Fourth of July's high.

"I thought it was going to snow!" Max had grumbled when he bounded into the Rose Room this morning at dawn, eager to see what Santa left under the tree.

"That's Lily Dale for you," Bella had heard herself say, smiling. Spoken like a true local.

Max forgot all about the disappointing green Christmas outside when he spotted the heap of gifts under the towering Fraser fir in the parlor. Not just the metal detector Bella had bought him at Mitch's, but stacks of other gifts sent her way in preparation for today, courtesy of various "Santas" in their lives.

"How can I ever repay you?" she'd asked around a lump in her throat whenever someone new showed up to furtively deliver Christmas morning gifts for Max.

Odelia, Calla, Drew, Luther, Mitch—even Pandora.

They had all brushed off her gratitude, but she did think of a way to thank them—with an old-fashioned Christmas feast. She and Max decorated Valley View from porch to parlor—freshly painted a lovely Sylvan Mist—and well beyond.

The more the merrier, she'd told herself whenever she thought of another name for her guest list. They'd all accepted her invitation.

Caught up in a flurry of holiday preparations, she's occasionally managed to forget the horror of what happened and of what might have happened if—

"*If* is a dangerous word when you're thinking about the past," Drew had told her the other night. "The future, too, for that matter."

"Why?" Max, who'd overheard, had asked.

They'd been trimming the tree with ornaments from the basement along with some Drew had let Max pick out—a glorious mishmash of delicate baubles and plastic toys, with a *Ninja Zombie* action figure riding the crest alongside the gold filigree star that's graced many a Valley View Christmas tree.

"Wasting brain power and energy on conjecture is dangerous," Drew had explained to Max, who was tossing vast clumps of tinsel at one small section of the tree.

"I don't get it, Dr. Drew."

"When you use *if* related to something that might happen or could have happened . . . why bother? Just be glad that it didn't happen, and move on."

"Well, I can't move on if Santa doesn't bring me a snowboard, and I'm going to be sad that it didn't happen. Not glad."

"I have a feeling he might if you're a good boy," Drew had said, winking at Bella across the shimmery boughs.

The snowboard had already been wrapped and hidden in Bella's closet by that time. Drew had bought it as part of the Santa bounty and had been bringing it to her the day of the storm.

Yes, he'd arrived too late to save her, but she'd saved herself—and Misty.

"Don't worry, Bella," he had said the night that they decorated the tree. "I'll teach Max how to use it."

"*You* know how to snowboard?"

"Hey, I know how to do a lot of things that might surprise you. Some things with more skill than others," he'd added with a—maybe suggestive?—grin.

Maybe not. Maybe she just wanted it to be in that moment, on a cozy, happy, night.

It wasn't until she'd climbed into bed after midnight that she realized the significance of the day that had just come to an end.

Somehow, the one-year anniversary of Sam's death had come and gone without her awareness. The day that she'd been dreading was already behind her, as was her year of sorrow and change.

"Hey, I was right!" Max had exclaimed when he saw the presents waiting under the tree. "Santa *is* real!"

"He sure is, Max," Bella had said, wiping tears on the sleeve of her robe.

Now her son is in the parlor building a Lego ninja with Drew and the puppies he'd brought to spend the day, along with their sweet, nicely recuperating Mama.

"Hey, Mom," Max had said when he'd seen them. "Can I keep—?"

"No way! Chance and Spidey would never . . ."

Then she'd noticed that Chance and Spidey might, indeed, be okay with it. Hearing the happy, yappy crew, the cats had slipped into the room to investigate and were perched on the sofa, watching serenely.

After changing her "No way" to a "We'll see," Bella had retreated to the kitchen, where she's putting the finishing touches on the meal she just removed from the oven.

A full five minutes after Odelia offered to toss the salad, it still sits neatly layered in the cut glass bowl on the counter, dressing on the side in a crystal cruet. Odelia stands at the stove stirring, stirring, stirring the hot wassail she claims would have been much better made in a Crock-Pot.

For once, her moodiness has nothing to do with Pandora, who'd lugged her portable electric organ over to Valley View along with an enormous Yorkshire pudding and a sack full of instruments.

In the hall, Mitch's tenor accompanies her operatic trill as they work their way through a festive Christmas medley. Long-widowed and still saddened over Virgil's tragic loss, Mitch didn't seem to mind the sleigh bells Pandora had forced into his hand the moment he crossed the threshold or being bulldozed into singing every verse of "Jingle Bells" with her. They've moved on to "Feliz Navidad," sleigh bells swapped out for maracas and, for all Bella knows, Pandora's "Father Christmas" cap exchanged for a sombrero.

Ordinarily, the rhythmic shaking and Pandora's exaggerated Spanish accent would be enough to have Odelia spiking the already-spiked wassail.

So would the fact that Blue Slayton is here with Calla, helping add a few folding chairs to accommodate the dozen fine china place settings around the table.

But she's fretting about Luther, who should have been here long before now.

"I honestly think he's avoiding me," Odelia confides, still stirring the wassail.

"Why would he do that?"

"Because the other day when he told me Jiffy was safe, I grabbed him and hugged him."

"That seems like a reasonable reaction."

"I might have . . . uh, kissed him, too."

"You were joyful. I get it."

"Not that kind of kiss."

"I see." Bella bites back a smile, and Odelia goes back to stirring so hard that, if the wassail were cream, it would have been butter by now.

Moments later, the piano playing ceases.

"Isabella? You have guests!" Pandora calls.

"Guests?" Odelia echoes. "Then it's not Luther, unless he brought a date—is he bringing a date?"

"Of course not," Bella assures her, tilting her head to listen to the voices in the hall.

"By the way, I got one, too!"

Bella smiles. Jiffy, checking out Max's snowboard.

She hurries into the hall to greet the Ardens, just in time to hear Jiffy ask Misty if he can keep a puppy.

"Sure, why not?"

The reply doesn't come from his mom, but from his dad.

Bella was surprised when Misty had said Mike Arden was planning to drive here on Christmas morning from Pennsylvania.

Having been held for questioning and then released, he's not charged with any wrongdoing involving his son's abduction.

Not officially anyway.

Unofficially . . .

"We've got a lot of problems to work out," Misty had told Bella the other night over eggnog as the boys assembled the world's messiest gingerbread house. "I mean, obviously, he shouldn't have been messing around with her, even from overseas."

Her—his high school sweetheart, the woman who'd called herself Priscilla Galante. Mike Arden had admitted to reconnecting with her on social media last spring and even to what he calls an "emotional affair"—strictly long distance, according to Misty.

"He's been telling her I'm a lousy mother and that he worries about Jiffy's safety and that we're living in some crazy haunted town," she'd told Bella.

"So he sent her here to spy on you?"

"Pretty much. I should have known something was off about her when I saw that black aura. I figured it was just first-timer nerves. Guess I'm not as good at this as I thought."

Poor Misty.

But Bella is hopeful they can work it out—especially now that Mike is here.

Priscilla is spending the holidays in jail, reportedly still proclaiming her innocence. Luther—who has contacts everywhere, including Pennsylvania—said she envisions herself as a guardian angel who'd swooped in to save Jiffy after nearly running him over.

Bella can't help but think she's right in some twisted way. If she hadn't snatched Jiffy off the street, "Elvis" would have. She might have had poor judgment and perhaps some mental health issues, but he was an armed criminal.

Elvis—not his real name, of course—is spending this Christmas behind bars—and, most likely, every Christmas for the rest of his life for the murders of Virgil Barbor, who'd been in the wrong place at the wrong time, and Yuri Moroskov, who'd tried to double-cross him after he'd smuggled the four stolen sapphire-encrusted rings over the border. The woman who had come to Lily Dale searching for them—"Barbara"—has been arrested, too.

"She was a key member of the Amur Leopard, like Yuri Moroskov. Elvis was a fence," Luther had told Bella. "Lived in Niagara Falls, New York, but he performed his act every night in a casino on the Canadian side. You get to know all the border guys, coming and going like that. His costume was jewel-studded, and he wore a lot of heavy gold jewelry. Costume jewelry and fake jewels unless—"

"Unless he needed to smuggle something!" Bella had said. It made sense—Elvis, transporting gemstones and stolen treasures in plain sight, including the four golden rings that Jiffy had found in the grass behind Valley View.

"Four . . . golden . . . rings," Pandora had sung that day in the kitchen. There was no way Pandora could have known about Elvis and his lost treasure.

Coincidence?

Spirit?

It doesn't matter—not today, anyway.

"Hey, Bella, this is my dad!" Jiffy says proudly.

Mike Arden greets her with a warm handshake, thanking her for being a friend to his family while he's away. Then Pandora presses in with her array of musical instruments.

"Come, now, we're singing 'Frosty, the Snowman.' Would you prefer a tambourine or bongo drums?"

Bella heads back to the kitchen, thinking of Dawn and pretty certain she wouldn't cry over this rollicking rendition of "Frosty" the way she does over the one on *A Very Von Vogel Christmas*.

She and Lauri had been aghast when Bella had pointed out a familiar face in their scrapbook photo of Sean Von Vogel's last concert. There was their friend Lisa, front and center, in the VIP seats reserved for his biggest fans.

"All these years," Lauri said, "and I never looked at the crowd. I was just looking at Sean."

"Me, too. I can't believe it was right there under our noses all this time."

"It happens," Bella assured them.

Boy, does it ever.

The day after they'd returned home, Lauri had called Bella to confirm that Lisa had, indeed, taken the locket—a closeted Von Vogel fan all along.

They, too, have some relationship issues to work out. Bella is certain they'll manage to forgive and forget. Maybe there's even hope for Odelia and Blue, though when it comes to Odelia and Pandora . . .

"Ladies," Pandora calls from the next room, "do come join us for this next song!"

"Be right there!" Bella calls back.

"You, too, Odelia! You must!"

Odelia glowers. "What am I, her sing-along soldier, following commands?"

"Come on, it's Christmas."

"I know what day it is." But she allows Bella to steer her into the hall, where Pandora is organizing a group effort of "The Twelve Days of Christmas."

"I'm going to assign each of you a day! I'll lead us off as the partridge in a pear tree . . ."

"Of course she will," Odelia whispers to Bella. "It's in every verse."

"By the way, there are only eleven people here, so I can be two days," Jiffy pipes up . . . just as someone knocks at the front door.

Bella opens it to find Luther in a red silk shirt and Santa hat.

"Merry Christmas!" he says breathlessly.

"Where have you been? We were getting worried."

"Last minute road trip to New York City last night, and I just got back."

"New York? Spending Christmas Eve with a new lady friend?"

"Nope. It was the only place I could find *this*." He nods at the large gift-wrapped box in his hands. "Sorry I'm late."

"You're actually just in time to be twelve drummers drumming . . . and I'm guessing there are bongos involved."

They rejoin the group, and Bella watches him walk over to Odelia and thrust the box into her hands. She peels off the wrapping paper as Pandora plays the opening chords.

"My Crock-Pot!"

"Shush now—we're singing!"

And they're off, Odelia now beaming as broadly as everyone else.

"On the first day of Christmas . . ."

Feeling an arm around her shoulder, Bella looks up to see Drew. Silently, he points at the ceiling, and she looks up to see . . .

Mistletoe?

"How did that get there?"

"Secret Santa, I guess," he whispers slyly and pulls her in to steal a kiss as the others sing on, ". . . my true love gave to me . . ."